NURSING A GRUDGE

DIANA ORGAIN

$\mathcal{P}$RAISE FOR DIANA ORGAIN

"Engaging...[A] charming debut thriller."
—Publisher's Weekly

"A fun, fast, cozy read that will keep its readers entertained and anxiously awaiting the next installment. A must read."
—The Best Reviews

"A breezy and entertaining mystery."
—The Mystery Reader

"An over the top, good-time cozy mystery. With a feisty heroine and with lots of humor, plenty of intrigue and suspense, and a little baby cooing, this novel is a delightful treat to read."
—Fresh Fiction

"A straightforward whodunit ... chick lit meets noir in Diana Orgain's fun mystery."
—The Mystery Gazette

"If you were expecting warm and cute you'll be mistaken. Fast paced and fun, this book gives a true feel of the modern mom, trying to juggle motherhood and career (when that career happens to be solving crimes)."
—Rhys Bowen, award-winning author of the Molly Murphy series

"Skip your afternoon nap and cozy up to Diana Orgain's Maternal Instincts Mysteries. The series' plucky protagonist gives 'working mom' a whole new meaning as she endearingly juggles bad guys and binkies."
—Susan McBride, author of the Debutante Dropout Mysteries

"…you'll laugh so hard you'll forget the labor pains…"
— Louise Ure, Shamus Award Winner of *Forcing Amaryllis* and *The Fault Tree*

"A stellar debut…A winning protagonist and a glorious San Francisco setting. Highly recommended."
—Sheldon Siegel, New York Times bestselling author

"… Anyone who's been a mother or had one will welcome the arrival of this entertaining new sleuth."
—Gillian Roberts, author of the Amanda Pepper series

"You'll love keeping up with this amazing mother and sleuth in the fun, fast-paced "Bundle of Trouble.""
—Camille Minichino, author of the miniature mystery series

WHAT READERS ARE SAYING ABOUT DIANA ORGAIN

Five Stars! "Bundle of Trouble is one of the best books I've read in a long while!"

Five Stars! "AMAZING! It totally blow me away. This writer has really got that special touch."

Five Stars! "I couldn't wait to read this one; it just seemed like such fun. I had to laugh at the "To Do Lists" that Kate would come up with, which reminds me of myself."

Five Stars! "In addition to wanting to befriend Kate, I also enjoyed the suspense of this book. It made me wish that I could stay awake a little bit longer, so that I could read more. I will eagerly await the release of the next book in the Maternal Instincts Mystery Series."

Five Stars! "Loved this book! Did Diana Orgain have a webcam in my house when I was a new mom? Nice tight little murder mystery. Love to see more from this author."

Five Stars! "Funny and intriguing! It will keep you guessing who-done-it to the end. Kate is a frenzied mom looking for a stay at home job and she found it!"

Five Stars! "This book was right up my alley with very relatable and likable characters. The story was definitely a page-turner and I cannot wait for another one!"

Five Stars! "A very entertaining book that achieves a nice balance between the amusing tribulations of a woman adjusting to motherhood and an increasingly complicated puzzle involving difficult family relationships."

Five Stars! "A fine mystery, perfect for readers seeking something different."

Five Stars! "I picked it up and could not put it down."

NURSING A GRUDGE

DIANA ORGAIN

Copyright 2013 © by Diana Orgain

www.dianaorgain.com
www.twitter.com/dianaorgain
www.facebook.com/DianaOrgainAuthor
www.dianaorgain.com/about-the-authorcontact

ISBN-13: 978-1492934028

Dedication

For Tom, Carmen, Tommy Jr, and Bobby

ACKNOWLEDGMENTS

Thank you to all the readers who have written to me. Your kind words keep me motivated to write the next story.

1

To Do:
1. Catch up with old friends!
2. √ ~~Phone Jill and set a date.~~
3. Land a new client.
4. Buy Paula a present for new baby.
5. Get back in shape!

From inside Tea & Tumble, I checked my phone for the umpteenth time. My best friend, Paula, was due to give birth any day now, and I'd promised to babysit her toddler when the time came. The café was empty save for myself, my four-month old daughter and another pair of moms with their infants camped out in the corner.

Tea & Tumble was rated as the top pick for baby friendly cafes in the Bay Area. It was decorated in pinks and greens with a colorful, plush carpet in the corner of the dining area and a large leather couch. On the carpet, the two infants drooled over picture books, while their mothers were perched on the couch sipping lattes.

I glanced at Laurie, who cooed up at me from her baby carrier nestled at my feet. "Paula's going to have her baby any day now. Are you ready for a new friend?"

Laurie batted her hand out, grabbing at imaginary items.

"I'll take that as a yes," I said. I freed her from the infant carrier, then lowered my voice. "Then you can slobber over the book of the month club choice like those other two in the corner."

Laurie flashed me a wide, toothless grin.

"Besides," I said. "A girl can never have too many friends."

A gust of wind vibrated the windows of the café, and I glanced outside to see Jill parking her car.

I hadn't seen Jill since quite some time before my pregnancy, and I was looking forward to visiting with her and catching up on gossip.

She climbed out of the car, wearing an asymmetrical orange blouse that caught the wind and billowed about her. She reached inside the car and pulled out a tan coat that matched her leggings and set off her black, stiletto thigh-high boots. As she wrapped it around herself, she spotted me in the window and waved vigorously. She sprinted across the street in her stiletto boots, short blond bob flapping in the wind.

Dear God, I wouldn't be able to walk in those boots, much less run in them, but Jill looks chic and fashionable, as usual.

I placed Laurie up to the window and moved her little wrist back and forth in a hello. When I pulled her back into my lap, a man wearing a long, dark coat and a black skull cap with a Smith & Wesson logo on it turned the corner.

He raised an arm as if hailing Jill.

She didn't notice him and pulled open the door to the café.

The wind rumbled through the café as Jill stepped in.

The moms in the corner glared at Jill as she made her way toward my table, annoyed that their *tête-à-tête* had been momentarily interrupted. Jill ignored them as she clippity-clopped over to my table.

Jill pressed her frozen check against mine. "Hey, stranger!"

Jill and I had been chummy once, but had fallen out of touch. In fact, now that I thought about it, it'd probably been several years since we'd last seen each other. But since the birth of my daughter I'd felt the need to get in touch with old friends and build a community around her. I held her up. She was dressed in a little pink knit dress that my best friend Paula had sent while visiting Paris.

"This is Peanut," I said.

"Oooh, love the dress," Jill leaned in toward Laurie, who reached out and grabbed a fistful of Jill's blonde bob while shrieking with delight.

Jill's hand shot up to her head to save her hair from getting pulled out by the roots.

"Sorry," I said, detangling Jill's hair from Laurie's fist.

Jill laughed and rubbed Laurie's chubby knee. "Good to meet you, you feisty little thing."

"And sorry I've been so out of touch," I said.

She pulled off her coat and took the seat across from us. "Well, I can see you've been busy so, of course, I forgive you."

She didn't know the half of it. We'd only talked briefly to set up our lunch date and I still hadn't told her about my new career as a P.I. Since giving birth to Laurie, I'd managed to be involved in several murder investigations and basically had decided to launch a private investigation business. But since I didn't have a P.I. license, I was doing a semi-very-unofficial mentorship under Albert Galigani, an ex-cop, to hone my skills and become marketable.

"Do you know the guy across the street?" I asked.

Jill frowned. "What guy?" She glanced over her shoulder.

"The one on the corner wearing the Smith & Wesson skull cap," I prompted.

Jill remained turned away from me. "Why would I know him?"

I shrugged. "I don't know. I thought he called out to you when you were crossing the street."

She gripped the table in a rather alarmed way, then swiveled back to face me. "I don't know him."

Something about the expression on Jill's face told me she was nervous about the man.

I stared out the window, past the fog, and studied the man. He was Caucasian and looked to be in his thirties. He wore a long, dark coat and his skull cap was pulled down around his ears.

"He seems to be lurking," I said.

Jill waved away my concern. "This is San Francisco. There's always someone lurking."

The swinging double doors at the back of the restaurant creaked open and the hostess who had seated me approached. She handed us menus, then ran a hand over her frizzy red hair. "Anything to drink?"

"I'll take a cup of coffee," I said.

Jill bit her lip as she perused the back of the menu where the beverages were listed. "I'll take a Mexican hot chocolate."

Mexican hot chocolate? Yum!

I flipped my menu over and scanned the list.

The waitress nodded and turned to go.

"Uh. Wait. I think…"

I found the entry: "**Fiery Hot Chocolate** | Muy Caliente! Our own hot chocolate blend that really packs a kick. Starts creamy with a hand-scooped ganache topping and ends with a spicy wallop."

"Oh. I see. Fiery, spicy, kick, wallop. It sounds… um…"

Jill laughed. "It's not for the weak hearted. It's made with chipotle chili chocolate."

"I'll stick with the coffee."

The waitress looked at me through her eyelashes. I understood the look as a warning not to waste her time again.

What attitude!

She turned on her heel and disappeared through the swinging doors.

"So what have you been up to?" I asked. "Catch me up on your career. I understand you're the hottest restaurant critic around."

Jill sat to attention. "An accidental career. Who would've thunk it?"

I balanced Laurie on my lap, letting her dig her feet into my thighs as she practiced putting her weight on her legs. She could only keep herself upright for a moment before her legs turned to Jell-O again.

"You always had a discriminating palate," I said.

She giggled. "You mean I like to eat. And I know how to string a few snarky remarks together. Enough, anyway, to make people pay attention."

In the past few months, Jill had become somewhat of an internet sensation. Her reviews were everywhere and she was always popping up on the latest foodie blog.

"Your latest review went viral, right?"

Jill put a finger to her mouth and eyed the moms in the corner. Although they seemed engrossed in their own conversation, Jill leaned in and whispered. "Don't talk about that, though. My picture's not out there and I don't want people to know who I am. Not yet anyway."

I nodded. "Are you going to do a review of this place?"

"If I have time." Jill shrugged. "Maybe. It's just that something's happened recently that's kind of stuck in my craw."

I waited for her to continue, but instead of saying anything she rubbed at her chin.

"What is it?" I asked.

"I reviewed Brent Miles' latest restaurant. Or should I say his *attempt* at a restaurant." She made a face indicating how lacking she'd actually found it. "Anyway, he called me. It was very...well, frightening—"

"Frightening? What happened?"

"He threatened me." Jill leaned across the table closer to me. "He warned me that I need to recant the review. Said I better make it seem sincere or else."

"Or else what?"

She raised an eyebrow at me and shrugged. "I told him to stuff it. Just because he owns half of San Francisco he thinks everyone is ready to kiss his ass. Well, he can kiss mine now, because I'm not recanting anything!"

Her tone surprised me. I had always known she was tough but now she seemed downright ferocious.

The hostesses with the frizzy red hair returned with two steaming mugs in her hands. She placed my coffee in front of me, sloshing hot liquid over the top and onto the table. I pulled Laurie away protectively.

The waitress didn't even notice; she merely put Jill's mug in front of her and asked, "Ready to order?"

Jill smiled up at her. "Not yet."

The waitress smiled back.

Well, there you go. Jill got smiles, I got a coffee mess.

"Let me know when you're ready," the waitress said. She spun around and attended to the other moms that were camped out on a large leather couch in the corner of the tea house. One mom leaned in and whispered something to the waitress, then they all turned and stared at us.

I lifted my mug and sighed as I placed it back down into the puddle of coffee on the table. I needed another hand. "Want to hold Laurie?" I asked.

Jill quickly glanced at her immaculate blouse. "Um, yeah. Sure."

She didn't look at all sure.

I reached into the hulking diaper bag that was always with me now and pulled out a clean spit-up rag and handed it to Jill.

She looked relieved as she placed it onto her shoulder and took Laurie.

I quickly wiped up the liquid on the table and watched in horror as Laurie batted a hand dangerously close to Jill's hot chocolate. The other hand had already found its way into Jill's hair.

Jill grimaced.

I finished mopping up the coffee and much to Jill's relief took Laurie back, who squealed like a demon.

"Tell me more about your experience with Brent Miles," I said, hoping to distract Jill from Laurie's wailing.

"Oh no, let's not talk about him. He's boring." Jill's eyes roved out the window and she frowned.

I followed her gaze out the window. "What?" I asked.

The man with the skull cap was still on the corner. He seemed to be staring right at us. A chill ran up my spine and I hugged Laurie to me.

"That guy is still there," I said.

Jill fluttered a hand around dismissing him.

"What do you think he's still doing there?" I asked.

Jill shrugged nonchalantly. "He's probably waiting for someone."

I stared at him through the glass. He took something out of his pocket and looked down at it, most likely a phone. Jill was probably right; in a few seconds whoever he was waiting for would turn up. I tried to ignore him even though my P.I. senses were firing like crazy.

"He gives me the creeps," I muttered.

Jill turned away from the window. "I have news." She glanced at the swinging doors and whispered. "I got my own show over at the Foodie Network."

"What?" I whispered back, only my whisper was so loud, it bordered on being a cheer.

Jill's hand covered her lips, signaling me to keep my voice down.

"That's awesome!" I said, this time more quietly.

She nodded at me. "I just came from the studio. The set is amazing!"

The swinging doors to the back opened as our waitress walked through them. She stopped momentarily to check in on the moms in the corner.

"Shoot," I said. "We'd better order or she might yell at me."

Jill snorted and flipped her menu over.

I scanned the list. I was hopeless under pressure. I only made out words like saucy, spicy, savory and hot. It told me nothing.

The waitress stood before us poised with paper and pen.

I decided to order whatever Jill did, which turned out to be the Mediterranean Panini: prosciutto ham, fresh basil, tomato and feta.

Sounds good to me.

"Same for me," I said.

The waitress nodded at me. I'd just made her life easier and I was somewhat in her good graces now. She retreated through the swinging doors.

As soon as the waitress was out of earshot, Jill leaned in and whispered urgently. "I can't let Brent Miles know about the show. He can ruin things for me, Kate."

The skin on my arms turned to goose bumps. "Ruin things for you? How?"

Before she could answer, the sound of a dog barking erupted out of Jill's purse. I stared at it, surprised.

Jill giggled. "Like my ring tone?" She pulled her Tory Burch bag onto her lap and began to dig through the front pocket. "Brent Miles is weird, Kate." She pulled out her phone and grimaced. "Egad, I hope it isn't him calling right now!"

The vision of the skull cap man holding his cell phone flashed in my mind. I twisted in my chair to look across the street.

Skull cap man was gone.

"UC Med Center," Jill said.

I turned back to her. She was staring at her phone display an expression on her face somewhere between puzzled and cautious.

"I missed the call," she said flatly.

I grimaced. A hospital calling couldn't be good news, could it? Unless it was a message from her doctor, then it might be. Only judging by the look on Jill's face, it didn't seem hopeful. "Maybe they'll leave a message," I said.

Jill shook her phone as if that would speed up the voicemail alert function. "I hope everything is all right with Perry. He went hiking this morning." Her lips twisted and her forehead creased as she thought for a moment. "I hope he didn't sprain an ankle or something."

I nodded reassuringly. "And who is Perry?"

Her face lit up with a smile. "He is my latest conquest. He's hot, hot, hot Kate. I can't wait for you to meet him. 6'4", sandy blond hair, dimpled chin. Looks straight out of a Pendleton catalogue."

I laughed. "You usually go for the short, bald type."

Jill almost snorted out her hot chocolate, then clamped a napkin to her mouth. After a second she cleared her throat and said, "I do not."

I laughed again. "What about Henry?"

Jill chuckled. "I was 16 for God's sake, and he wasn't bald. He was…"

"Bald. He was bald. Even at 17, he had a receding hairline."

"Henry was very sweet. I can't believe you have such a cruel memory."

I feigned innocence. "I'm not saying there's anything wrong with short, bald guys. I'm just saying I thought they were your type."

"Nobody's type is short and bald."

"Let's see, there was Henry, then Richard, Brandon, Mitchell—"

"Okay, shut up. Maybe looks aren't that important. All the guys you mentioned were like, artistic, poets, you know?"

It was my turn to snort.

Jill pointed a finger at me. "And you're forgetting Gunter. Remember him?"

"Who could forget Gunter? He was a Nordic god."

Jill raised her eyebrows at me. "Only he was a little jerky. Perry is just as hot as Gunter, but sweet."

She blushed.

"Oh. A little rosy around the edges, are you? Is it love? How long have you been seeing each other?"

"A few months," she smiled. "We met at Bottle Top downtown. Do you know it?"

I shook my head. "Please, I don't get out."

She laughed. "You're out now."

I waved her off. "This is different. It's a baby-friendly place. What is Bottle Top, a club?"

"No, a swanky restaurant I reviewed," Jill said.

"So it's love, then?" I pressed.

"I gave it a pretty good review."

I laughed. "I meant Perry."

She smiled. "Him, too! I give him a *great* review!"

"Wedding bells?" I asked.

She blushed. "You know what, Kate? Maybe. Maybe, finally, yes."

Her phone beeped and she glanced at the screen, then frowned. She held up a finger. "One second, okay?"

I waved a hand at her. "Of course."

She tapped at the screen, then pressed the phone to her ear.

My stomach rumbled and I fidgeted with my water glass. When was my lunch going to arrive? The waitress hadn't even brought a bread basket!

I laughed to myself suddenly, thinking if I were a restaurant critic, I would be as harsh as Jill. I absently wondered what she liked about this place. Yes, the atmosphere was cozy and kid friendly, but where was the food, for God's sake?

Jill covered her mouth with her hand. I watched her face. It didn't look like good news.

Our waitress approached with steaming plates in hand. As she placed the dishes in front of us, Jill pushed back from the table.

"Kate. I'm so sorry. I have to go. Perry's at UC. He fell from Painted Rock."

"What? Is he okay?"

Painted Rock was a cliff on the north side of San Francisco. It was a featured attraction on the Land's End hike that ran from Ocean Beach and Sutro Baths all the way to the Legion of Honor. There were many notorious cliffs, one of which was Painted Rock, which boasted some of the most spectacular views of the Marin Headlands and the Golden Gate Bridge. The cliff literally dangled over the Pacific. A fall from there could be grave.

"I don't know." Jill pulled a credit card from her purse.

I waved her away. "I got it, don't worry. Do you want me to go with you?"

"Oh, thank you, Kate. But no, you have the baby. You can't bring her to a hospital." Her face crinkled at the word *hospital* and I could only guess what was rushing through her mind. She added, "I'll call you tonight."

She leaned over to kiss my cheek, then rubbed Laurie's knee. "Goodbye little baby. I hope to see you soon."

I nodded and watched her leave, an uneasiness overcoming me. I looked at the corner. Skull cap man was back, and this time he trailed after Jill.

Man!

Now I needed to pay immediately and the waitress had vanished again. I placed Laurie in her infant carrier, then fished around the massive diaper bag for my wallet. Why didn't I have a small, cute purse like Jill?

I rooted past the diaper wipes and a pacifier.

Oh right, fashion purses don't hold much baby paraphernalia.

Then I pushed aside my binoculars, and an UZI tactical self defense pen…

Fashion purses probably don't fit much P.I. equipment, either.

I finally located my wallet and peeked inside. I had $17. Not nearly enough to pay for the chichi lunch. Probably not even enough to pay for the coffee drinks these days.

I pulled out my phone and messaged Jill:

Skull cap man is on your tail. I will trail you.

I rose and walked toward the back of the restaurant. "Hello?" I called out.

Our waitress appeared and I handed her my credit card. "I have to leave immediately. Can you ring me up?"

She made a face. "Is something wrong with the food?"

"No. Nothing like that. Just personal business."

"Can I wrap it up for you?"

"No. Thank you."

The waitress froze, then slowly she looked over my shoulder at the moms in the corner and then leveled a glare at me. "Are you a reviewer?"

"What? No. I just need to leave."

I refrained from turning around and staring at the moms behind me. Maybe they had ratted out Jill, only somehow the message had gotten confused and now I was the target.

The waitress clutched my credit card and squinted at me. "Okay," she said, drawing the word out unnecessarily. "One minute."

Laurie began to fidget in her carrier seat. I returned to the table to pack up my purse. The moms in the corner were watching me. My phone rang. I answered quickly, expecting Jill, but instead my best friend Paula's voice filled the line.

"I'm in labor!" Paula screamed out.

"Yippee!" I hooted.

"Yippee? This is real pain, sister."

Suddenly a stern looking man strode out from the back room clutching my credit card.

The moms on the couch began packing up their gear.

"Do you have a ride to the hospital?" I asked Paula.

Laurie squirmed out of the carrier and onto the floor.

"Uh…hold on," I said partly to Paula and partly to the stern man.

Paula screamed into my ear. "Hold on? Hold on to what? You're actually putting a woman in labor on hold?"

I picked Laurie up; she began to cry.

My phone beeped with an incoming call, but I didn't dare tell Paula to hold again.

The stern looking man thrust my credit card at me.

Was I over my limit?

"Are you Jill Harrington?"

I shook my head at him and glanced at my phone. Jill was beeping in. I pivoted my body so the man wouldn't be able to see my phone screen.

He frowned. "Well, then you go by another name. Maybe you're Carol McCarthy? You're a crit, though." He pointed at my card. "You're not fooling anyone with this pseudonym! Kate Connolly? Please."

The waitress came out from the back and angled her phone at me. "I've got her picture now, Donald, don't worry. We'll be able to post this online and warn everyone about her."

Laurie wailed louder and I pressed the phone to my ear, trying to ignore everything, only now Paula was wailing, too. "Paula, can you get to the hospital on your own?"

She took three short breaths, then said, "Yes, but I need you to pick up Danny."

Danny was Paula's two-year-old son, and our plan had always been for him to stay with me when she went to the hospital.

"UC won't let him into the maternity ward without another adult present," Paula continued. "David's flight's been delayed and I can't reach—"

"UC? I thought you were going to California Pacific?"

Paula wailed again.

"Another contraction?" I asked.

She ignored my question. "Meet me at UC, not Cal Pacific. Our insurance changed. Don't you ever listen—"

She continued to scold me but I covered the mouthpiece on the phone and addressed the dour man standing in front of me.

"Look," I hissed. "I am *not* a food critic. My name is Kate Connolly. My friend is in labor and I have to meet her. Please run the charges on my card."

Of course, I didn't add that Jill was indeed a critic or the fact that if I'd been a critic I would have given the place the ultimate thumbs down.

The moms in the corner huffed past us with their silent, sleeping, perfect-angel babies. Laurie cried even louder and entwined her fingers in my hair. I yelped.

Mr. Sour grabbed the card from me and whipped around to hand it off to the waitress turned paparazzi.

"I don't believe you. I'm going to splatter your picture all over the web," she said as she turned on her heel.

My phone beeped as Jill's call went into voicemail.

Darn it!

I rooted around the diaper bag and found a pacifier. Laurie kicked out her legs and arched her back when she saw it. I put it in her mouth and returned my attention to Paula. "I'll meet you at UC."

Although I had a baby in tow, UC seemed to be the place I needed to be anyway: while I took charge of Danny, I could follow up with Jill.

Paula let out a deep moan.

"Don't drive. Take a cab!" I said.

She mumbled something.

"What?" I asked.

"Can you call me a cab?" she whimpered.

The waitress emerged from the back and slapped my credit card along with the printout onto the table.

"Yes," I said to Paula and hung up.

I glared at the waitress and signed my name on the receipt. She snatched it from my hand, returning my glare.

I strapped the buckles on Laurie's car seat.

There was no way she could squirm her way out now.

I dialed Yellow Cab and ordered one for Paula ASAP, then headed out.

Even though I was desperate to listen to Jill's voicemail, I couldn't stand the cafe one moment longer.

Once at my car, I secured Laurie's portable car seat into the base, then hopped into the driver's seat and dialed my voicemail.

Jill's voice filled the line. "Kate. That guy isn't following me, so there's no need for you—"

There was a rustling sound, then a high pitched yelp from Jill. The line went dead.

3

I dialed Jill and got her voicemail. I pounded on my steering wheel and let out a few choice swear words.

Laurie made a noise from her car seat.

I adjusted the rearview mirror and studied Laurie in the Elmo mirror that was pinned to the backseat. "Sorry for the swearing, sweat pea."

Laurie pointed at my reflection in her mirror and cooed.

I texted Jill.

R U OK? WHERE R U? I'M ON MY WAY TO UC.

Then I dialed my hubby, Jim.

He picked up on the first ring. "Great news, honey. Ramon is here," he said. He's cooking up a storm—"

"What? Ramon? What's he doing there?"

We'd met Ramon over the holidays when I'd been investigating the murder of a reporter. Ramon catered for the television station the victim had worked for.

"Cooking!"

My stomach growled. "Uh! Sorry I'm missing out. Hey listen, Paula's in labor. David's flight's been delayed so I'm on my way to UC. Can you meet me there and pick up the kids?"

"Kids?"

"I have to watch Danny. He's not allowed into the maternity ward and neither is our little jelly belly."

"Oh," Jim said. "Uh, the empanadas are nearly out of the oven and I— "

"Empanadas? Come on, Jim. I can't take—"

"Well, it's not only the empanadas. I have a sales call scheduled this afternoon. I really worked for this one, so I'd hate to reschedule. Can I call your mom? Maybe she can—"

A sales call, my foot! I knew he intended to dig into Ramon's dish unabashedly. But, okay, just because I didn't get to eat lunch didn't mean he had to starve.

"Okay, call mom. If she can come, you can stay home and eat. And try not to burn your tongue."

I pulled into the UC Medical Center parking lot like a chicken with its head cut off. Thankfully, Laurie had fallen asleep on the ride and she gave me no problems as I released her car seat from its base and snapped it into the stroller.

I wheeled the stroller to the hospital entrance and looked for mom. Instead, I saw my mom's boyfriend, Galigani, who also happened to be my boss and mentor, approaching.

Galigani was tall and dark with a thick mustache. He'd retired from the San Francisco Police Department before I'd met him and started his own private investigation service. Under his guidance, I'd solved three crimes and had hopes of having a new career as a P.I.

"Hey, kid!" he said jovially.

"What are you doing here? It's not your heart, is it?" I asked.

Three months prior, Galigani had undergone open-heart surgery.

He laughed. "If I keep hanging out with you and your mom, it might be. I'm here in lieu of Vera."

"Why? Where is she?" I asked.

He placed a hand on his chest as though he were crestfallen. "I'm that disappointing?"

I leaned in to kiss his cheek. "No. I didn't mean that. In fact, you'll probably give me less lip than Mom."

"Don't count on it," he said.

I pulled my phone out and checked the display. No word from either Paula or Jill.

"Come on. I need to get inside and check for my friends," I said.

Galigani frowned. "I have to go inside? I thought I was just picking up the kids."

I turned to him. "Are you afraid of the hospital?"

He looked at me like I was the dumbest person on the planet.

"Never mind," I said. "Do you have a car seat in your car?"

He shook his head.

"How are you supposed to take the kids then?"

He stroked his mustache and asked. "They need car seats?"

I returned his 'you're the stupidest person I know' look. Galigani simply looked back me, tilting his chin down so that he looked at me through his eyelashes. It was his best 'I only have disdain for you' look.

I whipped out my phone and sent a message first to Paula, then Jill and finally Jim.

Galigani continued to look at me. "Are you hoping that if you tap that thing long enough, car seats will appear out of thin air?"

"Funny," I said, without looking up. "You can take my car."

I dug into my diaper bag to retrieve my keys, while filling Galigani in on my lunch.

He frowned when I told him about Jill's last message.

"Let's check and see how her boyfriend, Perry, is doing. Maybe he's here and she's with him."

"You want to go into the hospital with me?" I asked.

Before Galigani could answer, a yellow cab pulled up in front of us.

My mother burst out of the cab in true Vera style. She wore a blue and red striped knit cap that was somewhat reminiscent of a barber pole with a feather sticking out of it.

I hate to admit that I hesitated before saying the word, "Mom."

Mom on the other hand didn't hesitate at all. She gleefully yelled at us. "Hey, gang! I brought the lady of the hour."

What was Mom doing in Paula's cab?

Out of the cab jumped Danny, Paula's two-year-old son, who pulled on mom's arm and said, "Mommy's stuck."

A clodhopper attached to a very swollen ankle poked out of the cab and remained frozen in mid-air.

I left Laurie in her stroller with Galigani and motioned for Mom to take Danny to the curb.

I peeked inside the cab. Paula was in a semi-reclined position, wearing a flowered maternity smock and leggings, a hand on her protruding belly and a miserable expression on her face.

I smiled at her. "Need a little help?"

"Help, yes, but you can save the forced gaiety. I won't be happy until this little sucker is out of my body!"

I grabbed her elbow and heaved her out. She was my best friend and I loved her like a sister. I knew her well enough to know that even if the contractions and labor pain were enough to put her in a bad mood, worse was having to suffer the maternity smocks and clodhoppers.

"You're in the home stretch now," I said encouragingly. "You'll be back to your fashionable self in no time."

Paula grimaced while Galigani secured a wheelchair.

Paula seated herself. "Ah. Thank you. Who said chivalry was dead?"

I paid the cabbie and joined my crew at the curb. Mom had already taken charge of the children. Danny clung to her leg while he fussed with the wrapper of a lollipop that she'd no doubt just given him, while Laurie squealed to be let out of the stroller.

"She was asleep," I complained.

Mom laughed. "She's a very smart girl. She knows when there's excitement."

"How did you end up in their cab?" Galigani asked Mom.

"Oh, I saw those dreadful rates for the parking garage, and there's no way I was paying that! So, I had to hunt out a city spot."

"She hailed us about five blocks ago," Paula said.

Galigani handed Mom my keys. "Are you taking the kids, then? I'm going to help Kate out with a few things."

Mom's eyes flashed with excitement. "A new investigation?"

"Labor here, people," Paula howled.

I gave Mom directions to where I'd parked and wheeled Paula into the hospital.

Galigani and I agreed that while I stayed with Paula, he would poke around and see if he could get any information on Jill's boyfriend.

After the hospital checked Paula into an observation room, the first words out of her mouth were, "When can I get the epidural?"

The nurse, a small blonde who looked not a day older than 12, said sweetly, "Oh, we need to see how far along you are before we can even get you admitted to Labor and Delivery." She tapped at a computer monitor then said, "I'll be back in flash. I just need to get you set up in our system."

Paula smiled sweetly back to the nurse, but as soon as she left the room Paula let out a stream of profanity that someone suffering from Tourette Syndrome would envy. She finished with, "I want the stupid, stupid, stupid epidural now."

"Hey," I said, rubbing her shoulder. "They'll get it to you soon."

She let out a series of deep moans that frightened even me.

Another nurse peeked into our room and asked cheerfully, "Everything all right in here?"

Paula replied quickly, "Oh, yes. Thank you. My friend rubbed my shoulder and I feel better already."

I frowned. The mere presence of the nurse had calmed Paula down.

The nurse proceeded to complete her check of Paula, including attaching as many monitors as possible. Neither Paula nor that baby would make a move or take a breath that wasn't accounted for.

While the nurse worked, Paula had a contraction but breathed right through it. No moans, no swearing, no yelling. But as soon as the nurse left, satisfied that Paula was progressing as expected, Paula let out another scream.

"What's wrong?" I asked.

"It's another contraction, dummy," she said.

I cringed. "Sorry."

The blonde nurse returned to check on Paula's IV, which again turned Paula into an angel. When the nurse left, Paula began to moan as if she'd been stabbed.

I squeezed her hand. "Is there anything I can do for you?"

"Don't touch me," she said.

"How come you're all nice to the nurses and mean to me?" I asked.

"I don't know them," Paula said.

I laughed. "Okay. I'm the punching bag until David gets here, huh?"

My phone went off and I crossed the room to get my purse. Paula asked, "What are you doing?"

"Checking my phone. When you called I was at lunch with Jill— "

"You can't check your phone now. I'm in labor! You're supposed to be my support!"

I grimaced. "Sorry. I didn't mean to offend you. It's just that—"

She moaned again.

"You want to watch some TV?" I asked.

Paula stared at me. "Watch some TV?"

"You know, to distract you a bit."

"Punching you in the nose might distract me."

"In your condition, I think I can take you," I said.

She didn't laugh though, instead she moaned again, only this time deeper and longer as if possessed. I crossed to the door.

When she recovered from the contraction enough to speak, Paula asked, "Where are you going?"

"Nowhere. I'm looking for a nurse, hoping one will come in soon to check on you so you'll be nice to me again."

Paula's face softened for a moment. "Sorry, Kate. You know I love you."

She was overtaken by another contraction and I called the nurse. "I think things are speeding up in here. Maybe it's time to move us to Labor and Delivery?" I said on the intercom.

A nurse came in to evaluate Paula. While Paula was distracted I checked my phone. Galigani had left me a voicemail and I itched to check it.

If I left the room, certainly Paula would notice.

"I'm just going to use the restroom," I lied.

Paula moaned softly and glared at me. In the glare I could definitely tell she was calling me on my lie. The nurse stroked

Paula's forehead and she seemed temporarily soothed with the acknowledgement of the pain.

I escaped into the private bath that was attached to her room. I quickly dialed voicemail and listened to Galigani.

"Hey kid. I haven't heard anything about your friend Jill, but I have news on the accident victim. It ain't good. Call me."

I dialed Galigani, and when he answered I ran the tap water to mask my voice.

"Hey," I whispered. "What's happened to Perry? What room is he in? Can we go see him?"

"He was DOA, kid."

I gasped. "Oh no."

"Yeah, terrible. The Coast Guard picked him up," Galigani said. "They're releasing him to the medical examiner. Do you think there's any reason for me to try and flag the case?"

"Flag the case?" I asked. "You think there was foul play?"

"No. Well, I don't know," Galigani said. "That's what I'm asking you."

"Oh. Well, no. I mean, he fell while hiking, right?"

"Seems so," Galigani said. "Although his girlfriend, Jill, is missing now, too…"

I swallowed past the fear building up in my throat. "Well, she's not exactly missing, is she? I'm sure she's going to call me soon."

There were escalated screams coming from the hospital room. "I gotta go," I said, hanging up.

I turned the water off and ran into Paula's room. "How are you?"

She gave me the evil eye. "Awful. The nurse said I'm not progressing at all."

Reaching out for her hand I said, "Oh, sorry."

"Don't be sorry about that. It's not your fault. Be sorry about the fact that you're sneaking phone calls in the bathroom when you're supposed to be here supporting me!"

I squeezed her hand. "Sorry about that, too."

She pulled her hand away. "And don't touch me!"

I laughed and seated myself in the soft chair by the window. "Want me to sing to you?"

"No."

"Did you bring a book? I can read to you."

"No."

"Okay, no TV, no singing, no reading. How about I play a meditation CD for you or something?"

She gave me a scathing look. "Meditation CD?" Her voice was filled with contempt. "Puh-leese."

"Those haven't caught on with you yet?" I asked innocently.

She raised a brow at me but didn't say anything.

After a moment of tapping my fingers on her food tray and eyeing her saltine crackers, I asked, "Did you bring a photo album or anything to look through?"

Paula stared at me. "What?"

"You know, in all the labor prep books they tell moms to pack some calming photos to look through. Like pictures of the beach with the little huts on stilts in Bora Bora overlooking the emerald water, or a picture of Danny or—"

Paula looked like she held back screaming at me in order to breathe her way through a contraction. When it passed, she said, "Okay, put on the stupid TV. Anything is better than listening to you."

I decided not to be hurt and flipped on the TV. My stomach rumbled and I eyed the saltine crackers on Paula's dinner tray. "Are you going to eat those crackers?" I asked.

Paula turned to me and seemed so upset that I could swear her eyes were glowing red. "What do you think?"

I leaned forward and snatched the crackers of the tray. "You're not supposed to eat at this stage of labor. It could make you sick.

I'm doing you a favor here." I ripped into the package. "I didn't get to eat lunch—"

"Sorry I interrupted your little *soirée* with Jill," Paula said sarcastically.

"No. You didn't," I said, stuffing a saltine in my mouth and ignoring her sarcasm. "That's what I was trying to tell you when you—"

Paula's shook her head. "Uh huh. I can't hear it now. Sorry. Pain."

Her face contorted, but she didn't moan or have a bout of Tourettes.

"You okay?" I asked.

Paula nodded. "Yeah, that one wasn't so bad."

"I'm glad. It really sucks to see your best friend in pain."

Paula smiled, not a full, normal Paula smile, but at least her lips twitched up instead of down.

"Tell me about Jill before I have a baby."

I filled her in as quickly as I could. Oddly, she didn't have a contraction during my story and she seemed almost herself.

When I was done we stared at each other.

"Did Galigani flag the body so the M.E. can take a look?"

I shrugged. "I don't know. You wouldn't let me talk to him."

"Call him," Paula said.

I looked at the monitor that was tracking Paula's contractions. "I don't think I'm supposed to use a cell phone near the equipment."

Paula followed my eyes. "Hey, look at my report there." She indicated a roll of paper that was spitting out of the machine periodically.

I picked it up. "What?"

"I haven't had a contraction in about 15 minutes!"

"So?"

"I don't think that good," she said.

"I'm sure it's alright. Want me to call the nurse?"

"I guess, but I already know what she's going to say." She sighed. "False labor."

4

I drove home from the hospital quickly, my thoughts a jumble about Jill, food and babies. Jill hadn't answered any of my messages and I needed to get home to my computer to find her address. I cursed myself for not being more tech-savvy. Surely there was a better way to access my computer than physically driving across town.

Not to mention, I still hadn't had lunch and Ramon had left freshly baked empanadas at our house. But mostly, I really did need to check in on Jim and feed Laurie. It was already 4:00 pm and she was due to nurse.

At home, Mom had dropped the kids off with Jim, who seemed to be managing quite well with them, as the house was silent. I moved into the living room and saw that he'd pitched a tent in the middle of the room.

"Hi honey, I'm home."

There was no answer. Jim's bare foot was sticking out from the tent, which at 6'2" was no surprise. I leaned down and tickled it.

He laughed. "How'd everything go?" he asked from inside the tent.

"False labor."

Jim peeked out, his blondish red hair rumpled. He frowned. "No baby?"

"Not yet. They sent her home. If she doesn't go into labor again this week, they'll induce her on Monday."

"What a drag," he said, emerging from under the tent.

"How did your sale thing go?" I asked, nuzzling myself into Jim's arms.

"Actually, I think it went really well," He kissed my face and squeezed me tight. "I have a follow-up presentation with them downtown and hopefully I'll close 'em then."

"Good for you, honey. So proud of you," I said, as I disentangled myself from his embrace and flopped onto the sofa. I was exhausted and hungry at the same time. I supposed it would be better to feed Laurie first and then eat on the way to Jill's place.

"Bring Laurie to me, would ya?" I asked.

I needn't have asked him, because he'd already scooped her into his arms.

He handed her to me. "She's asleep."

"And Danny?" I asked.

Jim cocked his head toward the tent. "He's napping, snuggled in his Thomas the Train sleeping bag."

I nodded. "You remember my friend Jill?"

"Of course. Jill's all the rage on Yelp. Ramon was here making me empanadas because he's going to be Brent Miles' next star."

"What?"

"Yeah, Brent Miles is opening a new restaurant. He tried Ramon's catering service and hired him on the spot. Get this, Ramon found Jill on Facebook, saw she was connected to you and is wondering if you can get her to recant her bad review of Miles' restaurant."

I guffawed. "I don't think I have a chance. Listen to this."

I brought him up to speed on the events of lunch and the hospital. When I mentioned the fact that Jill had been followed by a guy wearing a skull cap and hadn't returned any of my messages, Jim offered to go to her place and check on her.

"I was planning on doing that myself but I need fuel. Any empanadas left?" I asked.

I unlatched Laurie, who had basically nursed in her sleep, and passed her to Jim. He burped her while I fixed my blouse.

Jim laughed. "A tray full. I ate as many as I could," he said, as he patted his flat stomach, "but even I couldn't eat them all."

I took a plate of empanadas, delicious little pockets of warm dough stuffed with ground pork seasoned with garlic, onion, tomato puree, and dribbled with chipotle sauce, into Laurie's nursery.

Laurie's nursery doubled as our office, since we lived in a ridiculously expensive home in San Francisco that only had two bedrooms. It was either share an office with Laurie or move our computers onto the dining room table, which as it happened both Jim and I were against. We'd have to come up with a plan for when Laurie got bigger, but right now I needed to focus on Jill.

I powered up my PC and pulled up Jill's address. I recorded it on a post-it note, and then did a Google search on Brent Miles.

He was an SF personality, a former seminary student who'd made a fortune when he founded Brent Miles Campaigns, dedicated to promoting underdog political causes. He'd made a secondary fortune on commercial real estate and was now trying his hand at restaurant ownership.

Jill's review appeared in my search results. I clicked it.

"How on earth did my meal even find its way out of the kitchen? Can you say, zero quality control? My salad was wilted with the dressing slopped over the rim, made all the worse by the fact that I'd requested the dressing on the side. My burger was overdone yet lukewarm, served on a stale bun. The menu choices were a

huge disappointment. All I can report is that Mr. Brent Miles'
PHILOSOPHIE must be not to go the extra mile."

I grimaced. I could see how this review would scare people off from trying the new restaurant.

I poked around online a bit more and found a news article on SF Gate mentioning Mr. Miles. A former employee of Brent's had died in a freak hiking accident in Yosemite the previous summer. He'd plunged more than 370 feet to his death after climbing the Mist Trial in Yosemite National Park. It had been an unusually high water year and there were signs posted near Vernal Falls prohibiting swimming in the Emerald Pool, but apparently the employee had done just that.

Another hiking accident...

This couldn't be a coincidence.

My home phone rang again.

"Hello?" I said.

Galigani's voice filled the line. "Kate, I've been thinking about that hiker. You know, your friend's boyfriend?"

"Mmm-hmm," I said, eager to beat him to the punch. "Looks like a Brent Miles' employee had a similar *accident.*"

"Oh." Galigani sounded annoyed. "You know about that?"

I laughed. "I've been trained by the best."

"You haven't been trained! You only started investigating a couple months ago. Don't think that, either, that you know everything already. As soon as you start thinking that, then bam, something's gonna bite you right in the— "

"I don't think I know everything already!" I interrupted defensively.

Galigani harrumphed.

"I've only started looking into Brent Miles," I said. "And I thought it was a pretty big coincidence, too. That one of his employees died at Vernal Falls."

Galigani was silent for a moment. I felt like I needed to offer him something to soften him up a bit, but I wasn't sure what he was looking for.

I cleared my throat. "You know I always appreciate any advice you have for me."

This got a laugh out of him. Then he said, "Okay, kid, I'll fill you in. Can you come over?"

"Actually, I'm on my way to Jill's. She hasn't returned any of my messages."

Galigani let out a low moan. "That's not good. Yeah, you'd better head over there."

Jim came into the office and I hit the speaker button so he could hear my conversation with Galigani.

"So this is what I know," Galigani continued. "Brent Miles is broke. The commercial buildings he owns downtown are all mortgaged to the hilt. He's gambling what he's got left in the restaurant business. He has plans to unveil three new restaurants this spring."

Jim grabbed an empanada off my plate and said, "Yup. Empanada King."

Galigani laughed. "How did you know?"

"The king himself was here trying out a new recipe."

"Ramon?" Galigani asked excitedly.

Jim stuffed his mouth with huge bite and made an exaggerated 'mmm' sound.

Galigani laughed.

"So, are you guys thinking that Brent Miles is behind Jill's boyfriend's death?" Jim asked, "Like a threat or something for her to recant her review?"

"Exactly," I said.

"But that makes no sense," Jim said. "If he wanted her to change her review he'd threaten her about it, maybe, if he's that type of guy. But how is killing her boyfriend going to make her change the review?"

"Well, he did that too. He threatened her. And I saw skull cap man follow her. What if killing her boyfriend is a warning? You know, declaring that he's serious," I said.

Jim shrugged. "Maybe it was just an accident."

I stared at him.

"I know you guys are investigators and all. And you're always looking for drama...um...I mean, looking for something to investigate, but it was probably an accident. Did you know that hiking is the most dangerous sport after skateboarding?"

"I didn't know skateboarding was a sport," I said, wiggling my computer mouse to bring my PC out of sleep mode.

I showed Jim the story on Brent Miles employee's death in Yosemite.

Jim's face turned white. "You'd better go check on Jill."

I wrapped the remainder of my empanada in a paper towel and finished it on the road to Jill's house. She lived in the Russian Hill district of San Francisco, and I absently wondered how she afforded the rent. I mean, how much money could she be making from writing restaurant reviews? Although, with her new TV gig, rent probably wouldn't be a problem. Right now, I just hoped to find her safe and sound and tried not to let my mind race with possibilities.

In Russian Hill, the streets were winding and cramped, parking non-existent. After circling the block for ten minutes I decided to double park on the corner and put my hazard signals on.

With the sun setting and a light drizzle starting, I jogged up the block to Jill's. I could see Jill through her front bay window, curled up like a cat on the window seat. She was wearing grey sweats and holding a martini glass. She looked awfully comfy.

As soon as I'd had the thought I immediately felt guilty. People grieve in different ways. Who was I to judge?

Jill spotted me, a look of surprise on her face. She rose and disappeared from view.

I climbed up the steps as the front door flew open.

Jill embraced me. "Oh, Kate. I wasn't expecting you. I had terrible news at the hospital. I'm a nervous wreck."

"I know."

She pulled away from me. "You know?" Her voice caught and she began to sob. "We were going to get married," she said. "He's gone now. Dead. Just like that. How does something like that happen?"

She buried her face into my neck and I smoothed down her hair. After a moment I prodded her back to the bay window. There was a new tissue box next to the seat and I placed it between us.

She tucked her bare feet under her and wrestled the first tissue out of the box, managing to free a clump of them together. She tried to shove the clump back into the box, making a noise that was a cross between a growl and whimper in her throat.

I took the tissues out of her hand and sat with her. We sat in silence for a while until she cried her way through the balance of tissues in my hand. When she reached the final one, I asked. "What happened to you earlier?"

She blinked at me. "What do you mean?"

"Last time we spoke, you got cut off. I left you a few messages and I waited around for you at the hospital."

"You were at the hospital?"

I nodded. "Paula was in labor. Well, false labor."

The news caused another jag of crying.

After a moment, Jill said, "I'm happy for her, really. Another baby. I wonder if I'll ever have one."

I patted her back, letting the awkward moment settle between us.

"When I got there they told me he was DOA." She was hit by another bout of tears. "I didn't even get to say good-bye."

I sat silently holding her hand for a bit.

"His sister, Melanie, got there when I did. We left the hospital pretty quickly, and she's coming over here," Jill glanced down the street. "We need to get drunk." She picked up her martini glass. "Lemon drop martini. Want one?"

I shook my head. "I'm glad you're safe. I was worried about you."

Jill frowned. "Why?"

"The creepy guy seemed to be following you and then when you called, it sounded like you screamed—"

"Oh. I think...I think..." She looked confused and scratched at her forehead. "I twisted my ankle on the curb when I got to the hospital. I must have dropped my phone. I'm sorry Kate. I don't know." She paused and glanced around the room. "I don't even know where my phone is right now. It's been powering itself off. I have to take it in for repair."

She spotted her purse across the room, propped on a chaise with silk flowers embroidered on it. Jill's apartment was as dainty as she was, decorated in whites and pinks. Behind the chaise was a floor lamp topped with a delicate lace shade. She padded over to her purse, fished out her phone and turned it on.

My own phone buzzed in my pocket.

I read a text from Galigani.

36

Monitoring police scanner — Burglary at 123 Franklin. That's the victim's place. Cops on the way. Meet me?

I heard a gasp from Jill. I looked up and saw her reading her screen.

"What is it?" I asked.

"Melanie left me a message. She stopped at Perry's to get his cat. Someone was there and beat her up."

5

"Let's go," I said. "My car's on the corner."

Jill slipped on a pair of red flats, which were next to the window seat. She glanced at her dowdy sweats. "I can't go like this!"

I looked myself over and cringed at the chipotle stain that had seeped into my t-shirt. "I'm in jeans. It's fine," I said, deciding not to call much attention to my sloppiness.

"Give me a minute," she said crossing the room and disappearing down the hall. From her bedroom she called, "Do you want a fresh shirt?"

So my sloppiness had not gone unnoticed.

"That'd be great," I called back.

Sighing, I pulled out my phone and messaged Galigani. I told him about Melanie and that we were on our way. Then I messaged Jim and waited for Jill.

After a few minutes, Jill returned in tan slacks and a red blouse that matched her Wizard of Oz shoes. Her face was freshly scrubbed, make-up reapplied, and hair coiffed.

"I'm ready," she said, handing me a clean t-shirt. Printed on the front of the shirt was a logo for Escape from Alcatraz, a 1.5-mile swim that took place every year in San Francisco.

"Wow! Did you do the Escape from Alcatraz?"

She snorted. "God, no. A friend did it."

I nodded. "Let's go."

"Oh, Kate. You don't have to go with me. I'm fine. I'm sure you need to go home to the baby."

I waved off her concern. "I left Jim a message. He's fine watching her."

Jill walked to her front door, her hand poised on the knob. "No, really. I'll deal with Melanie on my own. You go home."

I shook my head. "I haven't had a chance to tell you yet. A few months back, I started my own P.I. business. My mentor, Galigani, is meeting us at Perry's place."

Jill's face paled. "What?"

"We think you're on Brent Miles' hit list."

I drove to Franklin Street, while Jill sat quietly in the passenger seat. She offered a few directions when I complained about no left turns, but other than that she remained silent.

On Franklin, the parking wasn't nearly as tight as I feared and I managed to nab a spot in front. Galigani's car was nowhere in sight, and I also noted the absence of police cruisers.

Had we missed everyone?

Jill hastily climbed out of my car and hurried up the walk to Perry's front door. Before we reached it, the door swung open and a short brunette holding an ice pack to her face appeared.

"Melanie!" Jill screamed as she rushed toward the woman. "Are you all right?"

Melanie lowered the ice pack, revealing a bruised eye. With her free hand, she gingerly touched her lip, which was swollen and cut.

Jill gasped. "Your face, my God!"

"Does it look as bad as it feels?" Melanie asked.

"Yes! You poor thing," Jill said.

Melanie stepped aside and let Jill and me into the apartment. "I called the cops but they haven't got here yet."

She looked me up and down.

Jill said, "This is my friend Kate. She was over when you called and she gave me a ride."

"I'm sorry for your loss," I said.

Melanie nodded. "Thank you. I'm still in shock. I feel like Perry's going to walk through the door at any minute."

She wandered toward the brown leather couch and motioned for us to take a seat, but we all remained standing. The apartment was tidy, with a masculine décor. Burgundy rug, brown lazy boy chair and matching mahogany side tables all screamed out "bachelor" and seemed directly incongruent to Jill's taste.

"What happened?" Jill prompted.

Melanie looked around the room, a lost expression on her poor, battered face. "I came to pick up Whiskers, you know? Where is he now?"

Jill shrugged. "He's probably hiding. Go on."

"I unlocked the door and came in, there was a rustling sound from the bedroom, I called out. I actually called out 'Perry.' Can you believe it?" She shook her head and gripped the couch. "Like it was him, in his bedroom. Like it was him that was going to come down the hallway, yelling at me for interrupting him or laughing or…"

She stopped herself short and sniffled.

I reached into my shoulder bag and searched for a hankie. I came up with a spit-up rag and decided not to hand it over; instead, I surveyed the room for a box of tissues.

"They're here," Melanie said.

"Who?" Jill asked.

Melanie jutted her chin toward the windows. "The cops. Finally. Took them forever."

Jill switched her weight from one red Dorothy shoe to the other. She looked as if she were about to speak, but instead moved toward the front door.

A lanky officer stood on the stoop.

"Got a call about an interrupted robbery," he said, matter-of-factly.

Jill motioned for him to come in. He surveyed the three us, eyes landing on Melanie. He grunted and took out a notebook.

I took out a notebook of my own. The officer, whose name tag read "Ross," raised an eyebrow at me. I smiled. He said nothing to me and turned to Melanie.

"Tell me what happened," Ross said.

I heard a car backfire and looked out the window to see Galigani searching for a spot to drop his rusty old car.

Melanie tentatively touched her split lip. "I came over to pick up my brother's cat. He was…"

"He had a hiking accident this morning," Jill said. "We've only just come from the hospital."

"So who lives here?" Ross asked.

"My brother," Melanie said. "Only…only now…" She teared up and her shoulders began to shake.

Jill put a hand to Melanie's shoulder. "Perry lived alone," she said to the officer. "We dated, but he lived here and I live in Russian Hill, Melanie lives across town, and Kate, well, she's just here for moral support. She didn't know Perry at all."

The officer frowned, but made a note. "Uh-huh. I'll need full names and relationships in a sec."

Galigani appeared in the open doorway. "Ross. How are you?"

The officer looked across the room and seemed surprised to see Galigani. "Oh, Albert. What are you doing here?" He glanced at Jill, Melanie and me as if expecting an explanation from us. Melanie and Jill looked equally confused.

"Galigani's my partner," I said.

"Partner?" Melanie asked.

"We're private investigators," I replied.

Galigani crossed the room toward Ross and touched his arm. "Perry Welgan is at the M.E.'s office. We may be looking at homicide."

"What?" Jill and Melanie said in unison.

Galigani glared at me and I cringed. I hadn't exactly mentioned the Medical Examiner's office to Jill yet, only that I thought she might be in danger.

"My brother had a hiking accident," Melanie said, her face looking more swollen than before. "What does his accident... what does it have to do with...homicide?"

Jill shook her head. "No, no. It's wasn't a homicide. He fell."

Melanie sank into couch. "Are you saying someone may have killed Perry?"

"Nobody killed Perry. Who would do that? He was liked by everyone. It was a horrible, tragic accident," Jill said.

Galigani bowed his head. "I'm sorry to upset you ladies. I spoke out of turn. Of course, the M.E. won't know anything for several weeks."

Ross nodded solemnly and turned to Melanie. "What can you tell me about the break-in, Miss?"

Melanie wrung her hands. "I came over to get the cat and there was a man here, in the back. Someone I've never seen before. He hit me in the face and knocked me down. Then he ran out."

While Melanie spoke, Galigani wandered over to the front door and examined the lock.

"Can you describe the man?" Ross asked.

Melanie shrugged. "It happened fast. All I really know is that he was tall."

"How tall?" Ross asked. "I'm 6'4". Was he my height?"

Melanie stood up and compared her height with Ross'. "No. Not that tall." She pointed to Galigani. "But taller than him."

"Everybody is taller than me," Galigani grunted.

Melanie laughed, then yelped. "Ouch. Don't make me laugh, it hurts my lip."

Galigani tilted his head in a sympathetic manner. "Sorry."

Ross asked, "Was the man Caucasian, Hispanic, African-American—?"

"He was white, his hair was sort of dark, but not very dark, and a bit curly…oh I don't know. I was so shocked, I guess his hair could have been any color."

After a moment Galigani asked, "Did you have a key to the apartment? Was the door locked?"

Melanie frowned. "I have a key. I used it, but now that you mention it, I don't think the door was bolted."

Ross glanced around the room at the windows. "Any sign of forced entry?"

Melanie shook her head. "I don't know. There aren't any broken windows if that's what you mean."

"Does this place have a back door?" Ross asked.

"No," Jill said.

"Was Perry in the habit of locking his front door?" I asked.

"Of course!" Melanie said. "I mean, this isn't the worst neighborhood in the city, but it is San Francisco. You have to lock your doors! Anyway, he would have locked it because of Whiskers. Where is he anyway?"

Jill tapped nervously against one of the side table. "Well, it's terrible luck, isn't it? First Perry's…awful accident…" Her eyes filled with tears and she blinked them away. "Now poor Melanie gets battered. We can just thank God that she isn't seriously hurt."

Galigani studied Melanie a moment. "Did your brother share anything disturbing with you, like strange phone calls, or maybe he thought he was being followed…"

"No," Melanie said. "Not to me, anyway." She looked at Jill expectantly.

Jill wiped at her eyes and shook her head. "No."

"So you were the only one getting calls?" Galigani asked.

"Calls?" Ross asked.

Jill turned toward me, but before she could answer, Ross asked, "Who were the calls from?"

Jill shrugged helplessly. "I think they were from Brent Miles. One was for sure. A sort of threatening call where he asked me to recant a bad review I gave his restaurant, *Philosophie.*"

Ross made a note in his book as if the information meant nothing to him, but Melanie took a sharp inhale of breath.

"Oh my God. He threatened you? What did he say?" she asked.

Jill waved her hands frantically as if she thought we were all on the wrong track. "No, no. I mean, he threatened my future as a critic, not my life."

Melanie looked dumbstruck.

Galigani and I exchanged a look.

Then after a moment Melanie pointed to Jill and said the thing I'd feared she say. "My brother is dead is because of you."

6

"Whoa," Galigani said. "We're moving way too fast here. We're still trying to figure things out. We need to—"

Melanie began to sob loudly. "I'm sorry, Jill, I didn't mean to blame you."

Jill clutched at Melanie's hands and pulled her into an embrace. "No, no. Don't apologize. I get it."

"I didn't know you were in danger!" Melanie said.

"No, no. I'm not," Jill said. "Please don't worry."

Galigani exchanged a concerned glance with me.

Ross said. "I'm going to take a look around the premises. We may need to cordon off the area."

Galigani nodded.

"Block off the apartment?" Melanie asked. "What about Whiskers?"

Jill pressed a hand to her temple. "Whiskers is the least of our worries."

Melanie shook her head. "No, he's just a kitten," she turned toward Ross. "We can't lock him out of the house!"

Galigani put an arm out toward Melanie. "Don't worry, we'll notify the SPCA with the cat description and your information, so you can be reunited."

Although it seemed like the chances of that were slim, Melanie appeared mollified, because she nodded and wandered over to the window to peek out. Ross left the room to examine the back of the apartment. I jutted my chin at Galigani, then nodded after Ross, signaling Galigani to poke his nose around with the uniformed officer.

Galigani eyed Melanie and Jill, then nodded at me and walked down the hallway toward what I presumed were the bedrooms.

I wanted to call after him to look for a black skull cap with a Smith & Wesson logo on it, but what would that prove?

It would link the man to Perry, but certainly not prove homicide.

Melanie turned away from the window. "So, you're a private investigator?"

I nodded.

Melanie looked at Jill, "Have you hired her to look into Perry's case?"

"Case?" Jill shook her head. "I don't think we have a case—"

"Well, what about the threats?" Melanie persisted. "We have to consider that Brent Miles could be behind this. I mean, what if—"

Jill pressed her fingers into her temples. "No—"

Melanie grabbed my arm. "I want to hire you. Oh, but..." She covered her heart with her hand and said, "But, I don't have any money. I...what am I going to do? I want you to look into this—"

"Mel, calm down," Jill said. "I know you're in shock, but please. All we know is that Perry had a tragic accident—"

"Your TV show! On Foodie Network! You're going to get some cash out of that, right? Are they giving you a signing bonus?" Melanie asked.

Jill's face flushed red. "No! I'm not getting a bonus. Where did you hear that?"

Melanie took a step back as if deflecting Jill's anger. She looked surprised and a little confused, but Galigani and Ross returned to the room before she could respond.

Ross had tucked away his notebook and had some business cards in his hand.

"I didn't see anything unusual, Miss, except that the television looked askew. Like someone was trying to wrench it off the wall. Can you tell if anything is missing?"

Melanie shook her head. "Only Whiskers, as far as I can tell." She turned to Jill, "Do you want to look around?"

Jill shook her head and shifted her weight impatiently.

Ross handed Melanie a card. "All right. If you think of anything else, call me."

I wondered about the television. Could they get fingerprints off it? Why hadn't Ross lifted any prints? Was there something about the burglary he wasn't taking seriously? Or was that something that was done later?

Could I learn how to dust for prints?

Galigani walked Ross to the door. They exchanged words I couldn't hear and then Ross left.

Galigani turned to us, looking grim. "I'm so sorry for your loss today, ladies. Please let Kate or me know if we can assist in any way."

Melanie leapt at him. "Please, oh yes, please."

Galigani nodded.

"We'll do what we can," I said. "Don't worry about the money. I'll work pro-bono."

Galigani gave me a strange look, then reached inside his jacket pocket for his business card.

Melanie took the card while Jill watched nervously, her face set in an expression I couldn't read.

I recalled her words, this afternoon at lunch, about Brent Miles really being able to mess with her career. Her television foodie show would soon begin filming, and Galigani and I were about to crawl into Brent Miles' life and make him miserable. No wonder Jill seemed upset.

And how likely was it that Miles had anything to with any of this? For all we knew, Perry could have slipped and fallen on his own.

What about the break-in then? A coincidence? Or an acquaintance of Perry's trying to help himself to some of the belongings Perry would no longer need?

My thoughts were interrupted by Jill saying, "I'll drive you home, Mel. You need some rest."

"How will you get home?" I asked Jill.

"Don't worry. I'll stay with Mel for a while, until she feels better, and then I'll take a cab."

We left the apartment together and then Jill and Melanie split off from Galigani and me.

"What was that look you gave me?"

"Pro-bono? You're not even supposed to be charging anyone. You have no license, remember?"

"Well, it's still my time."

Galigani snorted.

"Plus, I've always wanted to use the word pro-bono," I said.

"What you meant was that *I* would work pro-bono."

"I thought you were retired?"

Galigani laughed. "It's okay. You can't expect someone like that to pay a bunch of money to a P.I. Why do you think I drive my rattle-trap of a car? If I wanted to make money at this racket I'd be working for the likes of Brent Miles. Those are the P.I.'s that get the dough."

"The ones defending the bad guys?"

Galigani ran a hand through his hair. "No, the rich guys. Doesn't matter if he's guilty or not. And remember, we don't know anything yet. Brent Miles could turn out to be the good guy."

To Do:
1. Order dust kit!
2. Figure out what happened to Perry.
3. Buy Paula a present for new baby.
4. Get back in shape!

I slept poorly that night. My nightmares were filled with strange images from the hospital and Melanie's swollen face. I'd even dreamt about a lost kitten.

Poor Whiskers!

My stomach rumbled. I suddenly realized that if I was hungry, then Laurie must be famished. I slipped out of bed and walked down our short hall to the nursery that was doubling as our office.

Jim was holding Laurie while staring at his computer screen, engrossed in some graphics. Laurie had her tiny fists entangled in his hair, laughing as she pulled. Jim let out an exaggerated yelp every time she did it, which seemed to cause an even greater amount of glee for her.

"Good morning!" I said.

Jim swiveled in his chair. "Hi, honey." He kissed me and passed Laurie to me. "Someone's been missing you."

"No. She seemed perfectly happy with you."

Jim smiled. "Oh, you're just flattering me."

I yawned. "Thank you for letting me sleep in. I was exhausted."

He nodded. "I know. You're doing too much. You need to relax. I made you breakfast."

I squinted at him, suddenly suspicious. "Wait. You're letting me sleep in, you're playing with Laurie and you cooked? Something's up. Out with it."

Jim put a hand over his heart. "I don't know what you mean. I always make breakfast."

I guffawed. "No, you don't! And you never let me sleep in and you certainly don't play with the baby."

"Whatdaya mean?"

I leveled a stare at him.

"Okay, maybe I don't make breakfast as often as you do, but I do sometimes. And I've played with the baby before. She's just getting more aware of things, so it's more fun now. Before she was like a blob of goo."

I pressed Laurie to my chest. "A blob of goo!"

Jim laughed. "Well, you know, like a bowl of Jell-O."

"That's worse! You went from blob to Jell-O."

"Oh, but a Jell-O-y blob of goo that I love," Jim said.

I punched him the shoulder. "I know you're after something, and sooner or later you'll spill. But in the meantime, I'm going to scarf down my breakfast." I walked to the kitchen with Laurie in tow and found some dry toast on a plate and the coffee pot drained to about an inch reserve. "This is it?"

"What?" Jim called from the office.

"Dry toast and coffee dregs? That's what you call breakfast?"

There was no response from the office.

Conveniently silent!

I broke off a piece of the dry toast and gave it to Laurie to gum. She seemed delighted. How ungrateful was I? I should be happy like Laurie; dry toast was better then nothing.

I smeared butter and some jam on my piece, pondering poor Melanie. I didn't really have much to go on.

I moved into the living room and put Laurie on her play mat. I propped her up with a Boppy pillow where she practiced her balance for sitting. She wobbled to the left and then the right, and finally pitched forward, still clutching her piece of dry toast. She squealed out at me in protest, like I was a complete betrayer.

"Calm down, bunny girl." I repositioned her and she swayed only a bit, then steadied herself. "There you go."

She cooed at me, then immediately lost interest in me in favor of the toast.

I picked up my cordless phone and dialed Galigani. He picked up on the third ring.

"You busy?" I asked.

"I'm on hold with the M.E. Let me call you back."

I paced while I waited and finally decided to make a fresh pot of coffee. While I was waiting for the coffee to brew, the phone rang.

"What did you find out?"

"About what dear?" Mom asked.

"Oh. Mom. I'm waiting on a call. Let me call you back."

"Oh no, honey, I only called to find out if you need anything from the mall."

"No. Thanks."

"Not even something for Laurie? The little dresses here are so cute. Only $15. Really, how can I pass them up? I'm getting one for Paula's baby. We're certain it'll be a girl, right?"

"Yeah. Okay, grab one for Laurie if you think they're cute."

"What size? 3 to 6 months?"

Oh God! I didn't have a newborn any more.

She was already in the next size up.

Laurie cried out and I saw that she was face down on her play mat and struggling to flip herself over, because the

Boppy pillow had her tangled. Okay, maybe she wasn't so big after all.

"Yes, 3 to 6 months," I said flipping Laurie over.

My phone buzzed as another call beeped through. "I gotta go, Mom."

I switched lines. Galigani was on the other end.

"What did you find out?"

"Nothing. I was on hold forever and finally they got on the line and told me they're doing the autopsy today. So I'll have to call again tomorrow."

"What do you think they'll find? I mean, probably a broken neck or death due to drowning or something—"

"Unless he was killed beforehand and the body was dumped into the bay," Galigani said.

A chill ran down my spine.

"No!" I said. "That can't be."

"Why not? When was the last time he was seen?"

Oh God. I hadn't even asked Jill that. What kind of investigator was I?

"Ummm—"

Galigani laughed. "Did you forget to ask?"

"No. Forget implies that I'd intended to ask. I never even thought to ask her."

"Don't worry about it, kid. We all start somewhere," Galigani said. "I'll keep on the M.E. Why don't you talk to your friend again?"

"Okay."

"Oh, and if you're up for it, why don't you take the hike? It's a nice day today, weather's clear. You never know what kind of inspiration will hit you."

"You mean the Lands End hike?" A fluttering of nervous energy coursed through me. "Yes, we should definitely check out the scene of the crime."

"Want do you mean we? That hike is all uphill and I'm a desk jockey now."

"Oh, come on!" I nagged.

"Hell no," Galigani said. "And don't get caught up with calling it a crime yet. As far as we know it's an accident."

"Right." I hung up with Galigani and walked down the hall to Jim's office/Laurie's nursery. "Can you Google Land's End and find out if it's a stroller-friendly hike?"

Jim raised an eyebrow at me. "Uh. If it is, are you thinking family hike?"

I smiled. "The weather is clear—"

"Honey, I'd love to but I'm up to my ears with sales calls and I have to prep for my meeting downtown. Can I take a rain check? How about I stay home with Laurie?"

I sighed. Galigani didn't want to go with me, Mom was going shopping, Jim had work, Paula was at the popping point and it would be too tender for Jill. For some reason, I wanted a pair of extra eyes. There was no telling what I'd come across and it seemed logical to have someone with me. I thought of my seventeen-year old neighbor Kenny. I sent him a text while I nursed Laurie, then dressed for the hike.

Finally, I did a quick search online for some P.I. tools. I found a dust kit and a lock pick set and ordered both. After all, you never know when they could come in handy!

As I was heading out the door, I got a text back from Kenny.

GOT A HOT DATE WITH MY BUTTER-EYE.

I laughed despite myself. Kenny had recently started seeing a gal who worked at our local café who sported a tattoo of a butterfly. Hence, we'd nicknamed her butterfly. However, Paula's little boy, Danny couldn't pronounce butterfly and instead called her butter-eye.

I'd have to go it alone, but that was alright. I was ready for adventure. I packed extra water into a day pack for myself along with some protein bars and hopped into my car. The drive along the Great Highway was lovely. For once, there was no fog on the coast and Ocean Beach looked expansive and majestic. I pulled into the parking lot above the Cliff House.

An uneasy feeling crept into my chest as I noticed that Brent Miles' restaurant, *Philosophie,* was directly across the street from the entrance to the Land's End hike.

Surely that was a coincidence….

There were a few more pubs and diners down the street and, of course, the Cliff House was a San Francisco landmark. So, hey, I probably didn't have to read anything sinister into *Philosophie's* location, right?

I found the trailhead for Lands End and to my chagrin, the path was paved. I could have strolled Laurie after all—although bringing a four-month-old to the scene of a crime…or potential crime…probably wasn't one of my brightest ideas.

As I ascended, the pavement ended and the trail turned steep and narrow.

Okay, so, a stroller definitely wouldn't have been a good idea. The view was breathtaking. I could see the Golden Gate Bridge and the bay waters below me. I pulled out my cell phone and snapped pictures that immediately posted to my Facebook wall.

Within a minute I got a ping from Jill.

WHERE ARE YOU?

Yikes! I hadn't thought she would see my status so quickly. How would she feel about me taking the same hike as her boy-friend before he'd fallen to his death?

If indeed he had fallen…?

While I hesitated and thought out my reply, I received another message from Jill.

I hope you're not hiking Land's End.

What could I do? Shoot back a lame reply of "long story" or something like that? Commenting on the weather would sound completely asinine.

I figured calling her would be best.

She picked up on the first ring.

"Hi, Jill," I said lamely.

"What are you doing? Are you at Land's End?"

"Yeah. The Medical Examiner doesn't have any results back yet and I thought I'd take a look at the site."

"I wish you wouldn't." Jill's voice was shrill and nervous. "It could be dangerous. Perry was an experienced hiker and if he fell, then…"

Then what hope did I have?

That was the unspoken piece.

"When was the last time you saw him, Jill?"

"Uh, the last time?" Her voice broke up and I feared she was about to cry.

When was I going to get better at this investigative stuff?

"Jill, are you okay?" I asked.

"Yeah," she said in almost a whisper. "Uh, he spent the night at my house. So I saw him that evening. I knew he was going hiking in the morning, but I didn't know where. I figured he'd go to Mount Tam. I left the house before he got up, because it was my first day of taping at the Foodie Network."

Well, that answered that. If Jill had been with Perry the night before the hike, then it was pretty likely that he hadn't been dumped here as Galigani had feared.

I could see a bench on the trail up ahead. Good. Somewhere to rest.

"I wish I hadn't left him here at the apartment," Jill said. "I...I didn't even say goodbye. He was asleep—"

"You couldn't have known—"

"I know. You're right, of course you are," Jill said. "But I can't help thinking...well, anyway," She sighed. "I had to be at the studio. I had a meeting with the producer. It looks like I might have a sponsor. We're in negotiations."

I reached the bench and collapsed on it. Man, this hike was steep.

"A sponsor? Jill, that's fantastic!" I said with what little breath I had left in my lungs.

She was quiet for a moment.

"Jill?"

"I'm here," she said her voice filled with sadness. "It's that...it's just that it sucks, Kate. You know? Professionally, things are really jiving. Really couldn't be better. And then personally..."

"I'm so sorry," I said.

There was silence on the line and I let it be. I dug my toe into the earth. The trail was hard and compact, like rock instead of dirt.

The sound of a sniffle came across the line.

"I'm going to go lie down. Will you call me when you get home, so I know that you're safe?"

I agreed and we hung up.

I pulled water out of my pack and, after hydrating, continued up the hill.

Two hikers, a man and a woman, were on their way down. They smiled at me as they passed and I overheard them chatting about the views.

I soon reached Painted Rock. There was an official San Francisco Park and Recreation warning sign. It was dark wood with bright orange lettering that read, "People have fallen to their death from this point. Keep out."

It seemed pretty clear. There was a trail but the warning sign was directly in its path. You couldn't *not* see the warning sign. Perry would have had to have leaned into the shrubs to avoid it, so he had to have seen it. Why had he gone down the path?

I glanced at the dirt around the base of the sign and noticed that it seemed soft. How was that, if the trail dirt was rock hard? I pressed a finger against the sign and it wobbled back.

Could it have fallen? Perhaps Perry hadn't seen it? I took a step backward and studied the fork on the trail. One path led uphill, where the two hikers who'd passed me had come from. The other path was short and looked like it went right off the cliff.

Dare I take a peek at the edge?

As I mulled over my options I noticed the earth was dark in two small circles at the base of the uphill trail. I stuck my sneaker into one circle. The dirt was soft, almost like mud, and it stuck to my shoe. I crouched and fingered the circle. It was a hole with fresh dirt in it. The soil around it was as rock hard as the rest of the trail.

I crudely measured the distance between the two circles with my sneakers. Two full feet and a half, the second hole reached my instep.

I moved to the warning sign and measured the distance between the two posts. The same.

Could someone have moved the sign?

If so, the sign would have blocked the uphill path and left the path that literally went off the cliff unblocked.

Why was there a path that went off a cliff? What kind of sense did that make? Surely, someone could sue over this.

I thought of Gary Barramendi, a high-powered attorney I'd had the privilege of working with. Maybe he could help Jill.

Actually, since Barramendi specialized in criminal defense, he probably wouldn't be keen about a wrongful death case. I decided to let the idea go and focused instead on the sign.

Could I dust it for prints? I'd need to receive my dust kit first. Not to mention, get training on how to use it! I'd have to ask Galigani.

I took several pictures of the warning sign and saved them. I grimaced as I declined the automatic message to post the pics to Facebook.

How awful would that be?

7

When I reached my car at the bottom of the trail, I called Galigani and got his voicemail. I left him a quick message telling him the warning sign to the trail had been moved and asking him if we could fingerprint wood.

My stomach growled. I glanced at my watch. It was only 10am, nowhere close to lunchtime. Still, cold toast wasn't a substantial enough breakfast for a mother who was breastfeeding, and I was starving. I needed a *real* breakfast and the fact that *Philosophie* was across the street was too much to pass up. I had to go investigate.

Digging inside my diaper bag/purse I rooted past an old ball cap and found my notebook. The thought of the waitress who snapped my photo nagged at the back of my mind.

What if she'd circulated my picture claiming I was a food critic or something?

For good measure I pulled out the ball cap and buried my hair inside it. It seemed a ridiculous disguise, but at least something was better than nothing.

I walked across the street toward the restaurant. The lights were dim and there was no traffic in front.

Could it be that they weren't open yet?

Maybe they didn't serve breakfast.

I pulled open the door. They were open all right, just empty. Looked like Jill's review really had wreaked havoc.

The decor was a bit confusing. There were panels of quotes along the wall and the tables were made of scrap wood that some designer thought would look good together. The effect was dizzying.

I looked around for a hostess and saw none. While I waited, I read some of the quotes along the wall *"All the easy problems have already been solved." "Be nice to unkind people, they need it the most,"* and my favorite, *"When your dreams turn to dust, vacuum."*

It seemed that there was no hostess was on duty, so I seated myself and hoped for a waiter.

After a few minutes a man in his twenties approached me, wearing the customary server uniform of dark pants with a white shirt.

"Oh. Sorry, I didn't hear you come in." He handed me a menu.

I gave him my best smile. I considered asking to speak with Brent Miles, but then I wouldn't know what to say to Brent if he were here. I was totally unprepared. Totally in over my head.

Oh well, at least I could eat.

I perused the menu.

Soup, sweet corn fritter, chorizo, white fish crudo.

I waved the server back to my table.

"I was looking for the breakfast menu," I said as sweetly as I could muster. Better to make a friend of him if I wanted to get any intel.

His lips turned into a thin line, an expression somewhere between apologetic and sympathetic, and then he whispered, "It *is* the breakfast menu."

"Soup for breakfast?" I asked.

He rolled his eyes. "I know."

Dear God, no wonder Jill had panned the restaurant.

I forced a smile. "Well. I'm open to new things. I'll try it. Omelet soup it is."

The server looked relieved. "Okay, great. It's not as bad as you might think. Can I offer you a cappuccino, espresso, or regular coffee with that?"

"Sure, I'll have a cappuccino."

He returned in a few minutes with a steaming bowl of soup along with a cappuccino.

"How did you hear about us?" he asked, placing the soup in front of me.

I really hadn't thought this through. I had no idea what to say.

"I live in the neighborhood," I lied.

"Oh, I haven't seen you before."

"I don't get out much." At least that much was true. "I just had a baby."

Although now that sort of felt like a lie, too. Paula was about to have a baby. Laurie was already four months old, not even a newborn anymore.

The server placed a bottle of hot sauce in front of me. "Some like it hot," he said.

I smiled at his corny line.

"I've never had soup for breakfast," I said. "But I'll try it hot." I dashed some sauce into the soup and stirred. My spoon caught on something at the bottom of the bowl and I frowned.

The waiter laughed. "That's the hash browns."

This sent us both into a fit of giggles.

I had been trying to give the place the benefit of the doubt, but really, hash browns at the bottom of a soup bowl?

The waiter covered his mouth and whispered conspiratorially. "I could get the chef to make you a plain breakfast. Hash browns, sausage, omelet. Hold the soup."

I laughed. "Yes. Who wants soup first thing in the morning?"

He shook his head. "Our owner is a fitness fanatic; he thinks that eating hot soup in the morning can rev up the metabolism."

"Oh really?" I studied him a moment. Was he joking?

He nodded.

Wait a minute! If we were talking about revving up a metabolism, who isn't game for that?

I stirred the soup. "You know, it is good to try new things from time to time."

The waiter shrugged noncommittally.

"Who owns this place?" I asked, trying to bury myself in the soup and look as nonchalant as he did.

"Brent Miles."

He said it offhandedly, like there was no reason for me to probe further. But, of course, I did.

"Oh. Mr. Miles. Right. I thought..." I hesitated, letting him fidget a bit. "I thought I read something online about him opening up a restaurant in the neighborhood, but I didn't make the connection."

It looked like he was about to come unglued. Especially when I mentioned the words "read something online." Almost as if he were waiting for me to mention Jill's review.

When I didn't, he said, "Yeah. There was a lot of hubbub about him opening the place."

I tasted the soup again then gave it a liberal dosing of hot sauce. Who knew what was good for the metabolism; maybe it was simply hot sauce.

He looked around the restaurant, double checking that no one had come in during our conversation. Then he leaned in. "In fact, I'm not sure if we're going to make it. One of the reviewers wasn't too kind to us."

I feigned surprise. "Really? With this creative menu and all?"

"Well, that's one of the things she hated!"

I pressed my lips together to avoid putting my foot in my mouth.

He continued, "That, plus the fact that we're owned by Brent Miles. I think she had it in for him."

"How so?" I asked.

This was something Jill hadn't mentioned. Did she have an axe to grind with Brent? Why?

"Well, I don't really know. Just something I overheard him complaining about."

"Is he here?"

The waiter laughed loudly. "Here? He's never here. He opens one business and then he's off to the next. He doesn't care what goes on here. Unless we fail. It's a pride thing."

"Is he opening up another restaurant?"

"Yeah. Fine Mexican dining. Yucatan style. New chef. I think it'll be a hit."

Ramon, the empanada king!

I took another taste of the soup and grimaced. Too much hot sauce. I gulped down some water and watched the waiter raise an eyebrow at me.

When I was sure I could speak without coughing I asked, "Where's the new restaurant located?"

"Pac Heights."

I nodded.

I tried to take another sip of my soup, but I had completely ruined it with the hot sauce. Well, not that it was great to begin with, but now it was simply inedible.

I got into my car and turned toward home. I was disappointed that the outing to the restaurant had not satisfied any needs, including the growling in my stomach. Jill had been correct with her review of *Philosophie*—maybe even kind!

But what the waiter had said bothered me. What kind of history did Brent Miles and Jill have?

As I pondered that my cell phone buzzed. I looked at the display. Jill. I pulled out of traffic and stopped in front of a fire hydrant.

"Hey Jill, I have good news."

"What?" she asked.

"I found the area where Perry must've gone off-track at Lands End. The warning sign looks like it might have been tampered with."

Jill gasped. "What do you mean?"

"Well, all I'm saying is that there is clearly a sign there now that says…gosh…I'm sorry to have to tell you this, but the sign says *'People have fallen to their death from this point, keep out'*. The sign is loose around the base. I felt like I could've pulled it straight up and out, but I didn't want to do that because of the prints. I'll send Galigani up with a dust kit, see if he can get anything off of it," I said.

After a moment, Jill said, "A dust kit? You can do that? Pull prints off of a board like that?"

"Well, I can't do that but Galigani can. Sure," I said with a bit more confidence than I felt.

"Hmmm," Jill said. "That would be great. How soon can he do it?"

I thought about it for a second. It was a rather steep hike and with Galigani's condition, only a few months post open-heart surgery, I didn't know if he be able to make it.

I'd figure something out.

"Well, we'll need to do it as soon as possible. I left him a message before breakfast. I ate at *Philosophie*."

Jill made an over-the-top retching sound. "Oh, sorry. How'd you like it?"

"You were right about the food. I was hoping to spy on Mr. Miles, but he wasn't there."

"No, of course not. He doesn't get involved in any actual work."

"Do you know him personally?" I asked.

"Yeah. I worked at his last restaurant, *Tartare*. The one that closed because of the kitchen fire. Do you remember that? It was in the news."

"I do remember, vaguely," I said.

"Guy was a giant a-hole to work for, if you know what I mean."

"Do you think I can talk to him?" I asked.

"Oh, I don't know. He's not very accessible to the public."

"Maybe I'll just show up on his doorstep."

She laughed nervously. "Oh my God, Kate. You can't do that!"

"Why not? I already have his address."

"He…well, he's a VIP. A power player in SF. We can't go around pissing those kinds of people off."

But you already have.

"Are you scared that if I talk to him, he might get to your show sponsor and somehow intimidate them?"

"No. I…I don't know. There are limits," she said.

"Not when it comes to a murder investigation."

8

On the drive to Miles' place, the weather started to change. January in San Francisco could turn rainy at a moment's notice. Dark clouds were blowing in and I had to put my headlights and windshield wipers on.

I ducked my head and sprinted up the gravel path to Brent's mansion, feeling foolish. Certainly a house this size had staff. What were the odds I'd actually get to talk to him?

What would I even say if he was here? "Excuse me, did you kill Perry Welgan?"

Oh, ridiculous! I was wasting my time.

As I pressed the bell, I noticed the siding on the garage was badly scraped and dented. Before I could make sense of it the door opened and an elegant gentleman stood before me. He was at least six feet tall, wearing a light blue cashmere sweater, tan slacks and loafers. I recognized him from his photos online. This was definitely Brent Miles.

"Mr. Miles, I'm Kate Connolly. I'm a private investigator. I was hoping I could ask you a few questions."

He nodded and swung the door open. "Come in, come in. Some weather starting to blow in, huh?"

As I stepped in the threshold of the doorway, he said, "Barramendi sent you?"

I froze. "Barramendi?"

He frowned, a slight crease between his eyes formed. "My attorney. He said he was assigning a P.I. to the case."

I swallowed past the dry spot in my throat.

Barramendi had hired another P.I?

I'd only worked with him one time in the past, but somehow I'd hoped I'd get another shot to work with him. Obviously someone else had beaten me to it. Not that Barramendi owed me anything, but I couldn't help the feeling of betrayal that stuck in my craw.

This was going to be awkward.

"I've worked with Barramendi before. But no, he didn't send me."

The crease between his eyes deepened. "I don't understand, why are you here then?"

"I'm a friend of Jill Harrington."

His eyes locked on mine. He seemed to silently calculate something in his head then motioned for me to enter.

"Have a seat," he said, gesturing toward the living room. "I'm going to make a quick call to my attorney."

Why had he already hired an attorney?

"That won't be necessary, Mr. Miles. I just wanted to—"

"Are you working for Jill then?"

I nodded.

He took a deep breath. "Sit down. I'll be right with you."

He turned and strode out of the room. I gazed around but didn't sit. I felt better standing, as if by sitting down I would give up something up. After all, this was his home. He already had control, but I wouldn't let him tower over me.

Before I could snoop around the room, a loud engine rocked the windows and the gravel on the front path crunched and spattered between a vehicle's tires. I peeked through the shades and saw a Harley-Davidson pull to a stop. It looked like a classic or vintage bike: really big, and shiny, and well taken care of.

A man dressed in a leather jacket, black jeans and boots dismounted from the bike. He pulled off his helmet to reveal a head full of dark hair, but his face was turned away from me. He crossed to the front stoop. The doorbell sounded throughout the house.

I heard footsteps approaching from the direction in which Brent had disappeared, so I took a seat on the couch and attempted to look casual, as though I hadn't just been spying on his guest.

From my position in the living room I could see Brent open the door, but not the man on the doorstep that he was addressing with a curt, "Can I help you?"

I heard the man say through a thick Spanish accent, "Good afternoon, Mr. Miles. I'm Vicente Domingo. Mr. Barramendi sent me."

What?

Vicente who? So this was who Barramendi had hired instead of me?

I watched Brent step aside and motion for the man who had just stuck a knife in my back to step in.

Vicente came into the foyer and smiled. He was strikingly handsome. His dark hair was offset with sparkling green eyes that creased a bit about the edges when he smiled. He brushed some drizzle off his leather jacket, then rubbed his hands together to dry them.

"You have great timing, Mr. Domingo," Brent said, "as I've received a visit from Ms. Connolly. She's been hired by Jill Harrington to," he glanced at me and practically spit out his next line, "to investigate me, I think."

Vicente gave me an appraising look as if he was a matador assessing the bull before a fight.

I felt a little unnerved, recalling that normally the bull is slaughtered in those fights, but only after being weakened by lances and spikes stabbed in its back.

I stood.

Who did this guy think he was, anyway?

Vicente Domingo? V.D. in my book.

He was sexy, that was for sure, but a P.I. and my competition? I couldn't wait to run a check on him.

V.D. tapped his chin. "Connolly? I have heard very good things about you."

I cleared my throat to interrupt him. The last thing I wanted was to hear about my reputation from this guy. "Excellent, then we should have no problem getting a few things cleared up. Mr. Miles, can you tell me about the phone calls you placed to Jill Harrington?"

Brett frowned. "What?"

"Jill has reported receiving threatening phone calls from you."

Brent's face reddened. "She did, did she? Who did she report that to? You? The police? What did she say I threatened her with? She doesn't work for me anymore so I couldn't very well fire her!"

I realized now that I hadn't gotten any details from Jill on what she'd done at *Tartare*, so I asked, "In what capacity did Ms. Harrington work for you?

Brent looked taken aback and glanced at Vicente. Vicente shrugged, as if to say it was okay to answer my question, but he raised an eyebrow indicating to proceed with caution - aka don't give too much detail.

Whatever, the guy was acting like a lawyer.

"I thought you people did background checks and such. Are we starting from scratch?" Brent said.

Vicente studied me.

I took a deep breath trying to remain calm.

"She was a goddamn hostess. What else would she be?"

"What about the threatening calls, sir, did you make them?" I asked.

Brent snorted. "Oh, back to that? Of course not. I'd already fired her—"

Jill had been fired? Why?

Before I could ask, Vicente stepped forward and said, "What is Ms. Harrington alleging?"

"That Mr. Miles was phoning and demanding she take down a negative review."

Brent pinched the bridge of his nose. "Oh that? Well, yes I did phone Ms. Harrington one time and asked her to give us another chance."

I tried to contain my glee.

Brent Miles had just confessed to the phone calls.

"So, she declined to review the restaurant again and you had her followed," I said.

"Followed? What? No!"

Vicente ran a hand through his hair. "Ms. Harrington claims my client had her followed? What else does she allege?"

"The fact that she was followed is not an allegation. It's a fact. I saw the man following her myself."

Brent shook his head. "No, that's ridiculous. I admit to one call. I asked her to be my guest at the restaurant and to give me and my staff another shot. But she refused. She babbled something about integrity. Imagine that. She's a stupid girl with a pen who'd like to cut down a hard-working entrepreneur. She thinks she has some sort of right to post negative reviews. As if that has anything to do with integrity."

The sound of gravel crunching came from the driveway again, a car's headlights flashed along the front window. Suddenly there was a loud crash followed by shattering of glass.

Vicente jumped. "My bike!" he shouted.

Brent covered his eyes with his palm. "Shit. The wife's home and she just ran over your Harley. Thank God you weren't on it."

The three of us immediately exited out the front door and joined Brent's wife on the driveway.

She had a helmet of perfectly coiffed blonde hair. She was screaming in hysterics. But neither her screaming nor the drizzly wet weather had any effect on it; her hair didn't budge at all.

"Holy night! What is a motorcycle doing parked there?" she demanded.

"It isn't parked there anymore," Brent said.

"I didn't see it!" she screamed.

"Apparently not," Brent replied.

V.D. knelt beside his bike as if in mourning.

I watched them silently. The dented siding on the garage making sense; this was not Mrs. Miles' first fender bender.

Brent embraced his wife, and her hysterical shrieking subsided.

She asked, "When did you get a bike?"

"It isn't mine, it's—"

"Mine." V.D. stood up cradling a bike part that fallen off in his hands.

Brent's wife pulled away from Brent and stepped toward V.D. "What in the name of all that is holy is it doing parked in my driveway?" she yelled.

V.D. stepped back, suddenly looking surprised. "Oh. I—"

"Now honey. Let's not get upset. What's important is that you're all right," Brent said.

She took a deep breath and patted her helmet hair, which of course hadn't moved an inch.

"That's right, dear. Thank you."

Brent wrapped an arm around his wife's waist. "Let's go inside. I don't want you to catch cold."

We moved inside. First Brent ushered in his wife, then came me, followed by V.D. and finally Brent.

Brent thumped V.D. on the back and said, "Please don't worry. We have insurance."

We found our places back in the living room, where Brent properly introduced his wife, Lillian.

She seemed to recoil when Brent told her I was a private investigator and that I was here to ask questions about Jill and their relationship—although no greater than the displeasure she had demonstrated to V.D. about his parking in the driveway. After the introductions were complete, she capped everything by saying to Vicente, "If you're ever here again, don't park in my driveway."

With that she stormed out of the room.

Brett pinched the bridge of his nose again. "Sorry, folks, Lillian's recently had some news that is distressing her greatly. Please don't be offended. Vicente, of course I'll take care of the bike."

Vicente nodded, but his jaw was clenched and I noticed his full lips were pursed slightly.

I stood. "Mr. Miles, I'm afraid I need to cut our meeting short. If you will kindly give me the name and number of the gentleman who was following Jill I'll be sure to speak with him."

Brent stared at me. "I told you I had nothing to do with that."

V.D. said, "Nice try."

I feigned confusion. "Oh, right. Sorry. With all the excitement around here I forgot. So tell me, when is the last time you saw Jill?"

"I haven't seen her in ages. I wasn't at the restaurant the night she was there," Brent said.

I picked up my bag. "Thank you, sir. If I have any additional—"

"You can talk to my attorney, Ms. Connolly. I don't appreciate the unexpected visit to my home. Next time—"

"Right," I said over my shoulder as I headed toward the door. "Next time I could end up run over."

"Cheap shot," Brent called after me.

I crossed the street toward my car. I was fuming. Barramendi had a P.I. on his staff and it wasn't me.

And did the guy have to be so cocky?

I pulled on the handle of my car door and swung it open. V.D. appeared behind me.

"Wait," V.D. said. "Which direction are you going?"

"What?"

"I need a ride," he hissed at me.

"Pfft. Forget it. Call a cab."

Like I was really going to help the enemy!

"No. I need to talk to you. Can you wait until I get his insurance information?"

While I said, "Oh for crying out loud," he said, "Thanks," and walked back into the house.

I debated whether or not to wait for him.

How presumptuous for him to assume that I would wait.

And yet…what could he want to speak to me about?

I was extremely annoyed with him, that much was true, but for what? For getting hired by Barramendi?

That was totally sour grapes on my part.

If I were a polished professional I'd give him a ride and pump for information. Even if it didn't yield anything on the case, I might at least be able to figure out why Barramendi had hired him and not me.

What was I lacking?

Uh…probably experience.

Although it was true that I'd recently solved a few cases, before my venture into investigating I'd been an office manager. Not much experience solving crimes there. I'd left my day job to have Laurie and then started my venture as a P.I. almost by accident.

V.D. walked out the front door again. As with many things in life, if you don't make a decision quick, the decision will be made for you.

V.D. held his helmet in one hand and adjusted the collar of his leather jacket with the other. "Mr. Miles is calling a tow truck, so I'm free to go with you."

I unlocked my car with the key fob and motioned to Vicente to get in. I asked him for his address. He lived South of Market.

"So, have you been a P.I. for long?" I asked.

He looked at me, surprised, "Me? Yes, of course." And then, as if it hadn't occurred to him before, he said, "And you?"

Damn.

Why did I have to go putting my foot in it? Sure, he'd been doing investigations a long time. Why else would Barramendi have hired him? He was experienced, and he was probably good.

Instead of answering his question, I used one of my all-time favorite distraction tactics: I evaded his questions by asking one of my own, one I knew was sure to get his interest. "You been riding bikes a long time?"

He nodded, then in a sudden burst of emotion he said, "Can you believe she ran my bike down! It's a 1946 original Harley-Davidson Knucklehead!"

I refrained from snickering at the word knucklehead.

But just barely.

"It was pretty shocking, really, the way she blamed you," I said.

He grimaced and sighed. "I can't believe it."

From between our seats, my cell phone buzzed. I glanced at the caller ID; it was Paula.

"Hold on a second," I said. "My friend's about to have her baby. This may be the call."

Vicente took the opportunity to pull out his own cell phone and scroll.

Paula's voice filled the line: "This ain't no false alarm, sister. I am in labor now!"

"Yeah? Do you need me to pick up Danny?"

"He's here with his backpack on."

"Okay. I'm pretty close, actually. I'm in the Sea Cliff, but I have to drop someone off South of Market and—"

"What? You have to go South of Market?" Paula asked. "There's no way you'll get here in time."

"It won't take me—"

"I knew I should have asked someone more dependable to watch Danny," Paula said.

"What? More dependable? I'm dependable."

"No offense, Kate…uh! Contraction. I didn't mean it in a bad way. It's just…uh…"

"Forget about it, I know. I'm on my way," I said, hanging up. "Look, my friend's in labor. I have to pick up her little boy, so I can't take you home."

"No problem," Vicente said. "I can go with you."

I pulled the car over to the curb. "Get out."

"I'm good with kids." He smiled and fixed me with a piercing stare. "Drive."

9

I turned the car around and drove toward Paula's house.

Who did this man think he was, telling me what to do?

V.D. dropped his cell phone into a cup holder then leaned over and started to fiddle with the knobs on the radio, turning it on and searching out a station.

"What are you doing?" I asked, making no attempt to mask the anger in my voice.

He looked over at me, surprised. "Real Madrid is playing today."

I flipped the radio off.

"Come on," V.D. said. "I've got money on the game."

"You can listen to it on your own time."

He looked confused. "This *is* my time."

"No. It's my time. My car, my time."

"Just because it's your car doesn't make it your time. And, by the way, if you hadn't been at Mr. Miles house, then my Harley never would have been hit."

I glared at him. "No. If *you* hadn't been there then your Harley wouldn't have been hit."

"I had to be there. I was hired by Barramendi."

Which begged the question: why had Miles hired Barramendi, a high-powered criminal defense attorney?

"So catch me up then. What do you know about Brent Miles?" I asked.

"Ah. You want information from me," he said, looking at me through his long dark eyelashes—a look I was certain had been cultivated in tapas bars all over Spain.

"Why else would I drive a man I barely know, who frankly I find extremely annoying, across the city and back?"

He flipped on the radio. "To learn about soccer, of course."

I turned the radio off. "Why did Miles hire Barramendi?"

"Do you really find me annoying?"

"Extremely. I said extremely. And yes. I do."

V.D. held out both hands in an almost pleading gesture. "Why?"

"Answer my question first."

He laughed. "Okay, what was it?"

"Why did Miles hire Barramendi?"

"Barramendi has been Miles' attorney for years."

"I thought Barramendi specialized in criminal defense."

"He does, but the firm handles everything. Miles has been a client with the firm forever, and when this came up," V.D. waved a hand around as if to dismiss any concern. "It was natural for Barramendi to be assigned."

"When what came up?"

V.D. squinted at me and remained silent.

"What? Come on, spit it out."

I was coming up to a red light and was tempted to hit my brakes a bit harder than necessary.

V.D. rummaged through his bag. "I want to give you something."

He handed me a postcard.

I stopped at the light and glanced at the card. "What's this?" I asked.

"Audition notice for my play."

"Your play?" I asked. "Are you in it?"

He certainly had the looks to be an actor. And as far as I could tell, he had the cocky disposition to go along with it.

I cringed. I had a college degree in theater and had dealt with many temperamental actors back then, and the last thing I wanted to do now was revisit working with divas.

"No." He laughed. "I wrote it."

I glanced over at him. "You wrote a play?"

He nodded proudly. "Yes, I'm a playwright."

"Now I've heard everything," I said.

"What do you mean?"

"I thought you were a private investigator," I said.

"Well, I am. But I write plays on the side. Just like, you know, you do all your other things on the side."

I did other things on the side? What did I do on the side besides have a family? Was there some rumor going around that I was distracted? Could that be why Barramendi hadn't given *me* the case?

"What other things?" I prodded Vicente.

"You know." He motioned to Laurie's car seat. "You're a mom and everything."

I held back my frustration and asked, "What's the play about?"

He smiled. "Murder, of course."

Turning onto Paula's street, I shoved the postcard deep into the bottomless pit of my diaper bag/purse hoping never to see it again.

I pulled into Paula's driveway. Her husband, David, was standing in front of their house, a dinosaur-decorated backpack in one hand and the other hand resting on his two-year-old son, Danny's, shoulder. Danny started jumping up and down as soon as he saw me.

David opened the back door and helped Danny into the car seat, glancing curiously at V.D. "Oh, Kate, I didn't know you had company."

"This is Vicente. He's a private investigator for Barramendi."

A confused expression crossed David's face. "Nice to meet you," he said to Vicente.

I could see Paula waving from their car pointing—no, rather, gesticulating—madly towards Vicente. "Who is that?" she mouthed.

I shrugged at her. It'd have to be a conversation for later.

At home, Jim was rocking Laurie in his arms as he paced the room listening to some talk radio.

"I'm adding one to the litter," I said, as I deposited Danny onto our couch. He had fallen asleep in the car after getting into an out-and-out battle with Vicente over which zoo animal was most like a human.

I don't know if I've ever been happier to see anyone get out of my car than I was when I dropped Vicente off at his place in South of Market.

Jim switched off the radio. "Is Paula really going to have the baby this time?"

"I sure hope so," I said.

We shuffled the children around as we converted the sofa into a bed and tucked Danny in. While we worked, I filled Jim in on the day's events. He agreed that there seemed to be some missing information.

What had prompted Miles to call his attorney?

I put Laurie in her crib and retired to the bedroom with Jim. I wanted to mull over again what I'd learned in the course of the day and try to figure out what I had missed, but as soon as my head hit the pillow, all thoughts seeped out of my brain and I was instantly asleep.

To Do:
1. √ ~~Order dust kit!~~
2. Figure out what happened to Perry.
3. Research the competition (Vicente Domingo)
4. Go grocery shopping!

My door bell rang early in the morning and I felt like my eyes were glued together. Thankfully Jim was already up, because I heard our door unlock and then David's voice.

There was a general tone of congratulations and some clapping each other on the back, then I heard Jim take off toward the kitchen, presumably to make coffee.

I rolled over and bumped into a child. I pried my eyes open and peeked out. Sometime during the night Danny had snuck into my bed. I rubbed him on the check to wake him. "Daddy's here, buddy."

Danny continued to snooze. I kicked off the heap of blankets and rose. It took me a moment to stretch out all the kinks from sleeping on only a quarter of the bed. How did one toddler take up so much room?

I slipped on my robe and headed down the hallway. "Do we have good news?" I called out.

"A beautiful baby girl. Chloe," David said.

I whooped as I entered the living room and patted David on the back. "Congrats! How's Paula doing?"

"Good. Only she's driving me crazy. She wants me to force them to let her leave the hospital right now."

"She's nuts," I said, chuckling. She should take advantage of the 24/7 care."

"I know," David said. "The last time she checked herself out early, we had to go back the next afternoon because she had postpartum preeclampsia."

"I remember," I said, recalling how Paula's feet had swollen like balloons.

David nodded. "Not to mention, the sooner she comes home, the sooner Chloe comes home and…" he shrugged. "The nanny doesn't start until next week," he admitted.

I laughed. "Yeah, you certainly don't want to be stuck on nanny duty."

David shook his head vigorously as Jim entered with three cups of coffee on a tray.

"Kate, you've trained him well," David said.

"I know, and with the way Paula spoils you, I'm sure you probably don't even *know* how to make coffee."

David, for his part looked dutifully shamed. He said, "I know how to *make* it, it's the cleaning the coffee pot part I don't like. So *messy*, all those wet coffee grounds."

We laughed as the doorbell sounded, so I didn't have a chance to explain to David that if he'd use a coffee filter, the grounds should stay *out* of the coffee pot.

Jim walked over to the door and looked out through the peephole. He didn't say anything but immediately swung the door open. Melanie stood on my door step, her face still viciously bruised and swollen, looking even worse than when I'd first met her two days ago.

"I'm so sorry to disturb you. Is Kate…does Kate live—?"

I stepped into her line of vision. "Melanie, come in."

"Oh, Kate! I'm so glad I got the right address," she said, crossing into my living room.

She clutched a tie-dye messenger bag that was slung around her waist as though it might protect her from another attack.

I quickly introduced her to David and Jim and led her to my kitchen nook to sit, giving the men a chance to put away the sofa bed while allowing us a bit of privacy.

Pouring her a cup of coffee, I sat down next to her.

"How can I help?"

"Please don't tell Jill I've come to see you."

"Why? What's going on?" I asked.

Melanie tinkered with the spoon on the table, then added some sugar to her coffee. "I have Perry's phone. They gave it to me at the hospital." She wiped gingerly at her bruised eye. "Damn, it hurts to cry."

I rose and grabbed a box of tissues from my counter and passed it to her.

She took a tissue. "Thank you. They gave me his stuff, you know, after they told me he was dead."

I nodded solemnly.

Wrestling her bag from around her waist, she dug out a phone, swiped at it and entered a password. "I think he was meeting someone at Land's End, Kate. I don't want Jill to know. It could be nothing, but if I know…" She sighed. "If I knew my brother at all, I'd bet he was meeting a girl there."

She handed me the phone and I reviewed the sent messages log. Perry had had a text conversation with someone. It was a local number with no name attached. He'd made plans to meet someone for a hike at Land's End at 8:00 a.m. on the day he'd died.

A chill ran up my spine. Could Perry have actually set a date with his murderer? Or was there a witness to what had happened? Or perhaps this was a random connection, a girl who maybe never even showed up and was therefore irrelevant? That didn't seem likely.

"Do you know whose number that is?" I asked.

"No. I called it, but got a generic out of service message."

"I can look it up. I have access to a reverse directory," I said.

Melanie eyes brightened. "Oh, would you, Kate? That would mean a lot to me."

"Yeah, come on."

She followed me into my office/nursery. Laurie was awake in her crib and staring at her mobile, the bears were dancing about and Laurie was swatting at them with her feet. Laurie cooed when she saw me and Melanie gasped.

"Oh, she's adorable! I didn't know you had a baby."

Before I could pick Laurie up, Jim called from the living room. "Honey, can you come here a minute?"

I indicated a chair next to my desk for Melanie to sit.

"Go ahead. I'll wait right here for you," she said, seating herself.

I joined Jim and David in the living room. They were standing near the front window.

"There's a guy on our corner, right now, wearing a Smith & Wesson skull cap," Jim said.

I stared at him. "What?"

"You think it's a coincidence?" he asked.

I peeked out the window.

I was vaguely aware of Laurie crying from the other room and Jim moving to get her from the nursery, but mostly I was fixated on the guy across the street. It appeared to be the same guy who'd been outside Tea & Tumble.

Same hat, same height—it had to the same guy. But why was he here?

I glanced at David, who had now retreated to my fireplace mantel.

"David, was that guy on the corner when you arrived?"

He shook his head. We shared a silent moment, both of us presumably thinking the same thing, because David tilted his head toward my office.

Had skull cap man been following me, or was he following Melanie?

10

Jim emerged from the nursery with Laurie in his arms. "I changed her, mommy, but I think she needs you now."

Laurie was desperately rooting around Jim's shirt and hitting his chest with her little fist.

Melanie was sitting where I had left her, waiting patiently.

"Did you notice anything strange on your way to my house?" I asked her.

She frowned. "What do you mean?"

"Well, maybe I should start someplace else. Come to the living room."

She followed me and peered out the front window.

"Do you know that man?" I asked.

"No, why?"

"It's the same guy I saw when I had lunch with Jill the other day. I thought he followed her when she left."

Melanie hugged her arms to herself. "Oh my God, do you think he's connected to Brent Miles and maybe even…?" Her voice trailed off and she stepped away from the window.

"He showed up after you arrived. Do you think you were followed?"

A noise came from down the hall and Melanie startled.

"That's Danny," I said to David.

David nodded and called down the hall, "In here, buddy!"

The sound of Danny's footsteps grew louder as he raced down the hall and into his father's arms. His hair was tousled and he rubbed sleep out of his eyes as he asked, "Where's mommy?"

"With your baby sister!" David said. "We named her Chloe."

Danny nodded excitedly. "I want to see Chloe and mommy."

David rubbed Danny's back while still looking out the window. He mumbled distractedly, "Yeah, I know. Me too. Let's have some breakfast and get dressed first."

I watched Melanie peer out the window again. After a moment, she said, "Kate, I can't be sure, but the guy across the street is the same build as the man who attacked me at Perry's house."

"We should call the cops," Jim said.

Melanie groaned. "Yeah, but they took forever to show up at my brother's place. This guy could be gone before they get here."

"The Taraval police station is pretty close to us," Jim said. "They should be able to get here fast."

I shook my head. "No, they'll scare him off and we won't get any answers. Let's use the station to our advantage."

Jim nodded. "You want to set up a trap?"

I smiled. "Of course."

We came up with a plan while I nursed Laurie, and David got Danny dressed. We'd called my seventeen-year-old neighbor Kenny and asked him to babysit, instructing him to come around the back of the house. Melanie was to leave through the front door and see if skull cap man would follow her. If he did, Jim and David would follow him. If he didn't, I would leave after Melanie and see if he tailed me. Either way, Jim and David would follow closely behind him.

I had Melanie call my cell and we put both phones on speaker. Melanie slipped her phone into her shirt pocket and we tested our connection. When we were convinced that we had full audio access to her, we sent Melanie on her way.

She was to head toward the Taraval Police Station. If she was tailed and something went wrong, like Jim losing her, then she was to park in front of the station.

Kenny knocked on my back door. It was refreshing to see his smiling face and dyed green hair.

Jim unlocked the door and let him in.

"S'up, familia Connolly!" He said, giving Jim a high five as he sauntered toward the counter. "Any breakie for the sitter?"

Our standing agreement with Kenny had always been to feed him. His parents were recent vegan converts and Kenny, being a growing boy, had a voracious appetite that tofu just didn't satisfy.

"You'll have to make it yourself," I said, securing Laurie into her baby swing. "We've got a bit of project going on here." I nodded to Melanie. "Ready?"

She rose. "Here goes nothing."

I walked her to the front door and saw her out, making sure she reached her car safely and that skull cup man saw me retreat back inside the house.

Jim, who was monitoring us from the garage door vents downstairs, had a clear view of Melanie, me, and skull cap man.

I went to the staircase and waited for Jim's assessment. We had agreed no one would look out the front window; we didn't want to spook our stalker.

Melanie's voice came through my phone. "I'm in my car now. I can't tell what he's doing."

"He's getting into a green Prius," Jim called from downstairs.

I reported this to Melanie.

"Okay, I'm trying not to turn around and stare. I'll keep my eyes on the road ahead of me and drive to Taraval Street," she said.

"We're going," Jim called up to me.

I could hear Jim get into the car with David.

"Where's daddy?" Danny asked.

"Hey, buddy, I make a mean Mickey Mouse pancake. Want to see?" Kenny asked.

Danny looked at me, concern furrowing his tiny brow. "Mickey's not mean."

I smiled. "He means delicious. A yummy Mickey Mouse pancake."

Danny jumped up and down. "Delicious!"

He had a little lisp when he said the word, which made me repeat it and hug him to me.

"Come on, let's crack the eggs, buddy," Kenny called.

Danny took off running toward the kitchen with Kenny.

I heard the car in the garage start up.

Melanie reported that she was three blocks away with a green Prius on her tail. I conferenced Jim into the call.

"You guys can open the garage. They're three blocks east heading toward the Taraval Police Station." I said.

"Roger that," Jim said.

I joined Kenny and Danny in the kitchen.

Kenny frowned. "How did the P.I. get left out of the surveillance?"

"I know," I said, feeling more than a little annoyed.

I placed a griddle on the stovetop for Kenny. Our home phone rang.

Kenny looked at me. "Want me to get it?"

I nodded and took over pancake duty. Not only did I get stuck at home, while everyone else was out gallivanting, but now I had to make breakfast!

DIANA ORGAIN

Kenny picked up the phone and frowned as he spoke. "Okay, okay, man calm down. I'll tell her. Hello?" Kenny stared at the phone, then repeated, "Hello?"

"Bad news," he said to me as he hung up the phone.

I frowned. "Who was that?"

"Dude said to call off the tail."

I froze. "What? What dude? Was that skull cap man?" I asked.

Kenny shrugged. "I guess so. He didn't really identify himself, just said to stop following him. He sounded pretty pissed."

"How did he get my number?" I asked.

The memory of the waitress from Tea & Tumble taking my picture flashed through my mind. Could she have posted my information somewhere? A chill ran through my body. I felt exposed, like a goldfish in a glass jar; even worse, I felt just as dumb as one. Things were getting away from me, events were out of my control and I was in the dark.

The corners of Kenny's mouth turned downward, but before he could respond, I said. "Damn!"

Danny repeated my swear word. I cringed. "No, Danny, don't say that. Bad word. I meant darn."

Danny pointed a finger at me. "Potty mouth, Kate!"

I clapped a hand over my mouth and Kenny openly smirked.

"What's going on?" Jim said through the speaker on my cell phone.

"Jim, you've been spotted and warned off," I said into the phone.

Jim cursed under his breath.

"Another potty mouth," Kenny said.

I hit Kenny in the arm. "This is serious!"

Kenny puffed out his skinny seventeen-year-old chest and said, "Don't worry, Kate. I'll protect you."

89

"Oh God," Jim said. "Protect you from what? What's going on?"

"Skull cap guy called our house," I said.

"Are you sure it was him? How does he have our number?" Jim asked.

"I wish I knew," I said.

I scrolled through the caller I.D. on my phone, but the call that had come through was marked as "unavailable."

"What do I do now?" Melanie whined.

"I'm pulling over. You carry on to the police station," Jim said.

I passed the spatula off to Kenny and rubbed at my temple. A headache was already forming. Whether it was due to lack of sleep or stress remained to be seen.

"I'm rounding the corner to the police station now and he's peeled off," Melanie said.

"Melanie, where do you live? We'll hightail it over to your place. See if he's heading there," Jim said.

I felt absolutely useless at home. As a budding P.I. or a P.I. in training or a P.I. wannabe or whatever the heck I was, *I* should have been the one fending off the bad guy.

Melanie gave Jim directions.

I grumbled.

Jim said, "What's that, honey?"

"Oh nothing," I said. "I'll do some research. Look up that number Perry called."

"Okay, we'll call you later," Jim said, hanging up and disconnecting me from Melanie.

I sighed. It was just as well; they'd fill me in as soon as something happened.

I took the phone over to my office, hoping something would happen sooner rather than later, and left Kenny and Danny eating their pancakes. I peeked in on Laurie. She was still sound asleep in the swing. I envied that she could sleep through all the commotion but was grateful for the quiet time.

After powering up my PC, I pulled up the reverse database. As I feared, the number came up as a pre-paid phone with no name attached to it.

I sighed.

An ominous feeling overcame me. If Perry had been meeting another woman, then it was possible she could have had a pre-paid phone, but it didn't feel right. Pre-paid phone equaled trouble in my mind.

My home phone rang again and I jumped. I squared my shoulders and prepared myself for a conversation with skull cap man.

"Hello?"

Galigani's voice filled the line. "Kate, got your message late last night. What's going on? We've got competition?"

The night before, I'd left Galigani a worried voicemail after dropping off V.D. Worried because a) I hadn't been the one hired by Barramendi and b) V.D. knew something I didn't.

"Yeah. Apparently Barramendi hired some Spanish playwright to look into things. Can you believe that?"

"Oh. Do you mean Vicente Domingo?"

"That's him. V.D."

Galigani laughed. "That guy's kind of tough to read and he doesn't play well with others. I'll tell you that much. Last year, I worked a case for the prosecution and he was working defense. He did NOT share information. Nothing. Not one single name or number, nothing."

"Is that customary for the prosecution and defense investigators to work together?"

"Sure. I mean, sometimes there's sleight of hand." Galigani sounded annoyed. "You know, someone trying to get ahead in their career at the expense of someone else. That especially happens in election years. But generally speaking, we're on the side of justice."

"So, why do you think Barramendi hired him?" I asked.

"They're first cousins."

"Ah, nepotism."

I felt relieved.

Maybe Barramendi doesn't think I'm incompetent after all.

I glanced at my cell phone. No update from Jim or Melanie. I could hear sounds of Kenny and Danny horsing around in the kitchen. All the commotion made it feel like Grand Central Station.

"Real question is, what spooked Miles? Why do you think he called his attorney?" Galigani asked.

"You've got me there. I tried to get it out of V.D., but the best I could do was a postcard about his play."

Galigani snorted. "A play, huh? Maybe you should get involved. You know the old saying, keep your friends close and your enemies—"

"Don't even go there!" And before Galigani could try to convince me, I said, "Hey, I have a situation developing here." I explained about Melanie's visit, Perry's mysterious phone friend and the skull cap man tail gone wrong. I ended by saying, "Why don't you come?"

"You have any food?"

"Mickey Mouse pancakes," I answered.

Galigani made a semi-gagging sound indicating his disapproval of my offering and hung up on me.

Fifteen minutes later, I opened the door for Galigani with Laurie in my arms. He was holding a pink pastry box.

"No wonder you're a heart patient," I said.

He smiled. "These are for *you*."

"Ahh. That's more like it," I said, putting my hand out to receive the pastries.

Kenny must have smelled the doughnuts from the kitchen, because he instantly appeared and snatched the box out of Galigani's hand.

"Let me help you with that," he said.

We watched in amazement as Kenny inhaled four doughnuts in a row.

I pulled the box from him. "Didn't you just eat pancakes? You're going to get sick."

Galigani seated himself on my sofa and said, "He's just filling up one of his legs, Kate."

I sighed, then broke off a piece of a chocolate-covered old fashioned and handed it to Danny, who had trailed Kenny from the kitchen and was now silently drooling over the box. Laurie let out a wail, not wanting to be excluded from the doughnutfest.

"Is it okay to give a doughnut to a four month old?" I asked.

Galigani and Kenny both answered at the same time. "Sure!"

I had my doubts. Really, Galigani and Kenny were the last people on earth to ask about either diet or child care, but now it seemed cruel to hold out on Laurie. I handed her a small piece. She kicked her legs in joy and gummed the doughnut while I hovered over her making sure she didn't choke.

Galigani waved me off. "She's fine. Look how happy she is."

I leaned back in my chair. I was still nervous, but figured I was close enough to perform the Heimlich should the need arise.

"So what do you know about tracking down a pre-paid phone?" I asked Galigani.

Galigani shifted on the couch and helped himself to a glazed doughnut. "Got coffee?" he asked.

I nodded to Kenny, who took it as his cue to get it. He got up and grunted, letting out an "Aww, man," as he walked out of the room.

"That's pretty difficult. Probably a waste of time. Do you have the name of any of Perry's buddies? Maybe someone knew of a squeeze he had on the side."

I nodded. "I'll get some names from Melanie. Let's not mention it to Jill yet."

Kenny returned with two cups of coffee. He placed one in front of Galigani and handed me the other.

"Hey, I don't actually know if you do this, but can you dust a sign for prints?"

"What do you mean? You don't actually know if I can do that? Hello? Former SFPD here."

"Right," I said. "The sign at Painted Rock looks like it's been pulled out of place. The dirt around it was loose. It looked like I could have pulled in straight up and out, but I didn't want to mess with it."

"Okay, where is the sign?" Galigani asked.

"Uh. That's the thing…it's kind of a hike."

Galigani grumbled. "So I gotta walk?"

"Well," I said, slowly, trying to think up a good way to disguise the fact that the *'walk'* was actually straight up a hill that felt more like a mountain.

"Sounds like exercise," Galigani said.

Kenny inhaled another two doughnuts. "Mmm, exercise."

"Or you can teach me how to lift prints," I said hopefully.

"Right. Put that on our list, but for now I could probably use some exercise."

I laughed. "Okay. Well, maybe you can teach me how to lift prints anyway. We can consider this my first lesson."

My cell phone rang and I jumped to answer it.

"Hello?"

"Honey," Jim said. "We're outside of Melanie's house. Looks like the guy didn't follow her home, but we're going to hang out here a while and be sure."

I glanced out my front window. Sure enough, skull cap man was on my corner.

"Don't bother. He's here."

11

Galigani took photos of skull cap man through my window and sent them to his ex-partner, McNearny, at SFPD. McNearny promised to look into it, but his tepid reply was not very convincing.

We brainstormed but came up with nothing better than either taking skull cap man for another wild goose chase or just plain going out there and talking to him. We chose to confront him.

We told Kenny to stay with the kids and watch through the window. At the first sign of trouble he would call McNearny.

Galigani and I left my house and crossed the street. I thought of Jim. If he knew I was about to confront this guy he would have never let me accompany Galigani, but then again, if I stopped and listened to Jim, I'd never get any experience. And I wasn't willing to let this creep skulk around my house while I had an infant and a two-year-old inside.

At least I knew Galigani was packing heat. Not that I expected he'd need it. If I thought that, I would've stayed in the house, hugging Laurie in a back room.

Skull cap spotted us, then turned and ran down the street. Unfortunately, Galigani isn't much of a runner, but I was working on it. So I took off after him, yelling, "Hey! Wait. We just want to talk."

Skull cap man jumped into his car and fired it up.

Galigani took a few photos of the license plate with his phone and emailed them to McNearny.

I shook my head in despair. "What do you think he wants?"

"Obviously, he doesn't want to talk. But let's see if Mac can trace the plates. If not, I might be able to."

Galigani was already heading up my staircase, but I remained outside.

Something wasn't right. This no longer seemed to be about Jill's review. Why stalk me? Could Brent Miles really be behind this?

I punched Jill's number into my cell phone, and after a few rings she answered with a whispered hello.

"Jill? Why are you whispering?" I asked, hiking up my front steps and huffing in her ear.

"On the set. What's going on?"

I explained about Melanie and skull cap man. I left out the part about Perry meeting someone on his hike. That could wait. It might help to know who he'd been meeting before blabbing it to Jill and causing unnecessary grief.

"A man following her? Was it her boyfriend?" Jill asked.

"Her boyfriend? No, no. Melanie definitely said she didn't know this guy."

Jill was silent a moment then said, "Well, I don't know that you can take everything Melanie says at face value. Because, you see, she's a terrible liar. I don't mean she can't pull off a lie; what I mean is, like, a compulsive liar. You know, like a pathological liar."

My stomach dropped. "But I don't get it. If this guy was her boyfriend, why would she pretend she didn't know him?"

"The other day at Perry's, she said someone broke in and beat her up. But, I mean, why in the world would that happen? Nothing was taken and the police didn't find a forced entry or anything. And Perry was well liked by everyone." Jill took a deep breath. "Honestly, I think her boyfriend Sam is abusive and I think she's too scared to say anything."

I took a moment to take in the information. Melanie's swollen face flashed before my eyes and it both saddened and angered me to think that someone she loved could have done that to her.

And yet...there was something nagging at me. What was it? Oh yes!

"What about the TV?" I asked.

"What?" Jill asked.

"The TV was wrenched off the wall, remember?" I asked.

"Oh, that doesn't mean anything. Perry probably tried to move it or something. He wasn't very handy. And the police didn't find any prints, did they?"

Before I could answer, Jill continued. "Anyway, it's not the first time she's shown up with bangs and bruises."

Oh no!

I hated the thought of Melanie being pushed around by anyone, much less someone she was in a relationship with.

"And Perry told me she had, you know, uh...issues. I think the last guy she was with...sort of the same sad story."

"Do you know where I can find her boyfriend, Sam? Like maybe you know where he lives or works?" I asked.

"I don't have his address. But I can forward you his phone and email. I have to go now. They're calling me to resume the show."

"How's it going?"

"Great. I'll tell you all about it later. Keep me posted."

Right after we hung up, my phone beeped with the message from Jill. It had an email and phone number for Sam Kafer.

While I sat on my front steps and thought, mom's car pulled into my driveway. She waved frantically at me as though she thought I might not recognize her. I smiled and waved back.

Mom climbed out of her car, in one hand she carried a shopping bag and in the other a god-awful teal and orange baby hat. The hat looked like something directly out of Dr. Seuss.

"The weather is turning cold," she said, thrusting the hat at me.

"What's this?" I asked, standing up and climbing my front steps with mom. "Is this for Paula's baby?" I asked hopefully.

I tried to keep my tone neutral. Something that didn't scream out, "Please don't make me put this on my baby!"

Mom shook her head. "It's for Laurie. I haven't seen her in the baby cap I knitted her for so long, I figured she must have outgrown it."

"Uh. Yeah. She did." I lied.

Actually, last month I'd donated it to the Salvation Army along with a turquoise scarf she knitted Jim and a mustard-colored sweater she made for me. But Mom didn't need to know that.

"It's okay," Mom said with a proud smile. "I made her another."

"Great."

"This is for Paula's baby," Mom said, indicating the shopping bag.

Nice. I'm sure Paula got a pretty, regular, off-the-shelf baby gift.

We stepped into the madness of my house. Galigani was on my computer in the office that doubled as Laurie's nursery. In my living room were Kenny and Danny amid an oversized Noah's Ark jigsaw puzzle that was strewn across my carpet. Laurie was in her swing greedily gumming the remnants of a glazed doughnut.

Mom rushed to Laurie and plucked her up out of the swing. "Who gave this baby a doughnut?" she demanded, glaring at Kenny.

Kenny startled as he glanced up from the puzzle. "It was Kate!" he said defensively.

Galigani entered the room and nodded enthusiastically. "Yes, yes, Kate was the one."

Mom kissed Galigani saying, "Are you the adult supervising here? If so, we're all in trouble." She hugged Laurie protectively. "If she's ready for solid food, then you have to give her something with some nutritional value. Bananas, carrots, squash—"

"I know." I flopped onto the couch and rested my head in my hands, trying to ward off an impending headache.

"McNearny's going to try to trace the plates, but my images are pretty blurry," Galigani offered.

"I spoke with Jill. She said Melanie is a pathological liar and is in an abusive relationship. She thinks the story about the break-in at Perry's was a fabrication."

Galigani grumbled something inaudible and headed back to my office.

"Where are you going?" I asked.

"I'll call Ross. See what, if anything, came from those prints." Then he whispered, "I'll be safe in here away from the food police," and gestured toward Mom and the empty pink bakery box.

"No, you are not safe. Have you been eating these?" Mom lifted the lid of the pastry box by the corner. She pinched it between her thumb and forefinger as if not wanting to disturb fingerprints.

Galigani covered his mouth and gave an uncomfortable cough.

"Aw. I ate 'em. Me and the kid here," Kenny gestured toward Danny, who had a ridiculous grin on his face alongside the smear of chocolate on his cheek.

Mom shook her head, apparently deciding the fight wasn't worth it. Instead her gaze fell on the postcard Vicente had given me earlier, which I'd haphazardly thrown on the coffee table.

She released the pastry box lid and picked up the postcard. "What's this?"

Uh-oh.

I tried to reach across the table to grab the postcard before Mom could reach it, but I was too slow.

"What is this?" Mom repeated.

"What? Nothing. Nothing. Here, give it to me."

Galigani left the room, knowing he was getting off easy about the doughnuts and choosing to get out of Dodge.

Mom read the postcard. "Auditions!" she said. "Are you planning on getting back on stage?"

"What? No! Of course not. It's just a flyer someone gave me."

"Who gave it to you?"

"An investigator. Someone Barramendi hired," I explained.

"Well, are you going to audition?" she asked.

"No."

Mom studied the postcard, which included a description of the play along with a picture of Vicente.

Danny climbed onto the couch next to me and used it as a trampoline, jumping up and down repeatedly. Kenny gave up on the puzzle and began to put away the pieces.

"My, my, my. Is this the playwright/investigator?" Mom asked.

"That's him," I said.

"Oh, he's handsome," Mom said.

"Yeah, he's good-looking enough," I answered.

"Are you sure you don't want to audition?" Mom asked.

"Why would I want to audition? Like I don't have enough things going on right now?" I motioned to Danny who was now attempting to do a headstand between the cushions of my couch, only he kept falling over sideways and whacking me in the head.

Mom ignored him and simply said, "Too much sugar."

Kenny finished picking up the pieces of the puzzle. "I'll take him to the park."

I nodded toward Kenny and helped Danny into his jacket, while he was chanting "The park, the park, the park."

Mom fingered the post card again. "Maybe I will."

"What?" I asked.

"I'll audition."

My jaw dropped.

Mom was going to audition for V.D.'s play.

"Well, then I can be on the inside track," she said. "Get the scoop from him. See what information he has."

"No, mom!" I pleaded. "Please don't audition."

I could tell by the look in her eye it was going to be difficult to dissuade her, and the fear grew in my belly.

"You can't audition for the play! Come on, Mom. What are you talking about? You have two boyfriends!" I glanced over my shoulder to make sure Galigani hadn't overheard me, although the truth was that they seemed more comfortable with Mom dating multiple people than I was. "And your life is busy," I said. "What about Laurie? She needs you."

At the mention of her name, Laurie kicked her feet.

Mom shook her head and gestured to Kenny and Danny who were leaving through the front door. "You practically have an army here with you at all times."

"But you need to knit hats and things for her! You can't be out auditioning for some stupid play."

Mother laughed. "You're afraid I'm going to take your spotlight."

I laughed. "No. Believe me, the spotlight is always on you, Mom."

"Then what are you afraid of?" Mom asked.

Indeed. What was it? That I thought she'd make a fool of herself? A vision of Mom onstage in a tight bodice dress wearing an orange wig flashed before my eyes. While ludicrous, I couldn't quite say it wasn't something I'd seen before. Mom could handle herself. She always hammed it up and people loved her.

What was it then? And then it came to me. She would be with V.D. and not me. As though by choosing to audition she was choosing sides...

I hugged mom. "I don't like the other investigator. I think he's pompous and...well, I'm probably just resentful. He's working for Barramendi and I was hoping I was on Barramendi's short list."

Mom rubbed my shoulder. "Well, you probably are, darling. You don't know why he was hired. I'm sure it has nothing to do with you."

"Galigani said they're first cousins."

Mom frowned. "Well, that's probably one reason to hire someone, but if we solve the case first then Barramendi will remember that, won't he?"

"I want to solve it on my own. Not because my mommy went and spied on the other investigator."

"I'm not spying. I'm auditioning for a play."

Galigani returned to the living room. "I have news. Sam Kafer is going to meet us at Lou's Diner near the Land's End. We can meet with him then go lift prints off the sign you said was moved."

Mom pocketed the postcard. "I think I'm going to do it."

"Do what?" Galigani asked.

"Spy on V.D." I said.

Galigani kissed mom's check. "Excellent!"

I sighed. I'd have to resign myself to it. There'd be no talking Mom out of it at this point, especially not with Galigani cheering her on.

12

Galigani and I decided that we wouldn't have time for the hike until after our meeting with Sam. Secretly I thought that Galigani would put off the exercise of the hike as long as possible.

As we drove to Land's End, Galigani filled me in on the details from Officer Ross. The police had lifted some prints from Perry's TV: one set matched Perry's fingerprints, another set had no match in the database, and the third print was only a partial, and smeared, at that.

I thought about Jill. She'd been pretty adamant that she didn't think anyone had really broken into Perry's apartment. Could Melanie have contrived the entire scene? If she was being abused and trying to hide it, why would she fake a robbery and call attention to herself? It seemed like the opposite of what one would want to do.

Galigani turned into a parking lot that was below the entrance to Land's End. We circled, looking for a spot. The lot was packed as it served both the hiking area and the nearby restaurants.

"Do you think that someone broke into Perry's place?" I asked.

Galigani shrugged. "Yeah. I assume it was the same guy who followed Jill and then Melanie."

"Skull cap man. Me too. What if it was Sam?"

"You mean, the woman made us go on a complete wild goose chase so we wouldn't think her boyfriend beat her up?"

I grimaced. "When you put it like that, it makes it sound ridiculous."

"No, no. Believe me. I've seen worse. Anything is possible. But it wasn't Sam's prints on the TV."

"How do you know that?"

"He's got a record. His prints are in the database."

I let the information sink in. "Record? For what?" I asked, and then added, "And how do you know this already?"

Galigani looked at me as if I was a piece of foreign matter and he didn't quite understand how I'd ended up in his car. "As soon as you gave me his name I ran a check. That's what I do. Gather information."

I nodded and indicated a parking spot that was opening up, hoping this might distract him from my lack of thoroughness as a P.I. intern/newbie/wannabe.

"What do you do? Just run off to meet the guy and hope he'll play nice and not lie to you?" he asked.

Obviously, he had not been deterred.

I tried not to look offended. "I operate on instinct." I smiled for good measure, feeling as if I'd been called to the boss's office, and prepared myself for the lecture that was sure to follow.

Galigani stopped the car, waiting for the other vehicle to clear out of the parking spot. He twisted in his seat and faced me. "You can't run off and meet with people without doing a check on them first. I thought we'd already had this conversation."

I grimaced.

Of course we'd already had this discussion. What was I thinking?

"You need to make a checklist. You do that, don't you?"

I blinked at him. "Yeah, I have a to-do list."

"No, not to-do. To-do's change every day or every hour even. A checklist, you know, certain things you need to do all the time when a certain thing happens. New person pops up on the radar, boom, run a background check. Easy as that. It's not rocket science."

"Right. I'll add it to my list."

He stared at me. "Add it to what list? You just told me you didn't have a checklist."

"I mean, I'll add the note to create a checklist on to my to-do list."

Galigani's eyes bulged and he looked as if he would propel himself out of the car right through the roof. I refrained from laughing, knowing that if he thought I was taking his scolding lightly, he'd crack. Instead, I lowered my eyes and tried to look contrite.

Thankfully, he said nothing more on the subject and pulled into the parking spot.

We got out of the car and crossed the street to Lou's Diner. Galigani and I went inside and found a spot at the counter. Galigani ordered himself a bloody Mary.

"Aren't you supposed to abstain from alcohol?" I asked him.

He smiled. "No. You?"

The bartender waited me out and I ordered a coffee.

"I can drink. I choose not to." I eyed Galigani. "I want to be sharp. What about your heart?"

Galigani sat straighter on the barstool. "Look, I gotta have a drink to be able to deal with you."

"Wow," I laughed.

Galigani smiled. "They have the best Bloody Marys in the city. You have to try it."

The bartender set our drinks before us. Galigani pushed his toward me and I took a sip. I had to agree. It was spicy and delicious.

"Yum!" I said.

Galigani nodded sagely.

"So what's the deal with Sam's record? What did he do?" I asked. Before he had a chance to answer, the front door opened with a bang.

We turned to look and in between the darkened restaurant and bright sunlight from outside stood the shadow of a large man, tall and imposing. He was about 6'4" and he let the door slam behind him.

"Galigani?" he asked, as he approached us.

I immediately noticed a circular bruise around his left eye. I checked out his hands. No marks that I could see.

"Yes," Galigani said, rising off of his barstool and extending his right hand. "Thank you for meeting us." He gestured in my direction. "This is my assistant, Kate Connolly."

He gave me a firm and aggressive handshake. "I'm Sam."

I tapped the area around my eye and said, "Ouch!"

Sam fingered the tender spot above his cheek next to his eye. "Yeah, I'm a plumber. Hazard of the job."

Galigani frowned. "Never knew black eyes were a side effect of plumbing."

Sam laughed, seemingly at ease with himself. "They are when you're breaking in a newbie who's eager to impress you. Guy was swinging a pipe around and talking too. I'm sure you know some people like that? They talk too much. Anyway, he hit me with a pipe by accident."

I expected Galigani to make a joke at my expense. Something to the effect of how he knew only too well the hazard of breaking in an inexperienced intern, who, incidentally, did talk too much. But he simply said, "We're looking into the death of Perry Welgan."

Sam's brows furrowed. "Why? I thought it was an accident."

"Well," I said, stringing out the word while glancing at Galigani for input.

Sam remained standing and crossed his arms in front of his chest. "Of course, I'll be as helpful as I can." Only his body language didn't exactly scream *openness*.

The bartender approached us and Sam ordered a Bloody Mary. Showed how much I knew. The entire city knew that this was the place to order a Bloody Mary and I'd ordered a coffee!

"Can I have one, too?" I asked.

The bartender nodded. "Folks want to see a menu?"

I shook my head, and he began to mix the drinks.

"What do you want to know about Perry?" Sam asked.

"How well did you know him?" I asked, glancing at Galigani to see how much information I should release.

Sam shrugged. "Good enough, I guess. I mean, Mel and I aren't that serious, but I'd met Perry a few times, helped him move a couch. That sort of thing."

Galigani didn't seem to be giving me any signal to shut up, so I continued. "Can you think of anyone who would want to hurt Perry?" I asked.

"No. Seemed a likeable enough guy."

"Well, you may know," I said, "Melanie came upon an intruder at Perry's place. Maybe there were looking for something or—"

Sam frowned. "What do you mean? Mel came across an intruder? When?"

"Day before yesterday," Galigani said. "She got banged up pretty good, too."

At that moment, the bartender presented the Bloody Marys to us with a flourish. "Best in town. Ain't that right, sir?" he asked Galigani

I tried not to let my irritation show. After all, he was just doing his job, but did the guy really have to interrupt us at the key moment when I wanted to watch Sam's face?

"Why didn't she tell me?" Sam wondered out loud.

"When the last time you spoke with her?" I asked.

"She called me from the hospital and told me about Perry. I wanted to pick her up but she told me she was with Jill. We're getting together tonight…"

He didn't finish the sentence, only took a sip of his drink and shrugged. "Chicks. Sometimes, I don't understand them."

How odd indeed that they hadn't seen each other yesterday. I would figure that Melanie would want the comfort of her boyfriend on the day she found out her own brother had perished, but then again, with Sam's bruised eye, who knew how comforting he was?

Galigani's phone buzzed and he glanced down at the display.

"How long have you and Melanie been dating?" I asked.

The left corner of Sam's mouth twitched. "Dunno. Don't chicks keep track of that kind of stuff? Probably about six months or so. Yeah, that's about right. We met in the spring."

His attitude about Melanie seemed so cavalier. It didn't seem like they were too serious. And, if he was responsible for her battered face, I hoped their relationship would soon be over.

Although, how was it that his face was battered too? Could Melanie have hit him? She was so petite I couldn't imagine her socking this guy in the eye.

Galigani murmured something next to me and I realized he'd received some news on his phone.

I glanced at him.

"Do you hike, Mr. Kafer?" Galigani asked.

Sam shook his head, a look of confusion on his face. "No."

"Were you working day before yesterday?" Galigani asked.

Sam nodded and took a sip of his Bloody Mary.

"Brent Miles is being detained by SFPD," Galigani said, indicating his phone.

I took a sharp inhale. This indeed was big news.

Sam looked confused. "Brent Miles? Who the hell is that?"

"Brent Miles owns the restaurant *Philosophie*. Jill Harrington, Perry's girlfriend, reviewed it, and unfortunately it wasn't a very positive review. We understand Mr. Miles may have been responsible for placing threatening calls to Jill in addition to perhaps having her followed," I said.

"We really don't have any evidence of that," Galigani interrupted, a strange look on his face that I took to mean, "Shut your trap."

I busied myself by sipping my Bloody Mary. Oh! It was so yummy.

"Mr. Miles is being investigated because of a related accidental death. It was also a 'hiking accident'. The night manager of another of Miles' restaurants fell to his death in Yosemite," Galigani said.

Sam frowned, his face registering shock. "Are you saying that Perry died because of some...some stupid review Jill wrote?"

Galigani and I exchanged glances.

"That's what we're trying to figure out," Galigani said.

Emotion crossed Sam's face and he pounded a heavy fist into the bar. "That is ridiculous. How could someone die over a restaurant review?"

Galigani pulled out a notebook and asked. "Can you give me the name of someone who can verify your whereabouts yesterday? You said you were working?"

The way Galigani asked it so calmly made me envy his training. However, no matter how smooth Galigani was, his question caused Sam to erupt.

"Are you asking me for an alibi?" he spat, as he rose to his feet.

Galigani sipped his drink and looked about as nonplused as if he was setting up a golf outing. "I'm not asking for an alibi,

I'm asking if someone can confirm your whereabouts." He raised an eyebrow at Sam. "Do you need an alibi?"

Sam's face contorted, his eyes narrowing and upper lip turning into a snarl. "You can call Dustin, he's the newbie that gave me this shiner." He pulled out his phone and recited a number at Galigani, who diligently wrote it in his notebook.

"Are you finished with me?" Sam asked.

Galigani shrugged. "Unless you think you have anything else to share with us?"

Sam slurped the rest of his Bloody Mary and wiped his mouth with his hand. "No, I ain't got nothing more to *share*."

The door to the darkened restaurant opened and a silhouette of a man wearing a dark leather jacket and holding a helmet appeared. The man stepped into the darkness of the restaurant.

Sam took the opportunity to leave, mumbling a good-bye and exiting through the door, his form getting swallowed into the bright sunlight.

The bartender cleared Sam's glass. "Another?" he asked Galigani.

Galigani shook his head. "Do you know the guy we were talking to?" Galigani asked him.

I studied the man with the helmet in the corner of the café. He was turned away so all I could see was his profile.

"He comes in from time to time," the bartender answered Galigani. "He's a tough character, huh?"

"Do you think he hits his girlfriend?" Galigani plainly asked.

The bartender shrugged. "I don't know his girlfriend."

"But you know him," Galigani pressed. "Is he the type of guy who could lose his temper with a woman?"

"Perhaps," the bartender said—although he said it under his breath and turned as he spoke, signaling us that the conversation was over.

I turned to Galigani. "So you don't think Melanie was beaten up by the intruder?"

Galigani shrugged. "We need to look at things from all angles. It's pretty suspicious that he had the bruise and he's got a record—"

"But the prints on the TV weren't his," I protested.

"That doesn't mean anything really," Galigani said. "Those prints could be from anytime."

The man with the helmet stepped forward into the light, his handsome face illuminated by the sunlight peeking in through the window.

Vicente winked at me, then flashed his dazzling smile at Galigani. "Yes, a record for assault and battery. It's definitely something that needs to be looked at."

13

I stuffed down my frustration and downed the rest of my Bloody Mary. What the hell was Vicente Domingo a.k.a. V.D. doing here? Had he followed us?

Galigani apparently wasn't frustrated; he looked completely relaxed.

"Ah, Vicente. We meet again."

Vicente extended his hand. "*Señor* Galigani."

Galigani shook his hand. "I hear your big-wig client, Brent Miles, is behind bars?"

Vicente shrugged. "Pfft. Not for long. Barramendi will see to that."

"And you have to make sure he stays out, right?" I asked.

"Of course." Vicente said, waving to the bartender and indicating he wanted a Bloody Mary by pointing to mine then to himself.

The bartender nodded his understanding and got busy concocting another drink.

"What do you have?" Vicente asked.

Information? He wanted information from us?

No way. Not without a quid pro quo.

"How did you find us?" I asked.

He cocked an eyebrow at me. "GPS tracking on your phone."

"You're tracking my phone?" I asked, dumbfounded.

Vicente nodded casually. "Yours, and his." He nodded to Galigani. "Even Sam Kafer's."

I inhaled sharply, trying to control my anger. I glanced at Galigani, wishing he'd blow his top all over V.D., but he said. "So, Kafer's on your list, huh? You work fast."

V.D. shrugged and accepted the Bloody Mary put in front of him by the bartender. "You know the procedure. Check out next of kin and all romantic relationships first. Kafer is the vic's sister's boyfriend and he has a prior. Elementary. And then the GPS of three of you together. Too hard to pass up."

GPS tracking? I'd have to look into that later. It didn't seem ethical, let alone legal, but if the competition was using it, I should be too. There was probably some tracking software I could get online. *Why was I always behind on everything?*

I excused myself to use the restroom and took advantage of the excuse to text Jill. Hopefully, V.D. wasn't tracking my text messages. I assumed *that* was illegal, but then again, what did I know? Just in case, I left Jill a cryptic message requesting she call me. Which she did immediately.

I decided to take the call in the privacy of the ladies room.

"Kate, I'm on break at the studio, so I can chat, but only for a minute. What's going on? Have you found anything out?"

"SFPD has detained Brent Miles. Person of interest."

"Oh my God!" Jill gasped.

"I know, but they probably won't be able to hold him long. He's got a top notch attorney, not to mention a P.I. who's following me around."

"He's following you? Why?" Jill asked.

"Well, tracking us. Me and Galigani. We met with Sam, Melanie's boyfriend. He's got a bruise on his eye. Blamed it on a co-worker. Do you know anything about it?"

Jill tsked, then said, "Oh. No. I...I don't know what to make of it."

I fiddled with the faucet on the sink, an idea forming.

"Jill? Did Perry think Sam was abusing Melanie?"

"Perry knew Melanie had a tendency to sort of pick the wrong guy. She's got a history of abuse. She swore Sam was different, but..."

I bit my tongue. I wanted to tell her that Perry had planned to meet someone on the hike, but I'd promised Melanie I wouldn't say anything. Besides, I hadn't figured out who he'd planned to meet yet. It could have been another woman, which she would want to know, but I also didn't want to arouse her suspicions unnecessarily. And I certainly wouldn't want to drag her through the emotions of betrayal if I was on the wrong course.

Could Perry have been meeting Sam? Perry could have given Sam the black eye, if he thought Sam was abusing his sister. It would make sense if they'd fought. Maybe it got out of hand and Sam ended up pushing Perry off the cliff.

And yet, what about the sign?

If Sam was abusive and he and Perry had fought over that, then Perry's going over the cliff would likely have been an accident, a crime of passion type of thing. Moving a warning sign was a premeditated thing.

No, my theory didn't seem to make any sense.

I sighed.

"What?" Jill asked over the phone.

I startled at her voice. I'd almost forgotten she was still on the line. "Oh. Sorry. I was lost in thought."

"About what? What are you thinking?" Jill asked.

"About that warning sign. I'm going to go up the hill and dust for prints."

"Be careful? Okay?" Jill said.

"Of course."

She rang off, after saying, "Let me know what you find out."

Galigani and V.D. were still chatting when I emerged from the restroom. I gave V.D. a curt nod and indicated to Galigani that we should go.

V.D. raised an eyebrow at me, but said nothing as Galigani and I left the bar. It took a moment for my eyes to adjust to the sunlight.

"What did he say?" I asked.

Galigani blew out a breath. "Not much. I told you the guy doesn't share. So I didn't either. We talked about the play-offs."

I laughed. "There's always football, right?"

Galigani nodded. I filled him in on my conversation with Jill and my ideas about Sam being the person Perry had met.

We talked as we began the steep incline of the Land's End hike. The wind was howling and I regretted not grabbing a hat or even a scarf. I thought of Laurie, realizing that soon it soon would be feeding time. I'd left Mom with several bottles so I probably had a little more time than usual to spend on the investigation.

"How much farther?" Galigani asked. A bead of sweat had developed on his brow and he wiped at it with the back of his hand.

How ironic. I was freezing and he was sweating.

"I think it's a little bit higher. Are you okay?" I asked.

He nodded. "The exercise is good for the ticker."

We followed the path along a twisty route and then a stunning view of the Golden Gate Bridge came into focus.

Galigani paused. He looked happy to have a credible excuse to stop.

I pointed to a bench that was up a steep incline. "Want to take a moment and enjoy the view?"

Galigani blew out air, keeping his cheeks puffed and giving the impression that he'd had it with the hike.

I placed my hands firmly on his back. "Come on. I'll push you up the hill."

"I can make it to the bench," he said, indignation in his voice.

Ignoring him, I began to walk, pushing him ahead while I leaned into the steep hill.

"Uh. It's much easier with a little engine that could behind me."

I laughed. "Weird thing is, I was exhausted the first time I did the hike, too. I think knowing we only have one more hill is making it easier for me."

We collapsed onto the bench as soon as we reached it.

"I should have trained you to dust for prints. Why didn't I do that? Then I wouldn't have—"

"The exercise is good for you. You'll thank me tomorrow when you can't get out of bed." I laughed.

Galigani didn't laugh, though; he grimaced and reached for his phone. "You think they can Medivac me out of here?"

Glaring at him, I pulled the phone out of his hands. "It's steep but it's only a quarter of a mile—"

"It was more than a quarter mile!" he growled.

I waved a dismissive hand at him. "Something like that. Quarter mile, half mile—"

He grabbed his phone out of my hand. "I'll check."

The wind seemed to be picking up and now that we were resting on the bench I felt colder than before. A lone raindrop landed on my wrist. "Come on. If you're rested enough to play with your phone then you can make it up the next little bit. Painted Rock is around the next bend."

"You say that as if the next bend isn't a mountain."

I grabbed his arm and helped him to his feet. His pride returned. "I got this," he said.

We walked in silence for the next few minutes. It was beginning to sprinkle, and each time a raindrop hit Galigani he grunted. When we reached Painted Rock, I gasped. "What?" Galigani asked.

I indicated the fork in the road. The main path continued up the hill, but on the other path—the one that went right off the cliff—the warning sign was gone.

"It's gone! The sign is gone." I looked around half expecting it to be in a nearby shrub.

Galigani frowned. "Are you sure?"

I nodded and indicated the large Painted Rock marker that was painted on the side of mountain. The dirt around the base of the sign had been soft and loose. I examined it now and found only two gaping holes.

"Do you think the cops pulled the sign?" I asked.

Galigani shook his head. "No. If they had, there would be crime scene tape."

"Vicente!" I screamed.

"What?" Galigani asked, puzzled.

"Could he have grabbed it? Maybe he thought it had Brent Miles' prints on it."

"No," Galigani said. His voice was emphatic and yet a skeptical look crossed his face. "It would be highly unorthodox."

"Is it orthodox to track down the other P.I.s working on the case using some phone GPS tracking thingamabob?"

Galigani's lips twisted, causing his mustache to work back and forth across his face. "Well, you've got to keep up with technology, but I can't see stealing a piece of evidence."

My hair, aided by wind, was swirling around my face. The sprinkles had turned to drizzle and I covered my face with my hands so I could focus. "Someone took it," I said.

"It could be unrelated. You said the base was loose. Maybe hikers took it home as a souvenir."

"Please. That's ridiculous!"

Galigani pulled his phone out of his pocket. "Really? Happens all the time. You'd be surprised how many kids take street signs and stop signs and all sorts of things. And the sign had a pretty menacing message, too, right?"

"People have fallen to their death from this point. Keep out," I said.

Galigani nodded. "What kid wouldn't want that on their bedroom door?" He began to photograph the scene with his camera phone. I sighed. It was a good thing I'd brought him along. He began to make his way down the short path, ominously close to the edge.

"What are you doing? Get away from there!" I demanded, remaining absolutely rooted to the safe ground where I stood.

"Having a look. What the heck you think I'm doing?"

"Hello! People have fallen to their death from there!"

He gave me a dismissive wave. "You have no idea how many times this cat has flirted with death. I've got nine lives."

"It's not you I'm worried about. If anything happens to you, Mom is going to kill me. Now get away from the cliff, please."

He ignored me.

"I'm serious," I said.

Proceeding to ignore me, Galigani got down on his hands and knees and examined the dirt. He pulled a plastic baggie out of his pocket and rooted around the ground.

"What are you doing now?" I asked.

"Soil sample," he answered.

The man carried around plastic baggies? I really needed to be better prepared if I was ever going to make it in this field.

Galigani shoved the baggie back into his pocket and stood. He wiped the dirt, which was quickly turning into mud, off the knees of his jeans and walked even closer to the cliff. "Oh my!" he said.

"What?" I asked.

"The view from here is amazing. No wonder people ignore the sign." He took a few pictures. "Especially those photographers."

He paced the edge of the cliff a bit, examining all the angles. I could barely avoid the image in my mind of him disappearing entirely off the face of the earth.

"I have to get home," I said.

Galigani proceeded to pace the edge.

"It's really started to come down now," I said, wiping rain from my face.

Galigani didn't answer.

"I'm hungry." I yelled. "My baby's hungry. I need to pay the sitter. Christ! Will you get away from the edge!"

He turned and began walking toward me. "Calm down," he said. He joined me where I stood on the main path.

We began to descend the path toward the parking lot. The dirt path was becoming slick from the rain. "Be careful," I said.

Galigani nodded and said, "I'm always careful," as he started to punch a number into his phone.

"Who are you calling?" I asked.

"SF Park Service. They gotta replace that warning sign right away. Without it we'll have another disaster soon. I don't know why they don't put a railing…"

Suddenly Galigani's foot slipped out from under him and he pitched forward. "Oh no!" I yelled, grasping at him. I grabbed hold of the sleeve of his jacket, but it wasn't enough to stop his fall, and he took a tumble down the path, pulling me with him. I fell to my knees, but he was completely laid out on his back.

Ridiculously, laughter erupted from me.

"Stop laughing," Galigani groused.

I continued to laugh. "I can't help it. I'm so glad you fell here and not off that cliff!"

He grunted. "Way to look at the bright side of things, kid. But I think there's something wrong with my foot." He propped himself on his elbow to get a better view.

I stopped laughing abruptly and took a deep breath.

His leg and knee were pointed to the right and his foot was angled grotesquely to the left.

I grimaced. "I guess we're going to need that Medivac after all, huh?"

14

The rain turned into an annoying drizzle as we waited for the paramedics to arrive. They took about fifteen minutes to get to us and, all the while, I got to listen to Galigani complain. Of course, I didn't mind. After all, this was my fault. I should never have pushed him out of his comfort zone. Now, he'd likely be in a cast for six weeks.

As the medics loaded Galigani into the ambulance, he handed me his keys. "You can take my car home, kid."

I took the keys. "I'll follow you to the hospital." I gave him my best charming smile, "Maybe they'll outpatient you."

He didn't answer me, only made a face and turned away. I glanced at one of the paramedics, who subtly shook his head. Most likely, Galigani would be admitted to the hospital.

I jogged over to his car and noted the scratched-up vintage Harley-Davidson parked next to it. I looked around for V.D. but he wasn't in the parking lot. I spotted him across the street in front of *Philosophie*, Miles's restaurant. He was locked in an embrace with someone…someone who had immovable blonde hair.

Mrs. Miles!

The one and only who had wiped out his Harley yesterday?

She pulled away from him and dried her eyes. It looked as if she'd been crying on his shoulder, and I didn't think she was all broken up about banging into his bike…

Was she distraught over her husband being hauled in for questioning?

Or was their relationship something else entirely?

How could that be, though? She definitely struck me as someone who'd only be interested in a man if they had dollar signs floating in their eyes, and V.D. was basically a starving playwright. All right, he could be making some money on the side with his P.I. business, but nothing compared to Miles. No. if Mrs. Miles was interested in him, she had an ulterior motive...

Could it be she needed his help in covering up a crime?

Mrs. Miles said something to V.D. to which he nodded. Suddenly, he turned and started walking in my direction. I jammed Galigani's key into the car door and twisted. The keys stuck in the side position and wouldn't budge. I tried to pull it out, but the key was slick from the rain, my fingers sliding off of it. I tried again, this time jerking so hard, the key actually broke off in my hand.

Shoot!

I stared at the broken key. This had never happen to me before. I cursed Galigani for having such a crappy car and an even crappier key. Then I immediately felt repentant. I'd only broken a key, he'd broken an ankle.

I could feel V.D. rapidly approaching and I considered my options. Could I head in the opposite direction and avoid him altogether?

"Hi, Kate!" he said, his voice full of cheer.

I groaned inwardly, then turned to face him. "Chummy with Mrs. Miles, huh?"

He frowned and glanced over his shoulder. "Oh. You saw us talking."

I smiled. "That's what you call *talking*?"

He laughed and cocked an eyebrow at me. "What do you call it?"

I waved an impatient hand at him. "Never mind." I pulled my phone out of my pocket, hoping that he'd get on his bike and leave.

He looked around. "Where's Galigani?"

I scrolled randomly on my phone. "Ummm. He's out of commission, right now."

V.D.'s eyebrows knit together, then a look of alarm crossed his face. "I saw the ambulance...don't tell me—"

"I won't, then."

"What?"

"I won't tell you anything. Look, I'd love to chat, but I need to make a call. See ya." I wiggled my fingers at him.

He leaned on Galigani's car. "Go ahead. Make your call. I can wait."

Seagulls chirped in the distance and the sound of the waves crashing against the Sutro Bath retaining wall made me want to lure V.D. to the edge of the parking lot and push him into the ocean.

I wiped the drizzle off my phone and dialed home. Jim's voicemail clicked on. "Honey," I said into the phone. "Galigani broke his ankle and I'm stuck over by Land's End. Call me when you get this message. I need a ride."

V.D. quirked his head. "I can give you a ride. Where do you need to go?"

I eyed the Harley-Davidson next to Galigani's car. "On that?"

"Yeah," V.D. moved toward the storage box on the rear of the bike. "I have an extra helmet."

"No."

He smiled. "Come on. I owe you a ride, and I don't like the feeling of owing anybody anything."

"Good. I'm glad you don't like it and you can continue to feel it, because I'm not getting on that thing with you. "

He licked his lips as if preparing himself for a challenge. "Afraid to get wet."

I held my arms out, indicating my shirt already drenched from the rain and subsequent drizzle. "I'm already wet."

"Don't be scared. I'm a good driver."

"I'm not scared. I'd rather take the bus."

Actually there was nothing I hated worse than the bus. But at this point, I wanted Mr. Arrogant Pants away from me.

I hiked around Galigani's car and headed toward the bus stop that was across the street in front of *Philosophie*. San Francisco was absolutely notorious for awful public transportation. I once watched a Muni bus driver pop over the curb of a crowded sidewalk and run over ten parking meters before correcting back onto the street. I figured since the bus practically never came, I could sit it out and wait for Mr. Harley-Davidson to whiz off.

I took a seat in the rain shelter and waited for him to leave. To my astonishment, a Muni bus turned the corner of the Great Highway and came lumbering toward me.

Darn it.

I couldn't really see V.D.'s face, but I imagined a smug smile. He put the extra helmet back in the storage box, then put his own on his head. He climbed on to his bike and revved it up.

The bus was upon me. I suddenly realized that I didn't even have cash for the bus. Not that I was going to climb aboard anyway, but for crying out loud, how unprepared could I be?

The bus doors opened and the driver looked at me expectantly. I waved him off and the doors closed. Before the bus pulled away, I was struck by brilliance. I stood and rounded the bus shelter and popped into *Philosophie*, all while the bus blocked V.D.'s view.

When the bus pulled away from the curb, I was safely tucked inside the restaurant. For all intents and purposes, V.D. thought I was on the bus.

I crouched behind a booth and turned my phone off, lest he be tracking my GPS signal or whatever the heck my phone was putting out. I watched as he mounted his bike and tore off after the bus.

Good. Now he was gone and I only had to figure out how to get to the hospital without a car, *and* without a serviceable phone.

I stood and glanced around the restaurant. It was totally deserted. Where was Mrs. Miles?

"Hello?" I called out.

The hostess with the frizzy red hair appeared. "Sorry, I didn't hear you come in. We're closed." She looked over my shoulder, checking to see if she had an unruly mob on her hands.

"Actually, I'm not here to eat. I...um...my friend had an accident while hiking and I—"

"Oh!" Her delicate brow wrinkled and a look of genuine concern crossed her face.

"Can I use your phone?" I asked.

"Yes, of course. Follow me."

She walked to the back of the restaurant. We passed the kitchen where the cook was bent over, checking something in the oven, and all that was visible was a chef's hat that seemed to float above one of the counters.

The hostess unlocked the office door and ushered me inside. She pointed to a black touchtone phone that sat atop a meticulously clean mahogany desk.

"Thank you," I said.

She nodded and closed the door behind her.

How odd that she'd leave me alone in the office, but hey, I wasn't going to look a gift horse in the mouth. I wiggled the computer mouse and a financial software program came to life.

I grumbled as I raked my eyes across the awful spreadsheet. It could have been in German or Arabic for all that I could make out of it. It looked like what you might expect from a restaurant, vendors like Antonio's Bakery, The Farmer's Market and Fresh Fish Daily. Certainly there was nothing that looked suspicious, from what I could tell.

Grabbing the black phone, I dialed Mom. Thankfully she picked up on the first ring.

"Mom, don't panic. Everything is fine. Galigani is alive."

"What?" Mom said, concern and panic suddenly in her voice. "Kate! What's going on?"

"Calm down. I said, don't panic."

"How can I not panic when you start a conversation with 'Don't panic'?" she shrieked. "What's happened? Are you alright?"

"I'm fine. It's Galigani. We went hiking—"

"Oh dear God! Is it his heart?"

"He fell and broke his ankle. They took him up the hill to UC."

"My poor Albert. Poor, poor, dear Albert—"

"Mom—"

"I'm on my way," she hung up.

"Wait!" a loud dial tone assaulted my ear. Shoot! I hadn't even gotten to the "I need a ride" part.

I started to dial her number again, when the hostess peeked in the doorway. "Everything okay?" she asked.

"Oh, I'm trying to get a ride to the hospital, but she..." I dialed Mom's number again, fearful that if I stopped to explain, Mom would be gone. I listened to the phone ring. "She's...gone."

Of course, Mom had a cell phone like everyone else now, but that number was programmed into my phone and I'd have to turn on my phone to look it up, not to mention the probability of Mom actually remembering to take her phone with her was slim to none.

The hostess frowned. "You need a ride to UC?"

I nodded.

"I'm off in a few minutes. I can take you," she smiled politely.

"Really? Oh, I…I wouldn't want to impose…"

"It's not an imposition, really. I live up the hill anyway."

I couldn't believe my luck. I'd have a ride and someone I could grill about Mr. and Mrs. Miles.

Perfect!

"I would so appreciate it," I said, sincerely.

She nodded. "Let me tell the chef I'm taking off."

She disappeared toward the kitchen, leaving me alone in the office. If there was only some information I could get here, then I wouldn't feel like such a loser. Something to help me crack the case, something V.D. wouldn't be privy to.

On impulse, I silently eased open the top drawer of the desk. Inside was a shiny silver and black Berretta handgun.

15

Crap!

I jolted upright and slammed the drawer closed as though it had bit me.

Whose gun was that? I couldn't possibly accept a ride from the woman I hardly knew! No matter what information I could glean from her, putting myself at risk was not an option.

I pulled my phone out of my pocket and turned it on. At this point, it didn't matter if V.D. found me here – so what? I called Mom's cell phone.

The hostesses reappeared in the doorway. "Oh," she frowned. "You have a phone."

"I…it's not working all that great," I muttered as way of explanation, sometime the reception…"

She nodded, seemingly satisfied. "Yeah. It's hit and miss around here. Ready to go?"

I held up a finger as I left a message for Mom, knowing full well it was in vain. "Okay, I'm in front of *Philosophie*, I'll be looking for you." I hung up and turned to the hostess. "I got in touch with her. She'll be here in a minute, but thank you so much for the offer of the ride."

"Oh." A hurt look flashed across her face, then she shrugged it off. "Yeah, sure."

I followed her back to the restaurant, and when we crossed in front of the kitchen she yelled out, "See you tomorrow, Ramon."

I turned toward the kitchen and came face to face with my friend, Ramon.

We both stared at each other in shock. I knew Ramon was going to work for Miles, but I'd understood it would be at a different restaurant.

"What are you doing here, Kate?" he asked.

"I…um…Galigani got hurt hiking the Land's End trail. He's at UC and I needed a ride…" it was all getting complicated fast and I didn't want to tell him in front of the hostess that'd I'd lied about having a ride. "What are you doing here? I thought you were going to be the chef of a new restaurant, Empanada King, or something like that?"

He nodded. "Yeah, but Miles was…" he glanced at the hostesses, who narrowed her eyes at him. "I was getting familiar with the kitchen here," Ramon clarified. "Anyway, I'm done now. I can take you to UC."

"That'd be great," I said.

The hostess leveled a gaze at me. "I thought you said you already had a ride?" I waved my hand around dismissing the idea, hoping she would be detoured. "Ah, it's a long story."

Her face was hard as she stared at me, then Ramon. Suddenly I got it. She was interested in Ramon and not at all hot on the idea of him giving me – some mystery woman who just appeared on the scene and friendly with him – a ride.

I quickly mumbled something about my husband not answering his phone. Her face brightened.

Ramon took off the chef's hat and then his apron. "No problem," he said, moving toward a white laundry bin and balling his apron in his hands.

The hostess grabbed some soiled towels that were on the counter and pitched them into the laundry bin at the same moment as Ramon tossed his apron in. She timed it perfectly so that their hands touched.

He smiled at her, but in a friendly way, not catching at all that she was into him.

"Let's go," he said motioning me into the dining area and towards the front door. We exited the restaurant, then the hostess locked the doors behind us.

"See you tomorrow, Jess," Ramon said.

"Yeah, sure, Ramon." She smiled coquettishly at him. "*Hasta mañana.*" She slung an oversize handbag over her shoulder and took off down the hill, toward an auxiliary parking lot nearby.

Ramon and I hiked across the street and back into the parking lot where Galigani's car was.

"She likes you," I said.

He frowned. "Who?"

"The hostess. Jess," I said.

Ramon stopped walking and stared at me. "Really? Why do you say that?"

I laughed. "Call it women's intuition. I could tell by the way she was looking at you."

He pressed his key fob and unlocked the car door. We climbed in and strapped our seatbelts.

"Where's Mrs. Miles, by the way? I saw her a few minutes ago outside. She was talking to their private investigator, but then she disappeared."

Ramon twisted in his seat to look at me. "They have a P.I.?"

"Yeah. The cops picked up Miles for questioning today," I said.

"I know. That's why I was at *Philosophie* instead of downtown. With all his troubles right now, the opening of Empanada King has been pushed out." He shrugged. "I hope everything gets straightened out soon."

I thought about the gun in the drawer and shiver went up my spine. "Ramon, are you sure you want to work for Miles? He has a ruthless reputation and I saw—"

"Kate, I'm sure he had nothing to do with that man's death—"

"How do you know that? Do you know one of Mile's employees fell to his death in Yosemite? Another hiking accident."

Ramon frowned. "I think if a man like Miles wants anyone out of his business he just has to wave around the cash. I don't think he'd start causing a bunch of hiking accidents. That's too—"

"I saw a gun in the office," I blurted out.

Ramon shrugged. "Lots of places have a gun around. You need to be able to defend against a customer gone postal."

"Really?"

"Sure." He stuck his key into the engine and started the car. "So, UC?"

"Yeah."

Suddenly I was feeling sulky. Maybe Ramon was right. Miles intentionally trying to kill people via hiking accidents did seem absurd. After all, Galigani had slipped and broken his ankle without anyone plotting against him.

Ramon backed out of the parking spot and headed toward UC. As we turned onto Geary Street and I glanced at the Land's End parking lot, my breath caught.

Behind the wheel of a green Prius was skull cap man. He was even wearing the same hat. I immediately ducked into my seat and kept my eyes on the passenger side mirror.

"What's going on?" Ramon asked, alarm in his voice.

"That car! Behind you. Can you read the license plate?" I asked.

Ramon glanced in the rearview mirror. "No. My vision is good, but he's too far away. Let me slow down…"

He pressed on the brakes and suddenly called out a series of numbers and letters. I repeated them to myself as I tapped them into the notes feature on my phone. "I got you!" I said excitedly.

"Got who? Who is that guy?" Ramon asked.

"I don't know for sure yet, but now I'll be able to track him. Is he following us?"

Ramon nodded. "I don't know. Let's see."

Ramon got into the left turn lane to get onto Lincoln Way. After a moment he said, "Well, so far it looks like he is."

"We need to lose him now. Can you lose him?" I asked.

Ramon smiled. "First you want him to get close, now you want him gone. Typical woman."

From my crunched position, I twisted and punched him in the thigh.

"Ouch!" Ramon said, rubbing at his leg. "Okay, okay, hold on. I'll get rid of him."

"Get to Sunset Boulevard. We'll lose with him with all those lights."

Ramon nodded. "My thoughts exactly."

I glanced at the phone in my hand. I turned it off.

Could skull cap man be tracking me through my phone like V.D. had?

Goose bumps appeared on my arms.

Why would skull cap man be tracking *me*?

Ramon dropped me off at UC, then took off. He was going home to try a few new recipes and I secretly envied the hostess, who I guessed sooner or later would end up at Ramon's sampling a few things.

I stopped at the front desk of the hospital and inquired about Galigani and also Paula. I knew she'd still be here with her brand new baby, Chloe. So it was a good time to kill two birds with one stone. Ah, one of my specialties. Multi-tasking.

The front desk gave me Galigani's room number, but when I got there Mom was standing in the doorway and wouldn't let me in.

"Mom! Hi," I said, getting close to kiss her checks.

"Well, you have some nerve showing up here," Mom scolded.

I frowned. "What are you talking about it? It's not my fault—"

"Yes it is."

"He fell. I didn't push him."

"You made a heart patient hike up a mountain!"

"I didn't make him. He wanted to go…well, maybe he wasn't crazy about hiking, but it's hardly a mountain. It's a trail—"

Mom waved a hand in my face, cutting me off. "He's asleep now. They're going to need to do surgery and probably put a pin in to set the ankle."

I pinched the bridge of my nose, fending off a headache. "I'm so sorry."

Mom tsked. "I'd just signed him up at Arthur Murray Dance Studio!"

I squinted at her. "You're upset because now he won't be able to be your dance partner?"

Mom looked offended. "Well, yes! But that's not the only reason. Can you imagine how much pain Albert's in? Poor, poor dear!"

"Okay, well, tell him I stopped by. Oh, and let him know his car is still in the parking lot at Land's End." I left out the part about breaking Galigani's key. After all, there's only so much scolding a girl can take.

Mom frowned. "How did you get here?"

"I got a ride with Ramon." I looked down the hospital corridor. "Well, if you're not going to let me in, then I'll go see Paula and the baby."

Mom perked up. "Is she here?"

I nodded. "15th floor."

She patted my arm. "All right dear, go see Paula. Tell her I'll be up later."

As I turned to walk away I had the evil thought that if Mom was to be busy playing nurse maid to Galigani that probably meant she wouldn't be auditioning for V.D.'s play.

I smiled all the way to the 15th floor.

Paula's baby, Chloe, was the cutest thing I'd laid eyes on since I'd left Laurie at home several hours ago. Chloe was wrapped tight in a pink and yellow striped blanket with a small patch of dark hair on the top of her head. She smelled like a mixture of baby powder and roses. I inhaled her scent as Paula ranted about the nurses.

"Honestly, I don't know why they won't discharge me. This isn't my first rodeo," she said.

"You just had the baby! You should be here at least 48 hours and anyway, try and enjoy the help," I said.

"I don't need their help. I have you," she smiled, but I nearly choked.

She laughed. "Don't worry, I don't really think you're all that much help."

"Hey," I said. "I'm *some* help."

"Barely," she said. "Now tell me what's going on with your investigation."

I brought her up to speed with the morning's events: Melanie being sure that Perry had been meeting someone at Land's End, her being tailed by skull cap man, meeting Melanie's beau, and Galigani's fall.

After commiserating with me about Galigani and promising to visit him on the 3rd floor, she asked. "Who do you think Perry could have been meeting?"

"I don't know and I feel awkward about asking Jill, because, you know," I shrugged, "what if he was meeting another woman?"

Paula closed her eyes and lay back on the hospital bed. For a moment I thought she was going to doze off, but suddenly her eyes flew open. "Have you talked to any of Perry's guy friends? Do you think you can ask one of them who he was meeting? They might know if he was two-timing Jill, right?"

16

Mom was kind enough to drop me off at home, but the ride did not come lecture-free.

When she pulled into my driveway, I was ready to bolt.

Mom unfastened her seatbelt. "Oh, stop acting like you want to get rid of me. You know I'm going to pop upstairs and see my grandbaby."

We got out of her car and headed up the staircase. There was a brown package on my front stoop. I bent to pick it up and examine it. Smiling, I ripped it open. "My lock pick set and dust kit."

Mom laughed. "Lock pick set? Are you going to break into your own house?"

"Now that's not a bad idea. I could try it out and get some practice."

Suddenly Jim flung open the front door. "Hey! I thought I heard voices. I'm on high alert since that wild goose chase!"

The smell of pepperoni pizza wafted through my living room. "Did you order pizza?" I asked, stepping into my front room.

"No offense, honey, but I'd starve if I waited around for you to cook."

Mom immediately found Laurie snoozing in her crib and brought her to the living room. She cradled her, still asleep, and rocked her back and forth. She simply stared at her and she listened to Jim and me.

"So, David and I left Melanie at home. She said she'd call us if she spotted skull cap man hovering on her corner or anything." Jim placed a slice of pizza on a plate and handed it to me. "And anyway, she said her boyfriend was coming over later tonight."

I made a face. "Yeah, some boyfriend. Galigani and I talked to him today. He has a black eye, and Jill said Melanie struggles with a history of abusive guys."

Jim frowned. "How does his having a black eye equal being abusive?"

I explained my idea about Perry and Sam fighting, then said, "He claims he got the black eye at work."

Jim shrugged and served himself a piece of pizza. "I guess anything is possible. Does that other P.I. know anything?"

"The handsome playwright?" Mom chirped. "The auditions are tomorrow at 10 a.m. Now that poor Albert is laid up at the hospital—"

"What?" Jim asked.

I filled him on Galigani's fall while Mom tsked at me.

Jim was wise to continue eating pizza and not comment on Galigani's broken ankle.

"Well, like I said," Mom continued, "now that Albert is in the hospital, I think I should audition for that play. It'll give me something to do."

"What about Hank?" I asked. Hank was my Mom's other gentlemen friend that took her out to dinner and dancing quite regularly.

Mom glanced at her watch. "Oh!" she said. "I have to get home and get ready. We're trying out the new restaurant down the street from my house. The specialty is fresh crab and garlic noodles."

Jim took a huge bite out of his pizza and said with a mouthful, "Sounds good!"

Mom handed me Laurie.

Suddenly, I had an idea.

"Mom, about the audition. Can you text me tomorrow when you're there?"

She squinted at me. "I thought you didn't approve?"

I leaned in to her and whispered. "I had an idea about where I can try my new lock pick set out."

"What?" Jim asked.

I walked Mom to my front door and said conspiratorially, "Vicente will be at his own auditions, right?"

Mom nodded enthusiastically. "Oh yes. You should spy on him. Like he's doing to you!"

"Who's spying on you?" Jim asked. "Skull cap guy?"

I didn't think Jim would approve of my plan, so I said. "Yes. I got his license plate. I have to call McNearny and see if he can run it."

Mom walked out the door and said over her shoulder. "It's a plan!"

Jim called out, "If you're making plans for tomorrow, I have a meeting downtown. I can't watch Laurie."

Shoot! If Mom was my decoy and Jim was going downtown, I'd have to get Kenny to babysit.

"No problem," I said.

Jim, seemingly satisfied, helped himself to another piece of pizza. I left him in the living room with what remained of the pizza and took Laurie back to the nursery/office. With all the shuffling about, she'd woken up and become fussy. I nursed her then put her in the Baby Bjorn carrier. I paced around as I dialed Galigani's old partner, McNearny, and left a message about skull cap's license; maybe SFPD could track him down. Then I made arrangements with Kenny to babysit and then called Melanie.

She picked up on the first ring.

I asked her for a list of Perry's friends.

"Well, if you want to talk to his best buddy, try Dustin Jasper. They've been friends for"—she stopped suddenly and became quiet. "I guess I should say they *were* friends, but I'm not used to the past tense yet." She sniffled. "My brother was the only family I had left. Our dad died when we were kids and my mom passed a few years ago of cancer."

"I'm so sorry," I said.

She gave me Dustin's number, then a call buzzed through for her.

"Kate, I gotta go," Her voice sounded decidedly more chipper and she said, "That's my boyfriend on the other line."

"Wait!" I said, but she'd already hung up.

I'd wanted to ask her about Sam, although I wasn't sure how to finesse it. I had to figure out if he was the cause of her bumps and bruises, but if he was, she wouldn't have sounded so elated with his call, right?

I made a note in my book. I'd check in on her tomorrow and have a heart to heart. Next, I called Dustin and made arrangements to meet with him in the morning. Then, I researched the victim from the Yosemite hiking accident. His name was Rick Link. He'd been the manager at *Tartare*. I found an obituary online and a surviving relative, Henrietta Link, his mother. After a little digging, I had an out-of-state phone number for her and dialed on a whim.

The voice of an older woman said, "Hello?"

I explained who I was and asked if she could tell me anything about Rick Link.

Henrietta turned out to be full of Rick stories and happy to share them with me. Rick as captain of the football team, Rick as Prom King, Rick moving to California and competing in the Escape from Alcatraz race. We chatted for about fifteen minutes before I asked about his death. Silence filled the air like a lead balloon. Laurie broke the silence by offering up a small coo.

"Oh, you have a baby?" Henrietta asked.

"Yes," I said.

"Then you can imagine," she said.

"No," I whispered.

"No!" She said immediately. "You shouldn't have to. No mother—" Her voice broke off and she choked back a sob.

"I'm so sorry," I said. "My friend's boyfriend had a hiking accident the other day." I continued to give her the information I knew about Brent Miles' restaurants and his being brought in for questioning by SFPD.

"Rick's death at Yosemite was an accident," she insisted. "He went swimming in the Emerald Pool." Henrietta's voice got high-pitched and she sounded in complete agony. "The park investigators all agreed. It was an accident."

"I understand," I said, rubbing Laurie's back through the Baby Bjorn. She'd fallen asleep and her breath warmed my neck, but it was little consolation. I felt terrible for wrenching at Henrietta's memories.

"You can ask the girl who went camping with him," she said.

"There was a witness?"

"No," Henrietta said. "A girl went camping with him, but she didn't go on the hike."

"Do you remember her name?" I asked.

"Uh…" She hesitated. "Oh, my memory is great for some things, but not names. I'm sure I have it written down somewhere.

She had blonde hair. I remember thinking it looked like a little helmet, or a halo or something. Sweet girl."

I froze.

A helmet of blonde hair?

Mrs. Miles!

"Was her name Lillian?" I asked.

"Lillian? Yes, I think it was. I'll look it up to be certain. You know, it's strange, a gentleman called a few days ago asking the same thing."

"Someone else called you? Do you know who?"

"No, I'm terrible with names," she said.

"Was he from SFPD?" A thought struck me. "Or did he have a Spanish accent? Vicente Domingo?"

Ugh! I was always one step behind.

"No Spanish accent...and I don't think he was with the police..."

Maybe it was Miles' lawyer then. There was no telling.

I gave her my phone number and she agreed to call me back when she'd verified the name of the woman camping at Yosemite. We hung up and I pumped the air with my fists. "I got you, Miles! I got you!" I yelled.

Laurie jolted awake and Jim came into the room. "What's going on?" he asked.

I danced around the room. "It's starting to make sense! Miles hired a criminal defense attorney, not for himself, but for his crazy wife who can't drive and pushes people off cliffs!"

Jim stared at me wide-eyed. "Honey, I think you may have just gone off a cliff."

I laughed. "I saw her with Vicente. They were talking, she was upset. She's desperate."

"What would be her motive?" Jim asked.

"I dunno. Defending Miles' reputation or fortune?"

17

To Do:

1. √ ~~Order dust kit!~~
2. Figure out what happened to Perry.
3. Find skull cap man.
4. Get Galigani a get well card.

I spotted a parking place between an Audi and a Volvo, and prayed that I could squeeze in. Parking around the new ballpark was sketchy and even I couldn't believe that I'd gotten lucky enough to nab a space. I triple checked the signs on the street to make sure I was clear. The last thing I needed was a parking violation.

The wind whipped me around as I slammed my car door shut and pressed the lock button on my key fob. The wind was so fierce, I immediately regretted not grabbing a jacket. Oh well, it was only a short jaunt to the apartment building. I could manage.

I put my head down and hurried toward Dustin's. He was the friend of Perry's I'd phoned yesterday, and he'd agreed to see me and answer any questions.

When I arrived, Dustin welcomed me in. Tall and thin, wearing Bermuda shorts, flip-flops and sporting a three-day growth of stubble, he stood in the entryway holding a coffee mug.

What did he do for a living to be able to afford such a care-free life of luxury in such an expensive city?

"Have a seat." He motioned for me to cross into the living room. His loft was designer decorated, with an orange weave throw rug in the middle of the floor and several stylish leather arm chairs. The view of the new Bay Bridge, complete with San Francisco's ballpark in the forefront, was simply stunning.

I stood at his window. "Wow!"

He smiled and joined me at the window. "It is nice, isn't it? I'm hardly ever home, so I forget sometimes how magnificent the view is."

"You're home now," I said.

He shrugged, "Yeah, right. I have a couple days in between trips. I'm taking off to Africa in a couple days…"

Must be nice, I thought.

He fell silent and I suddenly felt bad about feeling jealous. This man had lost a close friend.

"It's awful about Perry," he said, breaking the silence. "It's so sad. I miss him already. We'd been buddies forever. I can't believe this accident happened. He was supposed to go with me to Fiji, but then he bailed out at the last minute…and I keep thinking that if he'd come, he'd still be alive today."

I always found these moments heart wrenching. A friend coming to terms with loss. Feeling completely inadequate, I muttered, "It's not your fault."

Dustin remained lost in thought, staring at the view out his window and taking a swig of coffee. After a moment, he said, "Well, I guess when it's your time, it's your time. Perry could have had a freak accident in Fiji, right?"

Only what if it wasn't a freak accident?

I bit my lip and refrained from launching into questions like, "Do you have any reason to believe that there was foul play?" or "Can you tell me if anyone had it out for your friend?" Sometimes discretion was the better part of valor.

"Melanie told me you had some questions about Perry," Dustin prompted.

Then again, I hated to waste an invitation.

"I think he was planning on meeting someone on the hike. Do you have any idea who?"

Dustin cocked his head and studied me. "He was meeting someone?"

"I don't know, but according to some text messages that Melanie recovered, that seemed to be the case."

"Was he meeting Jill?"

"No. Jill was with me, having lunch. He must have been meeting someone else."

He frowned. "You met Jill for lunch? Why?"

"Oh, I've known Jill for a while. She got the call that Perry was in the hospital while we were together."

He turned away from the view and leveled a gaze at me. "Then you know about her and Perry."

I shrugged. "What do you mean?"

He took another sip of his coffee and wiped at the corners of his mouth with his fingertips. "I mean, he'd been trying to break up with her for a while. We were planning a trip to Mount Everest, Perry and I. When I asked him if Jill was interested in coming, he was all, 'You know, like, dude, she's old news'."

Jill was old news?

"Perry was planning on breaking up with Jill?" I asked.

"As far as I know, the relationship was pretty rocky. He may have already kicked her to the curb." He shrugged. "Let's just say, she wasn't in on the Everest plans."

Jill had thought they were close to being engaged. A part of me felt heartbroken. Poor Jill had been searching for a long time for the right guy, and when she finally thought she found him, he'd ended up DOA at the hospital. And now, what? Mr. Right had been ready to toss her aside like yesterday's lunch.

Dustin must have read something in my face because he said, "Don't worry, I won't say anything to her."

I nodded. "My impression is, she thought things with Perry were peachy keen."

Dustin raised an eyebrow. "So who was he meeting on the hike then?"

"Exactly," I said. We had a mini stare-down.

I imagined Perry meeting Mrs. Miles. Suppose Jill suspected he'd been seeing her and wrote the bad review to ruin her business, could that be?

And then again, I thought of the soup for breakfast at *Philosophie*. No, they'd probably earned their own bad review.

"Do you have any ideas?" I prompted Dustin.

He shook his head. "No. I have no idea. Perry had a bit of a wandering eye, but I can't imagine he'd take a date on a hike. He was more of a 'get 'em drunk and get laid' kind of guy. If he hadn't broken up with Jill yet, then he wouldn't invest that kind of time with a chick. I mean, hiking is an all-day thing. You have to really like a girl to take her on a hike. Probably if Perry were cheating, he'd just hang out at a bar...well, you know."

Not a woman then?

"Do you think Perry would have met with Melanie's boyfriend?"

Dustin scratched at his beard and mumbled. "Sam? I don't know. Did you ask him? Why would he meet up with him? As far as I know, Sam's not much of a hiker."

Now would be the moment to tell him I suspected foul play, but instead I asked, "How well do you know Sam?"

Dustin's eyes darted around the room. "I don't know him all that well. I know that he and Perry seemed to get along okay. I guess, I…" he shrugged. "Melanie deserves better."

I studied him a moment. His eyes had taken on a glassy faraway look.

Could it be that he had unrequited feelings for Melanie?

Dustin cleared his throat. "You don't think Perry's falling was an accident, do you?"

I shook my head.

Dustin drank his coffee. "Well, I have to say that Perry was a very adept hiker. You know, with the trip to Mount Everest we were planning, he was hiking all the time. I just don't see him following a trail that dead ends into the ocean…but I don't know. What do you think happened? Did he get disoriented? I mean, the trail is clearly marked, right? I don't understand why he would go down that path, but even if he did, he'd know when to stop. He wasn't the type to seek out problems." Dustin paused and we both looked out the picture windows again at the ballpark below.

After a moment, I said, "If you and he were planning a trip to Mount Everest, then he was the adventurous type, right? Maybe he was curious about—"

Dustin shook his head. "Nah, our hikes lately have been more about endurance and speed than curiosity."

"What if the sign wasn't there? What if it had been moved? Would he go down the trail then?" I asked.

Dustin frowned. "Why would the sign be moved?"

I pressed my lips together so as not to disclose the fact that I'd seen the dirt lifted around the base of the sign, and then, to make matters worse, the sign was now gone. After all, maybe Dustin had a reason to want Perry gone.

"When did you get back from your trip?" I asked.

Dustin arched an eyebrow. "Yesterday."

So he had an alibi—or at least he claimed to.

I shrugged. "Do you know anything about Brent Miles or his wife, Lillian? They own the restaurant, *Philosophie*?"

A look of confusion crossed Dustin's face. "Brent Miles? No, what does he have to do with Perry?"

"Jill gave the restaurant a bad write-up and says Brent Miles threatened her and asked her to recant the review." I held my tongue about Mrs. Miles in Yosemite. After all, I had confirmed it and I didn't want to burden Dustin with all my theories.

He finished his coffee and set the empty mug on a side table. "Sorry, Perry never mentioned the guy. I knew Jill was a critic, but I hadn't heard anything about the bad review."

I stepped away from the picture windows and headed toward the front door. "Thank you for your time." I stopped, dug into my purse and pulled out a business card. "If you think of anything that could help us figure out what happened to Perry, please give me a call."

On my way to the car, I made a mental note to verify Dustin's alibi. Although it didn't seem like he had a motive, I couldn't be too careful. Everyone should be a suspect until I could prove otherwise.

I started my car and pulled out into traffic. I'd left Dustin's apartment feeling a bit unsettled. Had I learned anything? Jill and Perry hadn't been as serious as she'd told me. Now the question was, did she know that? Or was she in the dark about Perry's real feelings?

Did it matter?

I struggled with the answer. If Jill knew Perry wasn't serious about her, then maybe I could tell her about my suspicions that he was meeting someone else at the hike without crushing her.

What about Sam? Dustin seemed to think that Sam and Perry got on fine, but I got the distinct impression that Dustin and Sam didn't get along fine.

But then again, did that matter?

I glanced at my watch. It was almost 10 a.m. Soon V.D would be holding auditions for his next play and it was my chance to snoop.

I pulled into a parking spot across the street from V.D.'s apartment building and waited. Mom was going to be at the auditions and she was supposed to text me when he arrived. While I waited, I scribbled some notes in my book and updated my to-do list. At three minutes before the hour I received a text from Mom.

HE'S HERE. COAST IS CLEAR.

I climbed out of my car and crossed the street. Standing outside Vicente's apartment building, I studied the mailboxes. Number 107 was marked "Domingo" in faded blue ink. I walked to the corner and waited for someone to leave the building so I could gain access. I tried to look normal, checking my phone for updates.

I glanced toward the apartment house and saw someone in the foyer approaching the front door. I hustled toward the glass doors. A young woman sporting a Goth haircut and dressed in black from head to toe pushed open the door and then actually held it open for me to enter.

I guess I look pretty non-threatening. Hopefully, I don't look like the type of person who is about to break into someone's apartment!

I sprinted up the steps to the first floor and located apartment number 107 on the right hand side of the hallway. The corridor was empty and I quickly pulled out the lock pick set I had ordered online. Adrenaline was pumping through my system and my heart was practically beating outside of my chest. I scanned the instructions on the lock pick set for the umpteenth time. All I had to do was insert the tension wrench and then put the pick in. It seemed simple.

I tried to relax, and slipped the tension wrench in. It went in easily, then I stuck the pick in and felt it catch inside the lock.

I smiled.

This breaking and entering could be fun!

Vicente hadn't dead-bolted the door. I had the lock on the doorknob open inside of 20 seconds. Who knew I had such a talent for this type of thing?

I stepped inside of his apartment: Standard brown carpeting, blue paint with taupe finishes, very sparse and tidy. There were several file boxes along the side of the room. It looked like he had some unpacking to do.

There was a couch and small dark coffee table and in the corner of the living room a table that was set up as a makeshift desk with a laptop and a few folders on it.

Footsteps from the unit above pounded around on top of my head. It made me feel like the floor could collapse on me at any moment.

I could hear the sound of running water. Must be the apartment next door. The units were pressed so close together that it practically felt like you were living with your neighbor.

I crossed to the desk and set the lock pick set down. As I opened my bag to stuff it in, my phone buzzed. I pulled it out and read a text from Mom:

R u in?

I texted her back.

I'm in.

Mom fired back.

Ooh. You are fast. Have to say Vicente is so handsome. He's flirting with all the girls. Even me!

I was tempted to text her back insisting that she was *not* a girl, but decided that I should probably focus on the task at hand. I slipped the phone into my pocket and opened the laptop. It was password protected. I sighed. I should have brought Kenny with me. He could hack into anything, but as it was I was out of luck.

I closed the laptop and picked up the folder, expecting some personal receipts or business to be in it, but instead a photograph of Sam Kafer stared up at me.

The sound of running water stopped. I actually heard a faucet knob squeak and the pipes rattle followed by a shower door.

An alarm went off in my head.

Holy Christ.

That wasn't the neighbor's shower…

I dropped the folder and hustled toward the door, fleeing into the hallway. I wasn't exactly what you'd call stealth. The door slammed behind me and then bounced open again.

Darn!

Regardless, I raced down the staircase and out the foyer. Hopefully whoever had stepped out of the shower would be hustling to get clothes on and in the meantime, I'd be gone like the wind.

I sprinted toward my car and jumped in.

I thought back to the girl who'd let me in. Apparently, I don't look like a typical criminal, so most likely no one would suspect me or stop me.

I revved up my car.

Why hadn't I considered that V.D. would have a girl there? It made complete sense.

I texted Mom.

Busted. He had company...

Mom replied.

No doubt. Seems like he's gotten three phone numbers in last five min.

I pulled out of the parking spot, relieved that no angry woman wearing a towel had fled out of the apartment looking to track down a burglar.

As I pushed my phone back into my bag a thought flashed into my head.

My lock pick set!

I'd left in on the desk.

Darn, darn, double-darn!

I repeatedly hit my forehead with the palm of my hand. It was all Mom's fault; if she hadn't kept texting me, then I wouldn't have been so distracted...

No, I couldn't blame it on her. It was my fault.

Now V.D. would know someone had been snooping around his apartment. Would he know it was me? Could he use the set to track me down, possibly pull my prints from it? Or maybe the person in the shower had seen me? She could be looking out the window right now at me.

As I rounded the corner of the block, I glanced out my driver's side window toward the building. I couldn't tell anything.

I cringed and hoped for the best, my thoughts turning to the folder on V.D.'s desk. Why hadn't I taken it with me? Obviously, he suspected Sam. Why else would he have his photo in a folder?

Darn it! It burned me up that V.D. might have evidence against Sam and I didn't know what it was. Part of me wanted to turn the car around and wait for whoever it was at V.D.'s apartment to leave. I could reenter after they vacated.

Oh, wait.

No, I couldn't.

My stupid lock pick was sitting on his desk.

I banged my steering wheel in frustration. If he could figure this thing out so could I.

I headed directly to Melanie's apartment.

It was time for some answers.

18

On the short drive to Noe Street, I ruminated over what I knew about the case. Melanie was Perry's sister. She'd been beaten up at Perry's apartment and I'd assumed her assault was related to Perry's death. That had seemed a given, and yet...

Jill had said Melanie was a pathological liar.

Could it be that the bruises on her face were really from Sam? Perhaps Melanie was too embarrassed or even scared to admit that her boyfriend hit her.

If Perry had been defensive about his sister dating a guy who beat her—and what brother wouldn't be?—then Perry could have confronted Sam. Maybe the confrontation had gone wrong. Perry beat Sam up, which would explain the bruise on Sam's face, and then Sam had sent Perry over the edge of a cliff.

It could have happened that way.

One thing was clear, Vicente was definitely following Sam's scent. I probably needed to look into him more carefully, too.

I was so aggravated with the case, my knuckles were turning white from my grip on the steering wheel. I turned onto Noe Street and compared the number displayed on my smartphone to that of a nearby house. I was still at least a block away. I began the infernal search for parking. On the next block, there was a Victorian style building down the street that had scaffolding against it with a huge black tarp covering it. The

155

tarp was presumably there to keep in debris and protect the new paint job from the weather. Granted, it was probably a bad time to paint, but the real estate market in San Francisco had begun a slight uptick and many owners were prepping for spring sales.

I pulled into a spot across the street from the Victorian with the scaffolding, which I now realized was Melanie's place. My front bumper encroached on the driveway, but I crossed my fingers and hoped I'd be back before the neighbors called my infraction into the Department of Parking and Traffic.

Melanie's flat was quiet. It looked like the work crew still hadn't shown up for the day. I climbed the stairs, counting them as I went. The building most likely had at one time been a single family dwelling and then had been converted to three units.

I reached the top floor, huffing and puffing.

48 stairs.

Wow. Climbing to the top floor of this apartment building was almost as aerobically challenging as the Land's End hike. I pressed the doorbell and waited, suddenly missing Galigani.

I felt guilty about his ankle. I'd have to pop in on him at the hospital, as soon as I finished here, and then…I glanced at my watch. Where did the time go?

I'd have to head home first and feed Laurie before going to visit Galigani.

I rang the doorbell again, this time pulling out my phone and dialing Melanie at the same time. Her voicemail clicked on. I left a message.

Where was she?

I rattled the door handle. Locked.

If I hadn't left my lock pick at V.D.'s I could have used the opportunity to snoop around inside Melanie's apartment.

I grimaced. Breaking and entering, twice in one day? What was I becoming?

The tarp covering the scaffolding flapped in the wind.

I grabbed hold of it and peeked underneath, examining the scaffolding. It looked pretty substantial…

Could I climb onto it and get a look inside her flat?

I gripped the cool black plastic and stretched for a foot hold.

A rumbling engine rounded the corner. I pulled my foot back onto the landing and pretended to be immersed in my phone. The rumbling engine belonged to a Ford pickup, which pulled right in front of the flat, blocking access to the driveway. Obviously, the driver was less concerned than I about San Francisco's infamous DPT.

A tall man in denim and work boots got out. He began unloading paint cans from the bed of the truck onto a dolly.

Darn it!

My plan was definitely foiled, there was no way I could hop onto the scaffolding without him shooing me off.

Oh well, it wasn't like I'd learn much by peeking in her windows. At the most, I'd find out if she was a tidy housekeeper.

I began my descent down the 48 stairs.

The man pulled his dolly, weighted down with cans of paint, under the tarp. He glanced my way. "Morning, lass."

"Good morning," I said.

I absently wondered if should question him. What could he tell me? Maybe Melanie's comings and goings?

"I was looking for my friend. We're supposed to get coffee…" I lied. "but she's not answering her phone."

He winked at me. "It's too bad I have work to do, otherwise, I'd get a cuppa with you, love."

I laughed. "Oh, I don't know that my husband would like that."

He wrinkled his nose. "Those husbands are a bother."

"Do you know my friend, Melanie? She lives on the top flat."

He shrugged as he grabbed a sanding tool and climbed onto the scaffolding. "Should I know her? Does she want to have coffee with me?"

I shrugged back at him. "Maybe."

He ascended higher. "Does she have one of the pesky things... what did you call it...a husband?"

"No. Not a husband. A boyfriend."

One that I think is extremely unfitting for her, frankly, but hey, what could I say?

He grunted. "I hate obstacles like that. She'd have to be cute. Is she cute?"

"Uh...yeah. She's cute."

What in the world had I gotten myself into? Now I was matchmaking?

He was at the top of the scaffolding. He peeled back the tarp and looked down at me. "Is she as cute as you?"

"Now you're just flattering me," I said, digging out my key fob and turning toward my car.

Suddenly, the painter let out a low string of cuss words, followed by a loud "Christ Almighty!" and a repeated rapping on the window.

A chill raced up my spine and I stopped in my tracks.

"What is it?" I yelled up at him.

The tarp thrashed about in the wind where he opened it and I could see him drop the sanding tool. He pawed madly at a window.

I raced up the flight of stairs. "What? What's going on?"

"Call 9-1-1," he yelled, as he yanked on the window frame. The glass suddenly took a nose dive and shattered at his feet. He cursed again.

"Is it Melanie? What do you see?" I asked frantically pulling my phone from a pocket. The phone slipped from my hand and skidded down the flight of steps.

Damn.

I chased after it.

"Stay down there, lass," the painter bellowed in his Irish brogue.

I glanced up to see him climbing into Melanie's apartment. "No! Don't go in there!" I screamed, frantically waving up at him.

All that remained visible of him was one tan work boot, which soon disappeared. I raced up the stairs, ignoring my dropped phone. "Hey! Hey! No, no, no! Don't go in there!"

Out of breath, I reached the top landing and scrambled onto the scaffolding. The scaffolding had an unexpected sway and give. A wave of dizziness and vertigo assaulted me. Spots formed before my eyes and my knees suddenly felt weak.

Oh! I was so high up and this...this scaffolding!

Why, I was practically suspended in mid air.

The scaffolding felt completely untethered and had a ceaseless rocking. A gust of wind rumbled and the tarp whipped across my face, stinging my cheeks in the cold. I yelped. All I could do to regain myself was grip the freezing metal of the scaffolding and try to breathe.

"Hey!" I called to the painter as I collapsed onto my knees, broken glass from the shattered window biting into my jeans. "Ah!"

A strong hand gripped my shoulder. "Lass! What are you doing?"

"Uh." The scaffolding lurched forward. "Oh God, this was a mistake." My stomach turned as I feared the scaffolding would give way.

The hand pulled me to my feet and toward the window.

"I shouldn't go in there! No one should disturb the crime scene."

And it had to be a crime scene, of that I was certain.

But even as the words tumbled out of my mouth, I found myself climbing in through the window. After all, I wasn't going to stay on the God-forsaken scaffolding that felt like it would collapse at any moment.

I crumpled onto Melanie's floor and tried to breathe. The only thing I registered about the room was that I was in a bedroom—that, and the fact that there was a pair of feet sticking out from a small space between the bed and the wall.

"What in God's name are you doing?" he asked.

"Hyperventilating!" I answered.

"I told you to stay down there and call 9-1-1," he chastised.

"Uh-huh," I said with my head between my knees.

A small grey kitten meowed and pressed its wet nose into the back of my hand. I moved my hand to pet it, but the cat ran and hid.

Whiskers?

"Are you afraid of heights?" the painter asked.

"I didn't think so—"

"You shouldn't be climbing on a scaffolding if you're scared of heights. We're up three flights! What if you got dizzy—"

"I am dizzy," I said, beginning to lift my head.

His hand pressed on the back of my head, pushing it down again between my knees. "Don't look, lass. Did you call 9-1-1?"

"I dropped my phone."

He groaned and removed his hand from the back of my head.

Without lifting my head, I shifted and glanced at the pair of feet. "Is she—"

"She's dead. Sorry, love." There was a rustling sound, then the telltale beeping of a cell phone. "I'm calling from 753 Noe Street," the painter said. "I...er...I found the occupant dead."

I chanced to raise my head while he was distracted, but he immediately pushed it back down.

"It's okay. I'm okay now," I said.

"No, you're not," he said.

"I am. I'm fine. I want to see her."

"Don't get up. You have blood all over your knees," he said.

Until now I had ignored the pain that was emanating from my legs. I looked down and saw shards of glass sticking straight out from my jeans.

He finished the call with the 9-1-1 operator and stood up. "Let me check the bathroom for some first aid supplies."

"We're not supposed to touch anything. The cops will have my ass. I'll wait for the paramedics," I said.

"Paramedics? No, I don't think they're sending any. I'm sorry, but she's dead." He squeezed my arm. "Were you very close?"

"No. We'd only recently met. She asked me to look into some things for her."

He nodded, seemingly satisfied that I wasn't going to fall to pieces on him. He turned and walked down the hallway, in search, I guessed, of first aid supplies.

I studied my torn-up jeans. Blood was dripping down the denim and onto my sneakers. The sight of it turned my stomach.

The painter returned with a bottle of disinfectant, cotton balls and tweezers. He wiggled his eyebrows at me and grinned. "Take off your pants, lass; it's time we got down to business."

"Not on your life," I said.

He turned serious. "You can trust me. I'm a gentleman."

"No. I'll wait for a doctor."

"I'm practically a doctor."

"You're a painter."

"Same thing," he said.

"No, it's not."

He made a face. "Sure it is, painting is all 'bout cutting out disease; mold, mildew, lead, you name it and then putting on a fresh, healthy finish."

"I don't think it's the same thing." I tried to straighten my legs and winced.

"There are a lot of similarities."

I tried to roll up my jeans starting at the ankle. I got as far as an inch and then it was clear that I wouldn't be able to roll them up past my knees.

He grinned wickedly. "You're going to have to take them down from the waist, love."

I flashed him a death stare, which he took well. He wiped the grin from his face, then handed me a throw blanket that was on the foot of Melanie's bed. "Here," he said. "You can use this to cover up."

I wrapped the blanket around my waist and lowered my torn, bloody jeans. He worked with incredible speed and gentleness. The disinfectant stung, but the overall sensation when he removed the glass from my legs was relief.

I looked around the room as he worked. What could I tell from the scene of the crime? Had Sam and Melanie had a final fight? The room looked relatively undisturbed, except, of course, for Melanie's corpse.

My eyes landed on her feet and I suppose I must have been staring, because the painter said, "She's not, you know."

"What?"

He flashed me his lopsided grin. "She not cuter than you."

"She's dead!"

"Well, yeah, I get that. But I meant, if one were to overlook that—"

"You can't overlook it! She's dead! " I nearly screeched.

He lowered his eyes and looked appropriately chastened. "I'm sorry. You're right." He secured the bandage on my knee and asked, "Do you have any cute single friends who aren't dead?"

"Christ, you're incorrigible," I said. "Are you done?"

He examined my knees. "You clean up well. Very pretty knees."

I pulled up my jeans in a huff and dispensed of the blanket. He laughed.

"Thank you for the first-aid," I said. "You surprised me."

He smiled. "I was a medic in the army."

"Ah," I said, limping over to Melanie's body. I studied her. Her bruised and swollen face was slack. I sighed and fought back the feeling of despair that threatened to overtake me. No, better to get right to work than to give in to anguish.

"Did you touch or move her?" I asked.

"Yeah, I tried to get her pulse."

"Was she face down?" I asked.

"Yes," he said.

I bent over Melanie and examined her. Of course, I couldn't tell anything from the body. She was dead. That much was certain. But I had no clue as to the cause or time. That was something the Medical Examiner would have to determine.

I glanced around the room. I couldn't help but feel like I needed to take advantage of being on-site. Something V.D. was not—ha!

As soon as I had the thought, I immediately felt bad. Melanie was dead and I wanted justice for her. It didn't matter if I were the one to solve the crime or V.D., as long as there was some closure...but...surely there was *something* I could pick up while being here that would bring me closer to solving the mystery.

"Were you here yesterday?" I asked the painter.

"Yes," he said.

"What time did you leave? Was everything normal? Did you see Melanie? Did you see anyone else?"

He held up a hand. "Whoa, lass. What's with all the questions?"

"I'm a P.I."

He was quiet for a moment then said, "I was here yesterday. Now that you mention it, she came home and it seemed like she'd been followed."

Fear churned in my stomach.

"Followed?" I asked in disbelief. "Guy in a green Prius?"

"No, two guys in a white Volvo."

Jim's car. The painter had seen Jim and David follow Melanie home to make sure she got home safe.

And she had. Only something else had happened after that.

"Did you see anyone else come or go?"

He shook his head.

"What happened with the window?" I asked.

The painter looked confused. "What do you mean?"

"It broke, I know, but was it closed? Or compromised? Why did it break?"

"It was open a bit at the top. I tried to lower it and it crashed out of the frame. But don't worry, lass, I can fix it. You get a new glass and—"

I tuned him out and looked around the room. Had someone come into Melanie's apartment via the window and scaffolding?

"Was there anything different about the scaffolding? Anything missing or moved or..."

"No."

"Does it always shake that way?"

He laughed. "I suppose you get used to it."

My gaze returned to Melanie. It didn't seem like there had been a forced entry. So it may have been someone she knew.

In fact, hadn't she and Sam had plans last night?

The phone on her nightstand buzzed. I leapt toward. The caller ID read out "Jill." I wanted to answer the call, but hesitated.

The cops would already be raging mad at me for being inside the apartment and they'd certainly pop a gasket if I touched anything, so I refrained from picking up Melanie's phone.

Although...

What if her phone went missing?

I could easily pocket the phone.

I felt the painter's eyes on my hand and backed away from the nightstand.

What was I thinking? Deliberately tampering with evidence?

Maybe I was a criminal!

19

An engine idled outside. I crept toward the window and peeked out. In the middle of the street, an unmarked police car was stationed with its hazard lights on. An arm reached out of the skylight and placed a revolving blue and white light on the top of the car. I prayed that it was any cop other than McNearny.

Although McNearny was Galigani's former partner at the SFPD and was usually helpful, he and I had had a rough beginning. He was, as a general rule, not always happy to see me. In fact, I was sure that if he never laid eyes on me again or heard my name, he'd be a happy man.

I must have been living life well, because Officer Jones stepped out of the car. I'd met him a few months ago, when I was working my first case. He'd been with McNearny then, but now he was alone.

I did a happy dance.

The painter frowned. "What are you so happy about, lass?"

"Much nicer cop then the one I was expecting."

The painter shrugged and said in a skeptical tone. "There are nice cops?"

A secondary vehicle turned the corner. I watched in horror as that vehicle double parked behind the first one and the hazard lights came on. Jones waited for the other driver to get out of the car and, as luck would have it, a stocky, balding man stepped out.

McNearny!

I groaned. Clearly, I wasn't living all that well.

"What is it, lass?" The painter asked.

"Uh…" I said.

The painter raised an eyebrow. "Good cop, bad cop?"

"Exactly," I said.

The painter patted my shoulder. "I can't see you having anything to worry about, lovie. We found the body, we didn't…" He took an involuntary step back and stared at me. "At least I didn't— "

"Oh, don't be ridiculous. I didn't kill her. It's just that…" I watched as McNearny and Jones headed toward the massive staircase, soon they were out of my line of vision. I limped toward the front door. "Never mind, you'll find out soon enough."

I opened the door to the officers. "Hello, good officers," I said cheerfully.

McNearny's face immediately betrayed him; he turned so beet red that the only thing missing was steam coming from his ears. "What the devil are you doing here?" he spat. "I should have guessed. Any time there's a homicide in the city you're never far behind."

"Already at homicide?" Jones asked, surprised. "How do we know that?" Officer Jones was younger than McNearny, with kind eyes and short dark hair that was gelled back. He smiled sympathetically at the painter and me.

McNearny ignored Jones and squinted at the painter. "Are you the one who placed the 9-1-1 call?"

The painter nodded and stuck his hand out toward McNearny. "Sean O'Neil."

McNearny shook the painter's hand, then reached into his breast pocket and produced a badge reading INSPECTOR PATRICK MCNEARNY. He showed it first to the painter and then flashed it at me saying, "So you don't forget!"

Jones smirked and patted McNearny on the back as he came further into the apartment. "No one can forget you, Mac."

The painter followed Jones into the apartment and gave him an accounting of our arrival on the scene. McNearny listened quietly and took notes only stopping to look up occasionally and scowl at me.

When the painter had finished, McNearny said, "And why exactly were you here, Mrs. Connolly?"

"The victim is the—"

"Whoa, we don't know she's a victim yet. We don't know cause of death or time or anything," Jones said.

"Right," I nodded. "Sorry, her name is Melanie Welgan, and she's the sister of Perry Welgan whose body was recovered after a fall from Painted Rock."

Jones let out a low whistle. McNearny growled and the painter simply looked at his hands.

Jones suddenly scratched at his forehead. "Didn't we bring in Mr. Miles for questioning on that one?"

"And Galigani broke an ankle hiking Land's End," McNearny rumbled.

Crap! Guilt overwhelmed me. Not only hadn't I been able to prevent Melanie's death, but it was probably my fault that Galigani was laid up in the hospital.

McNearny turned to the painter. "I'll need you to go downtown and get fingerprinted."

The painter frowned but nodded politely.

McNearny turned to me. "We have your prints on file, Connolly." He then exchanged glances with Jones.

Jones outstretched an arm and ushered the painter toward the door. "My car is outside. Why don't I pop you on over to the station?"

The painter walked with Jones to the front door, but stopped suddenly and flashed me a worried look. "Lass, you going to be alright?"

I smiled. "Oh, don't worry about me. I'm in good hands with old Mac." I patted McNearny on the shoulder who in turn grunted.

When they'd left the apartment, McNearny said, "I want to hear your theories."

"You do?" I was stunned, but suddenly felt proud. I was starting to command some respect at SFPD.

"Not really, but I should. At least, then I'll know what I can dismiss."

So much for respect.

I took a deep breath. "Miles is represented by Barramendi, the top *criminal* defense attorney in San Francisco."

He folded his arms across his expansive chest. "Tell me something I don't know."

"Barramendi hired a P.I."

McNearny cocked an eyebrow at me. "Let me guess, her name is Kate Connolly."

"No."

McNearny frowned. "No?"

"He hired some guy named Vicente Domingo, who I happened to know is looking into Melanie's boyfriend, Sam Kafer, as suspect *número uno* for the death of Perry."

"And you know this how?"

I couldn't very well tell McNearny that I'd broken into V.D.'s house, so I shrugged.

"Ah, I see." He rolled his eyes and said in his most sarcastic and dismissive tone, "Very helpful."

"Well, I do believe there may have been a history of abuse," I said.

McNearny uncrossed his arms.

"Abuse between Sam and Melanie, that is," I clarified.

"And you won't tell me how you know this either?" he asked.

"My friend, Jill. She was dating Melanie's brother. The first victim. The guy who fell off—"

"She's the restaurant critic?" McNearny pressed.

"Right."

"The one who panned Miles' restaurant, *Philosophie*?"

"Exactly," I said. I explained my theory about Melanie knowing the assailant and that Sam had plans to see Melanie last night.

McNearny paced around the room. When he got close to the bed, the kitten peeked out.

"Whiskers?" I called out.

The kitten came to me and I picked it up. He was all grey with a small patch of white from his chin to his belly. He was trembling, so I pressed him into my chest and stroked his ears.

"It's starting to look as if Perry's fall had nothing to do with Miles, isn't it?" McNearny asked.

Before I could respond, his eyes landed on a bloodstain on the carpet.

"Wait a minute. Look at this!"

I cringed. "Sorry, that's my blood." I indicated my torn-up jeans. I cut myself on the glass from the shattered window.

"Christ, Connolly!" McNearny exploded. "Next time stay out of my crime scene!"

After he collected his temper, he decided to walk me to my car. I'm sure his primary goal was to make sure I actually left, not chivalry.

He yanked on the front door and ushered me out.

"Got crime scene techs coming, you gotta go," he said.

"Can I keep the cat?" I asked. "I think it was Perry's. Maybe Jill will want—"

McNearny waved at me. "Keep it for now. I'll follow up with next of kin and see what they want to do."

I glanced around for a cat carrier, but McNearny was already hustling me to the door, and he didn't seem in the mood to help me with cat care.

We walked down the flights of stairs and crossed the street.

He immediately spotted my car bumper encroaching on the neighbor's driveway. He pointed at my car and said, "You're lucky the neighbor didn't call it in."

"I'm surprised you're not giving me a ticket anyway."

From the look he gave me I almost feared he would. But then his expression changed and he reached into his pocket. "How about I give you this instead?"

He handed me my cell phone.

I gasped. "Oh! I forgot about it. I dropped it—"

"When you were all in a hurry to go and bleed all over my crime scene?"

"No, I…" I tried to take the phone from him, but he pulled his hand back toward his chest. "Is there anything else you want to tell me?"

My brain went into overload and I suddenly felt like a petulant teenager. To my embarrassment I even stomped my foot when I said, "Give it."

His eyes narrowed. "There is something!"

"Well, I'm not hiding it! But it just occurred to me."

"Spit it out."

"The guy that was following my friend Jill, he also followed Melanie and yesterday he followed me..."

"Right. You left me a voicemail with the guy's license plate number."

"Exactly!" I said. "Who is he? Is he another P.I.?"

McNearny reddened. "You know I can't give you that information!"

"Why not? You were going to give it to Galigani." As soon as I said it, I regretted it. Galigani and McNearny were like brothers. They'd been on the police force together, there was an undeniable bond, but despite all that they still pretended they weren't sharing confidential information.

And if anyone were to suggest that it was, they were asking for trouble.

His eyes blazed with anger and he leaned into me.

I'm ashamed to admit that I actually held Whiskers a bit higher as if for protection from McNearny's fierceness.

"I was *not* going to give Galigani anything," he said, and then to spite me he added, "Least of all would I give him a broken ankle!"

He spun around in a fury, but before he could get out of earshot, Whiskers hissed.

20

I clutched Whiskers to my chest. "Already a little ally, huh?"

He purred.

When I got into my car, Whiskers' claws came out and he clung to my lap.

"It's okay, little guy. We don't have far to go."

He meowed loudly when I tried to pull him from my lap and put him into the passenger seat.

"Okay, you can ride just like this," I said, revving the engine.

Was it even legal to transport a cat without a carrier?

I had no idea and it seemed that the laws in San Francisco were constantly changing, each time taking a piece of our liberty.

I figured my best hope to avoid an infraction was to get home as quickly as possible.

But first, I wanted to call Jill and give her the news about Melanie. I shuffled Whiskers on my lap and pressed at my phone.

Nothing happened.

Darnit!

My phone was completely out. Broken. Kaput!

If I hadn't had a warm kitten on my lap to cuddle, I might have cried. As it was I decided to bury my face into his fur.

When I got home, Laurie was sitting on a blanket in the middle of my living room. She was propped up with her Boppy pillow and Kenny was serenading her with the trombone.

Whiskers romped into my house, and raced under the couch.

"Ah, cute kitty!" Kenny said, putting down his trombone.

"Yeah, he's only temporary. Don't get too attached."

Whiskers peeked out from under the couch and ran right to Laurie who flapped at him and cooed. He sniffed up at her.

Laurie absolutely adored him, squealing and grabbing at him.

"I'm nervous he's going to scratch her," I said, picking up the kitten and handing him to Kenny.

Kenny stroked the kitty's chin. "He doesn't look particularly fierce."

I picked up Laurie. "Well, she could pull his tail or something."

"Where'd you get him?" Kenny asked.

I flopped onto the couch and proceeded to fill Kenny in on Melanie's demise, V.D.'s prime suspect and McNearny's refusal to share any information on skull cap man with me.

Kenny made a face. "Pfft. I'm sure I can hack it. What's the license plate number?"

I gave him the information and he settled into my office to try to produce some magical results. Although I have no doubt that a 17-year-old musical prodigy can probably hack into quite a few systems, I still wasn't expecting much.

I grabbed my home phone and dialed Jill while I nursed Laurie. I was dreading telling her about Melanie, but figured it would be easier to hear from me rather than SFPD.

Unfortunately, I got her voicemail. I left an urgent message for her to call me at home instead of my cell, since that was now *"out of order"*.

While I fixed lunch, Kenny fiddled on the computer. After a few minutes, I heard him singing a victory song.

"What's up?" I asked.

"Registered vehicle is a Prius?"

"Yes!" I said, coming into the office.

Kenny wiggled his eyebrows at me. "Mark Zloky lives at Gate 5, Liberty Dock in Sausalito."

I frowned. "What kind of address is that?"

"Houseboat," Kenny tapped himself a drumroll on my desk. "By the name of"—tap, tap, tap—"Shady Lady!"

As I drove across the Golden Gate Bridge, I noticed a few clouds hovering above Alcatraz. It was a breezy day, and only a few sailboats were visible out on the bay. A gust of wind hit, and I could easily feel the sway of the suspension bridge. I remembered being afraid to cross it when I was little.

Today I was afraid of different things, like what Jim, Galigani or McNearny would say to me for running off half-cocked to investigate a houseboat in Sausalito.

Fortunately, Kenny was able to babysit Laurie a while longer, and if I hurried I would probably be home before Jim got back. If I returned home empty-handed, no one would even need to know about my trip. If I returned home with some worthwhile information, well then, the trip would be justified.

I took the first Sausalito exit, one of my all-time favorites. A cute little strip of shops lined the waterfront, selling everything from magic tricks to souvenirs to antiques.

I parked in the harbor lot and walked toward the docks across the short storefront strip.

There was a gelato store on the corner.

Mmmm. Gelato seemed to be screaming out my name.

Did it matter that I'd just had lunch? After all, lots of people had lattes and cappuccinos after lunch, right? Either that or they loaded their coffees down with sugar and cream. And what was gelato, except sugar and cream? So, I'd have a black coffee to go with it and call it good.

Hey, I'm a nursing mom. If we aren't entitled to these leaps of logic, then who is?

I bought the gelato and coffee, then walked through the harbor eating my ice cream on the short walk to Liberty Dock. I settled onto a bench in front of several boats and watched some sea gulls fight for crumbs.

There was a smattering of boats parked in the harbor. I spotted The Shady Lady. It was the third boat on the right.

A couple peeled off one of the boats. She was in her sixties and dressed optimistically in bright clothes; he was dapper, in dark clothes and a hat.

They were chatting as they passed me. She had a sweet, southern accent— tourists on holiday to see the Bay Area.

I suddenly thought of my mom and made a mental note not to mention anything about seniors on a boating holiday to her. Knowing her, she'd be ready to sign herself up for a steamboat cruise on the Mississippi.

I watched The Shady Lady for a few minutes, trying to figure out what I'd ask Mark if he were home. Who was he? Why had he followed Jill, Melanie and me? Did he have a connection with Mr. or Mrs. Miles?

The best way to get answers was to ask.

However, there didn't seem to be any movement on board or any sign of an inhabitant.

I walked the slick dock toward The Shady Lady, missing Galigani fiercely and wishing he were here to give me guidance.

"Mark?" I called out as I reached the boat.

When there was no answer, I climbed aboard.

It was a small vessel with an interior cabin below. I called out again. When no answer came, I peeked down the staircase to the cabin. There was a small door, but it was unlocked.

I called out again, "Anyone on board?"

When it was clear that I was alone, I wasted no time. I had no idea how long he would be gone and needed to find *something*, anything that could shed some light on why the guy had been following us.

The living quarters were down a short staircase. There was a small living room with a kitchen attached and a bedroom at the stern of the boat. I searched the main cabin, rummaging through every cabinet and cubby I could find, then went into the master bedroom and searched there. In the bedroom were a TV and a guitar. I searched the lone set of drawers and found nothing of interest.

The only thing I learned was that he wore a lot of dark t-shirts and jeans—which I'd already deduced from the few times I'd seen him. I didn't see any computer.

How could he not have a computer in this day and age?

With my luck, he had a laptop and it was with him.

Impatience bubbled up inside me, but I stuffed it down. There was no way I was leaving empty-handed. I sat on the bed, deflated.

When I sat on the bed I felt a small shift and noticed that a corner of the plywood the mattress rested on peaked out. I stood and centered the mattress. The bed was a captain's style bed. There was probably storage underneath. I yanked up on the plywood and it sprang open on hydraulic hinges, revealing a storage space large enough to hide a body.

I cringed at the thought!

Thankfully, there was no body there, only a cardboard box and...

Bingo! Inside the hidden storage was a laptop. I fumbled through the rest, some old clothes and stack of DVDs, then took the laptop and slammed shut the plywood. The bed looked a bit disheveled, so I straightened it up a bit and exited the bedroom into the living area. The boat rocked as I walked and suddenly it jolted hard to the right.

I heard footsteps overhead.

Damn! Someone was on board. Skull cap man!

How could I explain that I was rummaging through the guy's stuff?

I hurried back to the bedroom and did the only thing I could think of.

Hide!

I yanked up the mattress and climbed into the storage compartment under the bed. Then I pulled the plywood down over my head.

In the darkness I wondered about the sanity of that choice.

What the hell had I been thinking? Why was I hiding? What was I afraid of?

My subconscious served up the image of Melanie's bruised, lifeless face.

Oh, God! I have to get out of here.

But how? What if skull cap man was in for the day? Or, what if he decided to take a nap? Fortunately the plywood wasn't flush, and a sliver of light shattered the complete black that otherwise could have been suffocating.

I listened as skull cap shuffled around the room. There seemed to be quite a bit of rummaging. My heart was beating so fast and loud, I was sure he could hear it.

He was looking for something. I hoped he didn't decide whatever he was looking for was under the bed. I waited for him to get whatever he needed and get out. After all, it was a sunny day; didn't he want to be out and about?

What if he decided to take the boat out?

The movement around me seemed to come to a halt as the rummaging stopped. Suddenly the plywood above me creaked and the cracks where the light had been filtering in closed. He was sitting above me.

Great.

After a moment he got up and then...

Oh no.

Please don't open the...

Was there a way to hide myself further?

Where was my self-defense pen? I was so squished I couldn't even reach my back pocket!

A creak, then a flood of light. A silhouette of a man hovered over me for an instant.

I must not give him the upper hand. I threw the laptop in his face and jumped out of the storage compartment, slammed directly into his chest.

He fell back, stunned, screaming, "What the—?"

I lunged towards the bedroom door and grabbed the handle. I yanked, but it was locked. I realized I was screaming, too.

The man was yelling, too: "Kate! Kate!"

My heart was racing and I couldn't slow down enough to coordinate my fingers around the lock.

How did he know my name?

A hand reached out and grabbed my shoulder. I spun and kicked at the same time, missing his groin, but landing a kick square in his gut. He doubled over and I realized it wasn't skull cap man after all.

It was Vicente Domingo.

"Why are you...ugh..." He collapsed onto the floor. "Why are you fighting me? We're on the same side."

On the same side?

Relief flooded me. I put a hand on my chest, trying to slow my wildly beating heart, but with the other hand I still fumbled at the door. "What side are you on?" I asked.

"The side of justice. That's the same side you're on, right?" V.D. cocked an eyebrow. "Unless you want to tell me something?"

"I'm on my client's side." I blurted, although I didn't even technically have a client. "What are you doing here? Do you work with skull cap man?"

"Of course I don't work with him." V.D. lifted himself to one knee, one hand was still gripping his stomach, but with the other he reached for the laptop.

Damn.

"What are you doing here?" he squinted at me and then at the laptop.

I held my hand out for the laptop. "Give it here," I said.

"You kicked me hard," he said. His voice was filled with something more than a bruised ego. He looked at me, challenging me.

I said, "Give me the laptop. I was here first. It's mine."

He laughed cynically. "It's not yours," V.D. fired back. "And I have rights to this because I'm the one holding it and I'm the one who will walk out with it."

"It's illegal to steal someone else's property," I said, lamely.

"I'm not stealing it," he said. "I'm borrowing it."

We did a mini struggle. I pulled the laptop. He pulled it back and glared at me.

"Maybe we can work together," he said.

"No," I said, and with my increasing frustration I blurted out the inevitable, "You stole my client."

"What?" he asked. "You were planning on getting Brent to hire you?"

"No," I shrugged. "Mr. Miles isn't your real client, is he?"

V.D. looked confused, then suddenly said, "You think Barramendi would hire you?"

Ouch!

He started laughing so hard I thought he might split his gut.

Thankfully, it seemed the kick I'd given him served to curtail a bit of his laughter, because he clutched his gut and said, "Don't make me laugh. It hurts."

"Good!" I said.

He got serious for a moment and said. "I'm sorry, Kate. But there was no way Barramendi was going to hire you."

"Why not?" I challenged.

"Because he's my cousin and he owes me. Besides, I'm the only P.I. he ever hires."

I refrained from telling him that I'd worked for Barramendi in the past. Who knew, perhaps they'd had a family feud going on.

Frustration welled inside me and I turned to leave.

"If you want, I'll share whatever information I find on the laptop on one condition."

I took a deep breath and waited him out. "What?" I finally asked.

"You audition for my play."

I felt myself go cold. "I'm not auditioning for your play."

"Why not? You'd be perfect for the main character, you know."

"I wouldn't. I'm sure I wouldn't be."

"Of course you would be. She's a hottie." He gave me a lopsided smile.

Now what?

Was I going to argue that I wasn't hot?

"And I cast your mother in the mom role. You'd be perfect in the daughter role. Besides your mom says you're fantastic on stage. You trained in the theater, right?"

Oh God! I was going to kill Mom!

"I'm busy," I said. "Very busy. New baby plus new career equals super busy," I said.

"Well, it's only a staged reading at first," he said. "Not so much of a time commitment—"

I cut him off. "Are you crazy? We're standing in Mark Zloky's houseboat, stealing his laptop. Why are you negotiating with me over a staged reading?"

"You're right," he said. "Let's get out of here."

He unlocked the door and waved me ahead of him. I climbed up the short staircase, suddenly feeling uncomfortable walking in front of him. After all, he had just called me hot. Now he was looking at my rear-end.

I stopped at the top of the staircase and looked out into the main level of the boat.

The coast was clear. V.D. seemed to give no heed as to whether or not he would get out safely. I quickly climbed off the boat and made my way to the harbor. V.D. followed me, the laptop clutched under his arm.

I had to think of a way to get it.

21

"At least the weather is clear today," I said. "Nice day to be out and about."

He nodded in agreement.

"How about an ice cream?" I asked.

He raised an eyebrow at me. "You want to have an ice cream with me?"

I smiled. "Sure, we can discuss the case a little bit further."

He looked at me suspiciously. "Okay, and how about we talk about my play?"

"Yeah sure, you can tell me all about it," I said as we made our way down the main drag of Sausalito.

We walked into the same gelato shop I'd been in earlier. I ignored the look the girl behind the counter gave me. After all, drastic times call for drastic measures. I ordered myself a big double scoop of lemon meringue pie gelato in a waffle cone. Vicente ordered himself a Rocky Road.

We took seats by the window and watched the people on the main drag.

"Is Mr. Miles out on bail?" I asked.

"No, no. They didn't jail him, just brought him in for questioning," V.D. said.

I raised an eyebrow. "Do you think they asked him about Mrs. Miles?" Then added, "Lillian Miles," for good measure.

Vicente stuck his spoon into his Rocky Road cup and swirled the ice cream around. "I don't know. Why would they ask him about his wife?"

I suddenly felt superior. I was privy to information V.D. didn't have. Then a blast of self-consciousness attacked me and I wondered if he were simply pretending he didn't know anything in order to get information out of me.

I decided to steer clear of a potential landmine and asked instead, "How did you get started as a P.I.?"

V.D. licked the back of his spoon. "Well, my cousin became an attorney, and he needed people to start investigating things for him, and I needed a way to make a living. He encouraged me to get my license. I've been working for him ever since."

If Vicente was Barramendi's go-to P.I., why had he showed an interest in hiring me?

"What do you know about Mark Zloky?" I asked.

V.D. shrugged. "Not much. Nothing, in fact. I'm not even sure why you're interested in him." He patted the laptop. "I'm hoping this will shed some light."

I glared at him. Conflicting feelings battled inside me. I wanted so much to share my thoughts on the case with someone, but I realized I couldn't share them with V.D. I figured he'd laugh at me when I got things wrong and in general make me feel like a fool.

I focused on my lemon meringue ice cream and silently decided not to tell Vicente about Melanie. After all, McNearny needed time to notify next of kin, and there was a chance her death might not even be connected to Perry's…although I found that hard to believe.

We headed back to my car. His dented Harley parked next to my vehicle.

"So what's up with your phone?" V.D. asked.

I suddenly realized that he couldn't have tracked me through my cell phone. "It's broken," I said, turning toward him. "Did you follow me here?"

He laughed. "Of course."

My blood boiled so fast, it felt like steam was coming out of my ears, but before I could turn my wrath on him, he pulled something out from the carrier case on the back of his bike.

"I went by your place to give this to you, but I saw you leave so I followed you here." He held out a package wrapped in a plastic bag. "Does this belong to you, Mrs. Connolly?"

I took a step back, my anger turning to embarrassment. "No!" I said.

He smiled, an evil little wicked grin that said he knew I was lying. "How do you know? You don't even know what's inside." He waved the package at me, taunting me.

"What is it?" I asked. I could feel my cheeks burning hot.

He pushed the package into my hand. "Take a look."

I opened the package, already knowing what was inside: my lock pick set.

Ack, he knew it was me. I felt so foolish.

"This isn't mine," I said. I almost went so far as to say that I didn't know what it was, but since I'm a P.I. in training, that lie would make me look even more like a dolt.

He pressed his lips together. I'm sure it was to suppress another goddamn grin. After a moment, he said, "Really? It must be yours."

"No," I shrugged. "What makes you think it's mine? Where did you find it?"

"I fingerprinted it. I know it's yours. Do you think I'm a rookie?"

I was silent.

"And I found it exactly where you left it. Did you learn anything?" he asked.

He studied me intently, his expression changing from the charming guy to something else, like maybe there actually was something he was hiding.

What could that be?

I shrugged off his intensity and laughed. "Just that you…"

"What?" he asked.

"You suspect Sam Kafer."

Vicente's expression changed. "Why do you say that?"

"There was a big glossy…headshot…" I cut myself off. "Oh, God!"

He smiled again, that annoying, cocky, smug, childish "gotcha" smile.

"Sam was auditioning for your play, wasn't he?" I said.

Vicente nodded. "Yeah, I cast him today."

I absently wondered about Melanie's time of death. The Medical Examiner would probably give McNearny that information soon. Would Sam's alibi be that he was auditioning for V.D.'s play at the time of Melanie's demise?

I climbed into my car and said over my shoulder. "I didn't find anything else at your apartment that was useful because there was somebody there."

He laughed. "She scared you off, eh?"

"Yes." I closed the door to my car, then rolled down my window. "Now are you going to share the information you find on the laptop or do I need to break into your place and steal it back?"

"There aren't many things I share, Mrs. Connolly." He got on his bike and smiled at me. "But I like your Mom, so I'll let you know what I find."

On my way home I stopped at a pet supply store and stocked up on kitty litter, food, bowls, a few toys and even a scratching post. I wasn't entirely certain Jill would adopt the cat, and even if she wanted him, I didn't know when she would pick him up.

When I got to my house, I found Laurie playing on the floor with some plastic rings. Every time she pulled a ring toward her, Whiskers dove for it and Laurie squealed with delight.

I scooped Laurie into my arms. "How's mommy's little pea-nutty pie?"

Whiskers rubbed against my ankles then trotted over to sniff and paw at the pet store bags.

Kenny came into the living room gnawing on a crust of bread. "There's nothing in the fridge," he complained.

I laughed. "Didn't I just give you lunch before I went to Sausalito?"

"Cha, but that was over an hour ago!" Kenny complained.

I sighed. I would have told him he was a bottomless pit, but I remembered that I'd had two ice creams and a coffee since I'd left. "Order takeout," I said.

Laurie's pudgy hand pawed at my necklace. She was already rooting for milk.

"I don't have any money," Kenny whined.

I fished a twenty out of my pocket and pressed it into his hand.

"Were you able to talk to the guy on the boat?" Kenny asked.

"No, I stole his laptop instead," I said.

Kenny clapped his hands together in excitement. "Now we're talking! Where's she at?"

"It got stolen from me."

"What?" he asked.

"I know. It's ridiculous. Another P.I. swiped it out from under me. Long story."

Kenny grumbled and I caught him up on my trip out to Sausalito. When I finished, the only thing Kenny said was, "Does the guy know how to hack?"

"What do you mean?"

Kenny shrugged. "The other P.I.—is he a computer guy or does he have a computer guy?"

"I don't know. He's a P.I. playwright."

Kenny gave me a sidelong look.

"Oh God, you want to work for him now?"

Kenny placed one hand over his heart in a very dramatic gesture. "No, no, you know I...I..."

"Shut up," I said. "His number's over there," I pointed to my office.

Kenny leapt off my couch. "I'll let you know what I find."

After Kenny left I quickly fed the kitty then nursed Laurie. When I laid Laurie down for her nap, part of me wanted to nap right alongside her, but the other part needed to digest the case. When I figured out who killed Perry and Melanie, then I'd have myself a really good sleep.

I doodled in my notebook and tried to review what I knew, but my thoughts kept drifting to the second ice cream helping I'd had. I decided that I should go for an evening run as soon as Jim got home, so I changed into my running clothes and paced around my living room.

My phone rang and I dove for it, hoping it was Jill or Galigani. Mom's voice filled the line. "I was cast in the play."

"Congratulations," I said. "I heard you were trying to get me cast as well."

Mom laughed. "Oh, that was payback for breaking my beau's ankle."

I cringed. "How is he?"

"They've put him in a boot of some sort. A cast-boot thing… I think they're going to release him today. I'm on way to pick him up anyway."

"All right, tell him to call me when he can. I have news."

Mom pressed me for the news and as I began to tell her about finding Melanie, my phone line beeped. "Oh, Mom, we'll talk later. I gotta go. That's Jill phoning me on the other line."

I toggled lines over to speak with Jill.

She said, "Kate! I got your message. Sorry, I couldn't phone you earlier. I've been in the studio filming all day."

I broke the news to her about Melanie and listened sympathetically to her grief. She asked me the standard questions, "What happened?" "When," the rhetorical "Why," and finally the predictable, "Was I sure?"

I told her about my conversation with the Yosemite hiker's mother and the fact that she'd indicated a blonde woman named Lillian had been camping with Rick the weekend of his demise.

She gasped. "Lillian is Brent Miles' wife!"

"Right!" I said. "And another thing, I found out the identity of the guy following you. His name is Mark Zloky. We have his laptop. We're looking to see if there is a connection to Miles or his wife."

I hoped Kenny would get a chance to look at the laptop. After all, suppose V.D. hid or destroyed evidence that could link Mrs. Miles to creepy skull cap guy?

"What do you mean, we? Have the police arrested him?" she asked.

"Oh, no, no," I said. "I probably shouldn't have told you. I don't know that any of this will stand up in court...I think its probably not a legal...what's the term?"

"Search and seizure?" she asked.

The sound of my footsteps on my front stairs resonated through the living room and sent Whiskers skidding down my hallway. "Hey, one more thing. I have Perry's kitten."

"What?" she asked.

"Whiskers. He was at Melanie's. She must have found him. Do you want him?"

She sighed. "I'm allergic."

Secretly, I was thrilled, but convincing Jim was going to be a different story. We hung up as my front door lock clicked and the door swung open.

Jim smiled at me. "Honey! I landed the client!"

I hugged him. "Oh, I'm so proud of you."

"I called you a couple times, but you didn't pick up."

"My cell phone broke."

Jim made a sad face. "Oh, we'll have to get you a new one tomorrow, huh?" He headed for the kitchen and rooted around for a beer. "What's for dinner?"

"Uh..."

He laughed. "Why don't I buy? Where do you want to go?" He glanced at my outfit. "Were you planning on going for a run?"

"Yeah. I was waiting on you. Laurie's asleep. I have tons to tell you, but I'll tell you over dinner. I'm going to take a quick run on the beach, okay?"

He nodded.

Whiskers peeked around the corner of our kitchen. Jim leveled a gaze at the cat, but before he could turn to me I was already down the hallway.

22

The smell of salt air was refreshing and I took big greedy gulps of it as sweat dripped down my forehead. I was running through the knee-high sand that spanned the distance from the Great Highway all the way to the coastline. When I reached the water, I ran along the coastline toward the Cliff House, my legs throbbing as my heels pushed against the harder, more compact sand.

I let the rhythm of the run carry me as thoughts floated in and out of my head, relieved that I was finally getting my figure and tone back after giving birth.

The weather was still clear, although a bit cold, and the wind whipped at my ball cap, threatening to pull it off my head. I had an unobstructed view of the Farallon Islands and beyond, the mountains of Marin, including Mount Tamalpais.

The sun was getting lower in the sky, casting a streaked orange and pink glow on the horizon.

No matter how many times I witnessed the sunset on the Pacific Ocean, I never grew tired of it.

What was getting tiring was the running, though. I glanced at my wrist watch.

What?

I'd been running an entire seven minutes.

That had to be wrong.

Maybe there was another way to get back into shape besides punishing myself with a relentless run.

Forget hiking too. Apparently that was pretty dangerous.

What I could use was some martial arts training.

Before giving birth to Laurie, I'd enjoyed a kickboxing class at my local gym. But it was purely a cardio workout, not really any self defense training of any sort. I was sure V.D. had training. He was a serious P.I. and Galigani had been through the police academy. Was there an academy for private citizens? Surely security folks had to go through something.

I made a mental note to look up karate classes when I got home.

I spied my watch again.

Ten minutes.

Crap. I'd wanted to get to twenty. On the one hand, I could think that I was *already* half way done, but all I could think was that I was *only* half way done.

Half way seemed like a good time to take a break. I collapsed onto the sand and kicked off my left running shoe, then dumped the sand out of it.

One of the things that bothered me about running on the beach was that it was difficult to gauge the distance I'd run. I glanced around, straining to find a telltale street sign off of the Great Highway. There was a tunnel area up ahead that passed under the highway and connected the beach to one of the Avenues. I wasn't far from that, maybe only a block or two, so I decided that when I reached the tunnel, I could turn around and run home to enjoy a nice dinner out with Laurie and Jim.

I replaced my shoe, then stood and continued my run. A figure dodged out from behind the tunnel area, racing toward me menacingly.

My breath caught as I realized it was skull cap man.

Fear struck me immediately in my gut. Without thinking, without pre-meditating anything, I began to run in the opposite direction, trying to think of a way out.

I commanded my legs to move and pumped my arms as hard as I could, the previous run serving as an initial warm-up. My body now fueled and ready for flight, my feet hitting the sand with a speed I didn't know I was capable of. My lungs burned and my heart pounded through my chest until I thought it was going to explode.

Run, run, run, Kate!

I tried to remain calm as skull cap man advanced on me, hot on my trail.

A thousand thoughts collided in my head at once. Why was he chasing after me? If he was the killer, what was his connection to Melanie?

I felt his hand brush against my jacket sleeve. I shoved at him and kept running.

Suddenly he reached out and grabbed my ponytail; my head jerked back and the ball cap flew off my head.

"Get away from me!" I screamed.

Somehow his grip slipped. I evaded him and switched directions. I kept running, this time putting a greater distance between us. I focused on the tunnel. If I could make it to the tunnel and out to the other side, there were bound to be people around on the street.

It was either take the tunnel or risk climbing the stairs to the Great Highway. The problem with the stairs was that I'd have to traverse knee-deep sand.

No, it would be too risky to slow myself down on the looser sand.

I bemoaned my broken cell phone. Would Jim be missing me by now? Would he know that I was in danger? I could barely think of Laurie, my heart breaking when I pictured her little face and her toothless grin.

Skull cap man was swearing behind me, a vulgar string of obscenities hurled at me. He was closing the distance between us.

Suddenly I reached the tunnel and turned into it. My legs bouncing off the cement, giving me a feeling of speed as I pounded easily on the concrete without the added burden of having to pull my foot out of the sand.

Flashes of relief bobbed inside my stomach as I raced farther into the tunnel and away from skull cap man.

I was going to make it!

If I could get to the other side of the tunnel, people would be milling around the street and the café that fronted the beach.

I could yell for help.

But something was wrong in the tunnel.

It was dark, and remained dark the farther in I ran.

I swallowed past the panic, then I realized I'd made a deadly mistake. The tunnel had been closed due to new construction.

The tunnel dead ended.

I was dead ended.

Skull cap man was upon me, laughing. "Oh, Kate, not as smart as you think you are!" he snarled.

I hated him with an intensity I'd never felt before. I tried to marshal up all my resources, but I was huffing and puffing.

Could I take this man here in the tunnel? I needed a weapon. I needed leverage.

Right now, all I had was my head.

"What are you doing, man? I have nothing on you. You could walk away. I don't...I don't know who you are— "

"That's a lie," he spat. His face was inches away from me. I could smell his sour breath. Coffee and rotted teeth mixed together.

It was dark inside the tunnel and I couldn't study his features. There was something about him that was horrifyingly creepy, like I was staring into the eyes of a man without a soul.

"You've been to my place. You've been to my boat. Right, Kate?"

I hated the way he used my name. He said it with a mocking ring of familiarity, like we were long lost friends.

"No," I lied. "I don't know what you are talking about."

He reached out with one hand and caressed my cheek. I slapped him away. He recoiled and in that moment when he seemed off guard I knocked him in the nose with my elbow.

He doubled over. I pushed him hard, his head bouncing off the concrete with a sickening crack.

I fled.

I wasn't fast enough, though. Before I could run out into the sunlight he was upon me. He pushed me hard from the side, throwing me off balance. I struggled not to fall and kept moving forward, but he dove at my legs. He grabbed me by my ankles and dragged me to the floor.

He pressed against me, his weight on top of my arms, pinning me to the ground. "You're going to take a little trip with me, sweetheart. Don't worry, I'll make you comfortable."

He reached into his hip pocket and pulled out a small vial. He shoved it under my nose. I tried to push him off me but the fumes were too strong.

I tried to hold on to consciousness, praying for Jim and Laurie, then suddenly—blackness.

When I awoke, I was bound to a chair in a dark room and he was standing above me. There was a decided sway to the room and I couldn't figure out if it was me or the room. I looked out of the small circular window and spotted the twinkling lights from Alcatraz.

We must be on his houseboat.

What did he want from me? Why bring me here?

"Do you know who I am?" he asked.

"Yeah," I said. "You're skullcap man. Smith & Wesson man. You're responsible for Perry's death, probably Melanie's too."

His eyes narrowed as he studied me.

"Why did you do it? For hire? Brent or Lillian hired you, right? I'm sure…if you let me go…It's nothing personal, if you let me go, I'll pay. I can pay you."

He laughed. "You don't have any money."

"Why add another crime to the list? You can let me go and take off on your boat. Go to Mexico, live on the beach."

He smiled. "You know, those were my thoughts exactly."

Relief flooded me.

Was he really going to let me go?

"But I can't just let you go. You'd cause problems for her and then my final payment wouldn't come in."

Her? It was Mrs. Miles then, not Brent.

I swallowed my tears. "Final payment for what?"

He gave me a crooked smile. "For making you disappear, of course."

23

I needed to keep him talking. Jim would figure out where I was, wouldn't he? It was dark now, the sun had set. Jim would be missing me. Laurie would be hungry... Maybe, Kenny would pop over to the house and tell him about my trip out to Sausalito. Jim would figure it out, he had to. I had to believe that he'd come and get me.

"Take me to Mexico with you."

He froze in place. "Seriously?"

I shrugged. "You don't really want to kill me. You just want to get your payment. Let's head down to Matazlan. Make sure she wires you the funds and then you let me go."

I could tell the plea had done something to him, because his body language changed.

"I need the break, anyway," I said.

He laughed. "They're working you too hard, huh?"

I shrugged, not wanted to give away any more than I needed to.

I wondered if Brent even had any idea about her involvement. Would V.D. figure it out and call Jim?

"How much?" I asked.

"How much what?" he asked.

"How much did she pay you? How much is a life worth?"

"It started at 10k," he said. His tone was proud, and I tried not to cringe. So little for a human life. I wanted to choke on my tears.

"Ten for the first, but then I doubled it the second time around. I ain't risking no jail time for nothing."

"They can't pin it on you," I said. "They don't have any proof of you pushing Perry. They didn't find any witness, nothing."

He nodded, obviously proud of himself.

"Was Perry the first?" I asked.

He frowned. "Sure, what do you mean?"

I looked away from him and out the nautical window at Alcatraz...

"There was another guy, Rick Link. Died in Yosemite."

Skull cap rubbed at his chin. "Yosemite? No, no. That wasn't me."

Football captain...prom king...Escape from Alcatraz...

Nausea bubbled up inside me. "Oh my God! She said Lillian, but she'd meant Jillian."

"What?" Skull cap asked.

"Jill had the Escape from Alcatraz t-shirt. It was his, wasn't it? Rick Link's."

A crashing sound came from overhead, pounding and shouting. The boat rocked violently. Sirens sounded in the distance.

"Help!" I screamed.

Skull cap man dove for the door of the cabin, but wood splintered all around him as Jim broke through it in one fluid motion. Jim tackled skull cap like a linebacker while I cheered him on.

Directly following Jim was Vicente. He piled onto skull cap man and restrained him, while Jim came to me.

"Kate," Jim screamed, crushed me into an embrace. "Are you hurt?"

"I'm good, I'm good," I said. "We were going to Mazatlan."

He untied my wrists and then my ankles.

Before I could give him any explanations, he ushered me up to the top deck and off the boat. The sirens grew louder and at the end of the dock I could see Galigani directing a police cruiser to park. Two uniformed officers jumped out of the car and ran past us, climbing aboard The Shady Lady.

Jim squeezed my hand. "Thank God, you're okay."

"I'm glad you found me," I said. "Where's Laurie? Who's watching her?"

"The cat," Jim snickered. "And your mom," he said, ushering me toward Galigani.

Galigani stood at the end of dock, leaning on a cane with his foot in a boot cast. He ruffled my hair when I got close and said, "Hey kid. You're a sight for sore eyes. Glad we got here in time."

"How's your ankle?" I asked.

He scolded me. "Just because I led the charge in saving your butt, doesn't mean I've forgiven you for taking me hiking."

Jim and I both laughed and I leaned into him. "How did you guys find me?" "Vicente called me. He and Kenny got some information off the laptop that showed—"

"It was Jill," I said.

"You know?" Galigani asked.

"I pieced it together. She went hiking with the guy in Yosemite, right?" I asked.

"Right. His mother called the house after you left for your run, but I didn't know what she was talking about, said that the girl who'd camped with Rick was Jillian Harrington."

"Yes," Galigani confirmed. "Miles suspected her of stealing from the restaurant and I suppose the manager, Rick Link, may have had proof. So she got rid of him."

"Then Perry found out and blackmailed her," Jim said.

"How did Perry find out?" I asked.

"Same way we did," Galigani said, "Rick's mom."

Perry was the one who'd phoned her.

"If Jill didn't pay Perry to keep silent," Jim said, "he was going to ruin her career, not only as a restaurant critic, but also as a TV host on Foodie Network. So, she hired this creep," he gestured toward The Shady Lady, "to get rid of Perry."

"The guy went a little unhinged when Melanie interrupted his cleanup at Perry's. He figured once Perry was out of the picture, he'd help himself to the guy's big screen TV," Galigani said, "But when Melanie interrupted the heist, he got nervous that she could ID him."

Vicente emerged from the houseboat and swaggered toward us. "The police are reciting him his Miranda rights. How is Kate?"

"I'm fine," I said. "Thank you for calling Jim and for coming along to help."

Vicente smiled that charming, annoying smile. "Ah, come on, Kate. You know I couldn't let anything happen to my leading lady."

Jim cocked an eyebrow. "What?"

I buried my head in my hands. "He's making me take the lead in his play. Mom is already cast."

"And Kenny is going to play the trombone," Vicente added. "We're changing it up a bit. It'll be a musical."

Jim and Galigani laughed, a little too loudly if you ask me, but both said, "Ah! Brilliant. It'll be a sold-out show!"

To Do:

1. Enroll in Martial Arts Class!
2. Get Whiskers his shots.
3. Find next client!

~THE END~

Coming soon!

Vicente Domingo's story!

For a complete listing of books, as well as excerpts and contests, and to connect with Diana:

Visit Diana's website at www.dianaorgain.com.

Follow Diana on Twitter at www.twitter.com/dianaorgain

Join Diana on Facebook at www.facebook.com/DianaOrgainAuthor

Sign up for Diana's email updates at www.dianaorgain.com/about-the-authorcontact

Please enjoy the following excerpts from Diana Orgain's books...

Other titles by Diana Orgain
BUNDLE OF TROUBLE
Book 1 of the MATERNAL INSTINCTS MYSTERY SERIES
© 2009 Diana Orgain

A body has been dredged from the San Francisco Bay. Kate Connolly, pregnant and ready to pop, has reason to fear it may be her long lost brother-in-law. Battling sleep deprivation, diaper blowouts and breastfeeding mishaps she muddles through her own investigation, Mommy style:

To do:

1. *Find Killer*
2. *Figure out hideous breast pump.*
3. *Avoid cranky cop.*
4. *~~Send out~~ Make birth announcements – need pink paper.*
5. *FIND KILLER*

Enjoy the following excerpt for BUNDLE OF TROUBLE

1. *L*ABOR

The phone rang, interrupting the last seconds of the 49ers game.

"Damn," Jim said. "Final play. Who'd be calling now?"

"Don't know," I said from my propped position on the couch.

I was on doctor's orders for bed rest. My pregnancy had progressed with practically no hang-ups, except for the carpal tunnel and swollen feet, until one week before my due date when my blood pressure skyrocketed. Now, I was only allowed to be upright for a few minutes every couple of hours to accommodate the unavoidable mad dash to the bathroom.

"Everyone I know is watching the game. It's gotta be for you," Jim said, stretching his long legs onto the ottoman.

I struggled to lean forward and grab the cordless phone.

"Probably your mom," he continued.

I nodded. Mom was checking in quite often now that the baby was two days overdue. An entire five minutes had passed since our last conversation.

"Hello?"

A husky male voice said, "This is Nick Dowling . . ."

Ugh, a telemarketer.

". . . from the San Francisco medical examiner's office."

I sat to attention. Jim glanced at me, frowning. He mouthed, "Who is it?" from across the room.

"Is this the Connolly residence?"

"Yes," I said.

"Are you a relative of George Connolly?"

"He's my brother-in-law."

"Can you tell me the last time you saw him?"

My breath caught. "The last time we saw George?"

Jim stood at the mention of his brother's name.

"Is he a transient, ma'am?" Dowling asked.

I felt the baby kick.

"Hold on a sec." I held out the phone to Jim. "It's the San Francisco medical examiner. He's asking about George."

Jim froze, let out a slight groan, then crossed to me and took the phone. "This is Jim Connolly."

The baby kicked again. I switched positions. Standing at this point in the pregnancy was uncomfortable, but so was sitting or lying down for that matter. I got up and hobbled over to Jim, put my hands on his back and leaned in as close as my belly would allow, trying to overhear.

Why was the medical examiner calling about George?

"I don't know where George is. I haven't seen him for a few months." Jim listened in silence. After a moment he said, "What was your name again? Uh-huh . . . What number are you at?" He scratched something on a scrap of paper then said, "I'll have to get back to you." He hung up and shoved the paper into his pocket.

"What did he say?" I asked.

Jim hugged me, his six-foot-two frame making me feel momentarily safe. "Nothing, honey."

"What do you mean, nothing?"

"Don't worry about it," he whispered into my hair.

I pulled away from Jim's embrace and looked into his face. "What's going on with George?"

Jim shrugged his shoulders, and then turned to stare blankly at the TV. "We lost the game."

"Jim, tell me what the medical examiner said."

He grimaced, pinching the bridge of his nose. "A body was found in the bay. It's badly decomposed and unidentifiable."

Panic rose in my chest. "What does that have to do with George?"

"They found his bags on the pier near where the body was recovered. They went through his stuff and got our number off an old cell phone bill. They want to know if George has any scars or anything on his body so they can . . ." His shoulders slumped. He shook his head and covered his face with his hands.

I waited for him to continue, the gravity of the situation sinking in. I felt a strong tightening in my abdomen. A Braxton Hicks?

Instead of speaking, Jim stood there, staring at our blank living room wall, which I'd been meaning to decorate since we'd moved in three years ago. He clenched his left hand, an expression somewhere between anger and astonishment on his face. He turned and made his way to the kitchen.

I followed. "Does he?"

Jim opened the refrigerator door and fished out a can of beer from the bottom shelf. "Does he what?" He tapped the side of the can, a gesture I had come to recognize as an itch to open it.

"Have any scars or . . ." I couldn't finish the sentence. A strange sensation struck me, as though the baby had flip-flopped. "Uh, Jim, I'm not sure about this, but I may have just had a contraction. A real one."

I cupped my hands around the bottom of my belly. We both stared at it, expecting it to tell us something. Suddenly I felt a little pop from inside. Liquid trickled down my leg.

"I think my water just broke."

Jim expertly navigated the San Francisco streets as we made our way to California Pacific Hospital. Even as the contractions grew stronger, I couldn't stop thinking about George.

Jim's parents had died when he was starting college. George, his only brother, had merely been fourteen, still in high school. Their Uncle Roger had taken George in. George had lived rent-free for many years, too many years, never caring to get a job or make a living.

Jim and I often wondered if so much coddling had incapacitated George to the point that he couldn't, or wouldn't, stand on his own two feet. He was thirty-three now and always had an excuse for not holding a job. Apparently, everyone was out to get him, take advantage of him, "screw" him somehow. At least that's the story we'd heard countless times.

The only thing George had going for him was his incredible charm. Although he was a total loser, you'd never know it to talk to him. He could converse with the best of them, disarming everyone with his piercing green eyes.

Uncle Roger had finally evicted George six months ago. There had been an unpleasant incident. Roger had been vague about it, only telling us that the sheriff had to physically remove George from his house. As far as we knew, George had been staying with friends since then.

I glanced at Jim. His face was unreadable, the excitement of the pending birth diluted by the phone call we had received.

I touched Jim's leg. "Just because his bags were found at the pier doesn't mean it's him."

Jim nodded.

"I mean, what did the guy say? The body was badly decomposed, right? How long would bags sit on a pier in San Francisco? Overnight?"

"Hard to say," he muttered.

I rubbed his leg trying to reassure him. "I can't believe any bag would last more than a couple days, max, before a transient, a kid, or someone else would swipe it."

Jim shrugged and looked grim.

A transient? Why had the medical examiner asked that? George had always lived on the fringe, but homeless?

Please God, don't let the baby be born on the same day we get bad news about George.

Bad news—what an understatement. How could this happen? I closed my eyes and said a quick prayer for George, Jim, and our baby.

I dug my to-do list out from the bottom of the hospital bag.

To Do (When Labor Starts):

1. Call Mom.
2. Remember to breathe.
3. Practice yoga.
4. Time contractions.
5. Think happy thoughts.
6. Relax.
7. Call Mom.

Oh, shoot! I'd forgotten to call Mom. I found my cell phone and pressed speed dial. No answer.

Hmmm? Nine P.M., where could she be?

I left a message on her machine and hung up.

I looked over the rest of the list and snorted. What kind of idealist had written this? Think happy thoughts? Remember to breathe?

I took a deep breath. My abdomen tightened, as though a vise were squeezing my belly. Was this only the *beginning* of labor? My jaw clenched as I doubled over. Jim glanced sideways at me.

He reached out for my hand. "Hang in there, honey, we're almost at the hospital."

The vise loosened and I felt almost normal for a moment.

I squeezed Jim's hand. My husband, my best friend, and my rock. I had visualized this moment in my mind over and over. No matter what variation I gave it in my head, never in a million years could I have imagined the medical examiner calling us right before my going into labor and telling us what? That George was dead?

Before I could process the thought, another contraction overtook me, an undulating and rolling tightening, causing me to grip both my belly and Jim's hand.

When my best friend, Paula, had given birth, she was surrounded mostly by women. Me, her mother, her sister, and of course, her husband, David. All the women were supportive and whispered words of encouragement while David huddled in the corner of the room, watching TV. When Paula told him she needed him, he'd put the TV on *mute*.

When I'd recounted the story for Jim, he'd laughed and said, "Oh, honey, David can be kind of a dunce. He doesn't know what to do."

Another vise grip brought me back to the present. Could I do this without drugs? I held my breath. Urgh! *Remember to breathe.*

I crumpled the to-do list in my hand.

Bring on the drugs.

...Excerpt from BUNDLE OF TROUBLE
by Diana Orgain © 2009
Buy BUNDLE OF TROUBLE for your Kindle

MOTHERHOOD IS MURDER
Book 2 of the MATERNAL INSTINCTS MYSTERY SERIES
© 2010 Diana Orgain

Nights out are hard to come by for new parents. So when Kate's new- mommy club, Roo & You, holds a dinner cruise, she and her husband leave baby Laurie with Kate's mom and join the grown-ups for some fine dining on the San Francisco Bay.

But when one of the cofounders of Roo & You takes a fatal spill down a staircase, the police department crashes the party. Suddenly every mom and her man has a motive. Kate's on deck to solve the mystery- but a killer's determined to make her rue the day she joined the first-time-mom's club…

Enjoy the following excerpt for
MOTHERHOOD IS MURDER

1. At Sea

To Do:
1. Buy diapers.
2. Make Laurie's two-month check.
3. Find good "how to" book for PI business.
4. √ ~~Find dress for the cruise.~~
5. √ ~~Ask Mom to babysit.~~
6. Exercise.

I stared into the bathroom mirror and wondered how I'd failed to bring a hairbrush along on the San Francisco Bay dinner cruise. I ran my hands down the length of my mop, trying to tame the frizzies. If I put a little water on the problem, would it help or make it worse?

The door to the restroom flew open. Sara, one of the moms from my new mommy group, appeared. She looked worse than I did. Her lipstick was smudged and her hair had the volume of a lion's mane.

"Oh my God! Kate! I didn't know you were here." She took a step back toward the door, then hesitated, looking like she'd been caught with her hand in the cookie jar.

She was so prim and proper at dinner. Probably doesn't like to be seen looking so rumpled, but hey, if you can't look bad in the ladies room then there's no safe haven.

Sara ran her hands along the front of her black cocktail dress, which was wrinkled and wet, then squinted at her reflection. She jumped into action, grabbing a paper towel and fixing the smeared lipstick. "Your husband's been looking everywhere for you. The captain's called an 'all hands on deck.'"

"My hands too?" I asked, wiggling my fingers under the faucet to activate the automatic water flow.

Sara scrunched her mouth in disapproval.

"I guess I'm not up on ship rules," I said to her reflection.

"Everyone has to go back to their tables, now!" She grabbed another paper towel and frantically scrubbed at the wet section of her dress.

I stopped fussing with my hair and shifted my gaze from Sara's reflection to Sara.

If everyone was supposed to be back to their tables, what was she doing here?

"Why?" I asked.

"There's been an accident."

Goose bumps rose on my arms. "What kind of accident?"

"Helene fell down the back staircase." Sara motioned me toward the door. "Come on, come on."

We made our way through a dimly lit corridor toward the main dining hall. The cruise ship held roughly seventy-five passengers although tonight it was only about half full.

The change in atmosphere was immediately noticeable. Not to mention eerie. The dance floor was empty and the music was off. We crossed the bar area, which moments ago had been packed, and hurried to our dining table.

Most of the passengers were seated at their tables. The chatter that had animated the room was subdued.

I spotted Jim standing alone at our table, gripping the back of his chair. He surveyed the room. When he saw me, his expression relaxed a notch, going from grim to serious.

I hurried to him and reached for his hand.

He embraced me. "Kate! I was worried."

"I need to find my husband," Sara said as she rushed past us and headed for the main stairwell.

"What's happened? Sara said Helene fell down some steps. Is it serious?"

"I'm not sure. The captain asked everyone to return to their dining tables. Didn't you hear him on the microphone? Where've you been?"

Before I could answer my elbow was jogged by Evelyn, another mommy from our group.

She was eight months pregnant with her second child. Her blonde hair was pinned neatly back, and her green eyes flashed enhanced by the lime scarf she wore. The scarf was arranged to draw the eye toward her protruding belly, which she proudly stroked.

"Kate! How awful! Did you hear about Helene?" Her lips curled a bit, almost as if she were suppressing a smile.

Why was she smiling? Almost gloating.

"Sort of. Is she all right?"

"Ladies and gentlemen," the captain's voice boomed over the microphone. "Please take your seats. We will be a bit delayed in docking in San Francisco due to an unfortunate accident aboard. The U.S. Coast Guard will be joining us shortly. Thank you in advance for your full cooperation."

Evelyn squeezed my elbow and flitted off to gather her husband. Jim pulled my chair out for me.

"Coast Guard? What's going on?" I asked.

Jim's lips formed a line. "I was at the bar getting a Bud, when the brunette –"

"Sara, Miss No-Nonsense?"

"No. The other one, the one with the...with the..." Jim waved his hands around. "Fluffy dress."

I nodded. "Margaret."

Margaret was wearing a ballet tutu. I wish I could say it looked as ridiculous as it sounded, but the truth was it looked fabulous. Margaret was super tall, pencil thin, and had shapely legs. She looked as if she could have stepped out of a children's book – a cartoon character with spindly spider legs and a ruffle at her waist. But the gold top and shoes added something indescribable to the outfit. Making the cartoon Olive Oyl look glamorous and runwayish.

"Yeah, Margaret," Jim continued. "She ran up to us, looking a little dazed, and said

Helene fell down the back staircase. Said she was unconscious –"

"Unconscious?" I felt a shiver run down my spine.

Jim pulled out my dining chair. "The captain asked if there was a doctor on board."

I sat down and let him push my chair in.

We were the only ones at our table. Earlier, we had dined with all the parents from my new mothers' group: Sara, Helene, Margaret, Evelyn and their husbands.

We had christened them: Sara was Miss No-Nonsense; Helene was Lean and Mean,

Margaret was Tutu, and Evelyn was Preggers. We referred to the husbands as Cardboard Cutout Numbers 1 through 4.

Now, it felt almost irreverent to have given everyone a nickname.

"Where is everybody?" asked Jim.

I shrugged. "Helene, we know about, so her husband is probably with her, right? Wasn't Margaret's husband –"

"Alan?"

"Yeah, Alan, isn't he a doctor?"

Jim frowned. "A podiatrist."

"Okay. Well, med school and all. Maybe she twisted her ankle. Did you see the heels she was wearing?"

Jim tried to hide his smirk by sipping his beer.

I pushed his shoulder. "What's so funny?"

"You. We just heard that Helene may be unconscious and you're worrying about her shoes!"

"I'm not worried about her shoes! I'm wondering what happened to her and where everybody is. I mean, the woman practically kills herself wearing some ungodly high heels, just to please some man, who probably laughed at her –"

Margaret descended the main staircase and closed the distance on our table. I cut myself off despite Jim's snickers into his beer. She raised her hand in acknowledgment and sat down grim-faced.

"Where's Alan?" I asked.

"With Helene," she answered.

I shot Jim a smug look, which he ignored.

"How is she?" Jim asked.

Margaret's eyes clouded over and she shrugged helplessly. "I don't know."

We sat in awkward silence. I perused the other three tables in the dining room. The parties at each table were as somber as we were. The four-hour dinner cruise on the San Francisco Bay had now been delayed indeterminately and nobody looked pleased about it.

Margaret fiddled with a cocktail glass that lingered beside her half eaten dessert. She lifted the glass and examined the contents. Only two melting ice cubes remained. She stirred them with her straw, hoping, I suppose, to release any vodka that might be clinging to them.

After a moment of disappointing results, she returned the glass to the table. Her eyes flicked toward the bar.

"Can I get you anything?" Jim asked.

Margaret flushed. "No. God, no. Thank you." She picked up her discarded navy cloth napkin and wrung it.

From the main staircase Sara and her husband approached. Behind them Evelyn and her husband were struggling to keep up. Evelyn had one hand on her pregnant belly and the other on her husband's shoulder. They took their places at our table in silence. The men smelled of cigar smoke and looked relaxed. In contrast, both women had pinched expressions.

Now, there were only three vacant spots at our table. Helene's, her husband's, and Alan's. My eyes fell on Helene's empty spot. Sara gave me a tight smile, then put her hand on Margaret's to stop her fidgeting.

"Everything will be fine, you'll see," Sara said to Margaret.

Margaret lowered her eyes and nodded.

Suddenly we felt a bump and the ship jostled back and forth. Everyone in the dining room turned toward the sound. Through the starboard window we could see the U.S. Coast Guard vessel had arrived. Crew members were roping the smaller craft to our ship.

The Coast Guard quickly boarded our ship and disappeared out of sight with the crew members.

Margaret cleared her throat and eyed Evelyn. "Does anyone know what happened? I mean, did she just slip or what?"

I had noticed that the woman hadn't been very chatty with Evelyn throughout the dinner and now wondered what the look Margaret had flashed her might mean.

Evelyn shrugged and returned Margaret's look evenly. "How would I know? Ask Sara."

Sara pressed her shoulders back and sat a little taller.

"She was really out of it," Evelyn continued, rubbing her extended belly. "How much did she have to drink anyway?"

"I didn't think she had that much, did she?" Margaret asked.

Helene's empty place seemed to dominate the table. Her dessert plate still held the untouched apple turnover. The ice cream had melted and run over the edge of the plate onto the navy and white place mat. Next to the plate, two drained cocktail glasses loomed, and in the tall wine-glass only the stain of red wine remained.

A strange hush settled on our table.

Howard, Sara's husband, slouched into his chair and casually slung his arm around the back of Sara's. "Looks like we're going to be here awhile."

Everyone at the table looked at Howard, and then followed his eyes to the starboard window. The night and bay were dark except for a troubling light that was converging upon us.

"Oh good!" Margaret exclaimed. "That must be the hospital boat for Helene."

The craft nudged itself alongside us. Silence descended on the entire dining room as letters on the boat came into view: "SFPD."

...Excerpt from MOTHERHOOD IS MURDER
by Diana Orgain © 2010
Buy MOTHERHOOD IS MURDER for your Kindle

FORMULA FOR MURDER
Book 3 of the MATERNAL INSTINCTS MYSTERY SERIES
© 2011 Diana Orgain

Sleuth and first-time mom Kate Connolly and her baby are the victims of a hit-and-run, but escape unharmed. A witness identifies the car's French diplomatic license plates, yet when Kate and her hubby try to get some answers, they get le cold shoulder.

But there's something going on at the French consulate that's dirtier-and far deadlier-than any diaper.

Enjoy the following excerpt for
FORMULA FOR MURDER

1

To Do:
1. √ ~~Make holiday photo appointment for Laurie.~~
2. ~~Send out Christmas cards~~ Get them printed first—then send out Christmas cards.
3. ~~Complete~~ Start Christmas shopping.
4. Find a "Baby's First Christmas" ornament.
5. Get Christmas tree.
6. Finish background checks Galigani gave me.
7. Get new PI client. How do I do this?

I checked Laurie in the rearview mirror. She was sound asleep; as usual, the motion of the car had lulled her into slumber.

She looked adorable, wearing a tiny red satin dress with matching red booties. We were on our way to get her first holiday photos taken. I couldn't believe three months had evaporated; it seemed like she was born just yesterday. My best friend, Paula, had warned me the time would fly by, but this was ridiculous. How had I put off taking Laurie's holiday photos? Now it was the first week in December and I'd be hustling to get them taken, printed, and sent out as Christmas cards.

It's all right. From now on efficiency will be my middle name.

I cruised down the hill to the stoplight and stepped on the brake. Out of habit, I glanced in the rearview again and saw a silver SUV barreling down the hill.

218

Was the car out of control? It continued to speed and there was no telltale sign of the nose dipping as it would if the driver were braking.

They were getting closer! Almost on top of us.

I quickly looked for a way to avoid impact. The cars in front of me were waiting on the traffic signal and a steady stream of cross traffic moved through the intersection.

No! The SUV was going to hit us!

My eyes were transfixed on the rearview mirror. I held my breath, bracing myself for the crash at the same time my brain screamed for a miracle.

Please stop in time. Please don't hit me and my baby!

Adrenaline shot through me, and everything felt as though it was happening in slow motion. I watched in horror as the SUV swerved violently to the right, but there was no way it could avoid hitting us.

The impact jolted us forward and I banged my head on the steering wheel. My seat belt caught and tugged at me just as we slammed into the car in front of us, then my entire body jerked backward, the base of my head smacking into the headrest.

Laurie let out a shrill wail, piercing into my heart. My gaze shot right and I locked eyes with the assailing driver. He was young, maybe only sixteen or seventeen, with longish brown hair and peach fuzz on his chin. His eyes were wide in shock. The SUV revved and tore off through the red light.

The light changed to green, and traffic—which had been stopped all around us—began to move again.

The passenger door of the vehicle in front of us opened and a woman jumped out. She rushed to my driver's side. I unfastened my belt with only one thing on my mind.

Laurie!

My hands were shaking from the adrenaline pulsing through my system. I pushed open my door.

The woman asked, "Are you all right?"

"I don't know. My baby! My baby!"

The woman's eyes widened as she focused on Laurie in her car seat.

Why wasn't she crying? She had cried out on impact but now she was silent.

My heart was lodged in my throat. I struggled with the door handle, my hands fumbling it. The woman reached over me and easily opened the door. I dove inside the backseat to Laurie's side.

Traffic sped around us. One vehicle slowed then stopped. The driver yelled, "Is everyone okay? Do you want me to call a tow truck? The police?"

I swallowed past the lump in my throat and shouted, "Call an ambulance!"

My voice sounded near hysterical even to me. I examined Laurie, who upon seeing me started to fidget and then began to cry.

Was she hurt? Was I supposed to move her? Panic about spinal cord injury flooded my mind.

"What do I do?" I asked the woman. "I don't want to take her out of the car seat. What if it hurts her little spine?"

"Can we get the entire car seat out of the car? Traffic's not waiting, honey, and I want to get you two out of danger."

I unclipped the car seat bucket and pulled the carrier out of the car. The woman grabbed the carrier, and we crossed a lane of traffic to the side of the road.

She set Laurie's bucket down on a bed of ice plants. "My husband went after the guy," the woman said. "I can't believe he just took off like that!"

I nodded distractedly, my mind and attention on Laurie. "He was young, a kid."

The woman blew out her breath in a sharp huff. "Probably on drugs!"

I leaned in as close to Laurie as I could without removing her from the seat, trying to soothe her.

"Did you see the plates on the car?" the woman asked me.

I rubbed Laurie's check, she rooted toward my hand. She was either hungry or looking for soothing. "No," I answered. "Just him. Long brown hair, peach fuzz, wide-eyed doe look on his face."

"Foreign diplomat car. DL? What code is that? French?" she asked.

Sirens screamed from up the hill.

Help is on the way!

I pressed my check against Laurie's and whispered, "Shhh, little angel, pumpkiny pie, Mommy's here and help's coming fast."

The woman said something inaudible and looked up in time to see an ambulance accompanied by a police cruiser pull up to the curb. The paramedics jumped out of the ambulance.

An officer stepped out of the patrol car and began speaking with the woman.

One EMT leaned over Laurie and me. "How are you?"

"I'm okay. I think. My baby is only three months old. I didn't want to take her out of the seat. Because, you know, I didn't know if it was okay to move her. I'm scared of neck or spinal injury—"

"Right, right," the EMT said, flashing a light across Laurie's eyes.

I knelt in the ice plant and hovered over them, not caring about the dew that soaked through the knees of my jeans and chilled me.

The EMT looked at me. "Her eyes are responding okay, but I can't tell much without taking her out of the seat. You want to go to the hospital? It's down the street."

I nodded, trying to shove down the hysteria welling inside me.

The EMT picked up Laurie's bucket. Laurie was now seemingly beginning to panic, too, and her cry turned into a shriek, her tiny arms flapping about.

It broke my heart to see her in distress, not really able to calm her. Every fiber of my being screamed to grab the bucket from him, pull Laurie out, and cradle her.

Please just be hungry or fussy. Don't be hurt, don't be injured!

The other EMT helped me up off my knees. The woman seemed to be recounting the accident to the police officer. As soon as I got to my feet I followed Laurie into the ambulance. The EMT who had assisted me moved to the officer and said something I couldn't pick up.

The officer nodded and came toward me. He was slightly taller than me and had a stocky build. Somehow his build reassured me as though it made him sturdy and dependable. "Ma'am, I'll need a statement from you. If you leave me your information I can get it from you later."

I absently looked around for my purse. For the first time since the accident I saw my car. It was completely totaled. My trunk was smashed in and the hood looked like an accordion.

How had I walked away from that?

What about Laurie . . . could she really be all right?

Tears flooded my eyes. "I don't know where my purse is. I can give you my number . . . Can you call my husband?"

The officer jotted down my home number. "I'll tell him to pick you up at the hospital." He looked at me for approval.

I nodded. "Thank you."

"I'll be in touch, ma'am. I hope your baby is all right." Anger flashed across his face and his jaw tightened. "Don't worry: I'm gonna get the guy who hit you."

I thanked him, then jumped into the ambulance, anxious to be with Laurie. She was still crying. Not knowing how to best channel my distress, I broke down and began to sob also, my brain trying to process the fact that this was the second time in Laurie's short life that we'd shared an ambulance ride together. The fact that this time was not my fault did little to settle my nerves.

Why had the driver left the scene? Sure, he was probably scared, but didn't he know a hit-and-run was a criminal act?

The EMT attending to Laurie put a small blanket over her and glanced at me. "Are you in pain, ma'am?"

I searched my pockets in a useless effort to find a pacifier for Laurie and shrugged at the EMT. "I want to hold her."

"I know," he said, almost in a whisper. "It's hard to listen to them cry. Did you know just the sound of a baby's cry makes your blood pressure go up?"

I shook my head.

He continued, "Yeah, in all mammals except for rats."

We rounded a corner and arrived at the hospital. Laurie and I were unloaded and ushered to a small room. A nurse freed Laurie from the car seat, before I could protest, and laid her on a table to take her vitals.

Someone in green medical scrubs was asking me if I had any cuts or abrasions. I shook my head and felt a blood pressure cuff go around my arm. My eyes locked on Laurie, I didn't even bother to look at him.

The nurse hovering over her asked, "How old is the baby?"

"Three months," I answered.

"When's the last time she ate?" she asked, stripping Laurie of her beautiful little holiday dress.

"A few hours ago."

The nurse attached small metal pads to Laurie's chest. Laurie let out a sharp cry.

"I'm so sorry they're cold, sweetie," she said.

The man attending me dropped my arm. "Normal," he said.

I glanced at him in disbelief, then read the digital display: 120 over 80.

I closed my eyes. Did this mean I was a rat?

Surely if I were any kind of decent mother my blood pressure would be through the roof.

"Can you take it again?" I asked.

The man frowned. "You're fine."

I didn't feel fine. I felt like a failure.

How could my blood pressure be fine? I'm a total and complete failure as a mom.

"Do you want to see a doctor?" the man asked me.

Again, I shook my head. "No. Just a pediatrician for Laurie."

He nodded and left the room. The other nurse turned to me. "Are you breastfeeding?"

I nodded.

She handed Laurie to me. "Why don't you nurse her now and see if she calms down a bit. All her vital signs are very good. Do you still want a pediatrician to look at her?"

"Yes, of course!" I answered.

The nurse nodded in understanding and left the room, promising to send the pediatrician on call.

I squeezed Laurie and fresh tears ran down my checks.

"Littlest! Please be okay. Please don't be hurt," I sobbed.

Laurie's hand entangled itself in my hair and she yanked at it, letting out a howl.

I laughed and let her tug at my hair. "If you're mad at missing a meal, then you're probably okay, huh?"

I bundled her in a blanket, nursed her, and waited for the doctor while replaying the accident in my mind. Was there anything I could have done differently? Why did he take off? I know he was just a kid, probably only recently got his license. But how could he abandon us like that?

The door to the room opened and my husband, Jim, appeared. I leapt out of the chair, still holding Laurie, and fell into him. His strong arms engulfed us and made me feel safe for the first time since the accident.

In a rush of words I told him about the hit-and-run. He listened to me while he watched Laurie.

There was a soft rap at the door, followed by the creak of it opening. The pediatrician, a tall man with smooth olive skin and dark hair, stepped in. He had me place Laurie on the exam table, which caused me to go into full sob mode again.

He peppered Jim with questions regarding Laurie's health, as he examined her. After a bit, he subjected me to the same battery of questions.

He finally said, "I think she's fine. Of course, we'll have to monitor her for signs of distress for the next forty-eight hours or so. But newborns are mostly cartilage; it's probably you, Mom, who's going to be hurting."

He handed me a checklist of symptoms to watch for, including: vomiting, diarrhea, and lethargy, and then left the room.

I rebundled Laurie. "What did the police tell you?" I asked Jim.

"Not much. He said the guy in the car in front of you followed the assailant. He ended up losing him, but was pretty sure it was a vehicle from the French consulate's fleet."

A vehicle from the French consulate?

What did that mean? Why did he speed off? Why not stop?

"Was the car stolen?" I asked.

Jim shrugged. "I don't know, the cop barely gave me the time of day. Told me to file an insurance claim and gave me an incident number." Jim stared at me with a dumbfounded expression—one I'm sure matched my own.

After a moment, he said, "Of course, I didn't press him much. I only wanted to find out about you and Laurie and how you guys were doing."

I nodded.

"Why'd you ask if the car was stolen?" Jim asked.

"It was a teenager driving it."

Jim exhaled. "So it's some diplomat's kid."

"Maybe," I agreed.

He squinted at me. "Let's go there."

"What?"

"Let's track down the snot nose that hit you and Laurie."

"Shouldn't we let the police do that?"

Jim clenched a fist. "They already know it's a car from the consulate. You think they're itching to get involved with some diplomat's pinhead son? If they were, they'd already be over there, right?"

I pulled Laurie close to me and pressed my nose into her soft cheek. She was asleep but my squeeze caused her little hand to reach out. I placed my finger in her palm and felt her small hand wrap around it.

"You know the police aren't going to do a darn thing," Jim continued. "They want us to open an insurance claim. Let us take the hit."

Anger surged inside of me. "We already took the hit. Literally! Laurie and I."

Oh God, please let my baby be all right.

The doctor had said to watch for signs of distress.

Didn't I always?

I would be even more vigilant now.

"What about Laurie? I want to get her home. Make sure she's okay. I want her to be warm and fed and content . . ." My voice caught as a sob bubbled in my throat. "I want her to be okay."

Jim pulled Laurie and me into an embrace. "She's okay, honey. She's gonna be fine," he said, his voice full of emotion "You heard the doctor: She's all cartilage."

"She not all cartilage. She's a person! A tiny defenseless little person, with a heart and soul and . . ." Tears rolled down my face.

He tightened his grasp around me. Laurie squirmed between us.

"It happened so fast, Jim. One minute you're there, stopped at a light, and then the next . . . what if . . ."

"I love you guys so much. I can't stand the thought. All I can do is fight, Kate. I want to find the guy who ran into you. Accidents happen, I know. But you can't just leave a mother and child in the middle of the road after smashing their car to smithereens."

I nodded, swallowing back my fears. I picked up Laurie's discarded dress and handed it to Jim. "Let's go."

. . . Excerpt from FORMULA FOR MURDER
by Diana Orgain © 2011
Buy MOTHERHOOD IS MURDER for your Kindle

ABOUT THE AUTHOR

Diana Orgain is the bestselling author of the *Maternal Instincts Mystery Series:* BUNDLE OF TROUBLE, MOTHERHOOD IS MURDER, FORMULA FOR MURDER and NURSING A GRUDGE. She is the co-author of GILT TRIP from the NY Times Bestselling *Scrapbooking Mystery Series* by Laura Childs. Diana's FOR LOVE OR MONEY the first in her new *Reality TV Mystery* series will be published in Spring 2015. She lives in San Francisco with her husband and three children. Visit her at www.dianaorgain.com.

For a complete listing of books, as well as excerpts and contests, and to connect with Diana:

Visit Diana's website at www.dianaorgain.com.

Follow Diana on Twitter at www.twitter.com/dianaorgain

Join Diana on Facebook at www.facebook.com/DianaOrgainAuthor

Sign up for Diana's email updates at www.dianaorgain.com/about-the-authorcontact

Cocktails

& Other Stories

By Nicholas Trandahl

Nicholas Trandahl

Cocktails & Other Stories

ISBN: 978-0-9888466-7-8

www.swyerspublishing.com

Swyers Publishing paperback edition /August 2015

Dedicated to Brittany, the most evident of all the world's muses.

Table of Contents

DEAD TREES

Every good childhood needs a climbing tree. Mine was a cottonwood, probably a century old. It was tall and plain and its boughs were full and verdant. It was a chore to climb up the first five feet of the rough bark to get at the first thick limbs, but once you were there it was golden. It was a tree that was seemingly grown for the purpose of climbing.

We had a crabapple tree before the cottonwood, but one summer it got sick. All of its leaves died quickly and its tart, red fruit stopped showing up on the ends of its limbs. It was still fun to climb, however, until its brittle limbs began to crack dryly and split apart, leaving behind jagged treacherous edges. And then Dad said we couldn't climb in it anymore. It had gotten too dangerous.

Eventually my dad and my grandfather cut the crabapple tree down and tore the stump out. It was quite the family event and it preceded a family barbecue and lots of cold beer in the golden summer afternoon. Dad gave me a sip of his beer, and I

remember being a little disgusted at it because it smelled like his breath always smelled. I remember being exhilarated because all the adults were drunk, loud and happy, but then I remember being a little bewildered about why everyone was so damn overjoyed about tearing our old, short climbing tree to pieces. They were like pagans celebrating a gory sacrifice to their ancient horned deities.

So, after the celebratory destruction of the crabapple tree, my climbing tree became the cottonwood. But the spot in the yard where the late crabapple tree once stood became an eerie spot. Even just looking at the bare patch where the tree once stood elicited feelings of anxiety. It was like politely avoiding to stare at the face of an individual whose face had been long ago disfigured. Passing that area where it once stood was like passing quite close to the grave of a relative or a rotting, maggot-riddled corpse of a deer in the woods. Avoidance was paramount.

Eventually the grass grew over the ravaged dry spot of soil. But I didn't ever forget that the crabapple once stood there. And it still didn't feel right. It never would. It was a disgusting area of earth.

There are a lot of things like that in life. There are places and things that once were so very important that the solemnity of their absence, when they finally were vanquished or expired in one way or another, was

all-encompassing. Their absence retrieved in a person such primal and instinctual reactions that the wraith of their phantom existence was to be avoided at all costs. My missing crabapple tree is just an example, one of a great horde. Vanished things of personal import mark our individual haunted worlds like great ominous tombs in the fog. Their vacancy speaks volumes.

I felt the same sort of eerie emptiness three decades later, when I was on the cusp of forty years old, the night after a powerful wind storm. What had been blown away in the dark heart of the night when the crescent Wyoming moon had shone down in lapses between swiftly-scudding shreds of cloud? Something had blown away from my life in the fierce wind storm from the northwest that had torn over the small town in which I was a resident. The scariest notion was that I had a doom-ridden suspicion about what it was.

It was the next morning, about eight o'clock. The girls were inside, freshly awoken and innocently chipper in the wake of the Saturday night gales. Somehow they had unprecedentedly not awoken during the fierce winds that had slammed viciously into the house during the night. My wife was getting them breakfast, and she was probably having some coffee herself. On this morning, as far as I was concerned, breakfast and coffee could go to hell.

I wore an ivory-hued, cable-knit sweater like some goddamn Norwegian fisherman. My scruffy unshaven face and Scandinavian arctic blue eyes suited the sweater too. What didn't match were the plaid pajama pants and the shearling-lined suede slippers that clothed my lower torso.

I ambled from the backyard to the side of the house with a heavy load of cheap shingles loaded in one arm, and with my other hand I brought my cigar to my lips. I pulled in a mouthful of the honey-flavored tobacco, churned it around in my mouth a bit, and then I blew it out in a long steady breeze. Our two black cats, small skinny-bodied brothers, trotted after me loyally as they had been all morning throughout my repetitive chore of cleaning up the debris that littered our yard.

When I came around the corner of the house, I tossed the fallen shingles onto the ample pile that I had been stacking on the corner of our driveway that terminated beside our modest home. A pile of broken cottonwood limbs also rested nearby. The cats scattered when the shingles slapped onto the top of the pile, as they had with every single load. It was some sort of strange cat game, and I could imagine them giggling like simple-minded children as they scattered with quick bounds in opposite directions. I smiled and snorted softly through my nose as I shook my head. "You little idiots," I quietly remarked.

Hands blissfully empty of shingles and broken branches for the moment, I took another drag of my cigar and put my hands on my hips. Exhaling, I took a good long look up into the clear and crystalline blue sky of dawn, so new and pure at the start of Sunday. Sundays were the best days. A ghost of a smile still played upon my lips, lips sweet from the sugary natural wrap of the cigar. What in the world did I have to smile about, especially when such evil things had been uttered to one another scant hours ago?

I let my gaze drift downward and it settled on my kitchen window. My wife's face was there, oval-shaped and pale. It was a pretty face, but it was bitter. She wasn't scowling at me, but there was no love in her. She wore an emotionless mask as she looked at me from the window. I could imagine our girls eating cereal at the table right next to her. That made her melancholy presence all the more pronounced, more contrasted against their likely joviality and blissful ignorance.

The winds that tore through our landscape and our town weren't the only storm that befell our household the night before. We'd had our fights before. Who in the hell hasn't? Conflict is one of the most common ingredients to season a relationship. Right? That's what everyone says, isn't it? That's what they say

to feel justified in their own shitty romances. Well, the night before was beyond that.

Our argument that raged in ferocious and lethal quietness within our bedroom dwarfed the shrieking wind and the rumbling windows that roared without. In the argument, the subject of which was something trivial but exaggerated grotesquely through years of resentment, had fostered a blackened seed of finality that had suddenly burrowed threadlike tendrils into the pure flesh of our relatively happy marriage.

And now, on that clear Sunday morning with my yard strewn in windblown debris, I felt the absence of the continuance of our love. Its absence, like that of the destroyed crabapple from my childhood, caused the hair on the back of my neck to stand up and caused little eddies of anxiety to swirl through my belly. My wife's vacant features were unwavering as she observed me from the kitchen window. It was like she couldn't even see me, like I was unfamiliar. Her features also held within them the oddness and wrongness that had been there in that empty patch of ground where my first climbing tree had once stood in its life.

I blew out a mouthful of cigar smoke and averted my eyes away from hers. As I did so, I scratched some black adhesive off of my palms that the broken shingles had gotten on me. There was a connection between my marriage and that old crabapple tree. A

marriage is like a tree, needing sustenance to be bountiful and healthy. Both the tree and the marriage, in their prime, were symbolic of life and bounty, of fruitfulness. But one day, they'd both just become diseased and rotten. And now there were two dead trees in my life.

I marched back into my fenced-in yard and I casually observed the scattered black shingles that were clumped in broken heaps against the south and east fences and against my girls' swing set. A few sundered cottonwood branches were also scattered about in the damp green grass of the backyard. The cats were back behind me. They trotted past my slippered feet and darted playfully out into the yard where they got to hunting one another while keeping a simultaneous eye always out on my doings.

I gathered a couple of the nearest shingles. I was ashamed at their shoddy quality and at their inadequacy, especially knowing the winds that were so prevalent in Wyoming. I'd need to look into getting better shingles on the house. My girls deserved a house with good solid shingling. Then I looked up into the large old cottonwood that loomed raggedly and tall in the corner of our yard.

But they sure did have a nice climbing tree. And *every* good childhood needs a climbing tree.

FERTILITY

It was a Saturday afternoon in late June. A hot summer had very recently arisen from the pales tones of spring. I was watching my wife out of the front window of our small little home in the heart of the small town in which we lived. She didn't know that I was watching her, and I liked that. Reality is only achievable candidly.

I felt as though I was watching something sincere and flawless as she sat on her knees before the brick planter in the front of our house. She was wearing a straw sun hat, wide-brimmed and vintage, and a 1950s-style dress that was pale orange with large white polka dots. She reminded me of oranges and cream. The marigolds and zinnias that Rosie planted were colored warmly in yellow, orange, red and pink. The only cool shades in sight were the emerald green of the lawn the pale aqua of the sky. All else was colored in warmth.

Her name was Rose, but I called her Rosie. The extra vowel somehow made her name seem shorter,

denoting a shorthand style of familiarity and affection and fondness. Rosie. My everything. Truly, my everything. We had no children through our fifteen years of marriage, and we'd learned to be satisfied with that. It wasn't for lack of trying.

Rosie and I often joked about the intensity and frequency of intimacy in our marriage in comparison to the lackluster intimacies of our friends and other folks our age. Our romance had an earnestness that never seemed to diminish over the years like we were expecting that it would, like people warn you about when teasing you at your wedding. No, Rosie was just unable to get pregnant. She always had been. It was something to do with a disorder in her ovaries or uterus.

Rosie was thirty-five and was a kindergarten teacher at the local elementary school. I was five years older than her, and I had formerly written for a literary journal before I finally "made it" as a novelist. We had a modest little home that was a creamy pale yellow with plenty of reddish-brown brick and a white porch. I liked to sit on the porch in the early morning and drink hot tea as Rosie slept in. Rosie and I were *very* content with our lives and with one another. Our mutual contentment was present despite the tragedy that we wouldn't have children. We made our lives a certain way, a way that made it so that we were enough for

one another. We achieved this successful marital path through continual affection for each other.

As I watched her, I was overcome with a tickle of electric arousal in my thighs and butterflies stirring in my stomach. To me, Rosie had always seemed to radiate fertility, though Rosie was stricken with some brand of genetic infertility. She couldn't have children, of course, and yet my mouth watered with some instinctual and primal desire whenever I laid eyes on her.

Since it felt so primal and instinctive to me, I figured it as an animalistic response to fertility. That's what it felt like to me, and I watched her through the window as she quietly sang a song that I couldn't hear and planted flowers in the dark soil contained within the brick planter in the front of our house. I observed the plumpness of her belly that seemed to me to be the belly of some ancient goddess of sex and fertility. I observed the girth of her ample bosom that swayed and jiggled ever so slightly as she worked, and I noticed that the soft curves of her limbs had taken on a luminous tint in the robust afternoon light in those venerable waning days of June.

To me, ironically, Rosie was the avatar of fertility, but she was cruelly and coincidentally made infertile by a perverse world.

Rosie wore leather gloves that were weathered and soil-stained, and sweat and streaks of dirt adorned her attractive broad face, a face framed by a chin-length dark brown bob. Her pink full lips teased into a trace of a smile as she softly sang, and her large brown eyes danced with contentment and pleasure. Planting and tending her flowers ranked alongside baking and sleeping as Rosie's favorite pastimes, and I personally loved it when she partook in any one of those hobbies that she endeavored to lose herself in.

What a mother she would have been, I thought to myself as I brought the cool rim of a gin and tonic that I'd just made up for myself to my thin lips.

My drink was an unusually sour gin and tonic because I made mine with a couple ounces of gin, a few ounces of tonic water, and copious amounts of lemon and lime juice that I squeezed over the cold cubes of ice. The process concluded when I garnished the cocktail with a thin slice of vibrant lemon and one of lime. All the fresh citrus juice I put into the clearness of the gin and tonic water caused the drink to take on a pale minty cloudiness. I usually made a cocktail at night, after dinner when I wrote, but this Saturday afternoon felt like it called adamantly for a cocktail. I knew that

Rosie would feel the same, and so I returned to the kitchen to get something ready for her.

I filled a tall glass half-full with ice and pulled a pitcher of fresh lemonade that Rosie had made a couple days before from the refrigerator. The contents of the pitcher were opaque and pastel yellow, and slices of vivid yellow lemon swirled and tumbled happily within when I stirred the lemonade with a wooden spoon. I poured the tart liquid into the glass, filling it to about two-thirds full, and then I fished out of my antique, wooden liquor cabinet the bottle of gin that I'd just used for my own cocktail. I topped the cool summery drink off with gin, stirred it with one of my spiral-stemmed stirring spoons, and when I was finished with Rosie's drink I sipped it. Perfect.

My half-full gin and tonic in one hand and her full gin-spiked lemonade in my other, I made my way to the front door of our home and pushed open the screen door with my side. I came around to the front of the house and beheld Rosie working with her flowers. When I saw her voluptuous feminine form, I was again intoxicated with the aura of fertility and sensuality that she exuded like an expensive French perfume, or more like the subtle pear-scented perfume that she regularly wore. Little pieces of the song that she quietly sang, reached my ears in fragile fragments and I made my way towards her.

Rosie saw my approach, smiled voluminously, and said, "Hi, Honey Bee!"

"Hi, Rosie," I replied. As I neared, I took a good look at the warm-hued marigolds and zinnias. Their fragrance always reminded me of my childhood, of my aunt's nursery with its greenhouses, rows of young trees in black plastic pots, and Latin American workers. It was a pleasing and historical scent. It was an aroma that brought me back to days of hunting for slumbering snakes and frogs in the humid, amber afternoon light. Memory, I knew, was the product of everything that our senses gathered from the world. "The flowers look stunning."

"Do they?" she answered, turning to her horde of little floral children admiringly.

"Indeed they do. But you're more stunning, sweetie." As I said this I handed my wife, smiling on her knees in the dappled shade granted by the wide brim of her sun hat, her lemonade and gin and I kissed Rosie's soft cheek lightly as I did so. I loved her with a helplessness that was colored in the pastel tones of enormity and delight. Against the love I felt for her, there was nothing else in the world. It encompassed all the faraway corners and nooks of my pleasant reality.

Rosie took a long swallow, fluttering her eyelashes in surprise at the potency of the liquor contained in the tart lemonade. As the liquid passed

from the rim of the glass and through her soft rosy lips, I could hear the cubes of ice lightly tapping against the inside of the glass as their positions shifted. And when she was satisfied with her initial drink, she set the glass on the side of the brick planter, smiled warmly up at me as I nursed at my gin and tonic, and soundlessly mouthed, "Thank you."

Man, I loved her.

"How's your writing going?"

"Fine," I told her. "Slow," I elaborated.

I watched her for a few minutes more in the yellow-tinted summer light that afternoon, and finally she wiped the sweat from her forehead with a forearm and looked up into the June sky. "Do you think it's going to rain again tonight?" she inquired of me. "It'd be nice to have the bedroom window open tonight."

I continued to smile at her for a moment more, and then I followed her gaze up into the sultry, yellowed air. I answered with relief and joy swelling within my throat and my voice, "I don't think it's going to rain again … ever."

A WEEKEND IN THE WOODS

I

Their only son had left in August. After graduation, his life had revolved around all of his preparations for college. It seemed like Irving and Cecilia Scott had scarcely seen their son before his departure, and a few weeks before his first semester started Chet had taken off in the used sedan that they had bought for him for his sixteenth birthday, what seemed like epochs ago. It all had seemed to happen with a terrible suddenness.

On one evening late in the waning days of summer, Cecilia drifted through the large, clean, and empty spaces that comprised their townhouse. Two full glasses of red wine were in her hands. The lights were off and the rooms were dark, but a blue pall from the streetlights outside shrouded everything within. Occasional flashes of stark lightning threaded chaotically through the churning cloud cover that slipped ponderously slow over the city like a dark foam. The rain sounded rhythmic as it drummed in sweeping

waves upon the roof. Cecilia could feel a tension in the emptiness, a brooding expectation that had arisen in the home when their son had left and had remained stagnant and lurking.

How had one teenage body endeavored to make the home seem so much more full, so much more alive and vibrant? When Chet had went off to school a couple of weeks before, had he taken all the color with him? To Cecilia, it felt as though he did. And she knew that her husband felt the same way as well, though he seemed to hide it better. Irving was staying up later than usual, spending a great deal of time in his writing office pounding away on the keys of his computer with a mechanical repetitiveness. He was also smoking his pipe more and drinking more beer, as opposed to taking the time to make one of his cocktails at night when he wrote. He was stressed with this new parental change.

The front door of the Scott home was open, and the smell of the downpour and a flighty cool breeze whirled invisibly in the spotless entryway. Cecilia shivered slightly in the depths of her voluminous wool sweater as she stepped towards the threshold, and she wished a bit that the glasses of wine that she carried were mugs of hot chai tea. Then she stepped outside.

Irving's back was to her, and he sat on the top step of the concrete stairs that led up the door of the

townhouse. The shingled little awning above the door was perched darkly above him, sheltering him from the heavy rains. Cecilia smelled the aromatic traces of pipe smoke, and then she realized that he must have just finished smoking because the pipe and a closed matchbox sat on the concrete next to him in the shadows. Some scattered blackened dottle was in a diminutive heap on the step below. Irving kicked it off of the step when he heard Cecilia step towards him.

Cecilia sat down beside Irving silently, and she kissed his whiskered cheek before handing him a glass. He hadn't bothered to shave since Chet left home for college, but Cecilia had to admit that she found the dark stubble that shadowed his jaw and chin was quite attractive. She had forgotten the ruggedness that her author husband had been possessed of when they had first met in college about twenty-five years ago, before he had gotten his first novel published. He had been an avid backpacker and hiker in those days, an outdoorsman with a fondness for John Muir, Henry David Thoreau, and Jack London.

"Thank you," he stated quietly before he took a sip of wine, the creaky gruffness in his voice coming from several hours' disuse.

In response, Cecilia leaned against her husband's shoulder and looked with him out at the street. Great sheets of rain cascaded down upon the

reflective surface of the asphalt, and they sparkled and exploded on impact like shattering shards of glass that were sundered loose from the great dome of the night sky by the booming peals of thunder.

Cecilia was a lovely woman in her mid-forties, chocolate brown hair silken and long as it smothered her shoulders and framed her attractive girlish face. She was something of a writer, like her husband, but Cecilia wrote cookbooks instead of her husband's highbrow genre of literary fiction. Both of them had been successful in their writing pursuits and they thus lived comfortably. They were able to travel and enjoy their time.

Cecilia's physical form was one that used to be trim and athletic, but her middle-age had acquired a softness about her. She was apt to notice little rolls along her sides when she leaned certain ways and a soft belly was beginning to make itself known. Cecilia was as disgruntled with her body's newly-acquired mass as she was with the wrinkles that kept multiplying in the corners of her greenish-brown eyes and the multiplying strands of grey hair that appeared overnight in her dark hair. But, despite her own perceptions of herself, Irving found Cecilia's more feminine figure quite pleasant. He seemed to want to hold her more now than he ever had when they were younger.

Irving had also undergone physical changes that were more noticeable on the unfavorable side of forty. He was a broad-shouldered and wide-bodied man, tall but with a new-found belly softening up the waxing girth of his midsection. His dark brown jaw of whiskers also confirmed his age with the silver patches that were seemingly stained into it. He wore his brown hair short and combed back, and it had only started to thin a little bit. But his pale, minty green eyes, the eyes Cecilia had fallen for back when they were young in college, still held in them a youthfulness that only lifelong writers seemed to somehow possess until their coffins claimed them.

"We need to get away, Irving," Cecilia sighed after sipping her wine.

He sighed gustily himself, and replied, "I guess so, huh? Chet's gone. It's not as fun being at home with him gone."

"Nope. It's not. It's so depressing here now," Cecilia returned.

"In fact, this place fucking sucks. Let's move to Europe," stated Irving as he stared out into the downpour.

They snickered softly together and felt each others' warmth breathe into one another as though through osmosis. Despite their recent parental depression and loneliness, they were still hand in hand

against the universe. It was how they had always been, and Irving and Cecilia knew with adamant assurance that they would be together until the end of their lives. A lot of married couples say that with hope and uncertainty. But the Scotts were certain.

Leaning against her husband's muscular shoulder, Cecilia let her earthy, forest-hued gaze drift from the downpour to her husband's wrist that she held. A handmade scarlet and white bracelet of alternating braided threads was clasped about his wrist, and even in the darkness of the August night she could see that its color had faded greatly over the twenty years since their honeymoon.

They had honeymooned in Greece during the spring those decades ago, and a local springtime tradition of that Mediterranean country had been the crafting and gifting of red and white bracelets in honor of the spring. It was a tradition, so the locals had told them, from Ancient Greece, and later on folks would leave the bracelets in the boughs of trees. Cecilia and Irving had both returned home with them around their wrists and they had vowed to never remove them. Their bracelets were a symbol of solidarity for their eternal love for one another. Cecilia still hadn't forgiven herself for when she had lost her bracelet at a public swimming pool twelve years ago. But it made her feel better to

see that her husband still loyally wore his own. Irving wore it for the both of them.

Smiling very lightly and still caressing his wrist as she gazed at his bracelet, Cecilia finally said, "Okay. Let's go to Europe. Let's go back to Greece. I can get a new bracelet then."

"Not yet. It's August. These ones are traditionally made in the springtime, remember? And isn't Greece's economy shit now?"

"Probably. Everywhere is shit."

They were silent for a moment more, and then Irving said somewhat brightly, "Let's go to the woods, Cecilia. Let's go camping for the weekend. The woods aren't shit yet."

"Some of them are. Are there still forests out there that haven't been chopped down for pipelines or mines or for development? Are there still *real* forests?"

"Sure there are. Let's go camp. It'll be nice to get the hell away."

Cecilia removed her head from her husband's shoulder and looked at his handsome profile that faced out into the wet night. "You're serious?" she inquired.

"Sure I am."

Raising an eyebrow incredulously, Cecilia returned, "Well, a weekend in the woods is a far cry from moving to Europe. If I agree to go camping with you, do you agree that we can go to Europe?"

"Yes, we can go to Europe this fall. To *visit*. We can talk about *moving* there after Chet's been in college for a bit more time." Irving looked down into Cecilia's lovely face. "Agreed?"

When Cecilia nodded, he kissed her. Irving tasted of wine and pipe smoke, and his handsome whiskers teased her sensitive face. Cecilia held his face to hers so that their kiss could continue along with the rain and the night. Relief from the melancholy that came with their son's absence only came with Irving and Cecilia's love for one another.

II

The forested hills were composed of great smears of pine, blemished here and there with deciduous rifts that were kissed with a touch of early September yellow. The day was possessed of a very tolerable warmth, but the warmth was salted with a crisp hint of the coming autumn. A piercing azure hue colored the awe-inspiring sky and it was garnished with lacy little patterns of pale ethereal cloud.

It was in the early afternoon on a Friday in the first days of September, and Irving and Cecilia Scott rode in their neutral-toned SUV down a winding stretch of dirt road. They were clothed in cable-knit sweaters with lighter shirts underneath. Irving's Scandinavian sweater was navy blue and he also wore a pair of

broken-in comfortable jeans, admittedly a little tight around his burgeoning waist, and he was crowned in a tweed cap that went very well with the pipe in his mouth. Cecilia had always thought Irving as a man meant for a different era, and he was inclined to present himself as such.

Cecilia's large sweater was a creamy hue, and she wore black leggings and brown boots. It was an autumnal outfit that she'd seen in several women's fashion blogs lately. Her long brown hair was secured in two braids, one on either side of her head. Irving had smiled at her when he saw the braids and he'd told her that she looked like a Native American squaw. He liked that, and she was pleased that he liked that.

The windows of their vehicle were down and a ribbon of Irving's pipe smoke drifted swiftly out. No music was playing and just occasional statements from the GPS application on Cecilia's smartphone broke the silence of the wind rushing over the vehicle. The faint babble of the woodlands and the hills could also be heard just over the din of their transportation, and it chattered in the voice of rustling leaves and crying birds. Just in leaving the city that morning, the middle-aged couple had already touched upon a kernel of contentment and they were holding it close and basking in its radiance like it was an enchanted jewel. They felt that the weekend would be good for them.

"God, do you smell that, Irving? I *love* the smell of the wilderness."

Cecilia's husband only smirked in response, puffing away on his pipe like the beatnik writers that he worshiped. His writing and his fondness and nostalgia for that literary period made him seem a man from his parents' generation. Irving had always felt like he should have been born forty years earlier. Then he could have been contemporaries with his idols when their prose was up-and-coming in the fifties and sixties. Irving would daydream about ambling through the same circles as those writers that he almost praised as gods; Truman Capote, William Burroughs, and John Cheever. Cecilia had always been surprised at her manly husband's taste in pseudo-homosexual literary influences. But she also felt so fortunate to be with a man with a refined literary palate and an open-minded and sensitive taste.

Irving and Cecilia had packed their tent, used only once several years ago, a couple of camping chairs, some of their warmest quilts, paper plates and plastic utensils, a couple tin mugs, a cooler full of ice, food, shandy beer, some citrus, a bottle of club soda and a bottle of dry gin. Each had also packed a full backpack of clothes, toiletries and other personal items.

Irving's backpack contained his paperback copy of John Cheever's complete collection of short stories, a

notepad and some pens, and his pipe tobacco. Cecilia's contained a campfire cookbook that a friend of hers had written, some spices and herbs in little glass jars, her iPod, and stowed away in the bottom of her pack was a short, silky, pink nightie with white lace trim. She intended to surprise Irving with it when he came into the tent at night.

"You were so lucky to grow up in a countryside similar to this," began Cecilia, looking wistfully out of the passenger window into the passing trees. "I had the city and beach."

"I like the beach."

"Me too, but as a kid this would have been so much better," Cecilia explained.

"I think Chet would fight you on that point, dear," quipped Irving with a smirk.

"He doesn't like camping, does he? We haven't gone in so long, I'd forgotten. I guess that's why we haven't gone. Chet would much rather have the beach," Cecilia pondered verbally.

"Chet would rather have the girls in bikinis," Irving corrected dryly.

The Scotts laughed and then were quiet and peaceful for a little while. Irving finally asked, "Did you bring your bikini, dear? The water should still feel nice."

Cecilia crinkled her nose up in disgust and said, "Irving, sorry to break it to you, but I've gotten too fat for a bikini."

"Bullshit," was all he said.

"No, I'm not kidding. Have you looked at me lately, like *really* looked at my body? I'm a cow."

Irving picked a little chunk of tobacco off of his tongue and wiped it on his jeans before he glanced at his lovely wife. He said in a teasing seriousness, "You'd better quit saying bad things about my wife."

"Or what?" Cecilia teased coyly, returning her husband's look seductively from beneath her dark lashes.

Irving couldn't keep a straight face and smirked wryly as he replied, "Or you'll get punished tonight."

Cecilia smirked also and she shrugged. "I guess we'll have to see, won't we? I think that you're all talk."

The campsite was nice and private, a half mile or so off of the dirt road. It was a flat area on the top of a wooded slope that descended down towards a creek that could be heard faintly in the afternoon atmosphere. Surrounding the cleared area of the campsite were large solemn pines that swayed ever-so-slightly in the breeze, and the slope itself was shrouded in a mix of tall pine and young birch. In the golden-colored distance of the maturing afternoon, through

the spaces between the tall pines around the flat clearing of the campsite, Irving and Cecilia could discern the taller blue-green summits of the hills and low rounded peaks the studded the region.

The pair felt blissfully separated from the city and from humanity. They also felt separated from their son, but they were guilty to find that there was a bliss in that notion as well. They needed to be apart from the sorrow that was inherent in his absence from their home.

Irving and Cecilia worked together to put up their little-used nylon tent. It had the potential to be a wildly frustrating process and quite the ordeal, but the couple laughed at their helplessness and they finally had managed to get their shelter erected by early evening. The late summer sun had fallen behind the western brim of the world and it had splattered neon orange and scarlet tones up into the bruising purples and dark blues of the twilit expanse of the firmament. Stars had begun to wink feebly into being in the darker swathes of the sky.

The campsite had a ring of blackened and scorched stones at its heart, and the couple swiftly filled the heavily-used fire pit with dry branches and tinder. The tinder that Cecilia and Irving collected consisted of chunks of pine bark, fallen pine cones, and copious amounts of dry pine needles. The flat area that they

camped within was completely carpeted in the dry pine needles that over the years had fallen absently from the mighty pines encircling the area.

With a couple of matches it wasn't at all difficult for Irving to coax a hot yellow-orange fire out of the dry wood and the kindling that he and his wife had stacked in the fire ring. And as he got a fire going, Cecilia was in the tent layering quilts on the floor for cushioning. She finished it off by laying a heavy blanket on the top of the quilts for them to share when they covered up at night.

When night had truly fallen and distant frogs could be heard down towards the creek, the Scotts were done setting up camp and the pair had become tired and cozy. Irving set up a camping chair near the fire, opened up a shandy from the cooler, and he sat down and nursed his bottle of lemonade beer. Cecilia finally exited the tent, dusting her hands off on her hips, and she went over to her husband and lowered herself onto his lap. She took a sip from his shandy and Irving kissed the top of Cecilia's head.

Irving tugged lightly on the end of one of her braids and he said, "I really like these braids."

Looking at the hot flames of the campfire, Cecilia responded, "I'll keep them in if you keep your beard. Deal?"

"Deal," he answered.

They were silent for awhile then, and Cecilia and Irving just listened to the crackle of the campfire, the rustling of the surrounding pines, and the amphibious chorus of the frogs down at the creek. It was a peaceful night, and they were anxious for what Saturday would bring.

III

Saturday morning had dawned upon the woods early, and it held clutched tightly to its breast a fresh pastel coolness that edged just on the tolerable side of being uncomfortable. These were summer's last weeks, but a greedy autumn was already having her way with the landscape and the breeze. But the tired summer seemed to be giving into its younger, colorful sister happily and with gusto.

As golden amber light broke sideways through the quiet columns of the trees in luminescent shards Irving Scott crept quietly from the tent. The novelist wore his navy blue, cable-knit sweater that he'd worn the day before, a pair of sturdy khaki pants, and hiking boots that were bright and clean with disuse. Startled with the early morning autumnal chill that permeated the air and made his breath faintly visible, Irving slipped a black knitted beanie over his disheveled hair. When he was outside of the tent he knelt down and reached quietly within, so as not to disturb his sleeping wife.

Irving withdrew a pen and a notebook from his pack along with a tin of apple-flavored pipe tobacco.

There was nothing to rival the glory of quiet weekend mornings that were tumescent with the promise of writing. And Irving could not remember a weekend when he hadn't taken advantage of the solace to put solid, well-written prose to fresh paper or to an open hungry document on his computer. Writing in the evening with a freshly-made cocktail in hand at the desk in his writing office paled in comparison to those word-worthy dawns when the whole enormity of a man's life was entombed in a pleasant stillness, when creativity bubbled to the surface of a man so much so that to contain it would be a wild disservice.

Irving left his beloved spouse to slumber away in the campsite as he quietly trudged off from the needle-strewn flat ground that they had claimed as their temporary home. He hiked down the wooded slope, bracing his descent against the rough companionable trunks of the pines and the smooth, whitened, papery skin of the birches. The babbling song of the creek was slowly increasing in volume as the depths of the draw between the adjacent hills swallowed the writer up.

When Irving reached the side of the creek, he couldn't help but stand as still as the trees around him and observe the crystalline waterway. The golden glow of the rising sun scattered the undulating surface of the

water in a menagerie of yellowed crystals. Irving felt like he was looking into a stream of topazes. Close to the fern and grass-veiled bank of the creek, the reflective quality of the water's surface was lessened and Irving could see the darkened shapes of large trout inching about sluggishly beneath the surface. The creek, to Irving, had a youthful quality to it, a raw youngness. But, on the other hand, the youthfulness of the creek ran counter to the grain that also proclaimed its primeval agelessness in the world that the creek had been in since time had begun.

"Hello, gents," he said to the trout.

Turning about, Irving planted himself on some mossy roots of an older birch that grew along the water's edge and he leaned his broad back against the tree. Opening his pad of paper in the still sylvan air, Irving began writing some lines of fresh prose. He didn't put much thought into the story that he let flow from him in the inspired way that the morning and the woods bestowed. But sometimes inspired writing was the best writing that he did. On very idyllic mornings like the one in which Irving was currently sheltered, he had discovered long ago with the writing of his breakout novel that his higher self knew better than he *what* he needed to write and *how* he needed to write it. And so the novelist was obliged to let his higher self

take charge on that quiet peaceful morning in the woods, next to the trout creek.

It was around noon when Cecilia watched Irving's head and shoulders rise above the slope as he ascended the wooded hillside to the campsite. She knew that he had been down there at the side of the creek writing because last night, after they'd eaten some snacks and had made love tiredly in the tent, Irving had sleepily explained that he intended to hike down there to the water's edge early in the morning to get a little bit of writing done. Cecilia had spent her own morning sleeping, and when she had awoken and discovered that she was peacefully alone, she washed herself with baby wipes and got dressed. She then perused the campfire cookbook that she'd brought with for a recipe to utilize for lunch.

Cecilia's long brown locks were still braided, as they would be all weekend, and she had changed from her creamy cable-knit sweater and tights from the previous day into a pair of denim capris and a green wide-collared pullover. Part of the strap of her sports bra could be glimpsed against the lightly-freckled flesh of her shoulder. She wore a pair of running shoes, which she had begun to use less and less for the athletic purpose that they had been intended for.

"Hi, honey," said Irving happily as he climbed up onto the flat ground of the campsite, his pad and pen in hand and a joviality decorating his handsome features in the way that it always did after a morning of successful writing. "I could smell what was going on up here from down at the creek. What's for lunch?"

He went up to his wife and they kissed. Cecilia returned, "Hi, baby. Are you a hungry bear? There's pizza nachos melting up nice and gooey in the skillet. They'll be done soon. How was your writing?"

"Damn good," he answered in the smiling, almost-stoned state that he often was possessed of after a very inspired and successful session of writing.

"Good," stated Cecilia with a smile before she again kissed husband. Irving's free hand rested on the top of her bottom and he held his wife close against him as they allowed their kiss to extend beyond a mere moment. They savored the flavors of one another.

When they finally stood apart, Irving grabbed the tin mugs and the ingredients that he needed to fashion a couple of refreshing cocktails and he planted himself in one of the two camping chairs by the hot embers and heather-grey ashes of the campfire. Before him, the cast iron skillet was loaded with tortilla chips that were smothered in plenty of melting cheese, pepperoni slices, ribbons of dark red pizza sauce, and some diced red onion and green bell pepper. A dusting

of crushed red pepper topped the delicious-smelling mass.

Irving dropped a few cubes of ice into each tin mug, and then he sliced a lime in two. He squeezed a half of the lime into each mug, and then he stuffed the green, citrus, pulpy hulls into the ice and the pale, minty green juice. To finish the cocktails, he added a jigger of dry gin into each and then topped them off with fizzy club soda. Irving was stirring the rustic Gin Rickeys with his finger when Cecilia came over with a couple of paper plates and some napkins.

She carefully piled a steaming mass of oozing pizza nachos onto both plates and handed Irving his heavy plate with a napkin. When she was sitting in her camping chair next to him, he handed her a Gin Rickey. The Scotts ate their lunch with zeal and they drank their fresh cocktails throughout the meal. They carried light conversation, smiling often and laughing as much, and both Irving and Cecilia agreed that this was the best weekend that they had had in quite some time. They were losing themselves in the romantic throes of an idyllic adventure, an affair inscribed with serenity and wildness.

Time was supposed to fly when a person was having fun. That was the old saying, right? Well, for the Scotts, the day passed with a fortunate ponderousness

that was baffling because the husband and wife were having such a remarkably pleasant time that Saturday in the forest. After lunch they hiked around the surrounding area together. During their adventure Cecilia harvested some edible wild mushrooms and a few herbs that she was familiar with that she intended to use for dinner.

Irving took his wife down to the river and they had walked along the ferns and stones of the riverbank for awhile. Cecilia discovered a bird nest in a low birch limb, and in it were a trio of small, spotted eggs. They didn't know what type of bird the eggs belonged to, but they were careful to not touch or disturb the nest. Irving and Cecilia kept walking for a while longer, hand in hand and kissing occasionally, until the going became too difficult and the afternoon had ripened into a golden swell.

At suppertime, back in the campsite, Irving's mouth salivated almost uncontrollably and his soft stomach rattled with impatience at the aromas that had befallen the campsite. Cecilia had quickly cooked up in the skillet some mushrooms, butter, rosemary, sliced garlic and some shallots in a little fresh lemon juice and a bit of beef stock. The mouth-watering scent of the campfire mushrooms permeating the area made Irving quite thankful for his wife's culinary proficiency and he

marveled at her skill that was even evident in the wilderness.

They ate their meal greedily, forking every last bite of the meal into their mouths, and Irving made Cecilia and himself another down-and-dirty Gin Rickey. After dinner and their cocktails Irving opened a bottle of shandy and nursed it as his wife gathered a quilt from the tent. Cecilia sat sideways in his lap, her legs tucked up close to her body in a snuggly way, and she covered them in the warmth and security of the quilt as they watched the neon embers of the fire crackle in little eruptions of flame and sparks that illuminated the fallen twilight like magic. Irving hugged his wife close to his chest as the firelight was reflected in their glimmering eyes.

They conversed quietly for a while and then, under the privacy of the quilt, Cecilia's skilled digits unbuttoned her husband's trousers and she began to fondle him. The couple kissed deeply and passionately for many moments as Cecilia pleasured Irving. Finally, Cecilia's damp lips parted from her husband's and she whispered to him, "Come to the tent in two minutes."

When he obeyed her demand moments later, Irving found Cecilia atop their nest of blankets within the tent. She was wearing only the silken pink nightie that she had secretly stowed away in her camping pack, and she ran her attractive hands up her naked legs to

the white lace hem of the seductive garment. Her smile dripped with allurement as she slowly eased the bottom hem of her short nightie up to her waist.

"Jesus Christ," mumbled Irving in stupefied reverence. He stripped his sweater from his solid frame and crawled into the tent. Cecilia giggled playfully as her husband zipped the flap of the tent up behind him.

IV

Sunday morning dawned with a different flavor than the day before. It dawned with a melancholy for the Scotts because their camping trip was too soon coming to an end. And the bright sunny quality of the prior day had been supplanted by a grey overcast sky that absently wielded now and again a descending drizzle that was so fine that it was nearly a falling mist. The chill in the dim morning air was truly autumnal, a true prologue and sample of the season to come.

Cecilia awoke with Irving, despite his protestations that she keep on sleeping away the downtrodden morning, and she bundled up in her cable-knit sweater, her coat, tights and her boots. She climbed out of the tent with her husband and they stretched in the exhilarating coolness, observing their damp environs. And then they began to gather their items that peppered the campsite between soft, misty drizzles.

Cecilia folded and then skewered several thick slices of Applewood-smoked bacon and bell pepper chunks that she charred in the coals of their feeble campfire. As she whipped up the rustic breakfast, Irving loaded the wet camping chairs, cooler, and the quilts from within the tent into the back of their SUV. By the time that he was done, Cecilia had finished cooking the sizzling bacon and pepper skewers and handed one to her husband. They stood side by side, picking the delicious bacon and roasted peppers from their steel skewers with greasy fingers.

As she chewed, Cecilia voiced jokingly with a trace of a whine, "I don't want to go home. Can't we just live here, baby?"

"Sure, honey. We can write from anywhere, can't we? The woods are as good as Europe, right?"

They were silent for a moment longer, and then Cecilia soberly stated, "I guess we have no choice but to get used to Chet being gone. We've known it was going to happen from the moment he was born."

"I suppose so," began Irving. "It's not like he's dead or another planet or something. But it just sucks."

"Why do children have to grow up?"

"I don't know," he answered solemnly, chewing a piece of bacon. "But it sure makes me feel old. Damn old."

"I don't give a crap if *we* get old. You just keep getting handsomer with each decade, baby. But I don't want Chet to get any older. This is old enough. College age is certainly old enough, maybe too old."

"Indeed and agreed," Irving said flatly.

The pair finished up breakfast, broke down their tent, finished packing up the hatchback of their vehicle, and finally departed the wilderness. They were weary from their weekend excursion, contented at the treasures that it had blessed them with, but they were also infected with a trace of gloom because the weekend was coming to an end. They didn't use the GPS for their sojourn home, and they instead listened to the calming orchestral music that Cecilia kept her iPod loaded with.

As they drove out of the mountains and woods, Irving smoked his pipe and Cecilia ran her fingers lightly over his right hand that rested on her upper thigh. Her fingers caressed his red and white bracelet, as she was often to do. She sighed gustily. Irving glanced at his wife and he lifted the back of her hand to his lips. "I love you," he whispered.

Cecilia smiled faintly at her husband and she said to him, "I love you, too."

Hours later they had returned to the urban morass of the city that they lived in. It was early afternoon and the cloud cover and rainfall that had enveloped the forest seemed to have followed them back to their home. Hesitant rain sprayed forlornly over the city beneath the lurid sky that was encompassed with countless shades of smoky slate. They made their way into the residential landscape of the suburbs that skirted the hub of humanity, and they pulled into the garage of their suburban townhouse with simultaneous sighs. As Cecilia and Irving exited the SUV in the cool darkness of their garage, they stretched and Irving muttered, "Let's not worry about unloading all our shit right now. I'll take care of it in the morning, okay?"

Yawning, Cecilia replied, "Sounds good."

They entered their home together. Within the darkened rooms of their townhouse, chambers that were clean and empty as they had been since Chet left, they discovered that something had changed. Cecilia's hand found the soft warmth of her husband's and she whispered, "It's different, isn't it, baby?"

Irving was looking ahead into the darkness of their large living room with the scarcely-used television and leather sofa. But he found the darkness to be of a different quality than it had been when they had left for their weekend in the woods. Their home was still absent of their grown son, but the rooms had seemingly

become resigned to his absence. It seemed as though the home had accepted it and moved on over the weekend. It was an attribute that the residence shared gently then with its two middle-aged occupants.

"Yeah," he finally answered. "It *is* different."

He and his wife smiled, and their smiles were optimistic.

CAMPFIRE

It was morning, just after seven, and the June sky was blue and more glittery and bleached to the east. There was the nest of the sun. The air chimed with the luminous salt of the coming solstice.

A lacy ribbon of wind, a breeze in the final weary days of a stormy spring, whispered through the grey-green boughs of the tall stalwart ponderosa pines. But towards the forest floor, the tall emerald grasses that were like vertical splinters of enormous gemstones and the young oaks with their bright green manes stirred only a little bit. The verdant things that were low to the ground swayed softly in that final whisper of the venerable and wizened spring.

A campfire had been newly ignited that morning in a buried fire pit lined with scorched metal, and the lighting of the fire had proved to be a somewhat more arduous process than it had been in the prior dusk-swollen evening. In the morning everything had been sodden from the night before, and the fistfuls of damp pine needles that the man had collected and stuffed

alongside napkins in the spaces between the chunks of cut pine took a bit of time to get smoldering in thick acrid plumes of opaque smoke. But finally the campfire had ignited, smoke giving way to tongues of newborn flame. The fire was coaxed into dangerous life when the warmth of the morning sun was ascending betwixt the legion of pines that were to the back of the man as he sat in his blue nylon camping chair.

The man was seated before his flickering and famished construct, all red-orange and seductively swaying in the primal rhythms of heat and warmth. It was proving to be a good morning, a peaceful morning with things that are brightened and corrected. There was no day in a person's life like a day beginning and ending in the woods. Such a day, a day like the one that the man had recently awoken into, was pregnant with a slow-burning promise of contentment, of new sights and sounds and the natural glory of hours at ease and spent well. The man wished that the net cup-holder of his camping chair was filled with a bottle of cold beer. But he thought it more appropriate to wait until the sun was higher in the sky, more aware of its terrestrial constituents and their cheap vices.

The man's family, his wife and children, still slumbered within their familial dome tent. The lot of them had been late in getting to sleep. The night before, after the sun had made a concealed descent

through the thickening morass of silvery slate-colored clouds, and after a dinner of charred bratwursts and hot dogs that had been quickly and heartily consumed by the family, they had all quietly watched the flickering force of a storm slip closer in the swelling tide of dark clouds that had flowed in overhead unerringly and ominously from the east. The lightning had almost been an unending constant and the children had begun to get nervous when the distant rumble of thunder could be gleaned increasingly often from the weakening solidity of the firmament's unmarred silence. It was truly the proverbial calm before the storm.

The man's children had brought their own small dome tent, bright red and in the form of a bulbous smiling ladybug. The intention of their parents was for the children to sleep in their own diminutive tent so that the man and his wife could sleep alone in their own larger tent. The pair had planned to have some great rigorous sex after the children were asleep in the neighboring abode. The floor of the parents' tent was thinly cushioned and the air would be cooling in the darkness, but their quiet but frequent exhalations would ensure that the humidity in the tent died away slowly and not with the natural quickness promised by the coolness in the night air. The man had imagined dewy skin, moans and pleasured cries choked back behind bitten lips, but only just barely. He imagined his

wife's fair hands clutching fistfuls of their slippery nylon sleeping bags, red marks on their pained knees afterwards. But those intimate hopes had been dashed in the same manner that the man had dashed the embers of the fire with the half bottle of tepid beer that had belonged to his wife before they had all retreated to the solace and safety of the parents' tent. The man and his family still held out a weakening hope that somehow the thunderstorm would circumvent them, sparing them everything but a distant booming show of force.

However, the storm hadn't bypassed the campground. It arrived with a stark flash of crackling lightning that painted with sudden illumination the shocked and terrified faces of the man's family as though they were carved of pearlescent ivory or marble, huddled figures in the voluminous light of midday. The storm marked its entrance with a churning groan of thunder that followed a strobing flash of electricity and with a waxing deluge of driving rain.

Bookending the furious primal display of the storm, serving as both its prologue and epilogue, were tumultuous cascades of marble-sized hail that hammered at the slick nylon walls of the tent. The hail drummed the world in an all-encompassing way, granting no reprieve, as though the storm sought to batter every ant and blade of tall grass into soft

49

woodland loam. The family sedan outside was a silent victim to nature's percussive onslaught. Also victims were the trees that loomed overhead, stoic and grim, slender sylvan bodies slick with the descending rain.

Before the storm had arrived with its proboscis of hail and lightning, sound and violence, the man's wife had confided quietly to her husband with hopelessness and little dread that one of her greatest fears, possibly paramount among her jittery arsenal or trepidations, was the fear of camping in a storm. The helplessness of the situation seized itself upon her, strangling sense and courage from her in a sudden and merciless way. The man felt otherwise. He was brave and invigorated, confident, and he told his wife and children that they'd all be fine. He told them that there was nothing to fear and that they would all be safe and sound within the protective construction of the dome tent. The man had grinned when he assured his family, thunder rumbling overhead and lightning illuminating the thin walls of the tent, that all would be well.

The sky exploded overhead and the vast swathes of the hail bombarded their localized environs. The children were terrified and they covered their heads with their blankets as the man and his wife held them protectively, but not so protectively that the children would suspect the anxieties of the adults. The children cried over the sound of the natural cacophony,

and their bitter voices, angelic and light no longer but instead as strained and desperate as soldiers in a hellish firefight, exclaimed that they would rather be at home in their beds than camping.

The man's wife had entered into a state of panic. She said things that scared the children and herself, and she actively tried to pollute the entirety of the camping trip in all of their minds, even though this had only been the first night of the trip. The memories of the children were impressionable, the man knew, and he tried to keep calm, to reassure his children and his wife that the storm would quickly pass and that they would still have a grand time with the rest of their camping trip. The man reminded them all that the next day they would go swimming in the nearby lake, the wife and the children because the man didn't like to swim.

All of the man's efforts didn't hold water to the familial fear born in the thunderous breast of the storm. The wife, in her delirium, became hostile towards the husband. With resentment she attacked the man for his calmness and his confidence when the world thundered and flashed terribly. She called him insane, and she seemed to blame the turn of the weather on him. It was a common tactic for the man's wife to lash out when she felt vulnerable and ashamed of herself, when she

thought of herself as weak in any way, and the man was the most frequent target of her verbal scourge.

The man and his wife had despised one another then, and they had one of their children sleep in between them as a sort of buffer. The crashing of the storm-wracked sky and its angry ebb and flow of precipitation waned off into indiscernible droplets, and the family had finally drifted off one at a time into a restless slumber. The man suspected that he was the last to fall into the fitful fuzziness of sleep after the storm gave up on its relentless assault. His stomach was churning with an emotional magma because of the argument with his wife. Their fights caused him so much more anxiety and pain than any storm could possibly hope to achieve.

But a part of the man was cheered at the thought of waking up on the welcoming doorstep of a fresh new day, a dawn in which he could slip stealthily from the stuffy interior of the tent that was packed with sleeping bodies. He would step out into the swelling amber sigh of the morning with its crisp young air, rattled apart and rebuilt from the chaotic night before. His wife and children would be slumbering for a while longer. The promised solitude that the morning would bring was something that the man always savored, not because he didn't want to spend time with his family, but because, in solitude, the man was better able to

gather together the pieces of himself that life was apt to scatter asunder like the ashes and charred detritus of the campfire, like the wet green oak leaves that were plastered all over the exterior of the family car from the heavy rain and the hail. Every day a man that is sensitive and intelligent has to put himself back together again from the day before. Emotions and an open mind are portals by which a person can see life's ordinary brutalities and domestic barbarism.

The man's gaze ascended up the slender trunk of a young oak tree that struggled skyward across from him, beyond the crackling campfire that he had carefully crafted. His vision stopped within the rustling embrace of the apple-green foliage of the tree. In the assertive radiance of the rising sun, the healthy green of the innumerable oak leaves with their undulating rounded edges, was a startling hue, an almost alien vibrance that was nearly uncanny. Those leaves of the young tree were the greenest thing that the man could remember seeing. The man smiled at the sight.

The earthy and masculine aroma of the campfire washed over him in a way that was truly purifying, holy in the same way as the smoke that shamanistic tribesmen waved into their faces before some sort of dire struggle. The late spring breeze that morning was a caressing thing, and it pleasured the sensitive skin of the man. June was ripe, full, and mature, and it seduced

the man in the way that only a month, a singular and separate time of year, can seduce a person.

The man sat in his chair by the campfire all alone, in a communion with the flames of the fire and the heady green realm of nature that proclaimed with its silence that it was all that was wild, that which was most vividly alive. The man had another urge to pull a bottle of beer from the cooler, and that urge expanded with the sunlight to retrieving one of his cigars from the interior of the hail-dented car.

The man, intoxicated with the comforting enormity of the world, thought of childhood and youth, of bong hits and skateboarding with his friends. He thought of sex, of love and life and the rosy glow of the setting sun, of neon orange and red spread over the purple and blue bruise of the horizon like an obscene rouge. The man thought of his children, his lovely children, and he thought of his gritty days apart from them when he was a soldier in training or deployed overseas to a wasteland that was choked of verve and greenness. And the man thought of the vast indeterminate breadth of the wide world and his place within all of it, so insignificant and so very precious.

He was still smiling dreamily, contentedly, when the doorway of the tent unzipped and his wife's pale foot and shapely calf slipped out into the fresh kiss of

the spring morning. He loved her as he watched her exit into the temperate smoke-scented air that they shared.

LESSONS

The first week in May brought with it still cloudless air, humidity, and the heat of the encroaching summer. The persistent sun painted everything in a warm glow, but the shadows were left with the cool dampness of dew. It was some serious snake-finding weather. But one had to contend with the little slugs that peppered all the cooler shadowed areas that were the essential haunt of serpents.

When I was a little kid most of my summer days were consumed with thoughts of snakes. A couple cousins and I operated a "snake club" in the tool shed of our grandparents, and the rare occasions when our families would all get together were comprised of hunting for Garter snakes and gathering them, contending with their smelly defenses as we measured them and stored them in plastic buckets that we then sprinkled with grass clippings and twigs before finally letting them slither free. We took pages of notes, and even enlisted one of our younger cousins, then just a toddler, as a guard with a watergun.

The guard with a faux-firearm was essential because all youthful activities are infected with a hint of violence and barbarity. It's our training for what we are and what we see when we get older. The water gun was a tool for the desensitization of violence and the commonality of seeing the tools for violence throughout our lives in America.

As an adult, a father, I felt that it was my duty to steer my children in an alternate direction. I didn't want them desensitized to guns, to violence, and to bloodshed. I wanted those things to remain shocking to them, appalling to them. I would rather that they experience life and joy, little things that the world shares with us gently. I wanted familiarity to color. Things like nature, the sky, sunshine, rain, and love. And, yes, even snakes.

And so this fondness and kinship for snakes remained, even as my relationships with my cousins and other family members deteriorated throughout the decades. It is a fondness that also bled over into the imaginative and absorbing minds of my children. My youngest child, my four-year old boy Duncan, was currently in the throes of snake-fever and he followed me about our lush backyard that May afternoon with a red plastic pail and thick gardening gloves that my wife, Duncan's mother but my oldest child's stepmother, left sitting on our back porch more often than not.

Duncan wandered out into the flat grassy expanse of our yard, hunched over and prowling the grass for snakes. Smiling, I wandered over to the cooler mulch-covered area against our back porch where my wife grew flowers and laid slabs of flagstone decoratively. "Duncan," I said, "come over here. Let's look under this rock."

He trotted over, unruly blond hair bouncing with his footfalls, and he wiped his little nose with his grubby hand as he watched me pull a cool piece of grey flagstone up onto its side in the damp mulch. There were no snakes in the space beneath, only diminutive little bugs and worms and the small ever-present slugs that left their sticky snot-like trails wherever their painstakingly-ponderous wanderings took them.

"Dad, I don't think we have snakes."

"We do, buddy. We do. Trust me," I answered distractedly as I gently lowered the flagstone down so as not to crush the lives from the menagerie of little creatures.

I sighed when I stood up with my hands on my hips. The afternoon sunlight felt great, and I basked in it for a moment. It wasn't even summer and I already had a nice tan going. Denna, my wife, wouldn't be tanning anytime soon because she typically wore a wide-brimmed sun hat in the yard and she used copious

amounts of sunscreen. Denna *always* smelled of sunscreen and lotion.

"Dad!" shrieked Duncan suddenly, dropping his pail and pointing with both small hands to Denna's yellow tulips in the bed of mulch bordering our porch.

I crouched next to flowers and slammed my quick palm down over a coiled Garter snake. It was a small one, young, with twin yellow-orange stripes running parallel to one another down its dark back. And it was instantly dripping in odorous waste, its defense mechanism, as I lifted it up so that Duncan could observe the harmless serpent. Its taffy-pink tongue swept in and out of its mouth and my son stroked the dry scales of its head a bit roughly. "Is it sick?" Duncan asked concernedly. "It smells sick."

"Nope. He's not sick. They just smell gross when they get scared. Sometimes that will scare bad animals away."

"Bad animals like Hexer," stated Duncan forlornly. He was referring to our black cat who had brought a couple dead snakes to our front door already in the last couple weeks.

"Yep. But it doesn't really work against Hexer, does it, buddy?"

"Nope. He's *so* mean," said Duncan, and then he quietly added, "I hate him."

I tussled Duncan's hair and remedied, "Oh, Duncan, don't say 'hate'. You don't *hate* Hexer. He's just doing what he thinks cats are supposed to do. He's not really a bad animal."

Duncan and I were about to move on to another area when Denna came out onto the back porch and called out, "Sweetheart, your daughter's home. She had a problem at school."

"Keep hunting, buddy. I'll be back soon," I told Duncan, patting his narrow shoulder as I walked away. Denna must have seen the concern on my face as I approached the stairs that led up onto the back porch, and she held up her hands in a calming way.

"It's not that bad, Ross. Harper's not in trouble or anything. The principal just talked to me when I picked her up from school. He told me what happened."

"Well, what happened?" I inquired when I climbed the stairs and moved past Denna into the house. She smelled of the coming summer, lotion and sunscreen, and her body was warm as I moved past it.

"It was a situation with another girl in class. I think it was another 'bully' situation."

"God damn it. That shit fucking pisses me off," I growled, as I hesitated near the doorway, still communicating with my wife.

"Why don't you go talk to her about it, sweetheart?"

I nodded tersely and went to Harper's bedroom. The door was closed. She was only fourteen years old, a freshman in high school, and had identified as transgendered for about half of her life. At eight or nine she had told Denna and I, and her mother as well, that she felt like she was a boy inside. We became very defensive as parents at that point, keeping a too-wary eye out for any slight against our vulnerable daughter and her confusion about her body. We still referred to her as a female and she hadn't yet protested that point, but Denna and I both expected Harper to completely assume a masculine identity once she was done with high school.

Ever since she had started high school in the fall of last year, the bullying situation seemed to have gotten worse for Harper. The culprits were some of the females in her class. Most of Harper's friends were boys that skateboarded, boys that she didn't view in a romantic light at all but instead viewed as masculine contemporaries that shared her same taste in hobbies, dress, and the obnoxious deathcore metal music that Harper had playing in her room all the time. I taught Harper to skateboard at a very young age, and she had been in love with it ever since.

"Harper, can I come in?" I asked as I knocked on her door.

"Sure."

When I entered her room, a bit of a messy space with plenty of posters on the walls of skateboarders and deathcore bands, Harper was sitting on the side of her bed unwinding the cord of her earbuds that were plugged into her smartphone. She was short and skinny, like I was when I was a kid, and she had her hair cut short on a boyish way. Much to her constant chagrin, though, her angular face and beautiful blue eyes were unavoidably feminine. She was wearing skinny black jeans, flat-soled skateboarding shoes, and a black shirt with an indiscernible band logo on the chest.

She was silent, and she wouldn't look at me as she toiled with her electronics, but I finally asked, "Denna said something happened at school?"

Harper just sighed heavily.

"What happened?"

Harper began, still not looking at me, "It was that cunt Molly Joseph again, Dad. I hope she gets hit by a train. Like, for real."

Cringing inwardly at the vicious adjective that Harper had bestowed upon Molly Joseph, I sighed and sat down at the end of my daughter's bed. I just corrected my son for saying 'hate' and here was my daughter dropping the c-bomb. Scratching my jaw, I said, "Please cool it, and watch your mouth. Will you tell me what happened, Harper?"

With a huff she dropped her smartphone and her tangle of earbuds to the carpeted floor that was strewn with discarded clothing, her tattered and beaten skateboard, and scattered tools and skateboarding-related items such as bearings, a screwdriver, and a forgotten urethane wheel here and there. "Molly has been relentless this week."

"More so than usual?"

"Yes. Today, all during English she was saying things about my hair and clothes and stuff. That really doesn't bother me, you know? But then she called me a 'lesbo'. Dad, I just flipped."

My back was still to her, Harper sitting on the side of her bed and me sitting on the end of her bed, facing the door to her room. "What did you do?"

Harper laughed feebly through her little upturned nose and explained, "I got up, turned around and flipped her desk backwards."

I turned and looked at her over my shoulder with an eyebrow raised in surprise, and I asked incredulously, "With her in it?"

"Yep. Her desk flipped backwards and she smacked into the floor," answered Harper. She snorted humorously through her nose and continued, "Her hair is long, and it got caught between the back of her chair and the floor because she was in the chair, you know?

Her book and papers and stuff that were on the top of her desk slid back and hit her in the neck and shoulder."

"Holy shit!" I exclaimed. "That's crazy, honey! That was probably way out of line, right?"

"I know, Dad! Jesus. I don't need to hear it from you, too. I've heard it from everyone else. I know I fucked up, okay? Miss Werner was furious and sent me to Principal Faulk's office. He chewed me out, and then after school Denna bitched me out. I know I shouldn't have flipped out, but I just had enough, Dad. Do you get it, that I've had enough?"

I was silent for a moment in her dimly-lit bedroom, sitting on the end of her bed. It was disturbing to think of my kind, small-statured daughter being violent to another teenage girl. And I suddenly questioned my wisdom at neglecting to include things like violence and anger among the more peaceful lessons that I endeavored to show my children. Was I robbing them of valuable lessons by shielding them from the darkness of the world? I quietly answered, "I know, Harper. I know."

With a sigh, I fell back then and laid down on my back on my daughter's bed, my feet still resting on the floor. Harper laid back then too, perpendicular to me, and the back of her boyish head rested on my chest. "I'm just sick of all of it, Dad. Sometimes I wish that I was just a liar and a fake. I could act like the girl that

everyone thinks that I should be instead of the person that I actually feel like."

"Fuck them. Fuck anyone that wants you to change, honey.

She instantly rebutted, "That's easy for you to say, Dad. But you have no idea what it's like every day. Kids are assholes. You have no idea what it's like to be me. Can you imagine if tomorrow you had boobs and girl parts, and everyone expected you to grow your hair out and wear dresses or whatever? But inside you were still yourself; a boy?"

I didn't answer for awhile, really trying to imagine that frustration and agony, and I finally answered, "No. I can't."

Harper exhaled loudly in a way that stated, *I told you!*

A moment later I inquired quietly, "What do you want to do?"

She knew that I spoke not of what she wanted to do in that moment, but instead about what she wanted to do about her life, all of our lives. What did she *need* in order to thrive? My intelligent and unique daughter knew exactly what my simple statement meant and she answered passionately, "I want to leave here! This place is so small and close-minded. It's not healthy for a family like us. We're too different. We don't do anything normal. Why can't you buy a truck

and go hunting all the time and drink canned beer? Why can't we start going to church or something? If we did some of that crap that they do around here, then maybe we wouldn't stand out so much. Maybe *I* wouldn't stand out so much."

"What? So you want us to go to church?" I asked with a smirk. "You want me to kill a deer?"

A little frustrated, she answered, "God, Dad, I don't know! I just can't stand this. Why in the hell are we here when we could be anywhere else, somewhere bigger and less full of rednecks and bigots? Why'd we come here from Denver? I'd feel a lot safer there. Do you know that yesterday I saw four guys with pistols at their hips at the grocery store? At the *grocery store*! Why in the hell do people need guns to go grocery shopping in this small town?"

Smirking, I answered, "They think that the guns will protect them from a dangerous person or a terrorist or something."

"A *terrorist*?" Harper echoed incredulously. "It was a store full of families. Those idiots with their guns just made *themselves* the dangerous people."

"I agree. That's what this place is like though. A lot of places in America have become like this," I explained to my daughter. Then I answered her initial inquiry about why we'd moved, "You know why we

came here, Harper. Your grandpa was sick, and I had to take over the newspaper."

She lifted her head quickly off of my chest and turned to look me in the face. "Dad, Grandpa's dead now. He's been dead for like two years! Can't we get the hell out of here?"

"It's not that easy. What would I do with the paper?"

Her head crashed back down on my chest as if it were a pillow. I barely had time to tense up to absorb the impact. Harper said defeatedly, "I don't know. Sell it. Sell to someone and let's get out of here. You can go back to writing and being a teacher. And I know Denna would love to go back to Denver. You know she misses it, Dad. And I don't want Duncan to grow up to be an ignorant hick like the people here. I don't want him to start school here."

"What about you?"

"If we were somewhere else I could actually *enjoy* my high school experience instead of dreading it every day."

"Harper," I began, running my fingers through her thick short hair, "ignorant people are everywhere, even in the city. Your whole life, people will judge you just like they judge me and everyone else. That's what people do. You did it yourself, calling them 'hicks' and 'rednecks'."

Harper was silent for a moment, but then she finally said a bit sheepishly, "Well, if the shoe fits ..."

We both chuckled quietly. And afterwards we both sighed and laid there in the golden afternoon light that leaked into her small chamber from the space between the dark curtains. "I promise something will change, Harper. I don't know if it's us moving back to Denver, or just Denna and I talking to this girl's parents or whatever. But I promise that something will change."

Harper didn't answer. I knew that what I said wasn't the response that she was entirely banking on. I heard Denna joyfully cry out something indiscernible outside, and then I heard Duncan's chiming laughter in the yard. He had probably already forgotten about looking for snakes. Coupled with the yellowed afternoon glow and my daughter's head on my chest, my fingers tangling in her hair and running along her hidden scalp, I felt very warm and very happy.

I hoped that the happiness that I felt deep in my breast would rise up from me like the little motes of dust that were visible in the rich radiance clefting into Harper's bedroom. And I hoped that my happiness would soak into my daughter and warm her in the way that I was warmed. We sang a duet together with the long rhythms of our breathing.

"Do you want to go skate for a little bit with me before dinner?" I asked, still running my fingers through

her hair. I couldn't believe, in that moment, that this young teenage woman, this smart and melancholy girl, was my daughter. As I caressed her head, I felt a marvelous and overwhelming fortune for being her father and I felt so proud of Harper.

"Sure," she finally answered. "I landed a switch heelflip today after lunch. Let me show you. I think I can land it again."

THE SHOE BOX

To keep his thin hands from shaking, Olly Black clenched the sides of the cardboard shoe box that rested on his lap. His stomach was on fire with nervousness and anxiety and his heart felt as though it fluttered with uncertainty. His chest was in pain from holding his breath, a nervous habit of his, and his mouth was uncomfortably dry.

The young man, only twenty-five years old, sat alone on a wooden bench in the grass at Downs Park, east of Baltimore, Maryland. He stared out over the blue-brown waters of the northern Chesapeake Bay that lay beneath an overcast grey sky heralding an early summer rain. A large white vessel, a cruise ship or something from the looks of it, coasted slowly southward out in the heart of the bay across the water from Olly's bench. He wished that he was on that ship, among the somewhat-relaxed populace of the vessel that likely had their fingers crossed that their cruise ship wasn't the next to offer up some terrible disgusting mishap on the high seas. Mishap or not, *that* situation

would have been preferable to the one in which Olly currently found himself firmly entrenched.

Olly Black was a writer, a novelist of small localized repute. Between sales royalties, book-signing profits, and advances from his publisher, Olly's writing career made just enough to pay rent and utilities at his small rental near Downs Park. Olly's three short novels of contemporary romantic literature that all featured dramatic feel-good stories centered around the Chesapeake Bay were known and well-read among local book clubs and reading groups in Baltimore and its surrounding satellite communities. And he'd amassed a small force of loyal local readers that were largely middle-aged, married women with a penchant for romantic fiction. The makeup of his fan base was attested to by the makeup of the attendees of his local book-signings, which were relatively frequent. He usually did about one signing a month.

But constructing and coloring the differing facets of Olly's life, more than even his writing, was the death of his marriage. That's how he viewed his life anyways. His writing felt as if it were only his shadow, but his flesh and his blood were constructed of his marriage to Amber and their painfully-recent divorce. That earth-shattering event was the most evident construct in his life, and it consumed him unmercifully. It was epic in scope and significance and in its wake Olly was left in a

grey desolate world that was aimless and without creativity, imagination or his beloved muse. Amber, his gorgeous Amber Black, had always been his muse, and he thought that she always would be until he could no longer lift a pen or press a key to write. He'd been devastatingly wrong.

Olly wasn't sure when Amber had fallen out of love with him, but he hoped that it had been a relatively recent turn of heart in this relationship. He hoped that it hadn't been years ago in the dawn of their marriage, when they were both twenty-one, that Amber had decided that Olly and his frustrating career were a bore. He hoped that his last two novels, the pair that he wrote after he was a married man as opposed to his debut that he wrote just out of high school, weren't dedicated to Amber under false pretenses. Just the idea of it made him feel foolish and played. It made him feel that his career as a romantic novelist was a sham.

What could he, a man whom the love of his life had suddenly abandoned, know at all about romance and the intricate musings of the human heart? It made Olly question it all. Maybe it wasn't just him, but all men. What could *any* man hope to know of the fragility of the human heart? Its secrets were uncovered only through the cracks that marred its surface after heartbreak, when it was already too late.

He wasn't sure what he was going to do about his rental home now that Amber had moved out and divorced him. Her paychecks as a nurse at a busy Baltimore hospital brought in far more than his books did, and with their finances combined he'd never had to worry about doing anything other than writing romantic fiction and being solely an author, fueling his creative craft with the golden radiance of his beloved wife and muse. That was out of the window now, abducted by the cold stormy spring a few months ago. Olly barely had money left to eat after paying the bills. His muse was vanished like the sun at midnight, and he was left abandoned and cold and alone in a grey ashen world without her.

Downs Park and the waters of the Chesapeake Bay used to bring him such joy and pleasure, such inspiration, but now the waters seemed far colder and angry. They seemed aloof and uncaring, more primeval and treacherous. The bench felt uncomfortable and rigid, painfully artificial. And the summer wind that blew into his face, carrying with it the earthy smell of rain and the salty scent of the water, was chilly and its seasoning was bitter and distasteful to the novelist. The whole world was ominous and antagonistic.

Olly's coppery red hair was cut short and dark reddish whiskers coated his jaw and chin and the area between his lips and his nose, not from any aim to grow

a beard or appear rugged but from a general disinterest in maintaining the upkeep of his experience. The man's face was thin and drawn, freckled, and he thought of himself as pretty unremarkable in appearance. Sometimes he was sure that he was even unattractive. He was too thin, too pale. And Olly was not successful enough, and he endeavored in a profession that American ignorance was killing.

He'd thrown on a pair of slim khaki pants, a pair of running shoes that he'd not used for their intended purpose since the quick divorce proceedings had gotten underway that spring, and a light blue button-up shirt that was un-tucked and its sleeves were rolled up his narrow arms to his elbows. In the fresh and terrible newness of new-found loneliness Olly's dark blue-green eyes, a hue of teal, were desperate and panicked behind the lenses of his black-rimmed glasses, and they were also bloodshot and tired from lack of sleep and from regular and unpredictable bouts of weeping.

He looked down at the shoe box clutched desperately in his hands and he sighed shakily in a manner that shuddered out ghostly between his parted teeth, as it was some sort of delicate death rattle. This was it. The contents of the box were the final traces of Amber that Olly had rummaged up for her in their rental … his rental. When she arrived at their favorite bench in Downs Park and took it away from him, Olly

knew that she was going to be out of his life forever. This was the end, and he knew it. He was terrified. He imagined that this is what it felt like right before committing suicide or as you were strapped to a clinically-sterilized table before a lethal injection.

And then, there she was. Her honey blond hair was shoulder-length and silky, and it flowed like golden serpents in the breeze as she walked towards him, a medusa. Her pristine fair face, dusted as it was with a faint coating of freckles and a gentle rosy tint, was grim in a pure angelic manner that didn't diminish her beauty the slightest. She wore jeans, stylish brown boots, and a long loose black shirt under a violet knitted cardigan. She appeared severe, humorless, and extremely beautiful in her new terrible manner. She was his angel of death.

Olly was never quite sure how he had been luckily enough to garner the attentions of Amber Miller. She was so obviously out of his league. But Amber had always told him that his debut novel, she'd read it when she had first enrolled in nursing school when she was nineteen, had shown her what true love really was. Olly was sure now, that she was lying. That line sounded ridiculous and false when he said it to himself internally nowadays. Was every sweet and lovely thing that Amber had ever uttered to him nothing more than a lie?

He'd met her at his first book-signing, and that meeting quickly led to dinner, an intense romance, and then on to an engagement. A wedding finally followed when they were twenty-one years old. It was Olly's dream come true. The rose-tinted dreams of every hopelessly romantic writer had been fulfilled. But then those dreams had been completely shattered, ground into the stones by the hard heel of a bitter and loveless reality.

Olly had always thought the universe had made a mistake by allowing the skinny, pale, soft-spoken writer to become the beacon that drew the attentions of a beautiful and intelligent, goal-oriented woman. Now it seemed to Olly Black, that moment in late June alone on the bench in Downs Park with a shoe box in his lap, that the universe had discovered its error and it had snatched love and bliss quickly and handedly away from him. Some sort of karmic balance had swung back into place, isolating the unremarkable novelist.

He stood shakily and awkwardly from the bench at her approach and he said in a voice possessed of equal parts false cheeriness and meekness, "Hi, Amber."

She lifted a palm lazily in greeting, and when Amber reached Olly in front of the bench, with the waters of the Chesapeake Bay distant and tempestuous

a short walk to the east, she said, "Hey, Olly. How are you?"

She asked the question reflexively and without thinking about it. She didn't really care how he was. To Amber, Olly was already a ghost of her past that was already forgotten. But to Olly, the inquiry signified genuine concern from the woman that he still considered his soulmate. The poor fool actually dared to hope.

He swallowed a lump in his throat and answered, "I'm not good, Amber. I'm not good at all. I miss you so much."

She scoffed in frustration. "Olly, it's done with. Please don't say things like that. We're divorced now. You're just going to complicate things."

She crossed her arms and turned her fierce gaze out over the waters of the Chesapeake Bay. Olly looked down in forlorn anguish, box still clutched in his white digits, and he responded quietly, "I know. But I can't take it, Amber."

"What, Olly? I can't hear you."

He looked up at her, though she wasn't even looking at him, and he repeated, "I can't take it, Amber. You're my everything. I can't write without you."

"Then you won't write," she answered coldly.

"I can't live without you."

"Then," she began, turning her piercing blue eyes to him like the double barrels of a loaded shotgun, "you won't *live*."

He couldn't even answer or respond to such a cold and callous statement. Tears ran in quick sudden rivulets down Olly's sunken cheeks. Finally, he inquired in a voice broken by sorrow, "How can you be so fucking cruel? I've never done *anything* but love you, but worship you."

Anger roared in those blue eyes of hers and she exclaimed, "That wasn't enough, Olly! Not at all enough! You needed to do more than love me. Your love and your books provided our marriage nothing. Your love wasn't enough to let us go to Paris or London like we always wanted to, like you *always* promised me. Your love wasn't enough to get us out of that rental and into a house to call our own. Your love wasn't enough to get us cars that were worth a damn. Your money was shit. Maybe you should have gotten a better publisher that could really market your work to a wider audience. Maybe you could've been a bit more proactive. Or maybe you could've left your immature author dreams behind and gotten a real goddamn job like me and like everyone else. You aren't a child and I certainly don't have to be your mother anymore."

Olly was again speechless and he looked down, wreathed in shame at her cruel, hot words. Amber

scoffed again and finally said, "Just give me my things, and you'll never have to see me or hear my bitchy words again. I promise."

Wordlessly, Olly extended the shoe box out to her with his two arms, and she took it roughly from him. "Bye, Olly. I hope you find someone that thinks that love is enough. Because that's all you have to offer."

At that, Amber turned on her heel and walked quickly back the way in which she'd come. And Olly knew that his ex-wife was walking out of his life for good. They had no debts, no assets, and no children tying them together. It was a clean quick break, but that didn't lessen the excruciating pain of it for Olly Black. Tears streamed down his cheeks openly as he watched Amber diminish, shrinking away from his vision and from his life. And with her went the radiance, the inspiration, and all the light of the world and of his life.

The world that was left to Olly felt like a tomb.

Then it started to rain.

THIRD DATE

She poured three spoonfuls of sugar on the thin wheel of lemon that drifted on the top of her glass of iced tea, and then she pushed the yellow slice of citrus down to the bottom of the glass. When it was forced down beneath the ice cubes, she stirred her cold drink with the straw and then she brought the straw to her pink-painted lips. Iced tea and lemon couldn't quell all of Lynn's butterflies, but it certainly didn't hurt any.

Lynn Fleck was a Korean-American in her mid-twenties. She was born in South Korea but was adopted by wealthy Americans from Pennsylvania when she was still a toddler. Lynn's black hair was cropped into a chunky pixie cut that flattered the broad planes of her Asian face. She wore understated makeup in soft hues that matched the pale pink strapless sundress she had chosen for her outfit on that hot day.

Finch Pepper, the older man that she had been seeing, was still inside his quaint home rummaging around for a book that he had promised to show Lynn. Finch owned a single-story home with dark brown

shingles and pastel pink siding, and it was located in the sunny, green countryside outside of Harrisburg, Pennsylvania. Lynn was sitting at a little iron table in the backyard. Her eyes spotted the fuzzy yellow and black body of a busy bumblebee that maneuvered loudly past the table and out over the lawn.

Finch's painting studio stood on the far side of the yard, and yellow tulips grew healthily in planters at the base of the studio's walls. Lynn had been quite impressed when she discovered that the man with whom she had gone on a blind date with in the city was, in fact, a successful painter. He had, actually, informed Lynn that the entirety of his income came from his art.

Their first meeting had been a blind date that was set up by a mutual friend. That first date had went surprisingly well, and for their second date Finch had asked Lynn to accompany him to an art show and dinner. His own abstract oil paintings had been on display at the show, and Finch had seemed both excited and nervous to have Lynn look upon his work. Lynn worked as a hair stylist and Finch recognized that what she did with hair was a creative art in its own right. Thus her opinion of his creativity carried some weight.

Lynn also suspected that Finch had a crush on her as well, and that he sought to impress her.

A large cream-colored umbrella blossomed from the center of the outdoor table and it dropped a circle

of cool shade upon Lynn, shielding her fair Korean skin from the summer glare. The tabletop was adorned only with her glass of iced tea that was sweating in the heat and a little bowl of sugar with a small serving spoon that Finch had brought out with them when they'd gone outside to talk and drink tea in the gorgeous weather. This was her first time being at his home.

"I found it," spoke Finch's clear voice as the slender, handsome man in khaki trousers and an un-tucked light yellow seersucker shirt stepped from the backdoor of his modest home with a hardcover book in one hand and a tall glass of iced tea in the other. The sleeves of his airy button front shirt were rolled up to his elbows and the first few buttons of the shirt were undone, revealing the lightly-tanned contours of his collarbone and throat. His tall angular face was clean-shaven, and his green eyes were bright and lively as he strode towards Lynn.

When Finch sat down, smiling as he seemed to usually be doing in her company, he slid the book across the table to Lynn and took a long drink of iced tea. She took the book gently in her hands and examined the book jacket that shielded the cover. It was a book in great condition but the dark coloration of the edges of the pages and the antiqued tones upon the white book jacket proclaimed it as several decades old. "Wow," said Lynn in true fascination. "It's beautiful."

"A first edition of *In Cold Blood*. Signed by Mr. Capote himself. I bought it online," explained Finch.

Lynn had mentioned on their first date that her favorite book was *Breakfast at Tiffany's*. However, that novella had been the only book of Truman Capote's that she had read. Finch was thrilled to learn the identity of Lynn's favorite novel because Capote happened to be his favorite writer, and he had been quite eager to show her the signed first edition of what Finch considered the author's best work.

Very delicately, Lynn opened the book to the title page and ran the soft tips of her fingers over Truman Capote's signature. "It's amazing, Finch. I bet it was pricey."

Finch chuckled lightly and returned, "Yeah. I paid a few thousand for it. I'm not sure if it was a sensible investment of my money. But I just really love the book."

"What do you love so much about Truman Capote's writing?" Lynn inquired.

"Well, I was born the same month and year that he died. I think we were both alive on earth for exactly one week. I can't remember if I found that factoid out first, before I read any of his work. Or if I read a story of his first and then discovered that fact. But I feel like he and I have a bond. I feel connected to him in a way. I

would have loved to shoot the breeze with him for a while."

"Well, I'm going to have to get a copy of this to read."

Finch furrowed his brow and gestured absently towards the expensive literary find that Lynn held in her lovely well-manicured hands. "Don't waste your money on a new copy, Lynn. Just take that one home with you."

"What?" stated Lynn in genuine disbelief. "I wouldn't dare take this home with me. I'd accidentally rip the book jacket or spill soup on his signature or something. I wouldn't trust anyone with this book," she went on to explain as she eased the covers closed and set the book gingerly down on the tabletop. "I especially wouldn't trust *me* with it."

Finch laughed again and said, "I insist, Lynn. I trust you. Don't worry about it."

"No, that's the problem. You might trust me, but *I* don't trust me."

They both chuckled at Lynn's humorous, self-deprecating remark. Finch responded, "I'm not going to force you to take it with. If you won't take it with you to read, then you can read some of it whenever you're here. Sound like a plan?"

"That sounds nice," Lynn replied. She felt another rosy swell of butterflies in her tummy at the

notion of making repeated visits out here to Finch Pepper's home in the country. She had a sudden flash of what their relationship could be like in month or two. The future suddenly excited her.

They drank some more tea and sat in a brief silence that was littered with threads of birdsong. "Your place is so lovely, Finch," stated Lynn. "I love it out here."

"Well, you're free to come back whenever you want. I love spending time with you."

Lynn felt heat in her cheeks at Finch's statement and she hoped that her blush wasn't too evident. Softly, she smiled and returned, "I love spending time with you too."

Finch returned her smile and laid his hand palm-up on the top of *In Cold Blood*. Lynn lowered her small hand on top of his and they held hands like that for a moment, gazing contentedly at one another. "Are you ready for lunch? Do you want to eat out here or inside?"

"Inside if we can," Lynn answered. "It's getting pretty hot."

They slid their hands apart and grabbed their drinks, and Finch grabbed his old expensive book. They made their way across the yard to the back door, the chirping patterns of birds and the buzzing of bumblebees heralding their departure. The air within

the home was cool and fresh and the rooms comprising the interior were clean and dimly-lit. Artwork, some of which was Finch's own, adorned every wall that Lynn could see. He took her to his dining room, and he motioned for her to have a seat at his circular table before he pulled aside some curtains that covered the dining room window. It was a large, clean window that flooded the room with natural light, and a diamond of light green glass adorned the center of the window. Lynn saw the splash of luminescent green that the little pane of glass spilled upon the surface of the table.

"I'll be right back. Make yourself at home," said Finch, and he went into the neighboring kitchen to gather their lunch.

Lynn sat there awkwardly for a moment, fussed with her shortly-cropped hair, and reiterated again, "I love your place."

"Thanks," responded Finch from the kitchen. He returned to the dining room a moment later carrying two small bowls, forks and a large olive wood bowl full of garden salad. He set a plate and fork before Lynn and at the empty spot at the round table next to her. And then he set the serving bowl of salad in the center of the table. "Does ranch work for you?"

"Sure."

"What about ground pepper?"

Lynn answered, "Sounds good."

A minute later Finch returned to the dining room with a pepper grinder and a bottle of ranch dressing. The pair piled some salad into their bowls and dripped dressing over the top before grinding some pepper in conclusion. They ate their light lunch with relish, conversing easily and closely and with a blooming familiarity.

When Finch took a drink of tea, washing down a mouthful of salad, he afterward asked Lynn, "So, tell me something else about yourself. Something I don't know."

Lynn raised an eyebrow and smirked. "Like what?"

"I don't know. Anything."

"You first," Lynn rebutted before she took a bite of salad.

"Okay. Well, ... I love the sound of church bells but I'm not religious at all. And here's another one for you; my favorite color is pink."

"Pink? Really?" returned Lynn.

"You bet. Best color there is. Seeing something pink is, for me, like instant relaxation and happiness."

Lynn smiled again and stated, "Well, I suppose that explains the house color."

"Damn right," replied Finch, grinning boyishly. "You still haven't told me something about yourself."

"Oh, my bad," she joked. "Let's see here. Um, well, my number one fear is probably being abducted by aliens."

"Abducted by aliens? I'd say that's a legit fear."

Lynn laughed, and so did Finch. When they were done eating, Finch asked, "Would you like to see my studio?"

"I'd be honored."

The artist led Lynn back out to the yard, and they crossed the lawn to the studio in the very back. The structure was halfway nestled in a thicket of young oaks that divided Finch's property from his neighbor's land. He unlocked it with a key from his pocket and pulled open the weathered wooden door.

When they entered the interior of the studio Lynn almost coughed from the smell of dust, but it wasn't an uncomfortable environment. It was just old. Finch illuminated the space by flicking up a light switch beside the door. The floor was weathered hardwood and the boards were spotted in various colors of paint. A large easel stood in the corner and canvases of various sizes leaned against each wall. Some shelving was against the far wall, and it held jars of brushes and innumerable tubes of oil paint. A heavily-used paint palette leaned against a leg of the easel, and Lynn thought that the smears of layered paint upon the

wooden palette appeared to be an abstract painting of sorts.

"Wow! This is a great old space, Finch. So this is where the magic happens," remarked Lynn.

"I suppose so," he returned. "It's probably not that much to look at, but this is one of my favorite places ever. This studio is kind of important to me. Just coming in here fills my mind and my world with color. I get *so* creative."

As Finch explained this, he had his hands on his hips and was looking around in appreciation at his studio's interior. Lynn was standing next to him, and felt butterflies again. She had a notion to make a move, but she didn't know if that would be too forward. It's not like she was that romantically conservative or something. Lynn was certainly not a prude. She guessed that she was so nervous because she really *really* liked Finch Pepper.

She turned towards him and put her hand gently on his muscular abdomen. Finch looked towards her, and Lynn leaned into him and pressed her pink lips against his partially-opened mouth. They began kissing, and very quickly the intensity of the kiss increased. Their arms wrapped around one another.

Lynn hadn't meant for her kiss to go any further than that, but now that it had started she felt like a helpless observer to the flame of passion that burned

hotter and hotter. With a sudden electrifying surge of anxiety and lust, Lynn knew that there was no stopping what she'd unleashed. Before she really knew what she was doing, Lynn was unbuttoning the front of Finch's seersucker shirt, revealing the lithe muscular torso beneath.

They were still kissing deeply as Finch's agile hands slid up the smooth length of Lynn's upper arms to her bare shoulders. And then, slowly and purposefully, his hands slid down the front of her shoulders to the elastic hem at the top of her pink, strapless sundress. He eased his fingertips between the soft resistance of the hem and the warm flesh of Lynn's upper breasts, and then he pulled the top of the dress down. Lynn's rotund breasts were revealed, and Finch pulled her into him as they continued to kiss.

She worked at the belt of his pants, but then Finch pulled his wet lips from her own. "Wait, Lynn. Let's go inside. There's nowhere to really … do it in here."

Her eyes looked desperately and very hungrily up into his and she nodded. "Okay," she whispered.

She barely had time to cover her breasts back up as he grabbed her by the arm and marched her from the studio, leaving the door open. Finch led Lynn hastily across the lawn, and when they entered the house he took her to his cool, dark bedroom. They started kissing

again in a lascivious way that was almost primal as they ardently removed every article of each other's clothing. When Finch knelt down on the carpeted floor to slide Lynn's delicate panties of pale yellow lace down her naked legs, she breathed heavily through her slightly-parted lips and slid her fingers through his short, messy, brown hair.

When they were both completely nude, Finch stood back up and they wrapped their arms around each other. He collapsed backwards onto the bed, pulling Lynn on top of him. In the slivers of early afternoon radiance that broke around the edges of the closed curtains of the bedroom window, Lynn and Finch made love, quickly and vigorously.

When it was over they laid side-by-side, facing one another. Lynn was extremely satisfied and her body felt heavy and sleepy. Finch's hand eased Lynn's short bangs out of her eyes and he smiled at her. She smiled back with warmth and pleasure.

"That was ... perfect," Finch said contentedly as his hand slid down the side of her face, down her neck, over one of her breasts, and to the wider curve of her hip. "How do you feel?"

Lynn practically purred and answered, "I feel *so* satisfied."

"Good," he remarked. A moment later he asked with evident hopefulness, "Do you want to stay the night?"

Lynn didn't directly answer Finch, but she inquired, "Do you think that was too fast? This is only our third date."

Finch raised his eyebrows thoughtfully and shrugged. He rolled over onto his back, and Lynn draped an arm, a leg, and a breast upon him. He answered, "Lynn, I would have done this on our blind date if it would have been socially-acceptable. Pretty much right away, I was crushing on you quite hard. You're funny, you're smart, you're gorgeous-"

"And my favorite book is *Breakfast at Tiffany's*," Lynn interrupted with a smirk.

Finch chuckled and continued, "Yes, indeed. An appreciation for good literature goes a long way with me."

"So you're okay with all this?" Lynn asked, her small soft hand caressing Finch's bare chest.

Smiling, he answered, "I'm more than okay, Lynn. So ... do you want to stay over? Tomorrow's Saturday. Do you have anything going on?"

Lynn leaned forward and kissed Finch's cheek. "I don't have a thing going on this weekend," she whispered when her lips left his cheekbone. "I think I do want to stay the night."

THE SECRET STORY
OF
SHANNON HAWTHORNE
A Novelette in Five Parts

I

The evening sky was flushed with a smear of scarlet, a subtle wound that timidly hued the face of the darkening air. The air was evidently coy because of its nakedness, an ancient and vast nudity that revealed to the earth when the last dry, dead leaf had carelessly fallen away from the branch that had borne it aloft since spring.

There were few things in all of the world that were as sorrowful and as painfully beautiful as the final exhalation of late autumn in New England. The landscape was dead, colors having darkened and blended into an indiscernible muddled tone, and a sterling stillness claimed sovereignty over the cold sky. The modest world, shamed and broken upon the wheel

of irredeemable time, was begging to cover itself up with the first obfuscating snows of winter.

Eyes glistened faintly upon a black silhouette of a person in the falling light. It was a thin figure of indeterminate gender robed in a bulky coat that warded off the autumnal chill. Those eyes observed the cold sky that grew voluptuously red before the early darkness of the night engulfed the idyllic landscape. They observed the biting, hollow sky and the bare, rattling limbs of the trees that extended their gnarled fingers into the cold, crystalline ether of early December.

The featureless face of the darkened silhouette and its wet eyes turned to somberly take in the surrounding environs. A shadowy arm ascended to the obscured face of the figure a moment before the orange ember of a cigarette brightened into a singular point of glowing warmth. The sagging planes and wrinkled crannies of an aged face were highlighted dimly and briefly in feeble orange light. And then the arm fell, and the ember fell along with it, tracing a glowing trail through the air. A chilling gust slithered by, and upon the wind a ribbon of dark smoke slid away from the silhouette with a soft sigh that seasoned the fading dusk.

Then the dark silhouette in the coat, and the elderly woman that it tightly cloaked, turned from the

crisp autumn panorama. The view that she turned away from was forged of a collage of black empty trees, a cold hint of icy mist rising from the shadowed vales and dark copses of the countryside, and the piercingly-cold and empty sky that had by then faded from its short-lived crimson blush that had bloomed in the west to a sort of scab-colored pall that was only barely discernible. The darkness of the sky was nearly inseparable from the black trees and hills that were scattered across the landscape like the innumerable legions of fallen oak and maple leaves that were heaped to rot or be burnt. The sight was tragic, but it was also darkly bewitching. It was poignant.

The darkness within which the woman existed was spiced with the late autumnal notes of chimney smoke and dead, brittle, sylvan refuse. The frosty air was writing an epilogue to the season of rot before the snows, by then already late in their arrival, bespelled the picturesque forms of rural New England with their luminous white enchantment. The firmament was, at that time, proclaiming with a ponderous melancholy the brief era of bleakness, of death. It described a silent emptiness that was uniformly colored in tattered robes of brown, burgundy and grey. The pitch of the seasonal prose had increased to the doom-ridden crescendo of autumn's conclusion.

She strode alone as, overhead, the scab-colored sky collapsed steadily in on itself to such a heavy, looming darkness that even the eternal radiance of the stars barely shone through. The untouchable cosmic specks appeared as faint, ghostly pinpricks of luminosity that were weak and spiritless within the great slab of the night. It was as if the death of November had also unprecedentedly poisoned the very cosmos as it did the leaves, the fields, and the warm and festive colors of the fall.

The darkened shape of the old woman continued to take slow and steady drags from her dwindling cigarette. The bright orange dot of the cigarette's ember occasionally flared brighter before it trailed a serpentine ribbon of lacy smoke. Her quiet, relatively-brief sojourn finally ushered her limping steps to a small, modest home, a cozy country house on the edge of a large forest that stretched off like a discarded cloak over the hills that contoured the land to the east of the Berkshire Mountains.

A single window upon the face of the dark structure of the home softly gleamed from within, shedding a warm amber light. That pleasant illumination spilled a rectangle of welcoming lambency out onto the fragile brown grass and the drifts of dead leaves that surrounded the country home. A familiar shape of a familiar person moved about within the

home, and the elderly wrinkled visage of the lone woman, the face etched in amber light from the window, smiled warmly and contentedly. She enjoyed the familiarity of things more now than she ever had throughout her long life.

Nestled in northeastern Massachusetts, the quiet country home was slumbering in solitude a couple of miles from an idyllic, small, rural community. The nearby township was one of those little places that, even in the violent and terrifying artificiality of the modern age, brought to a nostalgic individual's psyche images of Norman Rockwell-presented tranquility and Main Street Americana. It was a place that still relied on harvests as much as it did the tourists that came to take photos of the changing leaves and stay at the quaint bed and breakfasts. The technology was changed from the domestic equipment of midcentury postwar America and so were the residents. But what hadn't changed in such places were its spirit, essence and flavor.

It was that very essence that had lured the old woman to rural Massachusetts ten years ago, when she purchased the quiet, small country home as an aged, newly-made widow. She required the spirit of the rural idyllic foothills of the mountains and the small, sleepy townships that studded them because those pleasant surroundings served her as a perfect immersion into the

colorful and potent, nostalgic fuel that powered her prose, her creativity, and her imaginative sense of eternal wonderment. The nearby township where she had gone for groceries and other domestic necessities throughout the last ten years, the ordinary people that inhabited that community and lived their peaceful, simple lives there, and the surrounding New England landscape served the old woman as the utmost of muses for the novels that she still wanted to write. All of those simple and quiet things inspired all of the perfect words that she desired to put to paper, and they kept the woman largely contented and comfortable in the waning, subdued years of her lonely life.

Could this elderly woman have been anything but a writer, the way in which she observed in silence the world around her? This thin, stooped figure in the coat that had walked alone down from the hilltop, cigarette in hand, to her modest abode in the cold dark night was Shannon Hawthorne. Shannon's name would be instantly familiar to any individual with even a wisp of literary interest when it came to twentieth century American literature. It had been her own creativity and imagination, as well as the unerring prowess of her prose and the folks that had helped her throughout the years, that had made her a titan of American literature as far back as the 1950s.

It had been over ten years, since her husband had passed away and she had moved from Washington, D.C. to rural Massachusetts, since Shannon had written a new story, but her reputation still carried with it plenty of weight. Though Shannon wasn't currently possessed of the physical or mental strength to write fiction, much to her chagrin, she was glad to know that her place in literary history was assured. Her plethora of bestselling literary fiction novels were her true legacy that she would undoubtedly be remembered for when the imminent hand of death reached out to whisk her handedly from the world. She was somewhat ashamed to know that her legacy wouldn't necessarily be her two children who were then in their middle years and had children of their own that were starting their own families.

Shannon stomped out her cigarette with her suede moccasin on the pitted slab on concrete before the front door of her home. And when she entered the warmth and cozy positivity of her abode, she made her way slowly to the living room where she sat in a tall-backed cushioned chair that was set at an angle before the hot flames of a dutifully-tended fireplace. She sighed with relief at giving her cold aching joints a much-needed reprieve.

A middle-aged woman in her fifties, rather ordinary in appearance but certainly not unattractive,

came to Shannon's chair by the fire and she carried with her two mugs of steaming coffee. "Here you are, Mom," said the woman.

Shannon replied tiredly in a voice that was flinty with age, "Thank you, Tabby."

Tabby was Shannon's eldest child and her real name was Tabitha. Tabby had two sons, the youngest one having been in college for a couple of years and the oldest was married and raising his own family in Atlanta. Tabby had taken it upon herself to become the caretaker for her elderly mother. She had been unmarried for about ten years, having gotten divorced around the same time that Shannon's husband passed away quickly from lung cancer, and Shannon suspected that her daughter had little else to occupy her time now that her boys had all departed home to pursue their own lives.

Shannon, however, was begrudgingly thankful for Tabby's assistance around the house and in town. The old woman became irritated sometimes because Tabby was always pushing her mother to write again. Ordinary tasks had begun to be quite difficult, much in the same way that writing had become essentially impossible. Shannon was thankful that Tabby was available to assist her because Shannon's younger daughter, Samantha, lived in London with her husband, a British policeman or detective of some sort. Samantha

had an older son from her first marriage in a European university, and a nanny largely looked after her spoiled children from her current marriage. Shannon had always thought that Samantha was a selfish girl. They rarely spoke on the phone anymore and hadn't seen each other in years.

"How was your walk? Any ideas?" inquired Tabby as she sat herself down in a neighboring rocking chair and sipped at her own hot mug of java.

Shannon made a noncommittal noise and shrugged. The old woman took a drink and then finally replied dryly and tiredly, "I feel as though all of my ideas are as dead as the leaves outside. Dead. Dead. Dead."

"Mom, don't be so grim."

"How am I supposed to be peachy when senility hasn't granted me the relief of not being aware that my craft has left me?"

"Oh, zip it. Your craft hasn't left you," returned Tabby with a knowing smirk before she took another drink of her coffee. The crackle of the fire in the hearth was exclaimed by the silence that followed.

Shannon took a drink of her own mug, grimaced at the boldness of its flavor, and asked, "Well, Tabby, what do you suggest I write about? I'm unsure if I've got the strength in me to write a novel anymore, ... nor the time."

Shannon's eldest daughter and caretaker shrugged and answered, "So write a novella then. Or write another short story. You haven't written one of them in ages."

"About what, Miss Know-it-All?" Shannon returned with only a diluted vestige of acidity that she salted with humor. She took another drink, and through the steam drifting up from beyond the rim of the mug could be glimpsed a faint smirk.

"I don't know, Mom. Why don't you write something about your past? You've been alive for just about nine decades. You've lived through some pretty amazing events in American history. I'm sure you can think of something to write of."

The old woman continued to smirk and she responded, "I may have lived through a lot, Tabby, but those events are already the backdrop of my novels. And my own life was just a simple life, the boring life of an author. What is there to say that will engage a reader? What is there to tell that isn't already known?"

"The lives of authors aren't boring. That's crap. Surely there's something? I'm sure that you have a number of spicy tidbits that you've kept from everyone, even Samantha and I."

"I'm not so sure," replied Shannon. "Nothing that noteworthy, or proseworthy for that matter, comes to mind."

And yet, something did slip into Shannon Hawthorne's mind.

It wasn't an unexpected thing, for it was a person and a time in Shannon's life that had entered into her thoughts for what seemed to be ages. It was a man that Shannon had been confronted with for most of her life, for he plagued her thoughts. Like a faintly-seen wraith looking out from the darkened window of a haunted house, Shannon was often confronted with the handsome face of Ansel Cooper.

It had been rumored for many years that Shannon Hawthorne had been romantically involved with Ansel Cooper, the famous Beatnik writer that had committed suicide in 1962, a year after Ernest Hemingway finished himself off. Shannon had never admitted to more than just knowing Ansel as a literary acquaintance that she had encountered only a handful of times. Though Ansel had been married to a single woman until his suicide, some folks theorized that there had been something there between the two novelists, something romantic. But Shannon had always denied it all, vehemently. She had denied it even to her two daughters, and she had always denied it to her late husband who Shannon had married a year before Ansel's death.

"Well, Mom, I'm going to bed. Are you going to stay up for a while longer?"

"I may stay up for a spell longer, Tabby. I think that I'll go sit before my typewriter for a little bit and see if something comes to mind that I want to write about," explained Shannon.

"Alright, Mom. Good luck. Don't stay up too late, okay?" returned Tabby. The daughter rose from the rocking chair, her half mug of coffee in hand, and she went to her mother. Tabby kissed the short white hair atop Shannon's head and whispered, "Good night."

"Good night, dear."

Shannon stayed in the chair in front of the yellow-orange flames that flickered in the fireplace until Tabby stopped moving about in her bedroom and was likely asleep. And then, with a pained world-weary groan, her joints creaking like twisting wet leather, Shannon stood and limped through the warm dimly-lit confines of her home to her writing office that was nestled cozily in a back corner of the house. The office was Shannon's quiet special place, but the space had sadly fallen into dusty disuse. Shannon would periodically sit in there, however, and she would stare for long stretches of time into her memories. But she wouldn't write.

After Shannon entered the office she closed the door softly behind her. And then, staggering forward on thin sore legs, the elderly woman reached her large desk of dark-stained oak. She supported herself against

the sturdy solidity of the office furniture, and then she reached forward and turned on her desk lamp. The light that blossomed into being revealed all of the familiar planes and objects of the small office to the old woman, and she was helpless to smile warmly with eyes all aglitter in youthful wonderment. Places of solitude where creativity was born had always done that to her.

Centered upon the top of the desk was Shannon's oldest living friend, a dusty relic of over six decades that was impractical to anyone but her. The yellowed light of the desk lamp spilled its rich illumination upon a 1950 Smith-Corona Clipper typewriter. It was a gift from Shannon's father on her twentieth birthday. On May 5, 1950, her dapper and civilized father had come down to Washington, D.C. from New York City on a train. He worked for a large publishing firm, and he had been responsible for getting his friends in some magazines to publish some of Shannon's first short stories. Her father had always encouraged Shannon's gift of writing, and the brand new Smith-Corona model seemed to be a paternal offering to Shannon that was to woo her into crafting her first novel. The ploy worked swimmingly, exactly the way that Shannon assumed her father had anticipated.

The matte grey-green paint that coated the metallic body of the typewriter only helped to flaunt

the apparatus' gentle curves. And the forest-green keys were still and silent with experience and promise. Not a word of prose had been written by Shannon Hawthorne through any medium other than her Clipper since she had received it when she entered into her twenties. What stories it had seen. What stories it had crafted.

"It has been so long," Shannon spoke quietly into the stale unused air that the writing office was swollen with. The old woman pulled out her desk chair and gingerly eased her fragile body down into it. Breathing heavily, both from the exertions of moving about her home and from the nervous tingle of excitement that coiled in the crown of her stomach, her arthritic hands hovered above the typewriter. Shannon flexed the swollen joints of her fingers above the keys, and then she gently lowered them down onto the rounded concave surfaces.

"Ansel," Shannon whispered almost inaudibly. Her silvery blue eyes closed.

"Ansel."

II

It was early June in Washington, D.C., and the breeze smelled sweetly of lilac. There was an outdoor café tucked away among the townhouses and brownstone of Georgetown, and the sidewalk outside of it was strewn with a few tables of decorative black

iron. Lilac bushes exploding with copious clusters of pale purple blossoms, savory in their fragrant perfume, grew thickly in planters on the sidewalk between the tables of the café and the traffic of the city street.

Shannon Hawthorne had turned twenty in the beginning of May, and was freshly finished with a couple of typing courses that she had enrolled herself in. She had taken the courses with a retinue of young girls that were bound for menial secretarial work, but Shannon's reasons were different for seeking proficiency at maneuvering about the keys of a typewriter. During the courses, she had taken the time to write short stories that she had written during the prior evenings in longhand.

It would likely have been a costly investment, paying for and enrolling in the typing courses just for the sole purpose of typing up her short stories on the typewriters that were in the classrooms of the university, but her father in New York had paid for Shannon's enrollment. He knew that she had talent, and he was doing whatever was possible to support and encourage his only daughter's writing endeavors. That paternal support also happened to include Shannon's new typewriter, a 1950 Smith-Corona Clipper, that she carried with her wherever she went in its tan hard case. She was carrying it with her when she made her way to the café that was edged with lilac bushes.

Shannon was a lovely young woman with a fair oval-shaped face, thin lips painted a cherry red, eyes like slate-colored frosted steel, and wheat-hued, long, straight hair that she often secured on the back of her head in a ponytail that she had bound with a navy blue bow. The bow's coloration exactly matched the long skirt that the aspiring writer concealed her long legs with. Shannon also wore a white blouse and a mustard yellow cardigan. She was a narrow-waisted, healthy young woman, and it pleased her when people often thought that she was still in high school.

Anyone that engaged in some conversation with Shannon Hawthorne for any length of time grew shocked when they discovered that the innocent young woman with which they spoke was actually a published writer that currently had three short stories appearing in popular magazines. She had published them under a male pen name to ensure, firstly, that they saw print and to ensure, secondly, that she was paid well for them. That had been her father's suggestion.

When Shannon reached one of the outdoor tables of the café, she pulled out a chair, set the typewriter case atop the table, and also placed a ream of paper that she had been carrying with her on the surface of the table. After she sat down and opened up the case, carefully removing her new

typewriter from within, a waitress came to her and asked her what she would like.

"An English muffin with butter and a cup of coffee please," Shannon told the girl.

As she waited for the waitress to return with her breakfast on that fine June morning, Shannon opened the ream of paper, took out a fresh, crisp piece, and loaded it into her new typewriter. Anticipation stirred within Shannon to such an extent that she didn't even remember to thank the waitress when she brought the writer her breakfast. And then Shannon began to type, and the clacking of the keys filled the June air with a mechanical music that reminded Shannon of the staccato song of a clockwork songbird.

So invested was she in the first page of what she knew would become her debut novel, that Shannon barely nibbled upon her English muffin and she sipped only absently at her coffee until it began to cool. Shannon began to take larger drinks of the bold beverage when its temperature had become more tolerable. An obese man in shirtsleeves read a newspaper at one of the nearby tables of the café, but Shannon wasn't even aware of his proximity.

However, she became aware of the man soon enough. He was seemingly suffering from some sort of respiratory ailment because he was continuously growling in the back of his throat before hacking mucus

and spittle onto the sidewalk next to the table that he sat at. After he would spit, the man would just return to reading his newspaper as if nothing was amiss. When Shannon had first sat down, the man with the newspaper and his disgusting habit were only background ambience like the rustling lilacs and the sounds of the traffic cramming the city street. But after glancing up from her work and spying the older man spitting the viscous ooze from his lungs or throat into the growing syrupy puddle next to his scuffed-up wingtips, Shannon could scarcely focus on anything else other than the abhorrent and rude man.

Shannon was astounded that someone could be so oblivious to those around him, so uncaring and inconsiderate of others. In disgust, she absently pushed the English muffin away from her and grimaced. Shannon tried to write a few words more on her story, but she was forced to stop mid-sentence in barely-concealed frustration when the man started up his hacking and spitting again. "My god," she whispered quietly in disgust and bewilderment.

It was at that moment when a different man drifted casually and brightly into the area. This newcomer was very handsome and in his middle years, apparent because of the grey that was taking over the temples of his well-groomed brown hair that Shannon spied beneath the brim of the man's hat. His face was

clean-shaven, but it was also one of rugged experience, tanned from the sun with comely wrinkles in the corners of his small brown eyes.

The man wore a dashing jacket and trousers of matching charcoal coloration, a light blue button-front shirt, and a thin knitted tie of hunter green. A pocket square of identical green peeked out from the breast pocket of the jacket. Shannon was pleased with the hue of the tie and of the matching pocket square because the color reminded her of the lovely green keys of her new typewriter, the green of her father's eyes when it was raining outside. Lastly, the man carried with him a notebook and a couple of sharpened pencils.

The new man smiled and tipped the brim of his handsome hat to Shannon before moving past her to take a seat at a vacant table in the café. Shannon returned the man's unexpected smile, and she felt a little bit of color rise into her cheeks. Her fingers had grown idle and her Clipper was impatiently silent, and she thus heard the attractive man ask for the dutiful waitress to bring him some coffee and sugar.

Then, immediately following the man's order, the portly fellow with the newspaper began another fit of hacking up phlegm onto the sidewalk. Shannon's delighted little smirk that was left over from the silent greeting of the handsome man with the notebook morphed quickly into a disgusted grimace. The

newcomer took his coffee from the waitress with a nod and he raised an eyebrow in bewilderment at the fat man that sat at the neighboring table, rudely spitting in front of the pair and the swift passersby. It was as if the thin man couldn't believe what he was seeing and hearing in a public establishment for dining and relaxing.

The newcomer was silent, watching with revulsion. His coffee was held untasted in his hand. But when the man spit some more mucus into his steadily-accumulating puddle, the handsome man stated crossly, "See here, fellow, this is a café. People are trying to enjoy their coffee and breakfast."

The obese older man turned a withering glare at the newcomer and returned in an offended manner, "Pardon me?"

"I said that you are in a public place," replied the handsome man. With a well-manicured tan hand, he referred to Shannon and added, "And can't you see that there's a lady present?"

"So what? Why don't you mind your own damn business?"

The newcomer smirked and he stood up from his table, facing the loathsome older man down. He answered, still smirking but with his brown gaze fierce in its intensity, "I'm not going to mind my own business because I'm trying to enjoy this perfect June day, and

your damned hacking is ruining the experience. The contrast between the aroma of my coffee, the fragrance of those lilacs, and the perfume of that lovely girl against the awful sound of your spitting is too much to take. Take your foul manners someplace else before I remove you myself."

"Well, I never-," returned the fat man in a shocked and insulted way. It was as if he was confused about why anyone should speak out against anything that he did, even something as foul as his prior uncouth actions. The man stood up, tossed some change on the table to pay for his coffee, and then he slapped his rolled-up newspaper onto the tabletop. With a final scorned glance at the other man, the big fellow stormed off. The only signs of his having been there at all were his discarded newspaper and the terrible puddle of phlegm on the sidewalk.

"I'm sorry about that, miss," said the man as he sat back down at his table.

Shannon smiled and nodded, replying, "Oh, that's no problem. I should be thanking you, sir. Some people."

"Indeed. Some people," the man echoed as he sipped from his coffee and caressed the cover of his notebook.

Shannon returned to her typing with a renewed focus, and as she changed the paper a few minutes

later the stranger remarked, "That's a fine typewriter, miss. Is it a Smith-Corona?"

Shannon was pleased that the man was versed in writing paraphernalia. She replied excitedly, "It is. It's the brand new model, the nineteen fifty. I got it as a gift from my father for my birthday last month."

"Well, happy belated birthday," returned the man with a grin and a nod of his handsome head. He then added, "Are you a writer?"

Glancing up with a smile and somehow pleased with the interruption, Shannon nodded and replied, "I am."

The man stood up from his own table and he ambled over to Shannon's table with his coffee, notebook and pencils. "Do you mind if I sit with you?"

Shannon certainly wasn't about to turn down the handsome older gentleman that had saved her from the foul company of the crass fellow and his horrible spitting. She smiled attractively as she motioned for the man to have a seat at the table with her.

"What do you write?" inquired the man.

"Fiction. Short stories."

"That's marvelous," he returned. "Have you tried to get published yet?"

Nodding, Shannon looked up at him and she bragged, "I actually had three stories published. *The*

Saturday Evening Post bought my most recent story a few months ago."

The man raised his eyebrows in an impressed manner and remarked, "That's just fantastic. Congratulations. Are you working on another short story right now? What are you writing today?"

Blushing with pleasure, Shannon answered, "Actually, I'm working on my first novel. I was waiting to start it until I'd gotten a typewriter of my own. I wouldn't dream of writing a novel with pen and paper."

"Really? I pencil all of the first drafts of my own novels," explained the man.

"Oh, you're a writer?" Shannon asked delightedly. She was suddenly attracted to him even more. "Could I ask you your name?"

"You sure can. My name is Ansel Cooper. What's your name?"

Shannon couldn't immediately respond because she was at a loss for words. She had read both of Ansel Cooper's famous novels and she adored his romantic work as much as everyone else did. Cooper was a literary celebrity, and here he was, sitting at a table on a Georgetown sidewalk across from Shannon. "My name is … uh … Shannon. Shannon Hawthorne."

"I'm very pleased to meet you, Shannon," Ansel returned warmly, his handsome brown eyes hungry. "Tell me about your novel."

III

The purity of the fog bank was almost overwhelming to Shannon. It spilled around the slopes of the Colorado Rockies and settled into a thick opaque swell within the meandering gulf of the river valley that Shannon gazed down upon from the back porch of the isolated cabin. It was only September but still the lofty heights of the ancient peaks that surrounded the scene were crowned in the glistening snow that starkly opposed the livid azure emptiness of the sky that was stretched out forever behind them. She smoked a cigarette in silent stupefied awe.

Shannon had never been west of the Mississippi River, and a vast mighty place, a wild place, like the Rocky Mountains had always seemed to her a faraway place of fantasy, a realm too enormous and majestic to actually be real. Oddly, she was reminded of the sea. In her experience, only the Atlantic Ocean equaled in scope the withered ice-helmed crags of the Rockies. They were points of contrast to one another but they were also siblings in a way, siblings in the great, big, open womb of the world.

In the eight years that Shannon had been having an affair with Ansel Cooper, since that Georgetown encounter in June of 1950, Shannon had never once accompanied him to his cabin in Colorado. The rustic, isolated vacation home up in the Rockies was the final

stronghold of the sanctity of Ansel's marriage, the last remaining place between he and his wife that Ansel hadn't spoiled with his repeated infidelities with Shannon Hawthorne. Ansel's wife was a fixture at their Baltimore home most of the time. She was a statuesque Native American girl, a young Sioux that Ansel had met and fallen suddenly in love with when he went out to South Dakota in 1945 to hunt pheasants in the cornfields near the Missouri River.

Shannon had never seen Ansel's wife in person, only in newspaper articles featuring the popular American romantic novelist. Ansel had been careful in that respect, keeping his wife and his lover from encountering one another. But Shannon felt like she was familiar with Ansel's wife, that she knew her well. When she found herself with Ansel in his large empty Baltimore home when Mrs. Cooper was away, Shannon would often observe the photographs of Ansel's wife. Mrs. Cooper appeared so very exotic, so stoic and beautiful, and Shannon felt undoubtedly jealous of her.

Also, when confronted with photographs or mention of Ansel's wife Shannon felt inadequate because she loved Ansel, truly loved him. She suspected that she loved him more than his own wife loved him. But Ansel's whole talented heart didn't belong entirely to Shannon. She hoped that even half of it did. It was a

passionate relic, Ansel's heart, that was shared with his alluring wife as well.

Part of Shannon was repulsed at the selfish jealousy that she felt towards Mrs. Cooper, and yet she felt jealous nonetheless. Shannon had been with no other man than Ansel. He was her everything. In the field of love and romance, Ansel Cooper stood alone in Shannon's view. To have to share him with his wife boiled a brew of resentment in Shannon's heart.

Ansel's Sioux wife had gone back out to South Dakota from Maryland for her father's funeral, and the novelist had used that opportunity to fly himself and his lover out to Colorado for a secluded holiday that September at the Cooper cabin. Shannon had been over the moon at the chance to play the part of Ansel Cooper's wife, if only for a brief period of euphoric time.

In the eight years that they had been secret lovers, Shannon had written two novels that had garnered her several outstanding reviews, some awards, and quite the pile of literary prestige. She had also, ironically, developed a reputation as a feminine writer that needed no man to lean on and that was free from dabbling in romantic adventure in her plots as well as her personal life. It was widely thought that Shannon Hawthorne's personal life was rather dull and lonely, and perhaps it was. Excitement only breathed through

its clenched teeth upon Shannon when she was writing and when she was in the arms of Ansel Cooper, and the latter the pair had kept hidden from the world.

Ansel had also written two more novels of romantic fiction and they were as well-received as his first two tremendously-successful works. It was Shannon's hopeful theory that their forbidden love affair kept their muses and their creativity sated and satisfied. She hoped, secretly, that Ansel recognized it too and would never break her heart.

Shannon's father up in New York was as proud of his only child, the successful young author, as any father could possibly be of their child. He glowed and gloated to his publishing colleagues. *"Oh, Shannon Hawthorne? She's my daughter,"* Mr. Hawthorne would say to folks with a satisfied smirk. *"Aren't her books just the berries? You know, I got her her first start with her short stories. And that typewriter that she writes her masterpieces on; well, I bought that for her twentieth birthday. She doesn't use anything else to write."*

Shannon stood alone for a while on the back porch of the log cabin. A quilt was wrapped around her shoulders like a shawl. She watched the fog come in over the dark green slopes of pine and the diminutive splashes of yellowing deciduous trees that were scattered among the pine, and she watched the fog as it settled over the white thread of the river that ran

swiftly and coldly in the bottom of the valley. The fog consumed the river and the trees that painted the mountainous river valley, but the disappearance of the environment into the pale murk was not an ominous thing. It was a gentle and peaceful natural act that came quietly and softly into the depths of the rugged, mountainous terrain below Shannon. The peace inherent in the sight was incomparable.

"Come in, Shannon. You're going to go back to Washington with a cold if you stay much longer out there in that chill."

Shannon bristled with pleasure at the sound of Ansel's voice. She smiled, dropped her spent cigarette butt off of the back of the porch, sighed wistfully at leaving behind the picturesque view of the foggy, vast landscape below, and then Shannon turned around and went back through the open French doors that led her back into the cabin. When she entered the richly-lit and rustic warmth of the vacation home's interior, Ansel was there waiting for her with a freshly-made cocktail in each hand. His own tumbler contained what Shannon knew was a finely-crafted Old-Fashioned, Ansel's cocktail of choice. In his other perfect hand was Shannon's preferred drink, a simple whiskey and soda. Shannon didn't place her trust in a drink with more than three ingredients. It, to her, muddled the purity of the taste.

Shannon went to her lover and she kissed his mouth as she took her whiskey and soda from him. "This is the most beautiful place that I've ever seen, Ansel. It's enchanting," she said to him adoringly as she draped herself down upon the sofa. She spoke to Ansel as if he were the one that carved the mountains, planted the forests, and spilled the fog out from some golden celestial urn. "I've been wanting you to bring me here for so long."

Ansel, outfitted in a warm wool sweater and thick trousers, smiled and he followed his lover over to the sofa, sipping at his bourbon cocktail as he came forward. Shannon smiled up at him with intense affection and she reached her free hand tenderly out towards him. Ansel knelt down beside the sofa, and Shannon's cool fingers delicately caressed the warm wool that covered his breast. "I know, my darling," Ansel whispered very softly.

He leaned over her then, and they kissed passionately. Ansel's breath smelled of bourbon, as it usually did, but it wasn't a foul scent to Shannon. It was *his* scent and she loved it as much as she loved him.

Shannon didn't often tell the novelist that she loved him more than anyone else on heaven or earth, more than her doting father and more than her long-deceased mother. She had told Ansel often that she loved him in those early postwar years when they had

first started seeing one another in D.C. and Baltimore and other secret secluded locales of the Potomac and Chesapeake regions, but she quickly began to suspect that using the word 'love' with Ansel made him very uncomfortable. Ansel took romance and lust very seriously, as was evidenced by his fiercely romantic fiction, and Shannon had been depressingly forced to accept the fact that the word 'love' was reserved entirely for Ansel's wife. It was as though, as long as Ansel could avoid that word entering into his affair, then he was still the romantic paragon that everyone assumed him to be.

As they kissed, Shannon wanted to cry out into the heavens how much she loved Ansel, but she knew that the only response would be the reverberating echoes of her own shouts. And so she kept silent but for her pleasured moans as his hands slid upon and grasped the feminine features of her body. Shannon would speak her love for Ansel with her lips and her searching tongue as the pair embraced on the sofa in the throes of passion. Ansel's narrow fingers began to unbutton Shannon's blouse.

After their intimacies were concluded an hour or so later, they both rested prone in each other's arms upon a thick bearskin rug that dominated the floor of the living room. They were both still nude following the passionate event, and the darkening sky was perched

on the mystical precipice of night. The deepening blues and purples spilled in upon the pale, bare flesh of the novelists from the glass French doors. The night sky over the Rocky Mountains was almost unbearably exquisite, like a scene from another world or a snapshot of Heaven. The stars were garishly bright, and more of them were existing in that single sight than Shannon had seen all together throughout the twenty-eight years of her life.

Shannon was exceedingly happy. Those were the blissful moments with Ansel Cooper that she had relied on for sustenance throughout the prior eight years. The pleasure with him, the taste of his mouth, the skill of his body, and the warmth of his hands as they explored all of the geography that encompassed her body were what Shannon desired to fuel her creativity and feed her hungry muses. Ansel awoke the Erato within her.

As night fell, Ansel made them each another cocktail and the pair sat in chairs before the warm fire that Ansel created in the fireplace. He brought out a small table from the bedroom, a nightstand most likely, and he placed it before Shannon's chair that she was seated in like some sort of pagan queen upon a throne. She smiled at Ansel lovingly with excitement and pleasure seasoning her steely blue gaze as he strode naked past Shannon's chair and went to their combined

luggage in the darkness of a corner of the cabin. Ansel returned a moment later with Shannon's beloved typewriter and a stack of fresh unused paper that almost gleamed with a hungry white sheen. The unblemished face of the paper desired words above all else, and Shannon desired to place words, her words, upon the eager innocence of the paper in the perfect formations and patterns that she yearned to construct. Those were the flawless words that the artful and lyrical depth of her literary fiction demanded.

Ansel placed the typewriter on the small table before Shannon, and next to the Clipper he placed the stack of purely-ravenous paper. He winked at Shannon playfully, boyishly, and then Ansel gathered up his notebook and a couple of sharpened pencils. He went naked to the chair opposite Shannon and collapsed into it with a contented sigh. The firelight played upon the softened bare edges of the pair of romantically-involved novelists. Ansel smirked at Shannon as he crossed his legs and placed the notebook atop his knee. Shannon smiled back and she knew that she was suddenly blushing.

"How, after eight perfect years exploring every square inch of each other, can you still make me blush, Ansel?" Shannon asked her lover as she caressed the green keys of her typewriter as though they were fashioned from his supple flesh.

"I don't know, my darling. But I'm sure happy about it."

Ansel grinned and Shannon giggled as she shook her head. God, how she loved him!

IV

January of 1960 was an infamous time for Shannon Hawthorne, a new era dawning with sorrow. The first month of a new decade had tumbled down upon Washington, D.C. in a frozen crystallization of the world that seemed to perch everything on the tense, brittle edge of shattering like frozen glass.

The dawn colored the bitterly-cold sky in a buttery shade of pastel yellow. The coloration of the sky and the chunks of pale cloud that drifted sporadically about could have reminded a person of a warm morning in some fairer summer month. It was a disarming hue that told lies. Summer was far afield, and sorrowfully out of reach. That was how Shannon felt.

Shannon thought that the pale yellow of the morning that pressed in upon her through the small window in the bathroom of her new apartment was a sickly and diseased color. She squinted into the thick, buttery glow and, on her knees on the cold floor of her bathroom, she suddenly retched again into the toilet. When she was done, the novelist, with three successful

novels under her belt by that January, stood dizzily and wiped her mouth with a couple squares of toilet paper. Her morning sickness had only just truly started, but Shannon was already beyond being exhausted with her recently-diagnosed pregnancy.

The baby was Ansel's. There had been one other man recently as well, a kind young man that was five years younger than Shannon's nearly thirty years, but she was positive that the child wasn't his. She also felt a pang of guilt for sleeping with the young man. Shannon felt as though she was somehow cheating on Ansel Cooper, a preposterous notion for he was a married man. Ansel had come down from Baltimore sometime before Christmas, and Shannon was certain that the pregnancy was a product of that rendezvous. There should have been a glee adrift in the hormonal atmosphere around Shannon because of the child that was growing within her womb, but she felt only sorrow and bitterness.

The talented older man that Shannon had loved for the last ten years would never claim the child as his own. He was married, happily married according to the press, and Shannon was nothing to him but a mistress, a literary harlot that enabled Ansel Cooper to have erotic adventures outside of his marriage. She had been used from the start. For a while Shannon had suspected that Ansel felt as much, but it had been confirmed to

her only the day before when she had called Ansel's home in a sort of panic because she had seen a doctor and been informed that she was carrying a child.

Ansel's Native American wife had answered the phone and it was with a great deal of anxiety that Shannon had asked if she could speak with Ansel. Mrs. Cooper had been obviously confused about an unknown woman calling their Baltimore home and asking to speak with her husband, but warily she had yielded the line over to her husband. Ansel had been quietly furious at the insolence that he perceived in Shannon calling his home without his prior consent. He was further livid because his wife had been home and had answered the phone.

Shannon had risked pushing Ansel's extramarital affair out into the harsh light of reality. Ansel had a phobia about being seen as barbaric, adulterous or uncouth. He didn't want to be seen in the same light as Ernest Hemingway. It was at odds with the radiant and romantic prose that Ansel penned.

In their ten years secretly seeing one another, Shannon had never been the target of Ansel Cooper's wrath. It shocked her. It had wounded her. And worsening the ordeal for Shannon, was her heightened emotional state. Ansel had called Shannon a 'stupid bitch' and threatened to ruin her career if she ever called his home again. When she had quickly cried out

that she was carrying Ansel's child, he had called her a 'liar' and a 'whore'.

After Ansel had hung up the phone on Shannon, she had been left in a sort of shocked stupor. She felt humiliated and abandoned, discarded. Something that she had trusted in and thrived upon for the last decade had abruptly soured in the blink of an eye. Shannon hadn't been ready for it, she hadn't been prepared for it, and she was staggered. A day later she remained confused and lost and abandoned, as disorientated as a wayward traveler that had just pulled herself from the icy embrace of a frozen lake.

Shannon drifted slowly from the bathroom of her apartment on bare feet. She was wearing a white nightie that had been a birthday gift from Ansel on Shannon's twenty-ninth birthday last May, and she felt shamed and humiliated that she had chosen that garment to wear to bed after the explosive, vicious dialogue with Ansel. She wore the lingerie, she supposed, because she hadn't so easily thrown Ansel aside in the way that he had thrown her aside over the phone the day before. As sad and as pathetic as it was, Shannon still loved the novelist.

The radio in Shannon's living room was turned on at a low volume. Since the beginning of January, all that anyone had been talking about nationally over the radio waves was Senator John F. Kennedy. The young,

handsome Democrat from Massachusetts had, at the start of the month, announced that he was running for President of the United States of America. All of the radios were glittering with excitement, and Shannon's radio was no different. As the man on the radio talked that morning about the upcoming race to the White House, Shannon walked past and turned off the device.

Her aimless sojourn through the morning murk of her apartment, a bigger place that she had recently leased, brought Shannon to her bedroom. In the dim grey world of that room, Shannon looked with despondency at the bed that she had so recently arisen out of to begin that first day of her new life, a life devoid of Ansel Cooper. He still had a presence on her bookshelf, as he did with many other people, but Shannon knew that she would never know his touch nor his kiss again. She felt compelled to lie down in her bed and vanish again into a heavy and anxious slumber to helplessly dream about what the grim future would bring her.

Shannon was about to step forward to her bed when suddenly there was a trio of knocks on the door of her apartment. She stood there until the quick knock sounded again, and with a dejected sigh, Shannon turned about and left her bedroom. As she slipped a bathrobe over her lingerie, the three rapid knocks sounded a third time and a voice cried out desperately,

"Shannon, it's me Pete! I saw your car was outside. Can I please speak with you?"

Pete Fitzpatrick, the twenty-five year old man that Shannon had spent the night with a few weeks ago on New Year's Eve, was waiting outside of the door of her apartment, and that caused Shannon conflicting feelings of unease and relief. Any man that wasn't her father or Ansel Cooper made Shannon nervous, but she felt relief at the same time because she didn't feel so very alone at that moment.

"I'll be right there, Pete," Shannon responded.

She pushed her undone wheat-colored hair behind her ears, coughed nervously as she smoothed her robe out, and pulled open the door of her apartment. Pete was there and looked pitiful and desperate in his wrinkled clothes that had obviously just been thrown on without thinking, and, despite his wool coat and the striped scarf that he wore around his thin neck, he was apparently half-frozen from the January frigidity. His cute and charming, though angular, face was as white as milk beneath the cold-imbued ruddiness of his cheeks and the reddened tips of his nose and ears. His shaggy brown hair was messy and uncombed.

"My word," Shannon said when she saw him. "Come in, Pete. You look frozen half to death."

As Shannon brought him into her apartment, she could see Pete clench his hands into fists to keep them from shaking. She couldn't tell, however, if the shaking was from nervousness or from the cold morning. Shannon told Pete to make himself at home as she went into the kitchen to make some coffee, but when she eventually returned to the living room with a steaming mug of hot coffee in her hands Pete was still standing nervously in the same place that he had been standing when Shannon had initially left his company.

"Will you please tell me what's wrong, Pete?" Shannon inquired as she handed the obviously distraught young man the coffee.

Pete took a small sip from the coffee and then he replied, "Shannon, I love you."

"Excuse me?"

Pete set the mug of coffee on the surface of the coffee table and he gazed earnestly into Shannon's steely slate-colored eyes. Pete looked on the verge of tears. "I said that I love you. I can't get that night out of my head. Shannon, I can't get *you* out of my head. And I don't want to."

"Oh, Pete," Shannon began sympathetically, and she lowered herself onto the sofa because her knees felt weak. Shannon was about to explain to Pete how fast he was moving and that she didn't feel the same for him, that her heart was with another man, but she

131

suddenly stopped. Time stood still for a moment. Ansel had discarded her, and she was carrying his bastard child. But Shannon had suddenly been presented with a way out from the humiliation and the stains that would certainly be acquired on her burgeoning literary reputation.

Shannon said, "Pete, I'm pregnant."

His hopeful and desperate face only increased its already-evident attributes. Rarely would an unmarried young man be thrilled at the news of impregnating a girl that he had only spent a single drunken night with, but Pete Fitzpatrick was indeed thrilled beyond measure. His charming, boyish face broke into a grin and he returned, "You're pregnant? And ... and it's mine? You're positive?"

Shannon nodded and her blue-grey eyes filled suddenly with a shimmering bed of tears, guilty tears. A dark blossom of shame opened its acidic petals in the depths of Shannon's stomach as she lied to the oblivious young man about his paternal responsibility to the fetus that was beginning to develop within her, but Shannon pressed on deeper into her lie because there was no going back. She committed to it in an instant and she committed to it for all eternity. It was all, her whole future and the future of Pete Fitzpatrick, decided in a heartbeat.

Shannon had been presented with a way to fix everything and to conceal the evidence of her affair with Ansel. And only Shannon Hawthorne would ever know the truth.

V

It was October. The unfolding darkness and the stars of the autumn night could be glimpsed through the erratic rents in the charcoal-grey cloud cover that had settled over the Massachusetts countryside in a thick, viscous layer. A cold drizzle had descended from the clouds throughout the day, and, though night had fallen, the rains showed no sign for stopping completely.

It had been a couple of months shy of a year since Shannon had started writing about her affair with Ansel Cooper. She knew that she could never write as quickly and as fluidly as she had when she was younger, and yet there was a jubilant liberation that had been reincarnated with the act of writing again. Shannon had settled into the ancient act of putting prose to paper as if she had never left it, and she discovered that she was much more happy, content and thankful about her life.

Shannon discovered that she was thankful for her late husband, Pete Fitzpatrick, who had died years ago in Georgetown before Shannon had relocated to

Massachusetts. She would carry the guilt of lying to him about Tabby's paternity until the day that she died, but Shannon was also gladdened that Pete never discovered that he wasn't their oldest child's biological father. Shannon was glad that he was able to pass away ignorant that his wife had perhaps tricked him into marrying her to just cover up her decade-long affair with Ansel Cooper. Pete had loved Tabby more than anyone on the planet, and the little girl had loved him back with her whole heart. Tabby's real father committed suicide when she was still just a baby. Ansel never knew anything of his daughter.

Shannon had also discovered that she was very thankful for Tabby. Tabitha Fitzpatrick had lost her married name after her divorce eleven years ago, she had lost both of her sons to their own lives and the wider world, and the middle-aged woman had lost any hint of romanticism in her life. But she was still willing to give up whatever else she did still have to come to rural Massachusetts in order to take care of her elderly widowed mother.

The very idea of the sacrifice made by her eldest daughter humbled Shannon and moved her close to tears. She had certainly needed Tabby's assistance throughout the last several months that Shannon had been passionately typing up the romantic drama of her younger years and the enormous secret contained it its

melancholy conclusion. The older woman had come to rely heavily on the food that her familial caretaker made for her and reminded her to eat, and Shannon tried to not take for granted all of the domestic responsibility that Tabby had wordlessly shouldered.

Shannon sat in a rocking chair on the weathered concrete slab outside the front door of her country house, and she had a thickly-knitted afghan covering her legs. She smoked a cigarette and blew an indistinct plume of smoke into the darkening quality of the autumnal dusk. The oaks and maples around her home shivered their brown and orange leaves in the brisk evening air, and Shannon smiled at them.

A couple hours ago Shannon had given Tabby the recently-finished first draft of the novella that she had been typing since last December, the work that detailed the affair with Ansel Cooper and ended with Tabby's startling parentage. Shannon had told her daughter that she needed a younger and fresher set of eyes to look over the short manuscript. Tabby had laughed and told her mother that Shannon's eyes were fine, but that she was honored to give the novella a read-through before an editor or publisher.

Shannon knew that her eyes were fine. She knew without a doubt that the autobiographical novella was very well-written. In truth, she had wanted Tabby to read it because Shannon was a coward. It took some

of the responsibility away from Shannon. She knew that, while she was still around to do so, she had to let her daughter know the truth about who her real father was. Having Tabby read the information, instead of Shannon having to engage in the emotional conversation with her over hot mugs in front of the fireplace, was a much more preferable option to the elderly woman. Her writing could explain things far better than her words. It helped Shannon to ease the anxiety that she felt about Tabby discovering the revelation about her father.

She still felt a twinge of nervousness as the night grew bolder in its presentation. Enough time had transpired so that Tabby was likely finishing up the manuscript. Shannon let a big weary sigh drift out into the October gloom, and she dropped the cold butt of her cigarette onto the slab of weathered concrete that she rocked upon.

Shannon heard footsteps within the house behind her, and then the front door opened slowly. Over her shoulder an emotional voice addressed the old woman simply and timidly. "Mom," the voice began, and Shannon's eyes closed as she braced for the conversation that was about to begin. "Can we please talk?"

SHE OBSCURED THE LIGHT

It was the morning light that I noticed first. Not her. That much I must admit. I always noticed the warm glow of light before anything else. It's like I have always been drawn to it. But now I feel like a fool for having noticed the sun's photons before I noticed her. How paltry they were in comparison.

I was sitting in an aisle seat in coach on a flight from Seattle to San Francisco. My friend's wedding was over and done with, and I could cross that off of my list of crap I had to do over the summer. The bourbon had been phenomenal but my head still ached a little from all the Old-Fashioned cocktails that I had at the reception. The pressure in the cabin and the flight itself worsened things slightly. But I knew that in my familiar environment of San Francisco, my natural habitat, things would return to normal. I could get back to working on my novel and being generally content.

My agent had developed somewhat of a harpy-ish manner concerning the ponderous pace that my next book was being written. Writing about the fruits of

love is a tad difficult when the realm of romance has, for you, been barren for some time. You've got to lie to your muses to enlist their help in that respect, but pulling a fast one on one's muses is painstaking and toilsome work.

But back to her.

I was looking into the amber swell of light deluging into the cabin from the window two seats to my left. I was remembering the morning light in the way that only writers can catalogue the finer details of the world, the simple things that demand literary representation. I was remembering how the light looked for later use in my writing. But my view of the glow was being partially obscured.

I was irritated at first. I was doing work, just sitting there and observing the world and life surrounding me. That's work for writers. And this darker mass was carelessly hindering my work.

But then I focused my eyes into the foreground, and there she was. Just like that.

She was of a similar observant mind because she just stared out of the window immediately next to her, soaking in the light and the view from however many thousands of feet up we were. Her face wasn't visible to me, just to the yellow tangibility of the rising sun that she faced. Her legs were tucked up onto the seat with her, and her slender arms were wrapped around her

knees. She looked like a child that I'd seen before watching fireworks on the Fourth of July at a park looking out over the Golden Gate Bridge. The young woman was possessed of a sort of girlish innocence that did a favor to her fresh adulthood.

Her hair was done up in a bun on the back of her head and it was a chocolaty brown, but upon closer inspection the yellow light consuming the oval-shaped background brought out ribbons of caramel highlights. No wedding band or engagement ring graced the pale digits of her left hand. She wore a red men's button front shirt, loose-fitting on her lithe frame, and I prayed to the deities of romance that it was a brother's shirt or a thrift store find and not the article of a lover. Her legs and feet, which were completely visible because of the manner in which she sat on her seat, were adorned in tight blue jeans and brown sneakers. Her outfit was casual to a fault, and not elegant or feminine by any means, and, yet, I was still infatuated.

As I stared at the girl, oblivious to the portly businessman between us, I lost track of time and place, and I was jerked back into coherency by the repeated inquiry of a middle-aged flight attendant. "Sir, would you like a beverage?"

"Sure," I answered in a somewhat distracted manner. "Ginger ale and ice please."

I sipped at the champagne-colored, subtle contents of the plastic cup and watched the girl some more. Finally she broke her visage away from the morning light that richly illuminated the window, and I could see her face. She was possessed of a cuteness that I scarcely explain. Like treasures or royal jewels, the woman wore a fairy-like upturned little nose, long dark lashes that danced around dark brown eyes with a subtle cherry wood finish, and a light dusting of delicate freckles upon both soft cheeks.

I kept on staring like a careless fool, but I don't claim any responsibility over that. I can't. She had me enchanted. Truly. Those rich eyes glanced over at me first, and the rest of her face followed a moment later. She offered a close-lipped smile and my heart beat against my ribs. I may have smiled, and finally she raised an eyebrow and whispered, "Hello."

I blinked and returned a nod. "Beautiful … morning," I feebly returned.

I glanced into the face of the businessman between us and he was smirking. He very subtly shook his balding head as if to say, *Dumb kid. You need to learn some finesse.*

Well, balding middle-aged guy, I wasn't a 'kid'. I was almost thirty. I just looked really young when I shaved off my whiskers. And I'd like to think that I possessed a little bit of finesse. I liked to think that I

could drift coolly into and out of rooms at a trendy party in some hipster's loft like a modern, poor Jay Gatsby that was regrettably devoid of a mysterious past.

I pulled my gaze from the girl with regret, looked at my cup of ginger ale and sipped it. And then I kept my hazel eyes carefully directed down the fuselage of the airliner for the rest of the southbound flight.

It was just after noon when I ambled through San Francisco International with my single carry-on. I wanted to buy a bottle of water because my mouth was still dry with the waning vestiges of a hangover and I sought to squish it into non-existence as soon as possible.

As I stood in line in the little store, my eyes wandered over to the book section. There it was, my first book, *Glow* by Scott Church. There were three or four copies of the paperback edition on the bookshelf. That book had opened a lot of doors for me. I wasn't that well-known, mind you, but *Glow* had made several bestseller lists and garnered an award or two. The book had enabled me to live comfortably, if a tad bit frugally, on the royalties. My agent promised that things would get more comfortable for me once I'd written another novel as good as *Glow*.

"You know, I sort of recognized you on the plane."

The voice was like honey. It was as if her whisper from before was only a caterpillar that had so suddenly blossomed into the most wondrous butterfly I'd ever seen. I turned around in line and there she was. A backpack rested on her back and I noticed that the canvas fabric was adorned with pins and buttons of various illustrations, phrases and bands. The bands were an erratic mix that tumbled between music genres; Deftones, The Beatles, Bon Iver, Jimi Hendrix, Jimmy Eat World. She wheeled a large burgundy piece of luggage behind her.

"Excuse me?" I said, even though I heard perfectly what she had stated. I just needed time to fire up my conversational engines.

"I said that I recognized you on the plane, from your picture in your book. I loved *Glow*. It was such a pretty novel, *very* descriptive. I could picture everything perfectly," the young woman explained with a beautiful smile.

"Oh," I began. "Thank you so much. I'm glad you liked it."

"Are you writing another book anytime soon, Mr. Church?" she asked.

"Working on it," I answered. "Hopefully I'll finish it up soon."

She nodded, and I turned halfway back around. But then I stopped, turned back to her, and I said, "And you can call me Scott. What's your name?"

Her smile blossomed again, and she responded, "My name's Erika. Erika Cardinal."

"Cardinal? That's an interesting last name. It suits your eyes."

Erika's freckled cheeks faintly blushed and she looked down at her feet with a giggle. "Thanks. I kind of like it," she began. She looked back up at me and continued, "I hope I never get married. I don't ever want to change my name."

I shrugged and returned, "Oh, I wouldn't count marriage out. You'll break too many hearts talking like that. You can keep your last name even if you're married. It's the twenty-first century."

"Are you married?" she asked.

I breathed out a combined laugh and a sigh and answered, "Nope. Never been married. I hear it's pretty cool though."

She quipped quickly, "And I hear that it's sometimes a pain in the ass."

"True enough," I returned with a grin.

We were silent for a while as the line progressed forward towards the counter and the cashier. My palms and fingers were sweaty around the bottle of water I

held. Finally Erika broke the silence when she inquired, "Why were you in Seattle?"

I smirked as I turned halfway to her and I raised an eyebrow in irony as I stated dryly, "A wedding."

We both chuckled.

"What were you doing in Seattle?" I asked then.

"Oh, I'm from there. I got accepted into Berkeley. So I'm moving down here. Well I suppose I just *moved* down here."

"Wow, you got into Berkeley! Great job, Erika. So you just got out of high school?" I asked. I was only slightly put off by the decade or so difference in our ages, but it pretty much diminished as quickly as it came when she smiled warmly at me.

"Yep. Freshly-freed from high school's halls. Eighteen."

"Eighteen?" I echoed confusedly.

"In case you were wondering how old I was, Scott. I'm eighteen. I read *Glow* when I was a freshman," she explained. Her cheeks were very faintly flushed as she said this smiling, but her auburn eyes glimmered in coyness and a ghost of a challenge. It was as if she dared me to think that she was too young for anything in the world. She chomped at the bit to inform anyone that challenged her that she was more mature and more worldly than people twice her age.

"I've got you beat by a decade," was all I said in response. I didn't know what else to add, but I knew that her age didn't deter the smitten aura that I was surely cast with. And too soon it was my turn at the counter. I bought my bottle of water, and I turned around to walk out of the airport store. Erika was stepping up to the counter and her cute face glimmered with what I felt was expectation. "See you later, Erika. It was nice talking to you."

"You too, Scott. Good luck with the book."

Painfully then, I walked away, and when I was back out in the lofty cacophonous din of the brightly-lit airport I opened my bottle of water and took a couple long greedy swallows. My hands were shaking slightly with releasing adrenaline. I glanced back at the open entrance to the store and I saw Erika exit the establishment, wheeling that luggage behind her. She was moving away from me, and I hesitated with a lack of surety about what I should do. I'd had one conversation with Erika Cardinal, but I already missed her terribly. It was a bewildering and wonderful state of affairs.

I trotted after her as I screwed the lid back onto my bottle of water, and as I came up beside her I blurted, "Can I take you out to dinner sometime?"

She smiled and looked over at me as we walked. "I'd love to, Scott. But you'll be in charge of reservations

because I'm fresh off the boat, so to speak. I don't know where the good restaurants are yet."

"Of course," I returned with a grin. "I'll show you all the good places. San Francisco has loads of good places."

"Great. When?"

"What about this weekend?" I answered. I noticed that I was chewing on my bottom lip with anxious excitement. I think that she noticed it too because she smirked and blushed before she answered.

"That sounds wonderful. I look forward to it. I'm going to buy a copy of *Glow* so you can sign it for me."

I chuckled and remarked, "Don't waste your money. I've got a couple boxes of them at my apartment. I'll bring one with."

Erika and I exchanged our numbers and we went our separate ways into the vast humanity-thronged expanse of the airport. And as I ambled with a sort of new-found romantic confidence, I was dappled in the light of the California day that spilled in through the numerous skylights and windows overhead. I loved the light still.

But I couldn't have been happier that the girl on the plane had obscured it from me for that brief moment so that I was able to notice her. She might have changed everything for me.

WOMAN WITH A BOOK

Going on a vacation alone is like reading a really phenomenal story over and over again. The first few days are perfect, exactly what your life required. But then, quite suddenly as a matter of fact, something changes. The prose becomes too familiar, too mechanical. The words and the days lose their polished luster and they suddenly dull.

Then you find yourself alone, and you're sitting by yourself on some gorgeous beach in the midst of a sunburnt, engorged swell of cookie-cutter tourists that you both despise and resent. They're never alone either, not like you. The loud parents have their loud kids, and anyone seemingly worthwhile seems to be avoiding your desperate search. You ask yourself what went wrong, and you ask yourself what you need to do to change things, to experience something meaningful. You ask yourself *who* you need in order to turn this whole shitty mess around.

In that respect, traveling is a lot like life. It's a consolidated magnification of your life that poses to

you the same problems, asks you bluntly the same questions, and, to the observant ones, it offers the exact same answers. You just have to listen and watch very closely for the answers. Michael Nash did that very thing because he was one of the observant ones.

The clear blue sky wasn't the tapestry of crystalline purity that a person commonly accepts it as without challenge. Instead, it was an azure heap that was all-encompassing, all-consuming. Great solid slabs of darkened cloudless blue had been stretched over the beach by an industrious god. And Michael found the featureless shade of cobalt that painted the firmament to be an unbearably oppressive spectator.

A small tote, his beach bag, leaned against the chair that Michael was sprawled in upon the beach. A fine bronzed hand, his hand, lowered down into it, and his fingers nimbly maneuvered among the navy blue boat shoes, digital camera, writing journal, and pens that were contained therein. From his beach bag he withdrew a pair of sunglasses. When Michael placed the eyewear on the long convexed bridge of his nose, he realized that he had been squinting beneath the glare of the sun and the naked sapphire void that loomed overhead.

Michael's skin had darkened considerably in the days that he'd spent alone on the sunny Caribbean isle. And he was proud to see the bronzed coloration upon

his abdomen and chest that stood out darkly from the vertical gap that was exposed beneath the unbuttoned front of his white linen shirt. The sleeves of the shirt were rolled up to his elbows, and he was also satisfied with the color of the lean forearms that he possessed. The veins of his arms were healthy and stood out under his skin. Michael then looked down, past his knee-length khaki shorts, and he saw that his lower legs and his bare feet were also richly-colored by the sun.

He was happy with his appearance, and Michael almost smiled as he situated his hat more comfortably on his head. During the entirety of his vacation, when outside as he was apt to be, Michael had worn a straw fedora with a short upturned brim and an aquamarine hatband. He wore the hat not out of some stylistic statement, not entirely, but Michael was balding and the hat shielded his sensitive and vulnerable scalp.

His fingers drummed impatiently on his knee, and he let his eyes drift around the beach for something that would change the isolated gloom of his lonely thoughts. It was late afternoon and he was ready for another drink. Michael just didn't want to drink yet another rum cocktail on his own at the hotel bar. He wanted to converse with someone interesting. He wanted to have a meaningful encounter. He wanted the prose that his vacation had thus far been written in to

change into something worthwhile, something important.

Michael's lazily-searching eyes found no solitary individual of note that would be a saviour to him. He found no avatar of a redeeming quality that would gleam some purpose into the synthetic gulf that was his Caribbean vacation. He let his eyes slide from the dark saturated individuals that peppered the beach and the shallow waters of the clear blue sea.

He twitched his vision up to behold the dark Atlantic vastness that held a primal court all the way to the far eastern horizon. Men have always thought of seas as vast obstacles of separation that are meant to be overcome and defeated, conquered. But Michael had always thought of the ocean in a different way than most.

The undulating expanse of the sea made Michael think of togetherness and the sacred connectivity of all things. The land fell down beneath the heavy press of the dark, cold ocean, but then it rose again someplace else … everywhere else. Michael knew that all of the lands were connected to one another, pieces and forms of one omnipotent body that protruded here and there from the shrouding liquid surface of the world.

Suddenly flooded with the feeling of seaborne oneness that he had made himself familiar with over

the years, Michael sighed happily and the cobalt sky was suddenly not so oppressive to him. And then, seemingly as a reward for the turn in his thoughts and the discontented emotions, Michael finally found the person that had the potentiality to be the alleviating force to rescue his vacation from the dreary vaults of stagnation and lifelessness. Maybe the person would be the force to inject some meaning into it all.

Down the beach from him, laying back in a beach chair in a way that was identical to his own posture, was a woman. Late thirties, his own age, the woman's hair was bobbed to the length of her chin and it was dark like the night. Her eyes, which Michael knew in the depths of his soul were the most desirous feature of all her beautiful pieces, were hidden cruelly away behind the dark barrier of a pair of large impenetrable sunglasses. She was thin, but not unhealthily so, and she was darkly-tanned and small-breasted. The woman wore a white bikini and a sunhat that seemed old-fashioned to the man that watched her. Its large, floppy brim spilled relieving shadow down upon her lovely cheekbones and narrow chin, and over the fine contours of her collarbone and her rounded shoulders that were brown and glistening.

She was lovely to be sure, but Michael knew that he required the pleasure of her company more than he desired her in a physical or sexual way. A

promising paperback was opened, perched up atop her flat brown abdomen as she read its mysterious contents, and Michael hoped that it was a well-written literary work, a classic that was authored beautifully and with sophistication.

Michael cleared his throat, gathered up his beach bag, and up stood from the chair that he had been lounging in unhappily day after day of his vacation. He took off his sunglasses and began walking along the beach. His steps left unerring footprints in the white sand, and they artfully traced a path straight to the woman with a book, to what he hoped was his salvation.

PAGES

A more perfect writing environment couldn't have been cleaved out of the architecture of heaven and earth. The overcast afternoon sky was heavy with sodden release, mumbling sensuously in the language of thunder and spilling out diaphanous ribbons of cool rain upon my New Hampshire cabin in tender reliance. The layers of damp cloud that slipped ponderously by overhead were painted chaotically in smears of thick darkened slate.

The hammering of the rain almost buzzed in an ebbing cascade that swelled and receded upon the wooden shingles of my writing refuge, this sylvan place that I kept in the wooded country away from the bustle and distraction of the city in which I primarily dwelled. I had the curtains of every window pulled to the side, and the dim blue glow of the rainy afternoon illuminated the shadowy rustic interior of my cabin in a lurid natural light. I sipped at my mug of coffee that was too sweetened and stood looking out of a tall window in the main room, into the dark and slumbering green

of the old New England forest that encircled my abode. The forest was silent in the gentle downpour, and I could see no answers there.

I was alone at the cabin for a week or so, a few days yet remaining before I was to venture back home to the city. Solitude was the state in which my writing came to me in the best possible way and with the greatest ease and proficiency. I could hear my clock ticking away in a duet with the sound of the shimmering waves of cool September rain, and it stirred anxiety in my gut because I knew the awful truth of its ticking. The clock was counting away the seconds, minutes, hours, and days until I had to leave, returning from the solace of my blessed privacy to the city and my wife and children, my agent and editor, the woman waiting to cross the city street and the man that shopped for a suitable bottle in silence alongside me at the corner liquor store.

I turned to look into the murky gloom of the room that I stood within, and I imagined that my portly silhouette was fairly ominous against the dreamlike, darkening blue of the outer world that encompassed the window behind me. Maybe my typewriter, sitting heavy and silent atop my desk across the shadowed room, would be intimidated. Maybe it could then be coerced into spilling forth the secret way in which I was required to woo it into activity.

My typewriter, I knew, was a womanly object, all attractive curves and productive industry. You could scarcely believe the music that we made together when she and I were alone. My fingers would press out her frequent mechanical cries, and she would respond so lovingly and dutifully to my earnest touches, to our lengthy passionate unions. Together we had produced such lovely children, spawn laden in sophisticated prose that people throughout the world had seen.

There she sat upon the surface of my writing desk, silent and observant, tense with electric anticipation. I realized then that she wanted me, unbearably so, and I wanted her as much. I wanted to touch her, use her, press her keys. I wanted to fill her continuously with the creamy whiteness of pure and unsoiled paper, and I wanted to impregnate those pages with the most perfect words that I could fathom, my literary seed.

But my flexing and unsatisfied fingers were claimed with a dysfunction that concealed from me the sacred act of writing. Equally stricken was my aging mind that was refusing to swell with the stories that had regrettably come so easily when I was in my twenties and thirties. Now that my matured mind was capable of so much more eloquence and poetry, the literary dysfunction that deprived my spirit of the bold

blood of beautiful words had seemingly been infecting me more and more with each passing year.

I wanted to march to my typewriter, and I wanted to pound pleasurably upon her feminine artifice until she moaned out my fiction in holy ecstasy. The mood was in evidence. The environment that was most needed for my work had been granted. Alas, I did not approach her nor the immodestly-nude stack of paper next to the typewriter. The paper was agonizingly pure in its literary virginity, and I wanted to spoil it all, each and every piece, with the vulgarity of my inner self.

I went to the cabin's small bedroom and I put a warm sweater over my shirtsleeves. The dark air was cooling considerably. My bed, white sheets luminous in the swelling shadows, flirted in the edges of my vision. I thought of my wife, and then I was shamed and guilty to realize that I was neglecting my writing and sharing passion with another.

In the kitchen, I poured a stocky tumbler half-full with dark brown maple whiskey. It smelled like breakfast, and I swirled the aromatic and intoxicating fluid with a bored and almost careless motion. None spilled. And then I took a long sip that burned my throat in just the right way. Burn me. Chastise me. Inspire me.

Liberate me.

I knew what the alcohol was for, and I used it like the professional that I was or that I endeavored to

be. I had honed my craft over productive decades that were written in positivity among the tapestry of the literary world that I dwelled within and was enamored with. I knew how to lubricate the writing process so that words and ideas were thrust forward in a freer and more creative form. And so I took another drink of maple whiskey, a larger drink, and I returned out to the waning blue dusk of the cabin's main room.

Sitting down at my desk before the silhouette of my mistress that crowned the top of it, I placed my tumbler off to the side of the flat expanse of the top of the desk and I turned on the short desk lamp that was perched over the well-used altar of literature where I had wrestled in the throes of unparalleled lust and passion with those useful curves and keys countless times. In the sudden bloom of amber illumination, her beauty and all of her responsive parts were abruptly displayed before me, openly and without modesty.

I touched my typewriter only just barely, and she remained silent. My digits caressed the solid coolness of her immobile flesh, and I sighed inwardly with heady anticipation. My breath smelled of the maple whiskey.

I was almost there.

God, I was almost cured.

BESTOW

Light. An October sunset painted with a rich ancient glow, light hearty enough to swallow down and fill the lungs. A tangible light. The leaves crowning the trees were all of the shades of warmth, stalwart agents against the chill of the autumnal night.

She caused the kitchen to emanate great savory smells, aromas of melting cheese, a sauce made with white wine, chicken, ham. She made chicken cordon bleu, her culinary specialty. We ate it at an iron table with two chairs on our balcony, beneath the fading warmth and amber hues that were bleeding into rusty scarlet and cool violet. She wore a dark purple sweater dress with long sleeves and a low back, tall socks up to her knees. I wore a cable-knit sweater, a fisherman's sweater, and a loosely-wrapped scarf that was draped in lazy coils around my neck like a slothful serpent. We were clothed against the cold October night like those seasoned in such things. And we were.

We each had a glass of wine to accompany our meal, the wine that she had cooked our meal with. It

was white wine with a European note. I hadn't read the label of the bottle. I didn't want to discover that it was truly from California. We tore chunks from a baguette and we dipped them in our wine before eating them. We ate heartily, like country people in the Old World.

When dinner was over and Venus shown, piercing across the void like the forlorn lamp of a single lonely vessel at sea, we enjoyed small cigars, soiled plates and half-full wine glasses on the table between us. She poured the rest of her wine into my glass, filling it to terrifying heights that I was grateful for. We laughed too much about trivial things. Coils of blue-tinted cigar smoke settled about us in an aromatic haze.

All of the warm colors finally fled, seeping down into the western rim of the world like rain into a patch of hot parched earth. The curtain of the night was finally pinned to all of the edges of the skyline, and it pulsed with the flickering of the stars and with the rustic purity of autumn, of a sticky summer scrubbed clean with a warm wool rag that greyed the coarse bark of the trees and put to all of the leaves the hues of heat and fire. The night was alive.

Inside, our apartment was equally dark, lit only with the ethereal glow of the stars and of the dim ambience that softly settles within civilized habitation. But it was not a cold darkness like the night outside that was stretched over the balcony with the table and our

plates, and over all the rest of the land. And into the mild darkness I followed her. The wine flavored my steps, my pursuit.

A feminine laugh, crystalline and delicate, sensual and commanding, a laugh of improbable fragility and resolute solidity, escaped her supple lips, slipped between her perfect teeth, and it decorated the interior's shadows like sugar. I walked through the fragrance in her luminous sweet wake like confetti at our wedding. We still, after years, made that walk together. I reached fingers out and caressed the bare smoothness of her back, birthed from the darkness of her garment like a white rosebud from ink. My wine glass posed in darkness on a bedside table, dwindled contents barely colored.

She was blank before me, revealed before me as flawless and as pale in the quiet murk as a new piece of parchment. A pen descends. I will write a tale of our love, I know, of our storied romance, and I will punctuate it with passion. She grinned up into my face with both expectation and stimulation borne in earnest by the darkened indigo of her eyes.

"Bestow! Bestow!" was what her eyes cried up into mine through the rosy slab of shadows. "Bestow!"

"Oblige," answered my own gaze, steady and calm. It was a serious gaze, and I held it towards her as firm as a knife. I was the giver of gifts.

The moon was full and white, like a breast. Leaves still rattled in the hard cold limbs of the trees, and the leaves were made dry and vibrant by the year's last great season. The pale lights of the night had usurped the chromatic radiances of the day.

Light always begets light. Eternity carries a torch.

OLD EYES

A husband and wife were outside of their modest antiquated home doing yard work for most of a Saturday in July. It had thus far been a humid and sunny weekend, but they knew that it was going to start raining later that afternoon. And so they rushed to get done most of what they had put off throughout the last week.

They were a young married couple with a single daughter, a toddler that they doted on very lovingly. The husband, Drew, mowed the front lawn and the backyard of their home and then he cleaned up the rough edges and corners with a weedeater. The wife, Kayla, worked in the flowerbeds out in front of their porch, and she pulled weeds in the garden, also checking on the progress and condition of the produce that she was growing. Their daughter, Lucy, toiled in feminine mimicry of Kayla, and she was clothed in a pale blue sundress and a white sun hat that matched her mother's.

The temperature dropped late in the afternoon, and the clouds quickly slipped in from the east, heavy and dark and swollen with moisture. The clouds brought with them a cacophony of rumbling thunder and a light show of sky-fracturing lightning that was tinted pink. Drew and Kayla finished their day of yard work just in time. The lawn and the flowers looked clean and well-groomed in the descending sheet of rain that was spilled freshly over the neighborhood. Drew told Kayla, as he looked over their yard when they walked inside, that he thought that they did a good job.

Lucy, contrary to the behavior of most young children, laughed at the thunder. Her parents had thought themselves very fortunate about that because the place in which they lived frequently received storms in the summer. The little girl was prone to covering her belly button with a hearty chuckle whenever thunder boomed. Kayla had told her once that that's what children in Japan did. That bit of knowledge had somehow stuck in the young child's mind.

All three members of the family were dirty and sweaty from their busy laborious day, and so they put little Lucy in the bath before they made something together for dinner. They were going to be cooking up some chicken and rice. They had some strawberry ice cream in the freezer for dessert.

Lucy's bath was hot and filled with bubbles, and Lucy shrieked with pleasure when her parents dumped a little box of her plastic toys in the tub for her to play with. The little girl stripped down to just her socks, and before she could remove them, Drew picked Lucy up and put her in the water. Lucy screeched and belly-laughed, and both of her parents chuckled as their young daughter writhed in the soapy foam.

Even an innocent young child was aware of the taboo feeling of getting in the bath while still wearing an article of clothing. Kayla got her forearms wet prying the soaked socks from her daughter's slippery tiny feet. Lucy wanted to keep her socks on in the bath now that she saw that it made her parents laugh as much as it had made her laugh.

With Lucy content and happy in her bubble bath, Drew and Kayla shut the door of the bathroom, and they simultaneously sighed when they realized that they had been presented with maybe forty-five minutes of their own time to wind down after the hot, busy day. Drew went into the bedroom to change out of his grimy clothes and get changed into a pair of pajama pants and a long-sleeved t-shirt. Kayla followed her husband silently and mischievously.

As he peeled off his shirt that was damp with sweat and unbuttoned his jeans, Kayla came up behind him in the cool darkness of the bedroom and she

slithered her hands around his firm abdomen and down the front of his jeans and into his underwear. "Hey there," Drew whispered with a smirk. "What are *you* doing?"

"Hi, sexy husband," Kayla whispered into the side of her husband's neck. Her hands slid down his hips and thighs, taking his jeans and underwear down along with them. Aroused and completely naked, Drew turned and faced his wife. As he did so, she reached under her dress and slid her panties down her shapely legs that were sticky with dried sweat. "Do you want me to keep my dress on?" she quietly asked before playfully biting her bottom lip in expectation and scarcely-concealed lust.

"Take it off."

Drew and Kayla made love quickly and quietly in the comforting darkness of their bedroom. They were both panting with their swift physical exertions, and they were both smiling contentedly and sleepily after making themselves twice as weary in the lazy, sensual dusk of their tiring day. Kayla, lying naked on her belly atop the rumpled sheets of their bed, said with fatigue, "I could seriously go to sleep right now. Let's just sleep. Just lie down for a little bit."

Drew sat on his knees on the bed behind her, and he ran his fingers through his hair as he explained, "We still have a little time. Let's sit outside on the porch

and have a smoke while Lucy is still happy with her bath."

They both slipped nude from their bed. The bedroom was pregnant in wavering shadows, and rain drummed on the roof. The husband and wife quickly wiped themselves off with Drew's soiled t-shirt, and they changed into more comfortable clothing. Drew got into his long-sleeved cotton shirt and a pair of plaid pajama pants, and Kayla changed into a large button-front shirt of white linen that was hanging in Drew's side of the closet. She liked to wear one of Drew's shirts, and nothing else at all, whenever they relaxed inside of their home after they had made love.

Kayla went to her husband's desk and retrieved a pack of his honey-flavored cigars and a lighter. As she did so, Drew went into the kitchen and grabbed a bottle of cold beer from the refrigerator. "Do you want a beer?" Drew shouted to Kayla.

She replied to her husband that she didn't want a beer and then Kayla opened up the bathroom door to tell Lucy that they were going outside to look at the storm. Drew walked past her, towards the front door, as Kayla shut the bathroom door and he asked her, "How's Lucy Tootsie?"

"She's perfect," answered Kayla, smiling.

The couple went outside onto the front porch, and both Drew and Kayla were taken aback by just how

much the temperature had dropped in the thirty minutes or so since they'd been ushered into their home by the storm. The rain fell over the neighborhood in heavy sheets from a slate-colored, cloudy sky that growled with the reverberating rumbles of thunder. The lightning seemed to have lessened visibly, but when it was seen slicing into existence in short bursts from the underside of the clouds it was a vivid blue-white instead of the grotesque and lurid pink that it had been previously.

Drew and Kayla had a couple of chairs on their front porch and they sat themselves down in them. The chairs were close to one another and they conversed casually as Kayla opened the pack of cigars, getting a pair of them out, and Drew screwed off the top of his bottle of beer. Kayla handed her husband a cigar and crossed her bare legs, lighting her own cigar as she did so.

As Drew put the small orange flame of the lighter to the end of his cigar, Kayla noticed one of their neighbors in the kitchen window above her sink. It was an elderly woman and she lived in the house directly across the street. She and her husband were nice, but they were quiet to their young neighbors. They waved or nodded to them in passing but they were very sweet to Lucy. And for that, Drew and Kayla were very pleased and thankful.

When Drew's cigar was lit, he took a drag from it and took a long swallow of beer. He looked at his young attractive wife, smiled at her, and then he followed Kayla's gaze across the residential street to their elderly neighbors' home. He looked at the old woman toiling with the dishes just out of view beneath her kitchen window. She didn't see the young couple on their porch. Her tired wrinkled face was focused downward at what Drew and Kayla assumed were a small selection of dirty dishes, the diminutive refuse of the quiet elderly couple.

"Do you think that she resents us?" asked Kayla, aromatic cigar smoke wafting out from her supple lips.

"What?"

"Do you think that Mrs. Harris and her husband resent us?"

Drew took another pull off of his beer and he bit the damp end of his cigar in his teeth. Around the cigar he inquired curiously, "Why in the hell would Mr. and Mrs. Harris resent us? All the sex we have?"

Kayla quickly grinned at her husband, and then she directed her gaze back to the old woman across the street. "Well, yeah I suppose there's that. But I guess what I meant was do you think that she resents this time, this future that her and her husband have found themselves in?"

Drew still smiled, but the smile was faded somewhat with contemplation. He answered, "I don't know. I guess that it's something that I've never thought of before."

Kayla continued, "Just think about her in the postwar era, when her and her husband were our age; cocktail parties, everyone smoking, the bustle of a changing America freshly-birthed out of the Atomic Age."

"Christ! We're sure poetic tonight, aren't we?" voiced Drew with raised eyebrows and a smile.

"Maybe," began Kayla thoughtfully. "Or maybe it's just nostalgia. Maybe it's just empathy. I feel bad for her. Why aren't her and Mr. Harris hosting cocktail parties and chain smoking like they probably used to? It's like all they do nowadays is host other people their age for bridge or go to strange club meetings."

Drew chuckled softly, a sound that barely could be discerned over the heavy cascade of the rain, and he smoked some more of his cigar and drank some more of his beer. "I think that you're imagining that Mr. and Mrs. Harris were more exciting than they actually were back in the fifties and sixties. What in the world makes you think that they were hosting cocktail parties and all that? They never struck me as that social to begin with."

Kayla returned, not taking her eyes from the window, "It's just that sometimes I feel guilty when I think that they're watching us. Sometimes I feel like they have to be resentful of this future that they're stuck in. I feel like they miss the time when they were our age."

"Oh, okay," replied Drew with a shrug. "So we're talking about just getting older here, right? About being wistful and being jealous of people that are younger?"

Kayla replied, "I don't know. I suppose so. What do you think, Drew? Do you think that we'll resent the future when we're their age and we've left this all behind?"

Drew thought about his wife's question as he took the cigar from his mouth and took another drink of his beer. He continued to ponder the inquiry as he drank and smoked. The pair kept silent, their gazes unwavering.

The couple watched the old woman in the window across the street. They could see her clearly enough through the torrential downpour and the rumbling darkness. A little bit of pale lightning flashed, and then the electric luminosity faded away.

Suddenly their old neighbor looked up from her dishes, and her steady eyes took in Drew and Kayla watching her from their chairs on their front porch. Both of the young people felt ashamed then. They were

ashamed of their blossoming love and their attractive, healthy bodies. Both of them grew ashamed of the smoke and the toxins that they were tarnishing their young bodies with. Both felt ashamed of their current disconnected era. And Drew and Kayla felt shame as their souls withered beneath the emotionless old eyes that met them through the rain.

"Let's go inside," began Kayla. "Lucy's probably ready to get out of the bath."

COLORS IN DESCENT

They had once been young lovers, but now they were no longer young. During the summer their twenties had given way to their thirties, a fresh new decade that was yellowed and antiqued, matured from the pastel gloss of the prior ten years. No, they were young no longer, but they hadn't noticed it yet.

The man and the woman walked into the autumnal heart of the Apple Creek Forest on a Saturday morning. The day was pregnant with promise and the warm-hued leaves of the oaks, birches and maples shivered in delight at the passing of the pair. Outfitted for autumn, they wore warm sweaters, boots and beanies. The woman wore black tights and the man wore jeans. The man's eyes, a yellowed brown, glittered in the amber rise of the sun and his full brown beard took on a reddish sheen in the rich light. He carried a small backpack. Twin black braids descended from either side of the woman's beanie, and in the cold morning air of mid-October her breath could be seen escaping in ethereal plumes.

The pair walked side by side, but at times they followed one another. The hike of the two was an ever-changing, mercurial thing, and it was a route they'd taken so often and had known so well that their conversation was never impeded with discussion of their surroundings. They only rarely lifted their eyes from their trudging hiking boots, and when they did it was usually to gaze into the familiar face of their significant other to listen or to laugh. Apple Creek Forest was a second home to them, an arboraceous abode that served them as a frequent escape from their small town lives in the community of Appleham, the town itself a quiet idyllic place in Franklin County on the southwest edge of the forest.

When the coldness of the October morning stirred into a more tolerable autumn crispness with the crowning of the sun, the couple had reached a small forest glade in the depths of the wood. A small pond darkened the heart of the little dell, and within the center of the pond was a protrusion of stone. Fallen leaves of oaken umber, maple scarlet and birch amber were heaped in the sylvan basin and they floated in strange primeval formations upon the surface of the water.

"Are you ready to have a bite?" inquired the man, stepping to the edge of the pool and dropping his pack from his shoulder.

His inquiry went unanswered immediately as the woman breathed in and out audibly from the hike. She nodded with a slight smile. "Sure."

They both sat next to one another on a fallen log next to the pool, an old oak log topped in a crunchy frosting of fallen leaves and its long sides peppered in pale shelf mushrooms. He took off his beanie and messed up his short brown hair that was slightly damp from the hike and the heat of the headwear. As he rummaged through the pack for their lunch and something to drink, the woman said quite softly, "I just love this place."

"Me too," he answered, still rummaging. "It's *our* place after all."

She looked across the pool and then up in the patch of azure sky that loomed over the glade. A nostalgic smile spilled out across her lovely face, rosy-cheeked from the brisk autumn hike, and she asked, "Do you remember what those old guys told us when we first moved to Appleham and started hiking in here? They told us that there used to be a woman in the woods that sang magic songs."

He snorted through his nose and grinned as he pulled two bottles of water, a couple of ham and swiss sandwiches, and some plastic bags of sliced apples lathered in cinnamon and honey from the backpack. "Sure. I remember."

"I think that made me love this place more. I hate that there's no more magic in the world. Do you think there ever was?"

"What, like wizards and elves? Like Tolkien stuff?"

She smirked and shook her head as she took her lunch from the gentle hands of her lover, and responded, "Not really. But don't you feel like this place has power? Some sort of ancient power?"

"Yeah," he replied before taking a bite of his sandwich. "We've discussed that before, remember?"

She shrugged, reaching into the bag and munching on the glazed apples. Her fingertips were sticky and golden and she absently sucked the sweet honey from them. "Sometimes," she began, "I feel like we've discussed all there is to discuss. Do you ever feel like that?"

The man raised an eyebrow in inquiry and returned, "That sounds grim. What do you mean?"

"Well, we're thirty now. We're so much older than we were."

"Yeah?"

She continued with a melancholy that the man had gotten more and more used to over the years, "It's over, honey. Our twenties are over. And they passed without any fanfare or fireworks. Were we supposed to feel something? Did we miss something important?"

"I feel something. I feel older."

"Are you okay with that?" she asked concernedly. "I'm not sure if I'm ready for thirty. We were having so much fun in our twenties."

The man washed a bite of sandwich down with a swallow of cool water, and replied with a grin, "Well, sweetie, thirty is here whether you're ready or not. Time has a habit of advancing against our will. And of course we had fun in our twenties, but we still are having fun. Aren't we? We're still working and going hiking every weekend. We still travel. In fact we travel more now because we can afford it a little easier. We're going to keep having fun. I promise."

She sighed and leaned into the broad-shouldered form of her lover. He put an arm around her and held her against him as they finished their lunch. Finally she said quietly, "I love you so much."

In response he kissed the top of the head against his shoulder. The trees around them quietly rattled their limbs in a crisp October breeze. As moments continued to relentlessly pass more leaves were plucked from their homes in the boughs of the trees. The leaves fluttered down towards the forest floor to be forgotten and crumble away into loam. But the colors sure were beautiful during their descent.

COCKTAILS

"God, Porter, you're a stupid son of a bitch!"

My wife's exclaimed insult was a toxic and spined thing that burrowed under my pliable flesh. I was driving our convertible through the afternoon gleam of the city streets that were wild and hot with sultry summer light, and she was sitting next to me. Her lovely, forty-year old features were still elegant and refined, but her features were also cross with me. I glanced sideways at her, turned my features back to the road ahead a moment later, and I had legitimate thoughts about jerking our car into oncoming traffic.

My wife, Lauren, used to love me. Shit, I used to love her too. The love bled out of our marriage through various wounds, and chief among those gory rifts upon our companionable creation were our infidelities with one another. We never forgave each other, and we reached a point where we didn't seem to care anymore. Our twin daughters graduated from high school a year ago and they had both got accepted into Georgetown with scholarships. Those sweet, intelligent girls had

been the glue that held Lauren and I together, but the wounds opened anew with their departure.

About once a month, Lauren and I harkened back to John Cheever's postwar era and we hosted cocktail parties at our house. We'd been doing it for about five years now, and our guest list largely stayed the same. Everyone dressed in a postwar manner, and everyone really seemed to enjoy themselves. It was an antiquated and out-of-place ritual in our present achromatic age, but I was extremely wistful for that era in which I'd never been allowed to be a part of. I worked as an editor for a publishing house in Boston and Lauren and I had a pleasing brownstone in the Back Bay neighborhood. She had an office job with a law firm.

I reached under the lenses of my glasses with one hand and massaged my eye sockets. I sighed wearily and forlornly. My wife's insults and verbal attacks on me carried the agonizing weight of a scourge that flayed the flesh from my bones. I was helplessly aware that she was turning me into a broken middle-aged man instead of a happy, gracefully-aging middle-aged man.

"I guess I'll just get the fucking snacks this time since I have to return just about everything you bought. Do you need me to hold your hand through every

goddamn thing? Why in the hell would you get only spicy stuff?"

I wheezed out defeatedly, "I like spicy stuff, Lauren."

Any sort of reply on my part, when she was trying to bitch me out, instantly made her fume. "Well, nobody else likes a bunch of spicy fucking snacks with their cocktails. God, you're a selfish bastard. You never think about anybody else. It's always about Porter."

I was silent after that onslaught, and a few minutes later I pulled in front of the supermarket. She opened the door with a huff, gathered a couple bags of groceries that I had bought earlier in the day, and slammed the door shut behind her. As she marched towards the sliding doors of the supermarket, I said loudly, "I'll be out here in about ten minutes."

She didn't answer me. I didn't expect her to. I put the car in gear and drove a couple blocks over to the liquor store that I was most familiar with. Inside, I bought a couple bottles of dry gin, a couple bottles of bourbon whiskey, and a bottle of sour mash whiskey. The liquor store had a cooler of drinking supplies and paraphernalia as well, and I also purchased a bag of lemons, a bag of oranges, and a bag of limes.

While I waited for my lovely, tempestuous wife to get done returning the items that I had bought and purchase new snacks that she approved of, I read some

more of a manuscript that I'd been assigned to look over. It was a novella by a debut young writer. It was a promising literary work and I was enjoying her writing immensely. The best part of my job was having a hand in directing the prose of fresh, new talent. There was an amber, delightful realm, a timeless place, where all good literature lived forever in a paradisiacal quality with their authors. I did my best to get as many new writers there as I could, safe and sound. I was like the literary Ferryman helping them to that mythic realm by guiding them over the River Styx, a swirling dark place where clichéd fallacies and mean-spirited reviews swam hungrily, eager to consume hope and talent in equal measure.

Too soon my wife stormed towards our car, her hands clutching two new bags of groceries. She entered silently and slammed the door, sighing with exaggerated exasperation as she untangled the handles of the plastic bags from her fingers and put them on the floorboard. We drove back through the South End streets of Boston to our brownstone, and when I stopped the convertible in the parking space in front of our home, Lauren stormed from the car and entered our home. She left the door to our brownstone open, as well as the passenger side car door, and she left the groceries on the floorboard.

I wanted to scream in frustration or cry, but all I managed was a world-weary sigh. I grabbed the snacks and the paper bags of liquor bottles, locked the car, and went into my home. I was relieved to much more of an extent than I can hereby express when I heard the shower running in our bathroom and I saw my wife's blouse, jeans and panties discarded in the hallway. I had a few minutes' reprieve from her animosity. I was about to gather her clothing and put it in her hamper, but then I realized that that would probably set her off. She would accuse me of thinking that she was incapable of picking up after herself or something. It crossed my mind then to strip down and get in the shower with my wife, but she would probably try and have me arrested if I did that. We hadn't been intimate in months.

I went into the walk-in closet in our bedroom and I laid out an outfit on the edge of our bed; brown trousers, my tweed jacket with elbow patches, a soft pink button-front shirt, and a pastel yellow knitted tie. I pulled a pair of argyle socks out of my sock drawer, put them in my highly-polished oxfords, and lastly I got out a pastel yellow pocket square that matched my tie and a minimalist wooden tie bar.

As I waited for my wife to get done with her shower so that I could take one without fighting over hot water, I went into the kitchen and looked through the bland snacks that Lauren had purchased at the

supermarket. I sliced up the vegetables for a veggie tray. Afterwards, I filled all the decanters atop my antique liquor table with the newly-purchased alcohol and I sliced up some citrus for later that night. The guests would start arriving around five.

When my wife was done with her shower, she went into our bedroom with a towel wrapped around her voluptuous figure to get dressed and do her makeup and hair at the mirror of her bureau. I crept into our humid bathroom then, shaved, and then took a shower with what was left of the hot water. As I let the tepid water shatter against my weathered frame, I was suddenly struck with the notion that I had become an emasculated man. My wife dominated me so much so, and loathed me so much so, that I was riddled with anxiety whenever I saw her. I was afraid to touch her in bed, afraid to share any of my own opinions with her, and I was afraid to accidently contradict her in any way. She was like an angry dog that one had to tread very carefully around to avoid being mauled. The ultimate betrayal was revealed with the sweetness and domestic happiness that she displayed for our friends. What a liar. What a fake.

This realization made me angry, and I hurriedly finished my shower, dried myself off, and combed my hair before I styled it classically with some pomade. I walked into our bedroom with a towel gripped around

my waist. Lauren was sitting at her mirror in a cotton bathrobe, curling her bouncy reddish-brown tangles. Her fierce blue eyes were already surrounded in dark mascara and her lips, that artfully-thin upper lip and that soft gleaming lower lip, were coated in burgundy lipstick. She gazed into the mirror at me when I entered, and I instantly sensed an invisible bristle of irritation.

"Porter, I need you to help me clasp these pearls," Lauren stated with some exasperation, as she held aloft the small string of pearls that I'd bought her for our fifteenth anniversary. She absolutely loathed asking for my assistance in anything.

Silently, I came forward and I took the pearls from her hand. I took my time fastening the necklace on the back of her soft white neck, and I let my knuckles and fingertips caress the soft warmth and the tiny little hairs that were there. When I was done, Lauren didn't thank me or anything. She just went back to her makeup and hair. I gritted my teeth in sudden ferocity. I wanted to strangle the life out of her from behind and smash her skull into the mirror of her bureau. I looked at the flesh of her neck and upper back, and fantasized about how savagely I could destroy it … destroy her.

I breathed heavily out of my nose, and suddenly and without warning I slid one hand around her throat and gripped it forcefully. Lauren jolted in alarm at the

unasked-for contact that I initiated. My other reached around her torso, sliding beneath the cotton of her bathrobe. My firm searching hand cupped dominatingly around the short bristly hair between her legs, and my fingertips felt the heat from her and some moisture as well. Her eyes widened in alarm, and her painted lips parted to protest, but I placed my face beside her ear and we both stared at one another in the mirror.

"You fucking listen to me," I said quietly and evenly. "You are going to be wonderful to me at this party, and when everyone is gone I am going to tear your clothes off of you and I'm going to push you down on that bed and make love to you for the rest of the night. Do you fucking hear me, Lauren?"

My steady, serious gaze seared into her shocked visage and I almost smirked when I saw her eyes quickly dart over to our tall bed. Her bewildered alarm and shocked disbelief at my sudden dominating attitude towards her was certainly evident, but so was her arousal at the sudden control that I'd taken of her. Her crotch grew warmer and moister under the firm touch of my fingertips, her nipples became erect, and a blush spilled across the softness of her cheeks.

Lauren licked her lips and replied softly and with wavering force, "Porter, get your hands off me right now."

In response I increased my grip on her throat and between her legs, and I growled, "Do you fucking hear me? When everyone's gone tonight, you and I are going to sort some things out in here. I'm going to destroy you."

I held the pressure, and finally she nodded. Her glittering eyes looked into mine with worry perhaps, but there was so much excitement and delight in her look too. I had to literally bite my cheeks to keep from grinning. I needed to take control. She needed me to take control. I let go of her forcefully, and she watched my reflection. I stood tall and stared into her eyes in the mirror. I put the fingers that I'd had between her legs into my mouth and sucked her feminine flavor off of them. Exceedingly pleased with myself, I gathered my outfit into a pile in my arms and marched proudly from our bedroom to go get changed elsewhere in the house.

The first guests arrived probably fifteen minutes before five. It was a married couple that Lauren and I were friends with. Jake worked as an editor for the publishing house that I also worked for and his wife, Becca, was a librarian. Needless to say, they were an intellectual and bookish couple, and I enjoyed spending time with them. Privately, Lauren had begun to loathe Jake because she said that he and I were too much alike. She got along with Becca just fine, which I thought was odd because she was remarkably similar to the

woman that I had an affair with a few years ago. Lauren's fling had been with a lawyer at the firm that she worked for. I still worried about their relationship restarting because they still worked together. As far as I knew, their affair had never stopped.

We greeted Jake and Becca, and took their hats. "What would you two like to drink? Becca?"

"I'll have one of those gin and tonics that you made for me last time, Porter. Thank you," answered Becca.

"The one with lime *and* lemon?"

"Yes, that one," she said.

"Alrighty, an Evans gin and tonic. What about you, Jake?" I asked.

His hand on my shoulder, Jake explained, "Well, I'll have an Old-Fashioned to start, but I'll follow you to the kitchen. This manuscript I'm reading is freaking amazing."

Jake and I went into the kitchen, and he talked excitedly about the manuscript that he was going through for work. As he did so, I quickly made up his Old-Fashioned, muddling a sugar cube and a slice of orange in a bit of purified water with a sprinkle of bitters. I poured in the bourbon, stirred and handed his drink to him. His wife's drink was equally fast to make. I started with the gin over a couple cubes of ice, and then I squeezed the juice from a quarter of a lime and a

quarter of a lemon into the gin. I finished it with tonic water, garnished it with thinly-sliced wheels of lemon and lime, and stirred.

"Honey, what would you like?" I inquired loudly from the kitchen. As I asked, I thought about our encounter in the bedroom earlier. I thought about my hand around her throat and nestled in the damp warmth between her legs. I waited for Lauren to answer and I hoped that her voice had an element of timidity within it in anticipation of the control I was usurping from her when our guests had left later in the evening.

"I'll have a whiskey sour, … dear."

There was a nervousness in her voice to be certain, but there was also a layer of anticipation seasoning her response. Lauren, I knew then, was excited about what would happen when everyone had left. My wife was excited for the tables to be physically turned on her. I became almost aroused right there in the kitchen, and to keep myself in check I got busy on her cocktail. "Great," I explained. "I'll have one too."

My wife's fondness for cocktail parties was an anomaly to me. I wasn't sure where her fondness for them came from but I was smart enough to not look a gift horse in the mouth. Lauren didn't even really like to drink cocktails. She liked to play at drinking alcohol, sipping rarely upon a too-full glass of moscato or

moving an untasted cocktail around the house with her as she distracted herself, busying herself with unimportant and self-imposed tasks. In the morning, I would always collect her full-watered-down tumblers and dash their room-temperature contents into the sink.

I put ice in a pair of tumblers before I opened my steel shaker and put within it ice, simple syrup, sour mash whiskey, freshly-squeezed orange juice and freshly-squeezed lemon juice. I shook the ingredients vigorously, and strained the cold, yellowed beverage over the ice in the two glasses. A layer of foam crowned the top of each whiskey sour.

Jake and I returned to the living room, where our wives were standing, talking to one another. They both looked amazing in the postwar-era outfits that they wore. Becca even wore gloves. It felt like we were starting up a cocktail party in the late nineteen-fifties. I carried the whiskey sours, and Jake carried his Old-Fashioned and his wife's Evans gin and tonic.

The guests arrived in a sudden steady stream after that. My bachelor friend named Jerome was the next to arrive. Jerome was a novelist that was published by the publishing house that Jake and I worked for. Jerome was followed by another husband and wife couple that Lauren and I were fond of, Greg and Jesse. Jesse worked in Lauren's office, and I secretly suspected

that she had been urging Lauren to divorce me when she was sleeping with that lawyer. Greg was a good guy though, a registered nurse for Mass General Hospital Back Bay. Last to arrive was a young, flighty friend of Lauren's named Violet. Violet was a new paralegal at the law firm, and she was young, trim, and very sexy. She blossomed like the flower that she was named after when all of us older men buried our gazes into her narrow curves and gorgeous face.

I was terribly busy throughout the cocktail party, as I usually was, but I enjoyed keeping busy during the parties in that way. There was always at least one other person keeping me company in the kitchen as I whipped up cocktail after cocktail, and I fueled myself with shots of various liquor. After a couple hours of conversation, snacking and drinking that everyone present seemed to enjoy, the first guests began to depart. We were all thrilled to see Jerome and Violet leave our brownstone together. Greg shouted after them, "Be safe, you two."

We all laughed, and so did Violet and Jerome as they trotted down the sidewalk into the sultry darkness of the night where their cars were parked further down the street. They both got into his car, and drove away. I expected that Violet's car would still be there in the morning.

Jake and Becca were the next to take off, and they were soon after followed by Greg and Jesse. The

stillness and quietness of our house, after one of our cocktail parties, was always piercingly evident. My wife and I were always left in a sort of bewildering stupor, as though we were suddenly-abandoned children.

I busied myself with picking up everyone's tumblers, and I shook my head when I saw Lauren's initial whiskey sour, still two-thirds full with the ice cubes that had melted into the drink, on the coffee table. I mused to myself about how much liquor my wife had wasted over the years with her legion of forsaken cocktails and discarded glasses of wine. Lauren busied herself with gathering together the bowls of chips, salsa, dip, and the remnants of the vegetable tray.

We were both silent as we toiled, but the tension almost screamed at both of us. To say that you could cut it with a knife would be a gross understatement. Both my wife and I knew what was soon approaching. She and I knew that I hadn't spoken idly when I'd told her what the night would bring when the guests left.

We both left the detritus of the evening on the kitchen counters and in the sink, and then Lauren slipped past me to leave the kitchen. She stepped out of her heels, and briefly looked back at me from under her lattice of black lashes. I drifted coolly after Lauren through the journey she took through the rooms of our

house back towards our master bedroom. En route, I watched the sway of her hips and I watched her round bottom beneath the fabric of her knee-length pencil skirt. Her dark stockings slithered teasingly up the curves of her calves and up her thighs. From behind her, I could tell that she was unbuttoning her blouse.

My wife entered the breathless, vulgar darkness of our bedroom. I unfastened my belt and, loosening my tie with concupiscent assurance, I ambled into the darkness after her. I closed the bedroom door behind me.

OTHER WORKS BY NICHOLAS TRANDAHL

Short Story Collections
Cocktails & Other Stories

Poetry Collections
Lost Yellow

Novels
Clark's Turning Leaf
An Uncomfortable Life

CPSIA information can be obtained at www.ICGtesting.com
Printed in the USA
BVOW06s0022060915

416761BV00009B/138/P

15107853R00146

Made in the USA
Middletown, DE
24 October 2014